"Nothing is free, Go'el,"
Jaina Proudmoore said.

"Your knowledge and skills were bought at a cost. The . . . orc you left behind in your place has done much harm in your absence. If I have heard about what is going on in Orgrimmar and Ashenvale, surely you must have!"

Go'el's mien, which had been deeply peaceful, now looked troubled. "I have heard, of course."

"And . . . you do nothing?"

"I have another path," he said. "You have seen the results of that path. A threat that—"

"Go'el, I hear this, but now that task is over. Garrosh is stirring up trouble between the Alliance and the Horde—trouble that didn't exist until he started it. I can understand if you don't wish to undermine him publicly, but—perhaps you and I can work together. Form a summit of sorts. Ask Baine to join us; I know he has no love for what Garrosh is striving for. I could speak with Varian. As of late, he seems to be more reachable. Everyone respects you, even in the Alliance, Go'el. You have earned that respect because of your actions. Garrosh has earned nothing but mistrust and hatred because of his."

She indicated her cloak, which had blown about with the wind he had sent to bear her to shore. "You can control the winds as a shaman. But the winds of war are blowing, and if we do not stop Garrosh now, many innocents will pay the price for our hesitation."

WORLD OF WARCRAFT®

JAINA PROUDMOORE
TIDES OF WAR

CHRISTIE GOLDEN

POCKET BOOKS

New York   London   Toronto   Sydney   New Delhi

Pocket Books
A Division of Simon & Schuster, Inc.
1230 Avenue of the Americas
New York, NY 10020

First Pocket Books paperback edition May 2013

POCKET and colophon are registered trademarks of Simon & Schuster, Inc.

For information about special discounts for bulk purchases, please contact Simon & Schuster Special Sales at 1-866-506-1949 or business@simonandschuster.com.

The Simon & Schuster Speakers Bureau can bring authors to your live event. For more information or to book an event contact the Simon & Schuster Speakers Bureau at 1-866-248-3049 or visit our website at www.simonspeakers.com.

Manufactured in the United States of America

10   9   8   7   6   5   4

ISBN 978-1-4516-9791-9
ISBN 978-1-4391-7144-8 (ebook)

It is not light that we need, but fire; it is not the gentle shower, but thunder. We need the storm, the whirlwind, and the earthquake.

—Frederick Douglass

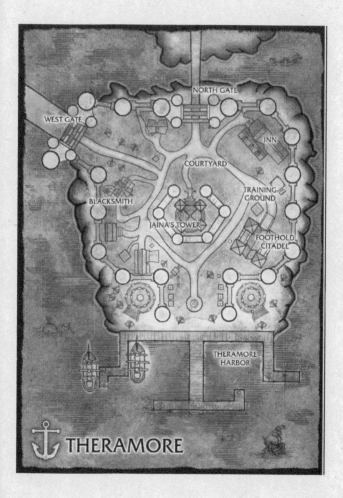

THERAMORE

1

The hour was close to twilight, and the vaguely warm hues of the afternoon were fading to colder blues and purples. Air peppered with swirling, stinging blades of snow whirled high above Coldarra. Other beings would shiver and shield their eyes, fluff their fur or feathers, or wrap themselves more tightly in their cloaks. The great blue dragon whose wings beat a slow rhythm paid no heed to such things as snow or cold. He had taken to the air in search of the crisp bite of the frigid, snow-speckled wind, hoping, perhaps futilely, that it would cleanse his thoughts and soothe his spirit.

Kalecgos, though young as dragons reckoned age, had already borne witness to tremendous change among his people. The blue dragons had endured so very much, it seemed to him. They had twice lost their beloved Aspect, Malygos—once to insanity for millennia, and then finally to death. Ironically, and poignantly, the blues—the intellectuals and the guardians of arcane magic in the world of Azeroth—were the flight most drawn to order and calmness, and the least able to deal with such chaos.

Yet even in the midst of this upheaval, their hearts had stayed true. The spirit of the blue dragonflight had chosen not the hard-line path represented by Malygos's deceased blood heir, Arygos, but the gentler, more joyful way offered to them by Kalecgos. And that choice had proved to be the right one. Arygos had in actuality been betraying the flight, not striving to be a devoted caretaker. He had promised to deliver his people to the evil—and quite insane—dragon Deathwing, once they had sworn to follow Arygos. Instead, the blues had joined with the reds, greens, and bronzes—and one unique orc—to help bring down that great monster.

But as Kalecgos flew across the darkening sky, the snow below turning lavender, he knew that with that victory, the flights, in a way, had also sacrificed themselves. The Aspects were no more, though the dragons who had once been Aspects lived on. The defeat of Deathwing had demanded all they could give, and at the end of that battle, though Alexstrasza, Nozdormu, Ysera, and Kalecgos still survived, their Aspect abilities were gone—poured into the final moment of the struggle. The Aspects had been made for this single act. With it accomplished, they had fulfilled their destinies.

There was a less direct effect as well. The flights had always had a surety about their roles, a firm understanding of their purpose. But now that the moment for which they had been created had come—and gone—what purpose was left to them? Many blues had already departed. Some had sought his blessing before leaving the Nexus—Kalecgos continued to be their leader, although the powers of an Aspect were no longer his. They had told him that they were restless and wished to see if there was some other place in the world where their skills and abilities would be appreciated. The rest had simply gone—present one day, vanished the next. Those who remained were either becoming increasingly agitated or surrendering to a bleak sense of malaise.

Kalecgos dove and wheeled, letting the cold air caress his scales, then opening his wings and catching an updraft, his thoughts once again brooding and unhappy.

For so long, even during Malygos's insanity, the blues had had direction. The question of what to do now had been thought and sometimes whispered. Kalecgos could not help but wonder if he had somehow failed his flight. Had they really been better under the leadership of an insane Aspect? The immediate answer was of course not, and yet . . . and yet.

He closed his eyes, not against the needle-sharp snow, but in pain. *Their hearts trusted me to lead them. I believe I did lead them well then, but . . . now? Where do blue dragons— any dragons—fit in a world where the Hour of Twilight has been prevented but only an endless night looms before us?*

He felt utterly alone. He had always deemed himself perhaps the oddest choice possible to lead the blue dragonflight, as he had never really felt like a "typical" blue dragon. As he flew, despondent and increasingly concerned, he realized that there was at least one who understood him better than most. He leaned to the right, angling his great form slightly, and flapped his wings, heading back toward the Nexus.

He knew where he would find her.

Kirygosa, daughter of Malygos, clutch sister to Arygos, sat in her human form on one of the magical, luminous floating platforms that encircled the Nexus. She wore only a long, loose dress, and her blue-black hair was not braided. Her back was against one of the shining, silver-white trees that dotted a few of the platforms. Above her, blue dragons wheeled as they had for centuries, ceaselessly patrolling, although there seemed to be no threat here, not anymore. Kirygosa appeared to pay them no heed, her gaze soft and unfocused. She was lost in thought, though what occupied her mind, Kalecgos did not know.

She did turn to look at him as he drew closer, smiling a little as she realized he was not one of the guardians of the flight's home. He landed on the platform and assumed his half-elven shape. Kiry's smile widened and she held out a hand to him. He kissed it affectionately and plopped down beside her, extending his long legs and folding his arms behind his head in an effort at nonchalance.

"Kalec," she said warmly. "Come to my pondering place?"

"Is that what this is?"

"For me, yes. The Nexus is my home, so I don't like to go too far, but it can be challenging to be alone inside." She turned to face him. "So I come here, and I ponder. Just as you seem to want to do."

Kalec sighed, realizing that his effort at casualness was lost on this perceptive friend he often thought of as a sister. "I was flying," he said.

"You cannot fly away from your duties, or your thoughts," Kirygosa replied gently, reaching to squeeze his arm. "You are our leader, Kalec. And you have guided us well. Arygos would have destroyed the flight and the whole world with it."

Kalec frowned, remembering the dire vision that Ysera, the former green Dragon Aspect, had shared with them all not so long ago. It was the Hour of Twilight— and an Azeroth in which all life was wiped out. From the grass and the insects to orcs, elves, humans, creatures of air and sea and land, to the mighty Aspects themselves, who had each been slain by his or her own unique powers. Deathwing had died then, too, along with the rest of Azeroth—impaled like a grotesque trophy on the spire of Wyrmrest Temple itself. Kalecgos shuddered, disturbed even now by the memory of Ysera's lilting but broken voice relaying the vision.

"He would have done that," Kalec said, agreeing with part of her statement but not all of it.

Her blue eyes searched his. "Dear Kalec," she said, "you have always been . . . different."

Humor flickered in him despite his dark mood, and he made a silly face, twisting his handsome half-elven features. Kirygosa laughed. "You see?"

"Different is not always a good thing," he said.

"It is who you are, and it is because you were different that the flight chose you."

The humor melted away and he regarded her somberly. "But, my dear Kirygosa," he said sadly, "do you think the flight would choose me again, now?"

Truth had ever been one of Kirygosa's most cherished ideals. She looked at him, searching for an answer that was both true and comforting, and not finding it. Kalec's heart sank. If this beloved friend, his sweet sister of the spirit, had no encouragement to offer, then his fears were more real than he had suspected.

"What I *do* think is—"

He would never know what she thought, for they were interrupted by a sudden terrible sound—the cries of blue dragons in despair and anguish. More than a dozen dragons were emerging from the Nexus, flying and diving about erratically. One of them abruptly swerved from his fellows, heading straight for Kalecgos. Kalec leaped to his feet, blood draining from his face. Kiry stood beside him, hand to her mouth.

"Lord Kalecgos!" Narygos cried. "We are ruined! All is lost!"

"What has happened? Slow down, speak calmly, my friend!" said Kalec, although his own heart lurched within his chest at the sheer panic and terror emanating from Narygos. The other dragon was usually calm and had been one of the more open-minded blues during the tense time when Kalec and Arygos were vying for the role of Aspect. To see him so distraught alarmed Kalecgos.

"The Focusing Iris! It is gone!"

"Gone? What do you mean?"

"*It has been stolen!*"

Kalec stared at him, sick with horror, his mind reeling. Not only was the Focusing Iris an item of immense arcane power, but it was also deeply precious to the blues. It had belonged to them for as long as anyone could remember. Like many such items, it was neither good nor evil in itself but could be turned to both benevolent and sinister purposes. And it had been used so. In the past, it had diverted the arcane energy of Azeroth and animated a hideous creature that should never have drawn breath.

To think it was now lost to them, lost and being controlled by those who might use its power—

"This is exactly why we moved it," Kalecgos murmured. Not two days ago, in an effort to avoid this very circumstance, Kalecgos, along with several others, had recommended moving the Focusing Iris out of the Eye of Eternity and into a secret hiding place. He recalled his argument to the blues: "*Many of our secrets are already known, and more of our flight leaves each day. There will be those emboldened by this. The Nexus has been violated before, and the Focusing Iris used for dark purposes. We need to keep it safe . . . and if much of Azeroth knows by now that the Nexus hosts this artifact, then it is certain that one day, it will again be vulnerable.*"

And that day had come, but not how Kalec had anticipated. The blues had decided that a small group would bear it into the Frozen Sea, off the coast of Coldarra, where it would be safely—he had thought—ensconced in enchanted ice. It would be securely hidden, a simple chunk of frozen water that was in reality so much more.

Kalec struggled for calm. "What makes you think it's been stolen?" *Please,* he thought, begging what power, he did not know, *please, let this be simple confusion.*

"We have heard nothing from Veragos or the others, and the Focusing Iris is not where it should be."

Some of the blues, those who had spent the most time with the artifact over the long centuries, were particularly attuned to it. Kalecgos had asked them to sense its progress. By this point, the Focusing Iris should have been on the bottom of the ocean, heavily warded, and those who had borne it there should have been back. There were other possibilities not nearly as dire, but Kalecgos was already in his dragon form and flying quickly to the Nexus, with Kirygosa and Narygos right behind him.

Because he *knew*—how, he did not understand—that the other possibilities were nothing but false hopes. And that two of the worst disasters to befall the blue dragonflight had happened while he had been first its Aspect and then its leader for only a few brief months.

Kalecgos landed inside the cold, cavernous interior of the Nexus to utter chaos.

Everyone seemed to be talking at once. Every line of their massive reptilian bodies screamed fear and anger. Some sat hunched and unnaturally still, and these alarmed Kalecgos even more. How few of them were left, he thought; how few had stayed, and no doubt these few wished they, too, had departed ere this doom had come upon them.

Retaining his true form, he called for silence. Only a handful obeyed. The rest continued to shout among themselves.

"How could this have happened?"

"We should have sent more; I *told* you we should have sent more!"

"This was a fool's idea in the first place. Had it remained here, we could have watched it every moment!"

Kalecgos slammed his tail on the ground. "Silence!" he bellowed, the single word ringing through the chamber.

The flight ceased talking at once, all heads whipping around to regard their leader. Kalec saw in several of their expressions a faint flicker of hope that this was some kind of mistake and that he would somehow make everything right. Others fixed baleful, sullen eyes on him, clearly blaming him for what had transpired.

Once he had their full attention, Kalecgos began to speak. "Let us first determine what we know to be true, not engage in wild speculation," he said. "The blue flight does not surrender to fears born of a fevered imagination."

Some of them lowered their heads at that, their ears drooping slightly in shame. Others bridled. Kalec would deal with them later. He had to establish the facts.

"I sensed it first," said Teralygos. He was one of the oldest of the blues who had chosen to stay. Once, he had sided with Kalec's rival, Arygos. Since the revelation of Arygos's betrayal and his subsequent death, however, Teralygos and most of the others had maintained their loyalty to Kalec, even after his Aspect abilities had been lost.

"Long have you been a guardian of our home, Teralygos, and great are the thanks all of us owe you," Kalec said, his voice full of respect. "What did you sense?"

"The path that Veragos and the others were to take was not arrow straight," Teralygos said. Kalec nodded. It had been decided that it would be too obvious to see several blue dragons bearing a mysterious object, flying straight for their goal. Instead, they had opted to travel in bipedal form. It was slower and more roundabout but would attract much less notice from any hostile forces. And if they were indeed attacked while on the ground, it would be the work of a blink of an eye to shift from humanoid-seeming to their true forms. Five dragons should have been more than a match for anyone who might be skulking about, thinking to ambush what appeared to be a simple caravan.

And yet . . .

"I knew every twist and turn of the route," Teralygos said, continuing. "I and others—Alagosa and Banagos— we followed each step our brothers and sisters took. And until barely an hour ago, all was well."

His voice, raspy with age, cracked on the last word. Kalec kept his gaze fastened on Teralygos but felt Kirygosa's head brush against his shoulder in a gentle reassurance.

"What happened then?"

"Then they halted. Before this, progress had not ceased for a moment. And after a pause, they began to move again, but not west, not to the Frozen Sea . . . southwest, at a speed far faster than the Iris had been moving before."

"Where was it when it stopped?"

"At the shores of the sea. Now it has traveled far to the south. And the farther it travels from me," Teralygos said miserably, "the less I can sense it."

Kalecgos looked at Kirygosa. "Take someone with you and go to the shoreline. Be careful. Find out what happened there."

She nodded, spoke to Banagos and Alagosa, and a moment later all three were airborne, broad wing beats carrying them out of the Nexus. By air, it was a short distance away. They would not be gone long.

He hoped.

"Oh no," Kirygosa whispered. She hesitated for a moment, hovering, trying to anticipate any possible lurking threat. She sensed nothing. The enemy was long gone. Only what they had wrought remained.

She folded her wings and dropped gracefully to the ground, bending her long, sinuous neck in grief.

The site had once been a plain, if unwelcoming, unmarred expanse of white—pure, clean, calming in its simplicity. The visitor would see nothing but snow, or the occasional brown-gray of rock. In some places, small patches of yellowish sand stretched into the hungry, cold ocean.

The snow had been turned to red slush. There were violent black gashes that looked as if lightning strikes had rent the frozen soil, which the whiteness had once blanketed. Boulders had been ripped from the ground or snapped off the faces of the cliffs and hurled great distances. Some of the boulders, too, were tinged with drying crimson. As Kirygosa and the others sniffed the air, they caught the lingering stench of demonic activity, the coppery reek of blood, and the unique, indescribable fragrance of myriad other magics.

More mundane weapons had been used as well; her sharp eyes caught wounds in the earth that had been made by spears, and here and there arrows had buried themselves up to their fletching.

"The lesser races," growled Banagos. Her heart aching, Kirygosa did not chide him for the insulting words as she might otherwise have done. He was right, although so far it was impossible to tell exactly which ones, or even which faction they bore allegiance to.

Kirygosa transformed into her human form. Tucking a lock of long, blue-black hair behind an ear, she respectfully approached the bodies of her slain kin. Five had started out, to protect the Focusing Iris. Five had been killed, giving their lives attempting to complete their task. Mild-tempered and wise Uragos, older than the others, the leader of the group. Rulagos and Rulagosa, clutch mates, appearing in human form as twins. They had fallen together, close to each other and in the same pose, arrows piercing their throats—as similar in death as in life. Tears filled her eyes as Kirygosa turned to regard Pelagosa. Kiry could recognize her only by her petite size. Pelagosa had always been among the smallest of the blues, young (as the dragons reckoned such things) but having a gift with the arcane that surpassed her years. Whoever slew her had also fought with magic, and she was burned beyond recognition.

Lurugos had perhaps resisted the hardest, given how far away from the murder site they found his body. Scorched, frozen, partially submerged, with arrows sticking out like quills in his shoulders and legs, he had not given up. Kirygosa thought that he might have even fought for a heartbeat or two after his head had been severed from his shoulders in a clean strike from a sharp sword.

Banagos, in human shape, came behind her and squeezed her arm. Swiftly she covered his hand with her own.

"I know little of the lesser races," Banagos said. "I see all kinds of weapons here and evidence that magic was used—demonic and arcane both."

"It could be any race," Kiry said.

"Then perhaps we were on the right track with the idea of killing them all," Banagos said. His voice was raw with grief, and his blue eyes were reddened with unshed tears. He had loved little Pelagosa, and they would have been mates once she had come of age.

"No," said Kiry sharply. "Such has ever been the sentiment of those who do not take time to think, Banagos, as I know you know. As I know Pelagosa always believed. They do not 'all' do this, any more than 'all' dragons attack wantonly and slay the younger races for sport. We understand why this was done. And it was not for hatred of our people. It was because someone wished to obtain the Focusing Iris for his or her own purposes."

"Five dragons," breathed Alagosa. "Five of us. Five of our finest. Who could possibly be strong enough to do this?"

"That," said Kiry, "is what we need to find out. Banagos, return to the Nexus with this grim news. Alagosa and I will stay here and . . . care for the remains of our fallen."

She had thought to spare him further pain, but Banagos shook his head. "No. She would have been my mate. I . . . will tend to her. And the others. You are closest to

Kalecgos. It is best that he hear this from you, and quickly."

"As you wish," said Kiry gently. She looked one final time at the bodies of the blue dragons, trapped in death in a form most of them scorned; closed her eyes in sorrow once more; then leaped skyward. Her wings flapped as she wheeled and turned back for the Nexus. Her thoughts were no longer on the fallen, but on their killers. Who was strong enough to have done such a thing? And for what specific purpose?

She knew very little, only enough to confirm their worst fears about the traveling party. She hoped that in her absence, Kalec had learned more.

Kalecgos knew that with every second that ticked by, the Focusing Iris was moving farther and farther south. And it was becoming harder and harder to trace. He had an advantage others in his flight did not. Though he was no longer the blue Dragon Aspect, he still led the blues. That tie to his flight, with echoes of what he had once been, seemed to enhance his connection to the Iris. When Teralygos had said he could barely sense the object any longer, Kalecgos had closed his eyes and drawn in three deep breaths. He visualized it in his mind, concentrating on it, on sensing and—

And there it was. "It is now in the Borean Tundra, is it not?" he asked Teralygos with his eyes still closed.

"Yes, yes, it is, and—" The words ended in a harsh, short cry. "It is gone!"

"No, it is not," Kalec said. "I can still sense it."

Many dragons sighed in relief. At that moment, a female voice said quietly, "They were all slain, Kalecgos. All five."

He opened his eyes and regarded Kirygosa sickly as she recounted what she, Banagos, and Alagosa had beheld. "And you cannot say if it was human or elf, orc or goblin?" he asked when she was done. "No scrap of a banner or distinctive arrow fletching?"

She shook her head. "What colors we found were random. There were no footprints. The snow had melted too much, and they were clever to both avoid the softer sand and refrain from tracking blood on the rocks. All we know, Kalecgos, is that someone likely knew where to find them, was strong enough to slay five dragons, and has absconded with the Focusing Iris. Whoever they were, they knew exactly what they were doing."

Her voice was low on this final sentence. Kalec nodded to her. "Perhaps that is true. But so do we." This was spoken with a certainty he did not feel. "I am able to sense generally in which direction it travels. And I will follow it and bring it back."

"You are our leader, Kalecgos," said Kirygosa. "We need you here!"

He shook his head. "No, you do not," he said quietly. "It is *because* I am your leader that I must go. It is time we acknowledged what is happening—how the flight is feeling. Many of our people have already left for the wide world. We once knew the role we needed to play; now we do not, and our most precious magical item, both tool and symbol, has been stolen, and good dragons lie dead for that theft. It is my job to guide and protect you. I . . . have not done so."

It hurt to admit it. "I have failed, at least in this, and perhaps in other things. You do not need me here, to worry and wonder along with the rest of you while others venture forth to retrieve our stolen orb. That is my task—and by performing it, I will indeed guide and protect you."

Glances were exchanged, but no one protested. They all knew this was the right path. He had meant everything he said. The failure was his; the recovery of the item was his duty. But what he did not say was that he *wanted* to go. He felt more at home interacting with the younger races than he did here, ostensibly leading his flight. He caught Kiry's eye, and she at least seemed to understand this deeper emotion—and approved of it.

"Kirygosa, daughter of Malygos," he said, "take the wisdom of Teralygos and others, and be my voice here while I am gone."

"No one can truly be your voice, my friend," Kirygosa replied gently, "but I will do all I can. If anyone can find the lost Focusing Iris in this wide world of ours, it will be you, who among us all know Azeroth best."

There was nothing more to say. In silence, Kalecgos leaped upward and flew out into the cold, snowy day, following the gentle tug that whispered *this way, this way.* Kirygosa had said she thought Kalec knew Azeroth better than any other blue dragon. He could only hope she was right.

2

Baine Bloodhoof looked about uneasily as he and a small retinue entered the city of Orgrimmar. The sole progeny of the late, much beloved and mourned tauren high chieftain Cairne Bloodhoof, Baine had only recently stepped into the position his father had occupied for so many years. It was a responsibility he had never actively sought, and he had accepted the duty with both humility and regret at the time of his father's death. Since then, the world had changed in every respect.

His personal world had shattered the night of his father's murder. Cairne had been slain in a mak'gora, a ritual duel, by Garrosh Hellscream. Garrosh, who had recently been named warchief of the Horde by Thrall, had intended to fight honorably, but someone else did not wish him to. Magatha Grimtotem, a shaman who had long harbored a hatred of Cairne and a desire to lead the tauren, had painted Garrosh's axe, Gorehowl, with poison rather than simple anointing oil. And so the noble Cairne had died by betrayal.

Garrosh had stayed out of the ensuing conflict that arose when Magatha made a blatant bid for conquest of the tauren. Baine had defeated the would-be usurper, banishing her and those who refused to swear loyalty to him. Afterward, he had vowed his own loyalty to Garrosh in the orc's role as warchief for a reason that was twofold—because his father would have wished it, and because Baine knew he had to do so in order to keep his people safe.

Since then, Baine Bloodhoof had not come to Orgrimmar. He had no desire to. Now he wished even more heartily that he could have stayed away.

But Garrosh had sent a summons to all the leaders of the various Horde races, and Baine, having pledged his support to Grom Hellscream's son, had come. So had the others. To disobey would be to risk open war.

Baine and his entourage rode their kodos through the massive gates. More than one tauren stared, ears flicking, at the towering scaffolding and the massive crane that moved above them. While Orgrimmar had never been as pastoral as Thunder Bluff, it was now actively martial. Looming iron construction, heavy and black and ominous, had replaced the simple wooden huts, "to prevent another fire," Garrosh had said. And, Baine knew, to evoke the so-called glory days of the Horde. To remind everyone after the chaos of the Cataclysm and the subsequent terrorizing of Deathwing that the orcs, and by extension the Horde itself, were not to be trifled with. To Baine, the ugly changes did not represent strength. The "new Orgrimmar" represented domination. Conquest. Subjugation. Its hard, jagged metal was a threat, not a comfort. He did not feel safe here. He did not think anyone who was not an orc could feel safe here.

Garrosh had even moved Grommash Hold from the Valley of Wisdom, where it had been under Thrall since the founding of the city, to the Valley of Strength—a decision, Baine thought, that reflected the nature of each warchief. As the tauren approached the hold, they were joined by a cluster of blood elves in their red and gold regalia. Lor'themar Theron, his long, pale blond hair in a topknot and his chin decorated with a small patch of beard, caught Baine's eye and nodded coolly. Baine returned the gesture.

"Friend Baine!" called an unctuously cheerful voice. Baine looked over to his right, then down. A sly-looking, obese goblin with a slightly battered top hat chomped a cigar and waved boisterously at him.

"You must be Trade Prince Jastor Gallywix," Baine said.

"That I am, that I am indeed," said the goblin with enthusiasm, giving him a toothy, somewhat predatory grin. "And delighted to be here today, as I am sure you are. My first official visit to Warchief Garrosh's court!"

"I don't know that I'd call it a court," Baine said.

"Close enough, close enough. Delighted, yes. How are you all doing in Mulgore?"

Baine regarded the goblin. He did not dislike goblins on principle, as some did. Indeed, he owed a great debt to Gazlowe, the goblin leader of the port town of Ratchet. Gazlowe had been of tremendous help to Baine during Magatha's attack on Thunder Bluff, providing zeppelins, weaponry, and warriors of a sort for (by goblin standards) a paltry fee. Baine simply did not particularly care for *this* goblin. Nor, his sources told him, did anyone. Not even Gallywix's own people.

"We are rebuilding our capital and fighting back the quilboar who are encroaching on our territory. The Alliance recently destroyed Camp Taurajo. We have erected the Great Gate so that they will come no farther," Baine said.

"Oh, well, sorry and congratulations, then!" Gallywix laughed. "Good luck with all that, eh?"

"Er . . . thank you," Baine said. Despite their small size, the goblins threaded their way through the flow of other Horde races to be first to enter Grommash Hold. Baine flicked an ear, sighed, dismounted from his kodo, handed the reins over to a waiting orc, and entered the hold himself.

This incarnation of the hold was, like everything else in the "new" Orgrimmar, more impersonal and martial—even the throne of the warchief of the Horde. Under Thrall's leadership, the skull and armor of the demon Mannoroth—whose blood had once corrupted the orcs and who was valiantly slain by Grom Hellscream—had been displayed on a massive tree trunk at the entrance to the hold. Garrosh had taken the symbols of his father's greatest victory and adorned his own throne with them, taking what Thrall had erected for the entire Horde to see and making them instead a personal tribute. He even wore part of the demon's tusks as shoulder armor. Every time he saw Garrosh, Baine's ears flattened slightly at the affront.

"Baine," said a gruff voice. Baine turned and felt the first surge of pleasure he had experienced since departing Thunder Bluff.

"Eitrigg," he said warmly, embracing the elderly orc. It seemed this honorable old veteran was the last who remained here of Thrall's original advisors. Eitrigg had served Thrall well and loyally, and had stayed behind at Thrall's request to advise Garrosh. It gave Baine hope that Garrosh had not concocted some reason to dismiss Eitrigg. It had been Eitrigg who had first noticed the smear of poison on Garrosh's weapon, Gorehowl, and who had told the young warchief that he had been tricked into slaying Cairne dishonorably. Baine had always respected Eitrigg, but that deed in particular had made Baine the orc's steadfast friend.

Baine narrowed his brown eyes at Eitrigg's expression. Keeping his voice as soft as possible—not an easy task for a tauren—he asked, "I take it you do not approve of the topic of today's gathering?"

Eitrigg made a sour face. "That is a pale statement. And I am not alone in my thoughts." He clapped the young leader on his arm, then stepped back, indicating that Baine should proceed to his people's traditional place on the left of the warchief's throne. At least Garrosh had made no effort to demote the tauren. Baine noted that Lor'themar was now on the right side of Garrosh, and next to the blood elves' sea of gold and red was the green skin of the goblins. Sylvanas and her Forsaken were directly opposite the orc, and Vol'jin and his trolls sat next to Baine. The orcs given the honor of being present—most of them Kor'kron, the formal guardians of the warchief—stood at attention, ringing the entire gathering.

Baine recalled his father telling him of similar meetings in Orgrimmar. At those gatherings, there were feasts, laughter, and revelry as well as debate and discussion. Baine saw no signs that anything resembling a feast had been prepared. Indeed, he thought as he took a tepid swig from the waterskin that hung at his belt, it had been a good thing that he and his people had brought their own water. Otherwise, in this desert city that baked under the sun, the iron buildings absorbing the heat, the tauren would even now be collapsing.

The moments crawled by, and the gathered leaders and their companions began to grow restless. Low murmuring broke out among the Forsaken. It seemed to Baine that despite the undead's frequent, chiding usage of the word, "patience" was not a universal discipline among them. His sharp tauren ears caught a sibilant whisper from Sylvanas, and the muttering subsided.

An orc clad in Kor'kron livery stepped forward. One hand had only three fingers, and a livid scar, pale against the darker hue of his skin, zigzagged across his face and down his throat. Red war paint, looking like streaked blood, adorned face and arms. But it was not these distinctions that made Baine's eyes narrow at the newcomer. It was the tone of the orc's scarlet-decorated skin.

Dark gray.

That meant two things. One, that the orc was a member of the Blackrock clan—a clan that had birthed many infamous members. And two, that he had spent years never seeing the light of day; he had dwelt inside Blackrock Mountain, serving Thrall's enemy.

Names, imparted in dire tones by his father, Cairne, filled Baine's head. Blackhand the Destroyer, warchief of the Horde and secret member of the Shadow Council, who had offered shaman up to become the first warlocks his people had ever known. That orc's son Dal'rend, nicknamed "Rend," had skulked for years in the depths of Blackrock Spire and opposed Thrall's leadership. There had only been a handful of Blackrock orcs whom Thrall had spoken of with respect. A handful, out of far too many. That this obviously seasoned veteran had the honor of opening the ceremonies—even ahead of the Kor'kron—made Baine uneasy about what was to come.

The veteran gestured imperiously. Several green-skinned orcs stepped forward. They held long, ornately decorated chimaera horns. With precise movements, they lifted the horns to their lips, filled their lungs, and blew. A long, deep, hollow sound reverberated through the chamber, and despite the current situation, Baine felt his spirit respond to the call to order. When the horns' blast had faded, the orcs who had blown them stepped back into the shadows.

The Blackrock orc spoke. His voice was deep and gravelly, and it carried throughout the chamber.

"Your leader, the mighty Garrosh Hellscream, approaches! Show him all honor!" The orc thumped his intact hand across his massive chest, turning to face the entrance to Grommash Hold.

Garrosh's brown body was covered with tattoos. Even his lower jaw had been tattooed black. Bare-chested, the orc wore Mannoroth's mammoth tusks, covered with spikes, on his shoulders. His waist was encircled with a belt that bore a carved skull—evocative of that of the great demon that adorned the throne. He clutched Gorehowl, the legendary weapon of his father, and lifted it high. Shouting and cheers filled the huge chamber, and for a moment, Garrosh stood, drinking it in. Then he lowered the axe and spoke.

"I bid you all welcome," he said, spreading his arms in an encompassing gesture. "You are true servants of the Horde. Your warchief calls you, and you come."

Like trained wolves, Baine thought, trying and failing to hide a frown. Thrall had never spoken so to his people.

Garrosh continued. "Much has transpired since I assumed the mantle of warchief. We have faced trials and danger, threats to our world and our way of life. And yet, we persevere. We are the *Horde*. We will not let anything break our spirits!"

He lifted Gorehowl again, and in response the gathered

orcs uttered a great cry. The rest of the Horde joined in, Baine included, for this was in support of the mighty Horde to which they all belonged. Garrosh spoke this much truth: those who called themselves Horde would never let their spirits be beaten down—not by a shattered world, not by an insane former Aspect, not by anything.

Not even by a father's murder.

Garrosh smiled around his tusks, nodding approvingly as he made his way to his throne, then raised his arms and called for silence. "You do not disappoint me," he said. "You are the finest representatives of your races—the leaders, the generals. And that is why I called you here."

He settled himself in his throne, waving to indicate that the assembled crowd, too, could sit. "There is a menace that has been present for too long, which we must now root out without mercy. A threat that has challenged us for years, to which we have, until recently, turned a blind eye in the mistaken notion that tolerance of a little shame will do no harm to the mighty Horde. I have said and say again, *any* shame is a great shame! *Any* injury is a great injury! *And we will endure it no longer!*"

A chill crept over Baine. He thought of Eitrigg's reaction to his earlier inquiry. Baine had half-suspected what Garrosh wished to say when the order was given for the Horde leaders to congregate. He had hoped he was wrong.

The orc continued. "We have a destiny to fulfill. And there is an obstacle to that destiny—one that we must crush beneath our feet like the insignificant insect it truly is. For far too long—nay, even a *moment* would be too long!—the Alliance pests, not content with their stranglehold over the Eastern Kingdoms, have wormed their ways into *our* lands, *our* territory. Into Kalimdor."

Baine closed his eyes briefly, pained.

"Chipping away at our resources and sullying the very earth with their presence! They are crippling us, preventing us from growing, from reaching the heights that I know—I *know*—we are capable of achieving! For I believe in my heart that it is not our fate to bow and scrape and sue for peace before the Alliance. It is our right to dominate and control this land of Kalimdor. It is ours, and we will claim it as such!"

Garrosh's orcs roared in approval. Most of them, anyway—those who stood with the Kor'kron and the Blackrock orc. Some murmured quietly to themselves. Many Horde members followed the Kor'kron's example, some bellowing with the same enthusiasm; others, Baine noted, with far less gusto. Baine himself remained seated. A very few of his own tauren applauded and stamped their hooves on the earth. The tauren had not been untouched by the recent changes. The Alliance, expanding from Northwatch Hold under false information that the tauren were planning an attack, had razed Camp Taurajo. The only residents it now had were looters. Many tauren died in the battle; others fled to Vendetta Point, sporadically attacking Northwatch Hold scouts, or to Camp Una'fe—the "Camp of Refuge."

In response to the aggression, Baine did what he felt was best to keep his people safe. The road to Mulgore had once been open; now what had been dubbed the Great Gate shut out any possibility of a massive Alliance incursion. Most tauren were content with the erection of the gate and did not burn for revenge. Others were still aching from the attack. He could not condemn these people. Baine did not rule with a tight grasp; the tauren followed him willingly and with love—perhaps mostly out of respect for his father, but with openness in their hearts nonetheless. Those who disagreed with Baine's decisions, like many Grimtotem or the tauren who chose to strike back at the Alliance from Vendetta Point, were expelled from Thunder Bluff but otherwise suffered no repercussions.

He returned his thoughts to the present as the cheering died down and Garrosh resumed.

"To that end, it is my intent to lead the Horde on a mission that will restore us to our rightful path." He paused, looking over the sea of faces, drawing out the moment. "Our first target will be Northwatch Hold. We will raze it. And once we have reclaimed that land as ours, we will move on to the next step—*Theramore!*"

Baine did not recall getting to his hooves, but suddenly he was standing. He was not alone. There was cheering, of course, but hard on its heels were cries of protest.

"Warchief! The lady Jaina is too powerful!" came a voice. It sounded like a Forsaken. "She has been passive and quiet. Rouse her, and we will have war on our hands—a war we are not prepared to fight!"

"She has behaved with fairness time and again, when she could have responded with force or deceit!" Baine shouted. "Her diplomatic efforts and her decision to work with Warchief Thrall have saved countless lives! To storm her realm with no provocation does not give honor to the Horde, and it is foolish besides!"

There were many murmurs of agreement. Other Alliance leaders were far less favored, and the lady Jaina had those who respected her among the Horde. Baine was heartened to hear the murmurs, but Garrosh's next words plunged the tauren back into despair.

"First," Garrosh snapped, "Thrall has given leadership of the Horde to me. Whatever *he* did or did not do means nothing now. I am the warchief, to whom you have all sworn loyalty. My decisions are what matter. And those of you who condemn my plan do not even know what it entails. Be silent and listen!"

The muttering died down, but not all of those who had risen took their seats.

"You respond to this as if the conquest of Theramore were the goal. I tell you now, it is only the beginning! I do not speak solely of destroying the human foothold in Kalimdor. I speak also, and even more vigorously, of the night elves. Let them flee to the Eastern Kingdoms as we crush their cities and take their resources!"

"Drive dem all out?" said Vol'jin, baffled. "Dey been here longer dan we have. An' we try something like dat, da Alliance be over us like bees on da honey! You just be giving dem de excuse dey been looking for!"

Garrosh turned slowly to the leader of the Darkspear trolls. Inwardly, Baine winced. Vol'jin had been among the most outspoken of Garrosh's critics after the death of Cairne. There was little love lost between the troll and orc leaders. Garrosh had forced the Darkspears into Orgrimmar's slums. Outraged at the insult, Vol'jin had ordered the trolls to leave Orgrimmar altogether. Now, the Darkspear ruler came to the city only when summoned.

"My soul is sick of the back-and-forth in Ashenvale that has gone on nearly since we set foot in this world," growled Garrosh. Baine knew the orc was still smarting from the latest defeat there at the hands of Varian Wrynn. "And I am even more sickened by our own blindness to what we should and must do. The night elves claim compassion and wisdom, yet they murder us when we harvest a few trees that would provide life-giving shelter! The night elves have lived here long enough. Let them now linger only as a bad memory. It is the Horde's hour to reign on this continent, and reign we shall! This is why Theramore is key, do you not understand?" Garrosh stared at the Horde members as if they were small children. "We crush Theramore, we stop the potential of Alliance reinforcements from the south. And then—we give the night elves their due."

"Warchief!" The voice was female, at once both musical and cold. Sylvanas Windrunner, former high elf ranger-general and now the leader of the Forsaken, rose and gazed at Garrosh with intense glowing eyes. "The Alliance may indeed not send reinforcements. Not at once, at least. They will turn and vent their wrath instead upon those of us in the Eastern Kingdoms—my people and the sin'dorei."

She looked at Lor'themar almost imploringly. The blood elf leader's face remained impassive. "Varian will march on my borders and destroy us!" The comment was addressed to Garrosh, but she continued to stare at Lor'themar. Baine felt for her; she was hoping for support from one who might reasonably be expected to give it, and finding none.

"Warchief! A word?" It was Eitrigg, turning with the respect he owed to his leader.

"I have heard from you already, my advisor," said Garrosh.

"*We* have not," Baine stated. "Eitrigg was friend to my father and advisor to Thrall. He knows the Alliance in a way few do. Surely you do not object to the rest of us hearing what such a wise elder has to say?"

The look that Garrosh shot Baine could have melted stone. The tauren met the gaze with deceptive placidness.

Nonetheless, the orc nodded to Eitrigg. "You may speak," he said curtly.

"It is true that the Horde has done much to recover from the Cataclysm," Eitrigg began. "And it has been under your leadership, Warchief Garrosh. You are right. Yours is the title. Yours are the decisions. But yours also is the responsibility. Think for a moment about the consequences of this choice."

"The night elves will be gone; the Alliance will be afraid to attack; and Kalimdor will belong to the Horde. Those will be the consequences, *elder*." Garrosh uttered the word not with respect, but almost with contempt. Baine noticed that two or three orcs frowned at the warchief's tone of voice and were listening intently to Eitrigg.

Eitrigg shook his head. "No," he said. "That is a hope. You hope to begin claiming this continent as ours. And you might. You would also begin a war that would involve armies from all over this world, Horde and Alliance, locked in a combat that would take lives and drain resources. Have we not suffered through enough of those costs?" The orcs who had been paying close attention now started nodding. Baine recognized one of them as a shopkeeper here in Orgrimmar. Another, surprisingly, was one of the guards, though not a member of the elite Kor'kron.

"Costs?" said a slightly screechy voice. "I hadn't heard Warchief Garrosh mention costs, friend Eitrigg." It was, of course, Trade Prince Gallywix. He was standing—not that anyone could tell. The crown of his top hat was all that could be seen of him, but it bobbed up and down animatedly with his speech. "What I hear is talk of profit for everyone. Why not expand, taking the resources of our enemies and driving them away at the same time? Even war is good business if you go about it properly!"

Baine had had enough. The greedy, self-absorbed goblin's quip about the blood of heroes and foes alike being spilled for profit pushed Baine's anger past prudent silence.

"Garrosh!" he said. "There is none here who can say that I do not love the Horde. Nor any who can say that I do not honor your title."

Garrosh did not speak. He well knew that he had not come to Baine's aid when it was needed, and yet the tauren still had acknowledged him as warchief. Baine had even saved Garrosh's life once. The orc made no attempt to silence Baine . . . yet.

"I know this lady. You do not. She has worked tirelessly for peace, knowing well that we are not monsters but people—like the people who compose the Alliance." His sharp eyes scanned the crowd, and any rabble-rousers who might have been tempted to protest his labeling humans, night elves, dwarves, draenei, worgen, and gnomes as "people" wisely held their tongues. "I have received aid and shelter in her home. She helped me when even members of the Horde would not. She does not deserve this treachery, this—"

"Baine Bloodhoof!" snarled Garrosh, closing the distance between himself and the tauren high chieftain in a few strides. Baine towered over him, but Garrosh was not cowed. "If you do not wish to share your father's fate, I would advise you to watch what you say!"

"You mean dying betrayed?" Baine shot back.

Garrosh roared. Archdruid Hamuul Runetotem stepped forward at the same time as Eitrigg. But another interposed himself between Baine and Garrosh—the Blackrock orc. He did not touch Baine, but the tauren could almost feel the fire of the other's banked rage churning.

The gray-skinned orc's eyes glittered, their coldness not tempering the heat of his anger but rather augmenting it. And Baine felt a prickle of unease. Who *was* this orc?

"Malkorok," said Garrosh. "Step down."

For what seemed an eternity, the Blackrock orc did not move. Baine had no desire for a confrontation—not here, not now. Attacking Garrosh, or this gray-skinned warrior who was clearly appointed specifically to defend him, would only further aggravate the young warchief and make him even more disinclined to listen to reason. At last, expelling air from his nostrils in a snort of contempt, Malkorok did as he was told.

Garrosh moved forward, shoving his face up toward Baine's.

"This is not a time for peace! The time for war has come—it is long *overdue*! Your own people have suffered from the expansion of the Alliance into your territory, unprovoked. If anyone should wish to destroy at the very least Northwatch Hold, it should be the tauren! You say that Jaina Proudmoore assisted you once. Are your loyalties now to her and the Alliance, who have killed your people . . . or to the mighty Horde and me?"

Baine took a long, slow breath and let it out through his nostrils. He bent his head to within an inch of Garrosh's and said, for that orc's ears only, "If I were ever to turn my back on the Horde and you, it would have been before this moment, Garrosh Hellscream. If you believe nothing else I say, believe that."

For a heartbeat, it seemed to Baine that an expression of shame crossed Garrosh's brown face. Then the scowl returned. Garrosh turned again to address the gathered crowd.

"This is the will of your warchief," he said bluntly.

"This is the plan. First Northwatch Hold, then Theramore, then we drive the night elves before us and take for our own what was theirs. As for any Alliance protests," he said, sparing a brief glance for Sylvanas, "rest assured, they will be dealt with swiftly. I am grateful for your obedience in these matters, but I expected nothing less from the great Horde. Return now to your homes, and prepare. You will hear from me again soon. For the Horde!"

The cheer, uttered so often and always with such passion, filled the hold. Baine joined in, but his heart was not in it. Not only was Garrosh's plan dangerously reckless, which surely should have been enough to condemn it, but it was based on treachery and hatred. The Earth Mother could never give her blessing to such an endeavor.

Garrosh waved Gorehowl above his head one final time, letting the weapon sing as the wind whistled through the holes in its blade, then lowered it. The Blackrock orc—Malkorok, Garrosh had named him—stepped right behind Garrosh before even Eitrigg, before even the Kor'kron. The orcs encircling the gathering snapped to attention and followed their leader out of the hold.

The crowd began to disperse. Baine saw the blue-skinned, red-haired troll leader moving toward him and slowed his own steps.

"Ju baited him," said Vol'jin without preamble.

"I did. It . . . was not wise."

"No, it wasn't. Dat why I stay quiet. Gotta tink about my people."

"I understand." The trolls were in more immediate peril from Garrosh's anger, living as close to Orgrimmar as they did. Baine did not blame Vol'jin. He glanced at the troll. "But I know what your heart is telling you."

Vol'jin sighed, looking somber, and nodded. "Dis a bad path we be walkin' down."

"Tell me, do you know who this Malkorok is?"

The troll scowled. "He be a Blackrock. Dey say he still don't like da light of Durotar, after bein' so long in Blackrock Mountain, servin' Rend."

"I suspected as much," growled Baine.

"He denounced his crimes in service to Rend an' asked for amnesty. Garrosh be givin' it to him, along wit' any others who swear to serve him wit' dere lives. Now da wahchief got a nice big dog wit' sharp teeth ta protect him."

"But—how can he be trusted?"

Vol'jin laughed a little. "Some might say, how can da Grimtotem be trusted? Yet you let da ones who swear loyalty stay at Thunder Bluff."

Baine thought of Tarakor, a black bull who had served under Magatha. Tarakor had led the attack against Baine but had pleaded for reprieve for himself and his family. Tarakor had proven to be as good as his word, as had all the others whom Baine had pardoned. And yet, somehow, to Baine, the Grimtotem seemed different from the Blackrocks.

"Perhaps I am inclined to prejudge," said Baine. "I think better of the tauren than I do of orcs."

"Dese days," Vol'jin said quietly, making sure he was not overheard, "so do I."

Garrosh waited outside so that those who wished to take this opportunity to swear loyalty to him could do so more conveniently. A goblin female was kneeling before him, nattering on about something, when Malkorok said, "There he is." Garrosh looked up and spotted Lor'themar.

"Bring him."

He interrupted the goblin, patted her head, said, "I accept your oath," and shooed her off as Malkorok approached with the blood elf leader. Lor'themar inclined his pale blond head in a gesture of respect.

"You wish to see me, Warchief?"

"I do," said Garrosh, steering them off a few steps so that they might speak with more privacy. Malkorok ensured they would not be disturbed by stepping in front of them and folding his massive gray arms. "Out of all the leaders, save Gallywix—who is supportive merely because he sees coins to be made—you are the only one who doesn't question your warchief. Not even when Sylvanas tries to play upon your sympathy. I respect that, elf. Know that your loyalty to me is duly noted."

"The Horde embraced and supported my people when no one else would," Lor'themar replied. "I will not forget that. And so, my loyalty, and that of my people, is to the Horde."

Unease stirred in Garrosh as he noticed a slight emphasis on Lor'themar's last word. "I am the Horde's warchief, Lor'themar. And as such, I *am* the Horde."

"You are its warchief," Lor'themar said, agreeing readily. "Is that all you wish of me? My people are anxious to return home and prepare for the war that is to come."

"Of course," Garrosh said. "You may go."

Lor'themar had said nothing inflammatory, but the unease did not dissipate as Garrosh regarded the sea of red and gold moving toward the gates of Orgrimmar.

"That one is worth watching," he said to Malkorok.

"They are *all* worth watching," the Blackrock orc replied.

3

I recognize that dirty cloak," the image of Prince Anduin Wrynn said, grinning.

Lady Jaina Proudmoore returned the smile. She and her "nephew," firmly related by affection if not blood, were conversing by means of an enchanted mirror Jaina kept carefully hidden behind a bookcase. When the proper spell was recited, the reflection of each respective room would vanish, and what had been a simple mirror would become instead a window. It was a variation on the spell that allowed magi to transport themselves and others from one site to another.

Anduin had once shown up unexpectedly when Jaina was returning from one of her secret visits with then-warchief Thrall. Clever lad that he was, the prince had figured out what she had been up to, and now they shared a secret.

"Never could fool you," Jaina said. "How goes your time among the draenei?" She could guess some of what he would tell her without waiting to hear the answer. Anduin had grown—not just physically. Even in the mirror, which rendered him in a palette of blues, she could see that his jaw was more determined, and his eyes were calmer and wiser.

"It's been truly amazing, Aunt Jaina," he said. "There is so much going on in the world that I want to be part of right now, but I know I have to stay here. I'm learning something new almost every single day. It kills me that I can't help, but—"

"It is the destiny of others to buy us a future for you to grow up in, Anduin," Jaina said. "It is *your* destiny to do precisely that—and do so well. Keep studying. Keep learning. You're right. You're exactly where you need to be."

He shifted his weight from one foot to the other and suddenly looked very young again. "I know," he said, sighing. "I *do* know that. It's just . . . hard, sometimes."

"There will come a time when you will long for these simpler, quieter days," Jaina said. Briefly her mind went back to her own youth. Loved by her father and brother, safe with her governess and tutors, Jaina had been filled with the joy of learning and the duties of a young lady, despite the military nature of her family. She had chafed against such things then, but now they seemed sweet and delicate as a flower's petals.

Anduin rolled his eyes in mock exasperation. "Give Thrall my best," he said.

"I'm sure that's hardly prudent," Jaina replied, but she smiled as she said it. She lifted the cloak's hood over her golden hair. "Be well, Anduin. It's good to hear how you are doing."

"I will, Aunt Jaina. You be careful." His image vanished. Jaina, who had been tying the hood down tight, paused in mid-motion. *You be careful.* He was, indeed, growing up.

As she had so many times before, she set out alone, taking care, as Anduin had asked, that she was not observed by anyone. She paddled the dinghy to the southwest, navigating the small islands of the area known as Tide-fury Cove. The occasional muckshell clacked at her in annoyance, but otherwise the waterways were undisturbed.

Jaina pulled up to the meeting place, surprised to see that Thrall wasn't present. She felt slightly uneasy. So much had changed. He had given leadership of the Horde to Garrosh. The world had cracked open like an egg, never to be the same again. And a great evil that had burned with hate and madness had rampaged across Azeroth to, finally, be defeated.

The wind shifted, caressing her face and blowing the hood off despite the fact that she had tied it securely beneath her chin. Her cloak billowed back from her slender frame, and suddenly Jaina smiled. The wind was warm and smelled of apple blossoms, and before she quite realized what happened, it had lifted her out of the dinghy like a large, gentle hand. She did not struggle; she knew she was perfectly safe. Cradling her, the wind deposited her on the shore with the same care it had displayed when picking her up. Not a drop of muddy water had touched so much as the toe of her boot.

He stepped out from his place of concealment behind a rock, and Jaina realized she still hadn't grown used to his new appearance. Instead of armor, Thrall, son of Durotan, wore simple robes. Red prayer beads encircled his throat. His large head of black hair was covered by a plain hood. The robes revealed part of his powerful green chest, and his arms were bare. He was indeed a shaman now, not a warchief. Only the Doomhammer, strapped to his back, was familiar to her.

He held out his hands, and Jaina took them.

"Lady Proudmoore," he said, his blue eyes warm with welcome. "Long has it been since we met so."

"Long indeed, Thrall," she said in agreement. "Perhaps too long."

"I am Go'el," he said, reminding her gently. Slightly chagrined, she nodded.

"My apologies. Go'el it shall be." She looked around. "Where is Eitrigg?"

"He is with the warchief," Go'el said. "While I now am leader of the Earthen Ring, I serve humbly. I do not think of myself as greater than any other member."

A hint of an amused smile quirked her mouth. "Many would consider you much more than a simple shaman," she said. "I among them. Or are the tales that you allied with four Dragon Aspects to help bring down Deathwing just stories?"

"It was an honor, and a humbling one, to so serve," Go'el said. Coming from anyone else, the words would have been simple politeness. Jaina knew them to be true. "I merely held the space for the Earth-Warder. It was all of us, working together—dragons and brave representatives of every race of this world. The credit for slaying the great monster goes to many."

Her eyes searched his. "You are content with *all* your decisions, then."

"I am," he said. "If I had not left to join the Earthen Ring, I would not have been prepared to undertake the task that was asked of me."

She thought of Anduin and his training, which was taking him far away from family and loved ones. "*There is so much going on in the world that I want to be part of right now, but I know I have to stay here. I'm learning something new almost every single day.*"

And she had told him he was exactly where he needed to be. Now Go'el was saying the same thing. Part of her agreed with him. Surely the world was much better off without the ravages and terrorizing of Deathwing and the Twilight Cult! And yet . . .

"Nothing is free, Go'el," she said. "Your knowledge and skills were bought at a cost. The . . . orc you left behind in your place has done much harm in your absence. If I have heard about what is going on in Orgrimmar and Ashenvale, surely you must have!"

His mien, which had been deeply peaceful, now looked troubled. "I have heard, of course."

"And . . . you do nothing?"

"I have another path," Go'el said. "You have seen the results of that path. A threat that—"

"Go'el, I hear this, but now that task is over. Garrosh is stirring up trouble between the Alliance and the Horde—trouble that didn't exist until he started it. I can understand if you don't wish to undermine him publicly, but—perhaps you and I can work together. Form a summit of sorts. Ask Baine to join us; I know he has no love for what Garrosh is striving for. I could speak with Varian. As of late, he seems to be more reachable. Everyone respects you, even in the Alliance, Go'el. You have earned that respect because of your actions. Garrosh has earned nothing but mistrust and hatred because of his."

She indicated her cloak, which Go'el had blown about with the wind he had sent to bear her to shore. "You can control the winds as a shaman. But the winds of war are blowing, and if we do not stop Garrosh now, many innocents will pay the price for our hesitation."

"I know what Garrosh has done," Go'el said. "But I also know what the Alliance has done. There are innocents, yes, but even you cannot place the blame for the current tensions squarely at Garrosh's feet. Not all the attacks have been initiated by the Horde. It does not seem to me that the Alliance is working particularly hard to find peace either."

His voice was still calm but held a warning note. Jaina winced—not at the tone of voice, but at the truth of what was said. "I know," she said heavily. She dropped down despondently on a rock jutting up from the soil. "There are times when I feel as if my words fall on deaf ears. The only one who seems to be truly interested in forging a lasting peace is Anduin Wrynn—and he's just fourteen."

"That is not too young to care about his world."

"But it is too young to *do* anything about it," Jaina said. "It seems as if I am struggling through mud simply to be heard, let alone actually listened to. It's . . . difficult to try to be a diplomat and work for real, solid results when the other side won't acknowledge reason anymore. I feel like a crow cawing in the field. I wonder if it's just wasted breath."

She was surprised at the frankness and weariness in the words. Where had they come from? Jaina realized that she truly had no one to talk to, to express doubts to anymore. Anduin looked up to her as a role model, so she couldn't explain how disheartened she felt at times, and Varian and the other Alliance leaders were—most of them—firmly on the opposite side of any argument she made. Only Thrall—Go'el—seemed to understand, and even he appeared at the moment to be denying how much his decision to appoint Garrosh as warchief of the Horde could cost.

Jaina gazed down at her hands, the words pouring out of her, uncensored. "The world's changed so much, Go'el. Everything's changed. Every*one*'s changed."

"Everyone and everything *does* change, Jaina," Go'el said quietly. "It's the nature of things to grow, to become something they were not. The seed becomes the tree, the bud the fruit, the—"

"I know that," Jaina snapped. "But you know what doesn't change? Hatred. Hatred and the hunger for power. People get an idea or a plan that works in their favor, and they dig in and won't let it go. They won't see what's right in front of them if it contradicts what they want. And the words of reason, of peace, just don't seem to be effective against that anymore."

Go'el raised an eyebrow. "Perhaps you are right," he said noncommittally. "We must all choose our own paths. Maybe there is something else you should focus on."

She gave him a stunned look. "This world has already been torn apart. Do you truly think I should stop trying to prevent its inhabitants from tearing *themselves* apart?"

Jaina stopped just short of adding, "Like you have done." It wasn't fair. Go'el had hardly been idle. He had indeed been doing much for Azeroth, but still . . . It was petty of her, but she felt as if he had let her down. She folded her stained cloak about her frame in what she realized was a defensive gesture. Sighing, she deliberately loosened her tight shoulders. Go'el sat quietly beside her on the boulder.

"You must do what you think is best, Jaina," he said. A slight wind stirred the braids in his beard. He looked off into the distance as he spoke. "I cannot tell you what that is, or else I would be just like these others whom you find so frustrating."

He was right. There had been a time when Jaina had easily discerned what the best thing to do was in a given situation. Even if it was bitterly hard to do it. Choosing not to stand with her own father as he fought the Horde had been such a defining moment for her. So had been walking away from Arthas when he instigated what became known later as the Culling of Stratholme. But now—

"It's all so uncertain, Go'el. More than it ever has been, I think."

He nodded. "It is indeed."

She turned to look at him searchingly. He had changed, in more ways than one. Not just his clothing, or his name, or his demeanor, but—

"So," she said, "the last time we met, it was to celebrate a happy occasion. How is life with Aggra treating you?"

His blue eyes warmed. "Well indeed," he said. "She honors me by accepting me."

"I think you honor her," Jaina said. "Tell me about her. I didn't really have much of a chance to talk to her."

Go'el gave her a speculative glance, as though wondering why she wished to know, then shrugged slightly.

"She is of course a Mag'har, born and raised in Draenor. That is why her skin is brown; she and her people were never tainted by any sort of exposure to demon blood. Azeroth is new to her, but she loves it passionately. She is a shaman, like me, and devotes herself entirely to healing this world. And," he added quietly, "healing me."

"Did you . . . need healing?" Jaina asked.

"We all do, whether we see it or not," Go'el replied. "We bear the wounds of simply living in this life even if we never have a physical scar. A mate who can see one for who one is, truly and completely—ah, that is a gift, Jaina Proudmoore. A gift that restores and renews one daily, and which must be tended carefully. It is a gift that has made me whole—made me understand my purpose and place in the world."

Gently, he laid a large green hand on her shoulder. "I

would wish such a gift and such insights for you, my dear friend. I would see you happy, your life complete, your purpose clear."

"My life *is* complete. And I know my purpose."

He smiled around his tusks. "As I said, only you know what is right for you. But I will say this with certainty: whatever journey you are on, whatever your path may lead to, I, at least, have found it to be sweeter by far with a life companion at my side."

Jaina thought with a trace of uncharacteristic bitterness of Kael'thas Sunstrider and Arthas Menethil. Both had once been so bright and beautiful. Both had loved her. One she had respected and admired; the other she had loved deeply in return. Both had fallen to the call of dark powers and the weaker parts of their natures. She smiled without humor.

"I do not think I am very wise at choosing life companions," she said. She forced down the frustration and unhappiness and uncertainty, and reached to place her small, pale hand on his. "I'm better when it comes to friends."

They sat together for a long, long time.

It began to rain as Jaina paddled back to Theramore after her meeting with Thrall. Though it made her cold and uncomfortable for the moment, she welcomed the inconvenience, as few tended to venture out in such inclement weather. She tied up the tiny dinghy to the dock, slipping a little on the wet wood, and under cover of the steady downpour, made her way to the magically concealed secret entrance to the tower, unnoticed. Shortly she was in her cozy parlor. Shivering, Jaina lit the fire with a murmured incantation and a flick of a finger, dried her clothes the same way, and put away the cloak.

She brewed some tea and selected a few cookies, set them down on a small table, and settled in by the fire, thinking about what Thrall had said. He seemed so . . . content. Calm. But how could he be? In a very real sense, he had turned his back on his people and, in handing the reins to Garrosh, had practically guaranteed that war would become inevitable. If only Anduin were older, he would be a valuable ally. But youth was so fleeting; Jaina felt guilty for momentarily wishing Anduin would miss a single day of it.

And Thrall—Go'el (it would take her some time to get used to the new name)—was married now. What would this mean for the Horde? Might he want his son or daughter to rule after him? Would he take up the mantle of the Horde again if this Aggra gave him a child?

"Save any cookies for me, Lady?" The voice was female, youthful, a little squeaky.

Jaina smiled without turning around. She had been so engrossed in her thoughts, she hadn't heard the distinctive humming sound of a teleportation spell. "Kinndy, you can always make your own."

Her apprentice laughed cheerfully, hopping into a chair opposite Jaina beside the blazing fire and reaching for a cup of tea and one of the aforementioned cookies. "But mine are only *apprentice* cookies. Yours are *master* cookies. They're ever so much better."

"You'll figure out chocolate bits any day now," Jaina said, keeping her face deadpan. "Though your apple bars are coming along quite nicely."

"I'm glad you think so," said Kinndy Sparkshine. She was perky even for a gnome, with a shock of bright pink hair pulled back in pigtails that made her look much younger than her twenty-two years—just a teenager by her people's reckoning of age. It would be easy to dismiss her as a chipper little thing with as much substance as the spun-candy confection her hair resembled, but those who looked into her wide blue eyes would see a sharp intelligence there that contradicted the innocent face. Jaina had taken her on as an apprentice several months ago. She hadn't really had much of a choice.

Rhonin, who had led the Kirin Tor through the Nexus War and still guided them, had requested Jaina's presence shortly after the Cataclysm had struck. He was more somber than she had ever seen him as he met her in the Purple Parlor, a special place accessible, as far as she knew, only by portal. After pouring them each a drink of sparkling Dalaran wine, he sat beside her and regarded her intently.

"Rhonin," Jaina had asked quietly, not even taking a sip of the delicious beverage, "what is it? What has happened?"

"Well, let's see," he replied. "Deathwing is loose; Darkshore has fallen into the sea—"

"I mean with *you*."

He smiled faintly at his own dark humor. "Nothing is wrong with me, Jaina. Merely—well, I have a concern that I'd like to share with you."

She frowned, a small crease appearing between her brows, and put the glass down. "Me? Why me? I'm not one of the Council of Six. I'm not even a member of the Kirin Tor anymore." Once, she had been, working closely with her master, Antonidas. But after the Third War, when the scattered members of the Kirin Tor had re-formed, it hadn't felt the same to her.

"And this is precisely why it's you I must speak with," he said. "Jaina, we've all endured so much. We've been so busy—well, fighting and planning and doing battle—that we've fallen behind on another, perhaps even more important, duty."

Jaina gave him a bemused smile. "Defeating Malygos and recovering from a world shaken like a rat in a mastiff's mouth seem pretty important to me."

He nodded. "They are. But so is training the next generation."

"What's that got to do—oh." She shook her golden head firmly. "Rhonin, I'd like to help, but I can't come to Dalaran. I have my own challenges in Theramore, and even though Horde and Alliance have been equally harmed by the Cataclysm, we still have so much—"

He held up an interrupting hand. "You misunderstand me," he said. "I'm not asking you to stay here in the Violet Citadel. There are enough of us here—but too few out there in the world."

"Oh," she said again. "You . . . want me to take an apprentice."

"We do. If you're amenable. There is one young woman in particular I'd like you to consider. She's extremely promising, intelligent, and fiercely curious about the world outside her limited view of Ironforge and Dalaran. I think you'd be a very good match."

And then Jaina understood. She reclined in the comfortable purple cushions and reached for the wine. She took a small sip and said, "And someone who'd do a fine job of reporting back to you too, I presume."

"Come now, Lady Proudmoore. You can't expect us to leave so powerful and influential a mage all alone out there in Theramore."

"Honestly? I'm surprised you haven't sent along an observer before," she said.

He gave her a rueful look. "There's so much in chaos now," he said. "It's not that we don't trust you. It's that we simply need to . . . well . . ."

"I promise not to open any Dark Portals," Jaina said, lifting her hand and mockingly swearing.

That made him laugh; then he sobered. Placing a hand on hers, he leaned in for a moment. "You do understand, don't you?"

"I do," Jaina said. And she did. Before, there had been no time for anything other than simple survival.

Any mage, anywhere, who had not actively allied with Malygos had been a threat to him. Now, with the world splintered, old alliances were splintered as well. And Jaina was both a powerful mage and a respected diplomat.

Thoughts of Antonidas, who had—after much badgering on her part—taken her on as an apprentice what seemed like ages ago, filled her mind. He had been a wise and good man, with a strong sense of right and wrong and the willingness to die to protect others. He had inspired and shaped her. Suddenly, Jaina very much wanted to give back to the world what it had given her. She was quite aware that she was a mage of no small ability, and now that the subject had been broached, she thought it might be a good thing to teach someone what she knew. She did not have to rejoin the Kirin Tor to help others understand and work well with magic, as she had learned how to do. Life was unpredictable, these days more so than ever. Additionally, she found she missed Anduin's occasional presence. Perhaps a young person would liven up the damp old place.

"You know," she said, "I recall a certain headstrong young woman who pestered Antonidas to take her as an apprentice."

"And as *I* recall, she turned out rather well. Some say she's the finest mage in Azeroth."

"Some say many things."

"Please tell me you'll teach her," Rhonin said, dropping any hint of anything other than complete sincerity.

"I think it's a fine idea," she said firmly.

"You'll like her," Rhonin said. His expression grew impish. "She'll challenge you."

Kinndy had challenged Pained, too, Jaina remembered. She smothered a smile as she thought about

Pained's reaction to the gnome girl. Pained was a night elf, a warrior who had stayed with Jaina ever since being assigned to the mage at the Battle of Mount Hyjal. She steadfastly served as Jaina's bodyguard, whether or not the lady actually needed her, unless Jaina sent her off on a more covert mission. Jaina often told Pained that she was free to return to her people at any point. Pained usually shrugged and said, "Lady Tyrande never officially relieved me of my duty," and would not reply further. Jaina didn't quite understand the night elf's stubbornness and inexplicable devotion, but she was grateful for it.

At one point, Kinndy had been studying while Jaina methodically went through her cabinet of reagents, writing up new labels for those that were almost illegible and putting aside items that had lost their potency for proper disposal. Chairs in Theramore were designed for humans, and Kinndy's feet didn't reach the floor. She had been swinging them absently, sipping tea as she perused a tome nearly as large as she was. Pained had been busying herself, cleaning her sword. Out of the corner of her eye, Jaina had noticed the elf glancing at Kinndy now and then, looking more annoyed each time.

Finally Pained burst out, "Kinndy? Do you *enjoy* being perky?"

Kinndy closed the book, marking her place with a small finger, and pondered the question. After a moment, she said, "People don't take me seriously. This often denies me opportunities to be useful. I find it rather frustrating. So, no. I *don't* enjoy being perky."

Pained nodded. "Ah. That is all right, then," she said, and returned to her work. Jaina had to excuse herself quickly in order to keep from laughing.

Unintentional perkiness aside, Kinndy had indeed

challenged Jaina. The gnome had more energy than any-one Jaina had ever met. The questions were endless. At first they were amusing, then annoying, and then Jaina woke up one day and realized she was truly a mentor. A master with an apprentice who would grow up to do her proud. Rhonin hadn't been exaggerating—he had prob-ably given her the best the Kirin Tor had to offer.

Kinndy was curious about Jaina's role as a leader as well as a mage. Jaina would have liked to have told the gnome about the secret meetings with Go'el—Kinndy seemed the type of person who might understand Jaina's reason-ing—but of course could not. Fond of the girl though Jaina might be, Kinndy was, in the end, honor-bound to report everything she knew to the Kirin Tor. Jaina's slip with Anduin had taught her to take extra precautions, and thus far, she was certain that Kinndy was still ignorant of the meetings.

"How is Master Rhonin?" Jaina inquired.

"Oh, he is well. He sends his best," Kinndy replied. "He seemed a bit distracted," she mused, pausing to take an-other bite of cookie.

"We're magi, Kinndy," Jaina said wryly. "We're always distracted by something or other."

"This is true!" she said cheerily, brushing at some crumbs. "But even so, my visit seemed rather rushed."

"Did you get to spend time with your parents?" Kinndy's father, Windle, was entrusted with the impor-tant duty of lighting all of Dalaran's streetlights with his wand in the evening. According to Kinndy, he so enjoyed the task that he sold wands that enabled others to experi-ence it themselves a time or two. Her mother, Jaxi, often provided baked goods for the high elf Aimee to sell at her stall, and the gnome's red velvet cupcakes were extremely popular. This heritage was part of the reason that Kinndy was so frustrated at her own—in her opinion—subpar pastries.

"I did!"

"And yet you still want cookies," Jaina teased.

Kinndy shrugged. "What can I say? Every tooth I have is a sweet tooth," she replied with the cheerful attitude that Jaina had come to expect, but it was clear something continued to worry the gnome. Jaina placed her plate down on the table.

"Kinndy, I know that you are supposed to report back to the Kirin Tor. That was part of the agreement. But you're also my apprentice. If you have any problems with me as your master—"

The blue eyes widened. "You? Oh, Lady Jaina, it's not you at all! It's just—I felt that something was off in Dalaran. You could sense it in the air. And Master Rhonin's behavior didn't help put me at ease."

Jaina was impressed. Not all magi developed the sixth sense that told them, as Kinndy had put it, that there was something "off." Jaina herself had the ability, to a degree. She couldn't always tell when things were magically amiss, but when she did get that feeling, she paid attention to it. And Kinndy was only twenty-two.

Jaina smiled a bit wistfully. "Master Rhonin was right about you," she said. "He said you were gifted."

Kinndy blushed, just a little.

"Well, I'm sure if there is something truly amiss, we'll hear about it soon enough," Jaina said. "In the meantime, did you finish the book I sent along with you?"

Kinndy sighed. *"An In-Depth Analysis of the Temporal Effects of Conjuration of Foodstuffs?"*

"That would be the one, yes."

"I did. Although . . ." She hesitated and wouldn't meet Jaina's eyes.

"What's wrong?"

"Well . . . I think there's now a smudge of frosting on page forty-three."

Night fell in Orgrimmar. The heat dwindled but did not dissipate; the hard-baked sand, devoid of vegetation, held the sun's heat, as did the large, newly constructed metal buildings. Orgrimmar, like all of Durotar, was hardly a pleasant place from a climate standpoint. It never had been, and now it was even less so.

That suited Malkorok just fine.

He found the heat of Durotar uncomfortable, as he had found the heat of the interior of Blackrock Mountain. And that was good. The best thing that had ever happened to the orc people was leaving the softness of places like Nagrand back on their homeworld of Draenor. This was a place that tested one's mettle, that tempered and tried one. It was not good to become too comfortable. And part of Malkorok's job was to see to it that no orc grew too comfortable.

Some orcs at the recent gathering had been too comfortable. Too secure in the rightness of their opinions. They had openly voiced displeasure and disagreement with one who was not just their warchief but the leader of their own kind. The leader of the *orcs*! The very arrogance of it caused Malkorok to grit his teeth in anger. He forced himself to stay silent as he moved quietly through the streets.

He had told Garrosh that they were all worth watching. Garrosh had initially assumed Malkorok meant that all the leaders of the various races composing the Horde should be observed. The Blackrock orc had a much, much larger view. When he said they were "all" worth watching, he *meant* the entire Horde.

Every member of it.

And so it was that he'd had some of his best orcs follow a few of the malcontents who had dared to stay silent while others cheered. Of course Eitrigg, well loved and respected, an advisor Garrosh had promised Thrall he would listen to, could speak with impunity.

For the moment.

But others who had sided with the old orc must pay the price of what Malkorok—and Garrosh—considered nothing less than open, unabashed treason. His mind went back to several years ago, when he had been in service to Rend Blackhand. He thought with satisfaction of what had happened to those adventurers unwise enough to enter into the heart of the mountain and challenge Rend. But even more vividly, he recalled what he himself had done to his fellow orcs who had muttered against Blackhand, thinking themselves safe in the shadows.

He had stalked them, carrying out his own implacable justice. Rend had commented once when one of the traitors had gone missing. Malkorok had simply shrugged, and Rend had given him a sneering grin of approval. It was never mentioned after that.

Things were different now. But not that much different. Now Malkorok did not walk in the shadows alone. Four Kor'kron, appointed specifically by Garrosh to obey Malkorok's orders as if they were his own, accompanied him, moving as stealthily as if they were shadows themselves.

Kor'jus lived in the Cleft of Shadow, one of the more

unsavory parts of Orgrimmar. One might assume that, with such a residence, Kor'jus was involved in shady business. However, the name of his shop, Dark Earth, was nothing more sinister than a description of the soil needed for his crop—mushrooms. While Kor'jus was, as far as Malkorok knew, a law-abiding citizen, the fact that he lived here made the Blackrock orc's duty easier. With a wink and a few gold coins, would-be witnesses nodded and looked away.

Kor'jus was kneeling, using a sharp knife to harvest mushrooms for sale on the morrow. He cut swiftly, close to the base of the fungus, tossed it in a sack, and moved on to the next. His back was to the door, which had a curtain partly drawn over the entrance and a sign that read CLOSED. Though he could not see his visitors, he sensed their presence and stiffened. Slowly he rose and turned around, his eyes narrowing at the sight of Malkorok and his companions standing at the entrance.

"Read the sign," he grunted. "The shop doesn't open until tomorrow." Malkorok noticed with amusement that the mushroom farmer tightened his grip on his small blade. As if that would help.

"We're not here for mushrooms," Malkorok said, his voice soft. He and the other four orcs moved into the shop. One of them closed the curtain. "We're here for you."

5

Dawn's light, gentle but persistent, found its way through the cracks in the curtains of Jaina's bed-chamber. Used to awakening at this hour, she blinked, smiled sleepily, and stretched. She swung her legs out over the bed, rose, threw on a robe, and pulled back the dark blue curtains.

It was a gorgeous morning, rose and gold and laven-der where the sun hadn't yet chased away the shadows of night. She opened the window and breathed deeply of the salty air, letting it tousle her bed-rumpled golden hair still further. The sea, always the sea. She was the daughter of the lord admiral, and her brother had once quipped that the Proudmoores all had seawater in their veins. A hint of melancholy touched her as she thought of her father and brother. She lingered for a moment longer, remembering, then turned from the window.

Jaina brushed her hair, then sat down in front of a small table. With a thought, she lit a candle and gazed at the flickering flame. She started every day thus, if she could manage it; it helped her focus and prepare for whatever might be thrown her—

Her blue eyes widened and she became instantly alert.

Something was about to happen. She recalled talking to Kinndy last evening (the gnome was no doubt still asleep; she could have been born a night elf, she liked to stay up late so much) about her visit to Dalaran and subsequent unease. *It's just—I felt that something was off in Dalaran,* Kinndy had said. *You could sense it in the air.*

Jaina was sensing something now, like an old sailor who could feel a storm approaching in her bones. She felt a vague fluttering of apprehension in her chest. Her morning ritual would have to wait. Quickly she bathed and dressed, and so it was that she was already downstairs and making tea when one of her most trusted advisors, Archmage Tervosh, knocked on the door. Unlike Kinndy, he didn't have anything officially to do with the Kirin Tor. He was, like Jaina, more comfortable on his own, and the two had developed a great and rewarding friendship, living in Theramore as a couple of mavericks.

"Lady Jaina," he said, "I—well—there's someone here to see you." He looked unhappy. "He won't give me his name, but he bears a letter of safe passage from Rhonin. I checked; it's genuine."

He handed her the rolled-up scroll, sealed with the familiar eye symbol of the Kirin Tor. Breaking the seal and reading, Jaina instantly recognized Rhonin's handwriting.

Dear Lady Jaina,

I ask that you give this visitor whatever aid he requires. His cause is frighteningly real and he needs all the assistance those of us who practice magic can offer him.

—R

Jaina inhaled quickly. What was going on, that Rhonin would say something like this?

"Show him in," she said. Looking as disturbed as Jaina felt, Tervosh nodded and withdrew. While she waited, Jaina poured herself a cup of tea and sipped on it, pondering. A moment later, a man with a hood pulled low over his head strode into her parlor. He wore simple traveling clothes that yet bore no stain of traveling such a great distance. A blue cloak made from rich fabric swirled about him as he moved with a lithe quickness. He bowed and straightened.

"Lady Jaina," he said in a pleasant voice. "I apologize for coming so early, and unheralded. It's not the way I would have wished to arrive."

With that, he pushed back the hood that had hidden his face and gave her an uneasy smile. He had the best of both human and elven features, blue-black hair that fell to his shoulders, and blue eyes bright with purpose.

She recognized him at once. Her eyes grew wide, and her teacup crashed to the floor.

"Oh, that's my fault," Kalecgos, former Aspect of the blue dragonflight, said. He waved a hand. The spilled tea disappeared and the teacup reassembled itself, reappearing empty in Jaina's hand.

"Thank you," Jaina managed to say. She gave him a slightly lopsided smile. "You've also taken away the chance for me to greet you in a proper manner. At least I can offer you some tea."

He returned her smile, but it didn't reach his eyes. "I would welcome some, thank you. And I regret that we don't have time for the formalities and pleasantries. It's nice to see you again, even under these circumstances."

Jaina poured tea for them both with a hand that didn't

tremble. She'd recovered almost at once. She had seen Kalecgos at the bonding ceremony of Go'el and Aggra, and had liked him immediately, although there had not been time for much conversation. She handed him a cup and said sincerely, "Lord Kalecgos of the blue dragonflight, I know well of your noble deeds and good heart. You are welcome in Theramore. The letter you presented instructs me to offer all aid I can, and that is what you shall have."

She sat down on the small couch and indicated that he join her. To her surprise, this being, so powerful and ancient, seemed almost . . . shy as he accepted the tea.

"It is an honor for me to work with you as well, Lady," he said. "You have a reputation also—one that I have long admired. Your understanding of magic and the solemnity with which you wield that power—as well as the more, shall we say, mundane powers of diplomacy and leadership—are to be respected."

"Oh," Jaina said. "Well—thank you. But pleasant as it is, I don't think you came all the way from Northrend to compliment and be complimented."

He sighed and took a sip of the tea. "Unfortunately you are correct. Lady—"

"Jaina, please. I don't stand much on ceremony in my home."

"Jaina . . ." He lifted blue eyes to her that no longer held any hint of lightness. "We're in trouble. All of us."

"Your flight?"

"No, not just my people. Everyone in Azeroth."

"My, that's a tall tale." Kinndy stood in the doorway, looking both confused and wary. "Or at least exaggerated. Surely not *every single person* in Azeroth will be affected by whatever trouble the blue dragonflight has gotten itself into now."

Her hair was a mess. Jaina suspected she'd put it up in pigtails quickly without even running a brush through it. Kalecgos seemed more amused than upset by the gnome's sharp tongue, and he turned to Jaina quizzically. Jaina recalled Kinndy's statement to Pained, that no one took her seriously. She felt sure that Kalecgos would learn to.

"Kalecgos, may I present Kinndy Sparkshine. My apprentice."

"How d'ya do," said Kinndy, helping herself to some tea. "I heard you talking outside to Archmage Tervosh. I got curious."

"A pleasure to meet you, apprentice Sparkshine. I am sure that anyone Jaina chooses to take under her wing is a worthy student."

Kinndy sniffed and sipped tea. "You'll forgive me, sir," she said. "Given all that's recently happened, I and the rest of the Dalaran magi are a bit . . . leery of your flight. I mean, you know—war and attempted slaughter of all other magi. Things like that."

Jaina winced inwardly. A twenty-two-year-old apprentice was all but accusing the former blue Dragon Aspect of, at the very least, bearing the responsibility for a previous Aspect's actions, and at the most, being deceitful himself.

"Kinndy, Kalecgos is a dragon of peace. He's not like Malygos. He—"

Kalec lifted a hand, politely interrupting her. "That's quite all right. No one knows better than I what my people have done to others who use arcane magic in this world. I have come to expect Kinndy's attitude from anyone who—well, who isn't a blue dragon." He gave the gnome a small smile. "A rather large part of my task as the flight's leader, if no longer its Aspect, has been to try to show that not all of us approved of the Nexus War. And that since the death of Malygos, we have not attempted to control or manipulate others who use the arcane."

"Isn't that the flight's job, though?" asked Kinndy. "Wasn't the Aspect entrusted with that very duty? And don't you still kind of perform that role, even if your unique abilities are gone?"

Kalecgos's eyes took on a faraway look. When he spoke, his voice was both softer and deeper, though it remained his own. "'Magic must be regulated, managed, and controlled. But it must also be appreciated and valued and not hoarded. Such is the contradiction you must deal with.'"

Jaina felt a shiver run along her spine. Even Kinndy looked subdued. Kalecgos's eyes once again became bright and alert, and he regarded both of them. "These were the words once spoken by Norgannon, the titan who gave Malygos the power of an Aspect."

"And so you make my point for me," Kinndy said.

Understanding now that Kalecgos would not take umbrage, and thinking that it might be wise for her to hold her tongue and let the two of them hash it out, Jaina leaned back against the couch's cushion and simply observed.

"All words are subject to interpretation," said Kalecgos. "Malygos chose to understand that he was the ultimate minder of magic. Because he disapproved of how others were choosing to manage magic, he decided to recover it all for himself and his flight alone—that only they could appreciate and value it. I choose to regulate, manage, and control my own magic. To lead by example. To encourage others to appreciate and value it. Because, Kinndy—if you truly appreciate and value something, then you wish to manage it well. You don't want to hoard it; you want to share it. And that was how I chose to be the minder of magic in this world. Now I am merely the flight's leader. I am no longer an Aspect. And in this new role, believe me, I more than welcome aid from the Kirin Tor and anyone else who is willing to help."

Kinndy pondered this, one foot swinging as it dangled off the floor. The gnomish culture was nothing if not logical, and Kinndy's methodical brain could appreciate what Kalec was saying. Finally, she nodded.

"Tell us about this thing that's going to affect everyone in Azeroth," she said. Kinndy wasn't going to apologize for her attitude, but she clearly had moved past mistrust of the blue dragon leader.

Kalec, too, seemed to understand the shift and addressed both women in his response. "You are familiar with the device known as the Focusing Iris, which has long been in the keeping of the blue dragonflight."

"That's what Malygos used to control the surge needles that diverted the magical ley lines of Azeroth so they flowed to the Nexus," said Kinndy. Jaina was afraid she was starting to put two and two together, but even now, she still hoped she was wrong.

"Yes," he said. "It was. And it is this ancient orb that has been stolen from us."

Kinndy looked as if she was going to be sick. Jaina stared at Kalecgos in horror. She couldn't imagine how he felt. She blurted out the first thing that came to her mind.

"Thank you—for being willing to ask for help," she said, reaching out and pressing his hand impulsively. He glanced at her hand, then her face, and nodded.

"I did not exaggerate when I said it affects all of us," he said. "I spoke with Rhonin, then flew directly here. You, young lady," he said to Kinndy, "are only the third non-dragon to know."

"I—I'm flattered," stammered Kinndy. The resentment she seemed to bear toward Kalec had utterly disappeared. She said nothing more about "tall tales." Kalecgos had been telling the truth.

"What do you know of the theft?" asked Jaina, anxious to turn the discussion to practical matters—what was known, what was yet to be discovered, and, hopefully, what could be done about it.

Briefly, Kalecgos filled them in. Jaina's heart sank with each word. *Taken by unknown foes who could overcome five dragons?*

"Did Rhonin offer any help?" she asked, surprised by how faint and hopeless her own voice sounded. Kinndy was turning the color of parchment and hadn't spoken in a while.

Kalecgos shook his blue-black head. "No. Not yet, at any rate. I was able to sense the direction in which it was traveling. Faintly, but it was there. That's what led me to Kalimdor—and to you, Jaina." He spread his hands in an imploring gesture. "I am the leader of the blue dragons. We understand magic. We have our own tomes, more ancient than any you have seen. But what we do not have are your resources. I am not arrogant enough to think that we know everything. There are magi not born dragons who have come up with things no dragon ever knew of. That's where you can help me—if you would."

"Of course," said Jaina. "I'll bring in Archmage Tervosh, and we'll all put our heads together."

"Breakfast first?" asked Kinndy.

"Absolutely," Kalecgos said. "Who can focus on an empty stomach?"

Slowly, Jaina's heart lifted, at least a little. Kalec could track the progress of the missing device. He was willing, apparently eager, to accept help. And he was right. Who *could* focus on an empty stomach?

Their eyes met and he smiled. Her heart lifted a little more. They had to believe they would recover it in time. And as Kalecgos, Kinndy, and she went into the dining room, she had hope that they would.

The five of them—Jaina, Kalecgos, Tervosh, Pained, and Kinndy—flung themselves into work and research. Kinndy returned to Dalaran, where, with Rhonin's blessing, she had access to the library. Jaina envied her the task.

"I remember when that was my duty," she told Kinndy, giving the gnome a quick hug. "There was nothing I liked better than poring through those old tomes and scrolls and simply learning." She felt a slight pang; the "new Dalaran" was beautiful, but she no longer belonged there.

"It was probably more fun when the fate of the world didn't rest on your research," Kinndy said morosely. Jaina had to agree.

Pained, who was in charge of Jaina's spy network, departed when she heard the news. "I will go into the field and learn what I can," she said. "My spies are diligent, but they might not understand what they need to look for in this situation." She eyed Kalecgos. "I assume you may be safe here, with this . . . person, my lady."

"I think my own skills and those of a former Aspect will keep me safe in the event of any threat, yes, Pained," Jaina said. Her voice held no amusement, as she knew how seriously Pained took her duties. The night elf's gaze flickered to Kalec, then back to Jaina. Pained saluted.

"Lady."

Once Kinndy and Pained had departed for their respective errands, Jaina looked at Tervosh and Kalecgos, nodded briskly, and said, "Let's get to work. Kalec—earlier you said that you were able to track the Focusing Iris. Why haven't you simply followed it? Why come to me?"

He glanced down, looking slightly sick. "I said I *had* been able to follow it. The trail . . . *vanished* shortly after I reached Kalimdor."

"What?" Tervosh was irritated. "It couldn't just stop."

"Yes," Jaina said, her voice heavy. "It could. Whoever stole this thing must have a great deal of power at their disposal if they could stand against five dragons. But they didn't know enough about it at that time to completely conceal the theft. That's why Kalec was able to track it."

"My thoughts exactly," Kalec said. "At some point, they either did learn enough about it or found a mage who was sufficiently powerful to hide its emanation from me."

Tervosh put his face in his hands for a moment. "That's—someone very powerful indeed."

"True," Jaina said. She lifted her chin in slight defiance of the bad news. "They may have a powerful mage, or more than one. But so do we. And we have the benefit of someone who knows everything about the Focusing Iris. We'd better settle in for a bit while Kalec brings us up to speed."

"What do you need to know?"

"Everything," she said firmly. "Don't just give us the basics. We need *all* the details. Even something that seems insignificant could prove useful. Tervosh and I must know what you know."

Kalecgos smiled ruefully. "That could take some time."

It did. He talked until it was time for the midday meal, when they paused briefly to eat, and then until dinner, and continued after that. Even a dragon's voice, it seemed, became hoarse if he spoke too long. The hour grew late, and that first night, the three all stumbled off to their various bedchambers with heavy-lidded eyes. Jaina didn't know how the others slept, but as for herself, she had nightmares.

She awoke the next morning feeling groggy and unrested. Her ritual did not restore her as it usually did, and the sky was overcast and lowering. She felt a heaviness sink into her chest, and sighed. Not wanting to look out on the gray day, she let the curtain fall and went downstairs.

Kalecgos gave her a warm smile as she entered the little parlor, but it faltered as he noticed her pallor.

"Didn't sleep well?"

She shook her head. "You?"

"Well enough. Though I was troubled with bad dreams. I blame your chef. That dinner tasted delicious, but obviously there was a fragment of an underdone potato hiding in there somewhere."

Despite the direness of the situation, Jaina found herself chuckling a little. "Then you are welcome to conjure all our meals, and that will teach you to complain!" she said, chiding him teasingly.

He gave her a look of mock horror. Their eyes met, and they both sobered.

"It seems . . . wrong to joke," Jaina said with a sigh. She began the preparation of the tea, measuring it out precisely as she always did, and setting the kettle to boil.

"It might seem wrong," Kalec said in agreement, helping himself to the eggs, boar sausage, and hot porridge despite his earlier teasing disparagement of the chef's abilities. "But it isn't."

"Surely humor is inappropriate at times." Jaina fixed her own plate and sat down next to Kalec.

"At times," he said, digging into the sausage. "But joy is never inappropriate. Not real joy. Not the sort of lightness in the soul that makes the burdens bearable." He gave her a sideways glance as he chewed and swallowed. "I didn't give you and Kinndy the full quote that I—well, 'heard' isn't the right word. 'Received,' possibly, from Norgannon."

The kettle began to sing. Jaina rose to tend to it, pouring tea for both of them. "Really? Why not?"

"Miss Kinndy didn't seem in the right frame of mind to receive it properly."

She handed him the tea and sat back down. "And I am?"

An odd look crossed his face. "Perhaps."

"Then tell me."

He closed his eyes, and again his voice changed, became deeper, became . . . *other.*

"'I believe that you will find that my gift to you is not just a profound duty—which it is—but also a delight—which it is! . . . May you be dutiful . . . and joyous both.'"

Jaina felt a strange twinge in her heart at the words. She realized she'd been silent, staring into Kalec's eyes, for several seconds when he quirked a blue eyebrow, inviting a response from her. She looked down at her bowl, stirring her porridge.

"I—was telling Kinndy the truth. I enjoyed studying," she said, stammering a little. "I loved it, actually. Loved everything about Dalaran." Her lips curved in remembrance. "I remember . . . humming as I went about my tasks," she added, laughing as her cheeks warmed with embarrassment. "The scents, the sunlight, the sheer fun of learning and practicing and finally mastering spells, of curling up with cheese and apples and scrolls . . ."

"Joy," Kalec said quietly.

She supposed it was. It was sweet, to linger in that long-ago moment. Then another memory crystallized . . . Kael'thas had approached her one such day, and then later . . . Arthas. The smile faded.

"What happened?" Kalec asked gently. "The sun went behind a cloud."

Jaina pressed her lips together. "Just . . . we all have ghosts. Maybe even dragons do."

"Ah," he said, regarding her with compassion. "You think of ones you loved and lost." She forced herself to eat more porridge, though the normally tasty breakfast food was now like sludge in her mouth, and nodded. "Perhaps . . . of Arthas?"

Jaina swallowed hard, then started to say something to change the subject. But Kalec pressed on. "We do all have ghosts, Jaina. Even dragons, even Aspects. Grief for her ghost nearly destroyed Alexstrasza, the great Life-Binder herself."

"Korialstrasz," she said. "Krasus. I saw him many times when he was at Dalaran but never really knew him. I had no idea who he truly was."

"Hardly anyone did. And yes, Korialstrasz. He gave his life to save all of us, and at first, we thought him a traitor."

"Including you and Alexstrasza?"

"We didn't want it to, but doubt crept into even our hearts." Kalec admitted this reluctantly. "And I have my own ghosts too, Jaina. One is a human girl. With," he added, giving her a little nod, "fair hair and a great heart. She was . . . so much more than just a girl, though. She was something beautiful and profound and unspeakably powerful, but her time as a simple young woman infused that power with compassion and love."

Jaina didn't look at him. She knew of whom he spoke—Anveena, who had been the Sunwell incarnate. Jaina was familiar with what had happened to Anveena. The girl who was not a girl had sacrificed one form for her true one, and in doing so, sacrificed her life.

"Another is a dragon, lovely as ice and sunlight, who was intended to be my mate." He seemed to recall Jaina's presence and gave her a quick smile. "I don't think you'd get along with her particularly well. She never understood my interest in the, ah . . ."

"Lesser races?"

"I've never called you that," Kalec said, and for the first time, Jaina saw a spark of anger in the blue dragon. "Those who are not dragons are not lesser. It took Tyrygosa a while to see that. You are simply . . . different from us. And maybe in some ways better than us."

Jaina raised her golden brows. "How in the world can you possibly say that?"

He smiled. "Cheese and apples and scrolls," he said. "And thus, you knew true, simple joy when you hadn't even entered your second decade. That to me makes you . . . astonishing."

6

It was not long before the explicit directives came. Baine hated what he was about to do, but if he refused, Garrosh would turn on him—and the tauren—with the full force of the rest of the Horde behind him. Baine harbored no illusions of the idealism of the Forsaken, the blood elves, or the goblins; they had their own agendas. The orcs were traditional friends to the tauren, but there were few malcontents. And the trolls simply couldn't risk it. If the tauren defied Garrosh so blatantly as to refuse this order, they would stand alone.

Baine crushed the missive in his hand and turned a bleak expression to Hamuul Runetotem. "Let us prepare," the high chieftain said. "At the very least, this part of the war Garrosh is getting us into has some scent of justice behind it."

The orders had been clear. Baine was to bring "at least two dozen braves," kodos, and weapons of war and approach Northwatch Hold from the west. The trolls would join them, though the trek from the Echo Isles to Mulgore was a long one. The orcs would be marching from Orgrimmar, and the Forsaken, the goblins, and the blood elves would take ships to meet them in the port town of

Ratchet, and then they would all move swiftly to rendez-vous with the tauren at Northwatch Hold.

Once, there had been only the dry land of the Bar-rens between Mulgore and Northwatch, and a little town called Camp Taurajo. Back then, the greatest problem had been fighting the quilboar. Now Baine would need to march his people past the ruins of Taurajo and through what had become known as the Fields of Blood.

Following the orders he so disliked, Baine amassed his people on their side of the Great Gate as quietly as pos-sible. They stood silently as instructed, the only sound the slight creaking of armor and the occasional stamp of a kodo. Baine could feel the tension; he marveled that the Alliance on the other side could not sense it as well. He had sent several scouts ahead, to make sure that the Al-liance recon would be taken unawares, and they had all reported back that only a few kept watch at this hour. Two tauren, taking care not to be seen, ascended the viewing platforms and made their own longer-distance reconnaissance. They could see better than humans in the dark, and besides, the Alliance soldiers were often foolish enough to keep campfires burning.

"High Chieftain," said one of the scouts, forcing his voice to be soft, "the trolls—the hills are thick with them. They only await your order."

"The number of soldiers is no greater than usual, judg-ing by the fires," said another. "They are not expecting an attack."

Baine's heart ached at what he was about to do. "Re-port back to Vol'jin. Tell him his people may attack at will. Once they have engaged the Alliance, we will open the Great Gate and follow up with our own weapons."

The scout nodded, turning and climbing up the hill

at the juncture where the gate met it. Baine looked out over the assembled crowd of tauren, their shapes barely visible in the light of the few torches they bore. There were several dozen braves and many others who would serve vital purposes when the conflict came in but a few seconds: druids, shaman, healers, and other fighters of all kinds.

He lifted his arm, making sure that it was seen, and waited. His heart beat quickly: one, two, three—

And then came the blood-chilling war cries. The trolls had attacked. Baine snapped his arm down. From the other side of the gate were the defiant shouts of humans and dwarves, the clang of weaponry, and the thud of ballista arrows striking home. On this side of the gate, two tauren grunted and strained, their massive bodies trembling with the effort, as the thick ropes were laboriously pulled and the gate groaned.

The Northwatch soldiers were taken completely by surprise. Tauren braves streamed through, bellowing and hurling themselves into the fray. The humans and dwarves didn't stand a chance. They were vastly outnumbered by furred and green- and blue-skinned bodies, and their weapons, while dangerous, needed time to be directed and prepped. There was no time for anything but desperate and ill-fated resistance.

One foolish soldier charged Baine himself, crying, "For the Alliance!" His simple military-issue sword snapped as Baine swung his mace. The piece went flying, flashing brightly in the faint light, and then was swallowed up by darkness. Baine swung again. The soldier's chain-mail armor offered no protection from the blunt instrument. The body hurtled a distance away from the force of the blow.

There were a few more shouts from tauren and trolls, and then the clang of weaponry ceased.

"Trolls, hold!" Vol'jin ordered.

"Tauren, to me!" Baine shouted.

There was a pause, and then whoops of triumph filled the night air. Baine looked around. It was over, mere moments after it had started.

"Dis bodes well for de attack," Vol'jin said.

Baine shook his head. "Not if any Alliance escaped. Under the cloak of night, they could warn Northwatch Hold."

"Den we best be about gettin' ta Nort'watch."

They took a moment to select a few scouts to go ahead and report back as the rest of the troll-and-tauren army regrouped and began the march east toward Northwatch. Vol'jin pulled his raptor up alongside Baine's kodo as they went.

"After we left Orgrimmar," Vol'jin said, "some of da orcs dat were noddin' dey heads when ol' Eitrigg was talkin' been kinda . . . absent."

Baine felt a jolt surge through him. "Garrosh is *executing* those who don't agree with him?"

"Not yet. Dem Kor'kron, especially dat gray-skinned one, dey be walkin' tru da streets jest waitin' to overhear somethin' they doan like. If dey do—well, some dey arrest right on da spot. Some dey come for all quiet. Dat mushroom seller, he close shop for a few days. He come back lookin' all beat-up, like he be in da wrong end of a fight. And some . . . dey doan come back at all."

"Political prisoners?"

Vol'jin nodded. "We trolls be keepin' our mouths shut."

Baine grunted. "Perhaps if Garrosh knew what the

Kor'kron are up to . . . He is a hothead, but . . . surely he cannot be ordering this."

Vol'jin made a dismissive sound and waved a gangly arm in disgust. "No one gets to Garrosh. I hear dat even Eitrigg only sees him when Garrosh feels like it, and den dat boy surrounded by his big ol' bodyguards. He be all, 'Da Horde can do dis; da Horde can do dat.' All confident, wit'out any reason for it. I can't say for certain dat he knows what's goin' on. But I can't say for certain dat he don't. Either way . . . I be more scared of Orgrimmar these days dan de darkest voodoo."

"Then . . . there is no stopping him. No reaching him, no reasoning. And insanity abounds."

"Dat's about da size of it, mon."

Baine growled softly, looking over his troops. An idea was forming. It was audacious; it was risky; and it might cost him dearly.

But it might save the tauren people.

It might even save the Horde.

"Why can't we find anything?"

The words burst as if of their own volition from Jaina, and she wished them back as soon as she had uttered them. Kalec, Tervosh, and Kinndy—who had returned from Dalaran with two entire trunks full of scrolls, magical items, and books that the Kirin Tor thought might help—all looked up from their various studies and stared at her.

She bit her lip. "I'm sorry," she said. "I'm . . . usually not like this."

Tervosh gave her a kind smile. "No, Lady, you're not," he said. "But then again, this is hardly a usual situation."

Normally, she was both idealist and pragmatist. "Practical" was what Arthas had dubbed her. The combination was part of what made her such a skilled mage. Her curious mind worked methodically around a problem until it was solved. It served her well in diplomatic endeavors too. While she cared deeply about the outcome of what she worked toward, she also *worked* toward it. She didn't just stomp her foot or weep or say whiny things like *Why can't we find anything?*

"The archmage is correct," Kalecgos said. "We're all under a lot of strain. Perhaps we should take a brief respite."

"We broke for lunch," Kinndy said.

"Four hours ago," Kalec reminded her. "Since then, we've not stretched or moved or done anything but stare at books. We may have lost the ability to even spot something if we do come across it."

Jaina rubbed her aching eyes. "I apologize again. Kalec may have hit on the very reason for, uh, why we haven't found anything." She put a little extra emphasis on the words to let them all know that she was fully aware of how she had sounded.

"I don't think—" Kinndy began.

"You're young," Tervosh said. "You can go forever. We old folks need our little breaks. You're welcome to stay here and keep perusing the documents, Kinndy, but I'm going to go and work in the garden for a bit. There are some herbs that need harvesting."

He rose and pressed his hands to his back. There was an audible crack. Jaina knew she, too, would creak as she rose after sitting in one position for too long. She and Tervosh were not, as he had joked, "old folks," but the seemingly endless energy of her youth, which had sustained her through her ordeals with the plague and the war with demons, appeared to elude her now that she had reached thirty.

"Care to show me around?" asked Kalec, interrupting her thoughts.

She started. "Oh! Yes, of course!" She rose, attempting to cover her embarrassment at being caught woolgathering. "I am very proud of the order and harmony we have here in Theramore. The Cataclysm damaged the city, but we rebuilt with a will."

They descended the long, winding stairs of Jaina's tower and stepped out into a surprisingly sunny day. Jaina nodded to the guards, who saluted smartly, and to the mounted lieutenant Aden. Kalecgos looked about with open interest.

"Over there is Foothold Citadel," Jaina said. There was a training area on their right as they walked by where Theramore's guards "fought" against practice dummies, their swords thunking against wood. Coming from their left, however, were the bright sounds of steel clashing against steel as the young recruits trained in the open air. Their commanders barked orders while priests watched carefully, ready to call upon the Light for healing the instant anyone was injured.

"It's . . . rather martial," Kalec observed.

"We're at the entrance to a very dangerous swamp on one side and the ocean on the other," Jaina said. They continued to walk, turning away from the practicing warriors and passing the inn. "We've got a lot to protect against."

"The Horde, obviously."

She gave him a look. "We *are* the most martial Alliance presence on the continent, but honestly, the majority of the danger comes from the wildlife and various unsavory characters."

Kalec put a hand to his chest and widened his eyes in feigned shock and hurt. Jaina smiled. "Don't worry. The only dragons I take issue with are the black dragons in the swamp," she said. "The Horde seems to keep to itself, as long as we do. And that's an arrangement I can live with, although there are many who don't understand that."

"Is the Alliance pressing for war?" Kalec asked quietly. Jaina grimaced.

"Ah, now you have found a sore spot," she said. "We'll discuss that later. How are your blues faring, Kalec? Most magi may resent them, as Kinndy did, but I know you have undergone a great deal. First the Nexus War, then finding and losing an Aspect, then this theft—"

"Now *you* have found a sore spot," Kalec said, but his voice was kind.

"My apologies," Jaina said. Their path was leading them out of the city, the cobblestones becoming less well tended and slightly muddy. "I meant no offense. And here I am, supposed to be a diplomat."

"No offense was taken, and a good diplomat can often see clearly what is troubling another," Kalec said. "It has indeed been difficult. For so many ages, dragons were among the most powerful beings in Azeroth. We alone had the Aspects to guard our flights and the world. Even the least of us had a life that must seem impossibly long to you and abilities that made many of my race feel superior. Deathwing—what is the phrase you humans use?—gave us a good helping of humble cake."

Jaina fought to keep from laughing. "I think the phrase is usually 'humble pie.'"

He chuckled. "It would seem that even though I like

the younger races more than most of my kin do, I still have a lot to learn."

Jaina waved her hand. "Human slang should not be high on your list of things to master," she said.

"I wish I could say that I had nothing more pressing to do," Kalec replied, sobering again.

"Halt!" a voice cried sharply. Kalecgos stopped, looking at Jaina with curiosity as several guards approached with drawn swords and axes. Jaina waved at them and they immediately put away their weapons and bowed as they recognized her. One of them, a fair-haired, bearded man, saluted.

"Lady Jaina," he said. "I wasn't informed that you and your guest would be passing through. Do you wish an escort?"

The two magi exchanged slightly amused glances. "Thank you, Captain Wymor. I appreciate the offer, but I think this gentleman will be able to protect me," Jaina said, keeping a straight face.

"As you will, my lady."

Kalec waited until they had passed out of earshot before saying in a completely serious tone of voice, "I don't know, Jaina; I might be the one who needs rescuing."

"Why then, I shall come to your rescue," Jaina said, keeping her face as serious as his.

Kalec sighed. "You are already doing so," he said quietly.

She glanced up at him, her brow furrowing. "I'm helping," she said. "I'm not rescuing."

"In a way, you are. You all are. We're . . . not what we were. I want so much to protect my flight, to take care of them."

Something clicked in Jaina's mind. "As you wanted to protect Anveena."

A muscle twitched in his cheek, but his steps didn't falter. "Yes."

"You didn't fail her."

"Yes, I did. She was captured and used," Kalec said, his voice harsh with self-loathing. "Used to try to bring Kil'jaeden into Azeroth. And I couldn't save her."

"You had no control over that, if what I understand is true," Jaina said softly, feeling her way. She wasn't sure how much Kalecgos was ready to share with her. "You were possessed yourself by a dreadlord. And once you were freed from that horrible existence, you went to her."

"But I couldn't do anything. I couldn't stop them from hurting her."

"Yes, you did," Jaina said, pressing him. "You let Anveena become what she really was—the Sunwell. And because of your love and her courage, Kil'jaeden was defeated. You were selfless enough not to deny her her destiny."

"And the Aspects were destined to lose our powers in order for us to succeed against Deathwing, I know," Kalec said. "It's not wrong, what is going on. But . . . it is hard. It is hard to watch their hope failing, and—"

"To know yours is failing as well?"

He turned sharply to look at her, and for a moment she thought she had gone too far. But it was not anger in his eyes; it was anguish. "You," he said, "are not nearly as old as I. How is it you are so insightful?"

She hooked her arm through his as they walked. "Because I'm wrestling with the same thing."

"Why are you here, Jaina?" he asked. She raised a golden eyebrow at his bluntness. "I've heard that you were considered one of the finest magi of the order. Why are you not in Dalaran? Why are you here, standing between swamp and ocean, between Horde and Alliance?"

"Because someone has to."

"Truly?" His brow was furrowed. He came to a stop and turned her to face him.

"Of course!" she retorted. Anger rose in her. "Do you *want* war between the Alliance and Horde, Kalec? Is that what the dragons have decided to do with their time these days? Go around stirring up trouble?"

His blue eyes showed hurt from the blow her words had landed.

She winced. "I'm sorry. I didn't mean that."

Kalec nodded. "What *did* you mean, then?" he asked, but there was no rancor in his voice.

She stared at him mutely. She didn't know. Then words came tumbling out from somewhere. "I didn't want to be part of the order after Dalaran fell. After . . . Antonidas died. Arthas killed him, Kalec. Killed so many of them. The man I had once thought I would marry. Had loved. I didn't . . . I couldn't be around that. I had changed, and the Kirin Tor had changed too. They're more than simply neutral . . . I think, perhaps without realizing it, they may look down on anyone who's not one of them. I had learned that to really foster peace, you have to embrace the people—all of them. And although I was the last one to suspect it, I do have diplomatic gifts," she said earnestly.

The hurt was gone from his kind face, and he lifted one hand to stroke her golden hair, almost as if he were comforting a child. "Jaina?" he asked. "If you believe that— and I am not saying you are wrong—why are you trying so very hard to convince yourself?"

And there it was. He had plunged a dagger in her heart, keen and sharp and so painful that she gasped as if it were a physical blow. She stared up at him, unable to drag her gaze away, feeling tears sting her eyes.

"They don't *listen*," she said, barely audible. "No one listens. Not Varian, not Thrall, certainly not Garrosh. I feel that I am standing alone on a cliff, and the wind snatches the words from my lips even as I speak them. No matter what I do, no matter what I say, it is all . . . pointless. It has no meaning. *I* . . . have no meaning."

As she spoke, she saw a sad smile of recognition touch Kalec's lips.

"And so, this we share, Lady Jaina Proudmoore," Kalec said. "We fear being of no use. Of no help. All that we have known to do is useless."

The tears spilled down her cheeks. Gently, he wiped them away. "But I do know this much. There is a rhythm, a cycle to such things. Nothing stays the same, Jaina. Not even dragons, so long-lived and supposedly so wise. How much, then, must humans change? Once, you were an eager young apprentice, curious and studious, content to stay in Dalaran and master your spells. Then the world came and ripped you away from your safe place. You changed. You survived, even thrived, in the new role of a diplomat. You had puzzles and challenges, but of a different variety. And that is how you served. This world—" He shook his head sadly, looking up into the sky. "This world is not as it was. *No thing, no one,* is as it was. Here—let me show you something."

He lifted his hands, his long, clever fingers moving. Arcane energy sparked from his fingertips. It formed a whirling ball, hovering in front of them.

"Look at this," he said.

Jaina did, forcing her foolish tears—where had they come from?—down and focusing on the little orb of arcane magic. Deftly Kalec touched it. It seemed to shatter and then re-form, with a difference.

"There—it's a pattern!" Jaina said, marveling.

"Watch again," Kalec said. A second time he touched it. A third. Each time, the patterns became clearer. There was a moment when, baffled and enraptured both, Jaina wondered if she was looking at a gnomish schematic rather than a ball of arcane energy. Signs and symbols and numbers whirled, then jumbled together, then arranged themselves in a certain formation.

"It's . . . so beautiful," she whispered.

Kalec splayed his fingers and drew his hand through the orb. As if it were mist he disturbed, it fragmented, then re-formed in still another way. It was a ceaselessly shifting kaleidoscope of magic, of precise patterns and order.

"Do you understand, Jaina?" he asked. She continued to stare, almost hypnotized by the exquisite patterns of formation, shattering, and reconfiguration.

"It's . . . more than spells," she said.

He nodded. "It's what spells are made of."

For a moment, she didn't follow him. Spells had incantations, gesticulation, sometimes reagents—and then understanding smote her so powerfully she almost stumbled with the revelation.

"It's . . . *math!*"

"Equations. Theorems. Order," Kalec said, pleased. "Combined in one way, they are one thing—in another, something altogether different. It is fixed and mutable, as is a life. All things change, Jaina, whether from the inside out or the outside in. Sometimes with only a single shift in a variable."

"And . . . we are magic, too," Jaina whispered. She tore her gaze from the ineffably beautiful swirl of lyrical, poetical math and began to form a question.

"Lady Jaina!"

The shout startled them both, and they turned to see Captain Wymor galloping toward them on a bay horse. He pulled the beast up so sharply it reared and mouthed the bit.

"Captain Wymor, what—" Jaina began, but the guard cut her off.

"Pained has returned with news," he said, panting from the short but intense ride. "The Horde—they are gathering. Coming from Orgrimmar and Ratchet as well as from Mulgore. It looks like they're set to converge on Northwatch Hold!"

"No," Jaina breathed, her heart, an instant ago so buoyed by the beauty and insight Kalecgos had shared with her, now heavy in her chest. "Please, no . . . not this . . . not now . . ."

7

It was Ol' Durty Pete's turn to keep watch in Corporal Teegan's Expedition encampment, located on the edge of the mysterious jungle Overgrowth, which had seemingly sprung up overnight. Despite his fondness for a "mug o' th' brew" on, well, nearly an hourly basis, the white-bearded dwarf knew enough to take his assignments seriously. He hadn't had anything to drink since nightfall, and it was nearly dawn.

He patted his blunderbuss—which he loved, even if it was becoming a bit erratic these days (unkind folks said it was Ol' Durty Pete who was erratic, not his gun)—and sighed. Soon his watch would be over, and he could open up that cherry grog he'd been saving for—

There was a rustle in the undergrowth. The old dwarf got to his feet with more speed than most would have given him credit for. All kinds of strange critters could be attacking. Raptors, plainsriders, those big nasty flower- or moss-things—

A woman, wearing a tabard that sported a golden anchor, stumbled forward, stared at him a moment, and then collapsed. Pete barely caught her as she fell.

"Teegan!" roared Pete. "We got oursels a problem!"

A few seconds later, one of the guards was attempting to bandage the young scout's injuries, but Pete thought sadly that it was pretty clear the little missy wasn't going to pull through. She reached out frantically, grabbing on to Hannah Bridgewater's arm as Hannah bent over her.

"H-Horde," the scout rasped. "T-tauren. Opened the gate. Heading east. Think . . . Northwatch . . ."

Her eyes closed, and her black hair, matted with blood, fell back limply against Pete's broad chest. He patted her shoulder awkwardly.

"Ye got yer message through, lass," he said. "Ye done good. Take yer rest, noo."

Teegan, hurrying up in response to Pete's call, shot the dwarf an angry look. "She's dead, you idiot."

Gently, Pete replied, "I know, laddie. I know."

Two minutes later, the fastest one among them, Hannah, was running as quickly as her long, strong legs would carry her, east to Northwatch, praying to the Light that she wouldn't be too late.

Admiral Tarlen Aubrey was, as usual, awake before dawn. He rose swiftly, splashed water on his face, dressed, and shaved. As he met his own eyes in the mirror, he saw that they had circles underneath them and frowned as he carefully shaped the beard and mustache that were his only concessions to physical vanity. Over the last few days, the Rageroar clan of orcs had appeared to be regrouping—what was left of them. Skirmishes had broken out, during which it had been reported that a few of the orcs had shouted insults along the lines that the Alliance would get what was coming to it, or had grunted defiant comments as they died, such as, "My death will be avenged."

Nothing out of the ordinary, not really. Confidence and arrogance marked almost every orc, in Aubrey's experience, and the Rageroar in particular. And yet, he had not gotten to his position without being alert to all possible dangers. It was odd that the Rageroar had come back after being defeated, and he needed to know why. He had sent out spies to confirm if the Horde was beginning to move toward war, and especially if its sights were on Northwatch Hold. None had reported in yet; it was too early.

Aubrey broke his fast with a banana and some strong tea and headed to his usual patrol route. He nodded a greeting to Signal Officer Nathan Blaine, who saluted smartly despite the early hour, and together the two men looked out over the sea. Dawn was full-on, and the ocean and dock were painted in shades of rose, scarlet, and crimson, the clouds hovering above limned faintly with gold here and there.

"'Red sky in the morning, sailors take warning,'" Aubrey mused as he sipped his tea.

"'Red sky at night, sailor's delight,'" Blaine finished. "But we're not sailing today, sir." He gave the admiral a lopsided but still respectful grin.

"True enough," said Aubrey, "but we are always sailors. Keep an eye out, Nathan." The admiral's eyes narrowed a bit. "There's something . . ."

He pursed his lips, shaking his head, then turned and descended the tower quickly. He left the sentence unfinished.

"A tad superstitious, isn't he noo?" said a dwarven guard to Blaine.

"Perhaps," said Nathan, turning back to the bay. "But I bet you still always step onto a ship with your right foot first, don't you?"

"Um," said the dwarf, his cheeks flushing a bit red, "aye. No sense in invitin' bad luck, noo, is there?"

Nathan grinned.

They were a sea of green and brown moving steadily down the Gold Road through the Northern Barrens toward Ratchet. Most of the orcs were on foot, though a few of the elite—including the Kor'kron, Malkorok, and the warchief himself—rode wolves. Some were mounted on kodos, the better to manage the drums of war that were sending a trembling pounding through the very earth itself.

Word had gone ahead, of course, so that at each town more could gather and join the march on Northwatch. Those who would not participate in the active battle, and they were few—the elderly, the very young, the mothers of suckling babes—nonetheless ran out to cheer Garrosh and his unquestioned victory.

Garrosh, tall and proud on his black-furred, muscular wolf, raised Gorehowl in response to the cheers but seldom dismounted. The pace of the march enabled the army to be seen from far enough away for the warriors, magi, healers, and shaman to fall in step without slowing down the river of Horde that flowed along the road. As they left the Crossroads, where their numbers had swelled, Malkorok brought his mount alongside Garrosh's. He thumped his chest in a salute, and Garrosh nodded acknowledgment.

"Any word?" Garrosh asked.

"It seems that Baine is indeed loyal to us, for the present," said Malkorok. "He and the trolls slew the Alliance scouts that hovered at the Great Gate and now march east to Northwatch, as they said they would."

Garrosh turned to Malkorok. "I commend you for your watchfulness, Malkorok," he said. "Surely now you see that I hold Baine in the palm of my hand. He is devoted to his people and would not risk them. He knows that I suffer no such hesitation when it comes to the tauren. His protectiveness of them is a trait to both admire and hold in contempt. And," he added, "to use."

"Even so . . . he spoke out so brazenly," Malkorok growled.

"Indeed," said Garrosh. "But he comes through when he is needed. As do Vol'jin, and Lor'themar, and Sylvanas."

"And Gallywix."

Garrosh made a face. "He is out only for profit and is as subtle as a charging kodo about it. As long as the Horde lines his purse, he will be loyal."

"Would that all our allies were so transparent."

"Leave Baine be, for now," said Garrosh.

"This is the task you set me to, great warchief," said Malkorok. "To root out those who would defy your leadership and thus become traitors to the glorious Horde."

"But if we are too suspicious of our allies, their patience will grow thin," retorted Garrosh. "No, Malkorok. The time is now to fight the Alliance, not each other. And what a fight it will be!"

"And if Baine or Vol'jin, or others, do plot against you?"

"If you have proof rather than irritated words, then, as always, you have free rein. Which I know well you have already exercised."

Malkorok's gray lips curved in a smile that was as malevolent as it was ugly.

• • •

The ships—Forsaken, blood elf, goblin—had come early to Ratchet, and Garrosh could barely contain his excitement at the sight. Ratchet's harbor was crowded with them, and Garrosh's hot anticipation of the certain bloodbath to come was quelled slightly as he realized that it would take some time to unload all the troops and supplies he had requested. This was the part of being warchief that he found tiresome, but it couldn't be helped.

The arrival of the orcs did not go unnoticed despite the activity in the harbor, and cheers went up. Garrosh waved and dismounted as three figures approached. One he knew—the corpulent and sly trade prince Gallywix. The others, a blood elf and a Forsaken, he did not, and he frowned.

"Warchief Garrosh!" said Gallywix enthusiastically, his piggy eyes bright and his arms outstretched in welcome. By the ancestors, Garrosh thought with a stab of repugnance, did the goblin think to *embrace* him?

He forestalled the gesture by turning to the blood elf. She had golden hair and pale skin, and wore the bright, gleaming armor that marked her as one of her people's paladins. "Where is Lor'themar?" Garrosh asked bluntly.

Her full lips pressed together in irritation, but when she spoke, her voice was calm and pleasant. "He has sent me to oversee the blood elf troops. My name is Kelantir Bloodblade. I trained with the lady Liadrin, and I serve under Ranger-General Halduron Brightwing."

"Neither of whom is here," said Malkorok, stepping protectively near Garrosh. "Instead we have this little third-ranking whelp."

Kelantir turned coolly to Malkorok. "You also have two ships filled with blood elves willing to fight and die for the Horde," she said. "Unless you are so sufficient in numbers and supplies that our feeble support will not be necessary."

Garrosh had never much cared for blood elves, and this female was getting under his skin. "You have a chance to prove your people's worth in battle today," he said. "Take care you do not squander it."

"My people are familiar with war and battles and sacrifice, Warchief Garrosh," snapped Kelantir. "You will not find us lacking." With that, she turned on her heel and marched back to the docks, her plate mail—*how can she even bear it on such a tiny, twig-fragile frame?* Garrosh wondered—clanking slightly as she strode.

"Warchief—" interjected Gallywix, but Malkorok silenced the loquacious goblin with a single glance. Garrosh directed his attention to the Forsaken, who, in contrast to the arrogance displayed by the blood elf, bowed almost obsequiously low. He was a warrior of sorts, if the blade sheathed at his bony hip was any indication. He had no hair—it apparently had rotted off by this point—and his skin was the pale green color of decay.

"Captain Frandis Farley, sir, commanding the Forsaken units in the name of Sylvanas Windrunner, in service to the Horde and your good self," he said in a rasping, deep voice. While his jaw moved properly to form the words, once he had stopped speaking, it seemed to drop into a permanently gaping expression.

"And where is your Dark Lady?" asked Garrosh.

Farley lifted his head, and his eyes gleamed with yellow light. "Why," he said, sounding surprised, "holding reserves and standing ready to command when, after your inevitable victory, the Horde marches on Theramore."

The response was audacious and cunning, and Garrosh

threw back his head and laughed. "Perhaps we should send you in to simply talk to the lady Jaina, and she will voluntarily surrender completely."

"My warchief flatters me. But that would deprive the Horde of a well-earned victory, would it not?"

"Fight as skillfully as you speak today, Frandis Farley, and your warchief will be well pleased."

"I shall endeavor to do so." Some foul substance gathered at one corner of the slack jaw and dripped to the hard-baked earth. "Now, with your permission, I will see to unloading the cargo my lady has sent."

Pleased with the banter, though still irritated at both Sylvanas and Lor'themar for sending underlings instead of coming themselves, Garrosh finally turned to Gallywix. The goblin had dropped his eager-to-please mask and chomped sullenly on his cigar, the top hat slipping over his low brow.

"You, Trade Prince, seem to be the only one who has come to Ratchet to lead your people into battle. I will remember this."

The mask slipped back into place immediately. "Well, I am not so much leading my people into battle as overseeing getting them here and settled, and making sure the supplies you requested were properly delivered, if you understand my—"

Garrosh absently patted Gallywix's top hat and walked down to the dock to get a better view of the ships and cargo.

At first, it would seem a strange choice. Other than warm bodies to physically fight in the battle ahead, the ships were filled not with swords or bows or armor, but with carefully stacked timbers, securely tied with ropes into tidy bundles, and carts bearing rocks.

But Garrosh nodded his approval. He sighed, forcing down his impatience, and indicated that some of the larger, more physically powerful orcs should give the slender blood elves and the—in some cases quite literally—skin-and-bones Forsaken some assistance in unloading the cargo.

Soon—perhaps within hours—Northwatch Hold would fall.

Victory was, after all, the Horde's destiny.

When Hannah Bridgewater, her clothes soaked with sweat and her legs trembling with exhaustion, was stopped by one of the Northwatch guards patrolling the western path, her message was relayed immediately to Admiral Aubrey. He swore, a single, harsh word, then recovered. To the guard who had brought him the news, he said, "Notify everyone to prepare for battle. The tauren and trolls are approaching from the west. Shore up our defenses there and—"

"Sir!" yelped Blaine. He stood, his eyes fixed on the signaler on the dock below, who was frantically waving the semaphore flags. "Horde ships are approaching from Ratchet—six of them! Fully armed battleships!"

"Six?"

"Aye, sir." Blaine strained for more information. "They appear to have the markings of—of goblin, Forsaken, and blood elf!"

Aubrey didn't reply. Trolls and tauren first, and now the Forsaken, the sin'dorei, and the goblins. The only ones missing were—

"Orcs," he snapped. "Tell Dockmaster Lewis to send some scouts to Ratchet. They'll have to dodge the remnants of the Rageroar, but they're used to that." He should have known the instant he heard the word "tauren" that they would not come alone. They hadn't pressed forward in an attack before, not after the late general Hawthorne had ensured that the civilians of Camp Taurajo would be allowed to leave unharmed. It wasn't like them.

He should have known the real threat would come from the north. From Orgrimmar.

As for the battleships of the other Horde races . . . "Tell cannoneers Whessan and Smythe to fire at will as soon as those ships are within range. We'll need to keep their troops from landing."

"Aye, sir."

Aubrey's mind was racing. How would the orcs manage it? The tauren and trolls approached by land, yes. The other races, by sea, yes. But there was no way that hundreds of orcs would be able to charge Northwatch Hold en masse directly from the north. The Rageroar orcs had been a thorn in his side but they had never been able to bring in many reinforcements. Their strongholds were merely small jutting islands between the hold and Ratchet. An army could never possibly—

He felt the sound before he heard it. It was not cannon fire; Light knew they had grown used to hearing that over the last few months. No, this was different . . . a deep trembling of the earth. For a second, Aubrey and most of the others, still raw from the tumult during the Cataclysm, thought it was another earthquake. But it was too regular, too . . . rhythmic . . .

Drums. Drums of war.

He reached for the spyglass hanging at his hip, hastened to the wall of the tower, and looked to the north.

Until this moment, the Rageroar stragglers had been glimpsed milling about near the base of the hold, sometimes even attacking the Northwatch guards in reckless, usually fatal charges. Now there was no sign of them.

"Belay that order to send scouts!" he shouted to Blaine. "The Rageroar have returned because they've joined with the Horde orcs. They'll be—"

The words died in his throat. He could see them now, cresting the hill—a great wave of orcs clad in everything from the cloth robes of their shaman and warlocks to mismatched pieces of leather to imposing plate mail. They lugged carts of wooden planks and boulders. The Rageroar had joined them, obviously expected, and the great green brutes heaved and tossed the boulders into the shallow waters with enormous splashes and roars. The infernal drums kept pounding, pounding, and the enemy was close enough so that Aubrey and the others could hear war chants being sung in Orcish. Behind the orcs were catapults, battering rams, other massive engines of war. But how could they possibly think—

It was when the orcs began laying the planks over the stones that Aubrey realized the insidious cleverness of the tactic.

"Shore up the gates!" he shouted. *What little there is of them,* he thought. "Prepare for attacks on three fronts— from the harbor, from the north, and from the west!"

They'd been able to handle the Rageroar. They'd been able to handle the few tauren skirmishes that erupted from time to time on the Fields of Blood.

But this . . .

"Light preserve us," he whispered.

8

The tauren and trolls had continued their march eastward as night yielded its reign to dawn. They had given the Alliance's Forward Command a wide berth and so far had met with no resistance. Forcing their way through the Overgrowth, they found the remains of an encampment, with the campfire extinguished but the coals still warm. There was no way to tell who had built it. Horde and Alliance both were in the area, and there was always someone wandering from one place to another. The Cataclysm had caused upheaval in lives as well as land. They continued cautiously, but Baine was beginning to wonder . . . was it possible that their approach was yet undiscovered?

They found a small sacred site of the tauren, and Baine called a halt. "This is a sign," Baine said. "Here is where our brothers and sisters were released from their bodies. Here we will pause, to prepare our hearts for battle and our souls for possible death. Our troll brethren, this is not your ritual, but you are welcome to approach here, to contemplate life and death and those who have gone before. And," he added, "we will ask our ancestors to bless us, and to guide us to do what is right and best for our people."

Baine did not suggest asking the ancestors to bless what they were about to do, for he was not at all certain they would approve. He did not think Cairne Bloodhoof would. There was a mixture of fierce battle anticipation and unease in the gathering of tauren and trolls; Baine knew his people well and could sense their divided loyalties. Loyalties that were in conflict in their leader's heart as well.

After a few moments—where some chanted, some knelt in prayer, and others simply stood respectfully—it was time to move forward. They were on the last leg of their troubled journey. The Great Divide yawned on their left, and the path curved slightly and bore them up into gently rolling hills.

"Looks like we caught a break," Vol'jin said.

"I don't think any runners made it through to warn them," Baine said.

Vol'jin peered up at him from his raptor. "Dey destroyed Camp Taurajo, mon," he said.

"Yes," said Baine. "They took down a military target. And their general refused to slaughter civilians. He could have given the order to massacre everyone. But he didn't."

Vol'jin's eyes narrowed. "Will you be showin' da same courtesy to dese Alliance?"

"I do not think there are any civilians in Northwatch Hold," Baine said. He did not add that he was fairly certain that Garrosh would order him to kill any prisoners he took. Yes, it was a military target, and Garrosh was displaying good tactical leadership in wanting to see it broken.

But Garrosh wasn't truly interested in Northwatch as a military target. To him, rendering it useless to the Alliance was not so much a strategy as a stepping-stone.

His true goal was Theramore. There were plenty of Alliance soldiers and sailors there. But there was also an inn. Merchants and their families dwelt there. And so did one who had never shown anything but friendship to Baine Bloodhoof.

They rounded a curve in the road. The view opened up, and Baine could see the gray and white stone of the towers of Northwatch. Just as he lifted a hand to call a halt to prepare for the rush toward the hold, the quiet of the Barrens erupted with the sound of gunfire. The trolls and tauren responded immediately, aiming their own guns and arrows up at the Alliance soldiers who were attacking from the hills.

Baine was furious. He should have expected this, but he had permitted himself to be lulled into a false sense of safety. And now his people fell in their tracks, paying the price for his foolishness.

"Forward!" he shouted, his voice carrying, fueled by his anger. "Shaman! Interrupt their fire!"

The shaman obeyed while the rest of the tauren and the trolls surged forward as swiftly as they could. The Alliance riflemen found themselves knocked off their feet, buffeted by sudden winds, or crying out in startled pain as their clothing caught fire. In the chaos that followed as the riflemen tried to regroup, the Mulgore contingent had reached the path to the hold and was engaged in fierce battle.

"The tauren are here!"

The cry was caught up and swept through the ranks of the orcs who were bearing down on the Alliance stronghold from the north. Cheers arose, and Garrosh, swinging

Gorehowl as he himself led the charge, spared a moment to give Malkorok a fierce grin. He could hear the sound of massive stones striking the already damaged walls of the hold, and he threw back his head and screamed his delight.

He wished that he had done this sooner. The Cataclysm had torn down some walls of the fortress, and the foolish Alliance had not made the effort to properly restore them. Now they would regret it bitterly and pay for that neglect with blood.

The orcs stormed over the makeshift bridges of boulders and planks. A guard charged toward Garrosh, wielding a pike. He was human, strong and deft and knowledgeable with his weapon, but he could not stand against the Kor'kron encircling the warchief. Screaming their battle cries, the orcs descended upon him, hacking with swords and slamming maces against his metal-encased body. A blow landed with a crunch that was audible even amid the sounds of the drums, battle, and cannon fire, and the guard crumpled. The Kor'kron and Garrosh ran over his fallen body, though Garrosh spared the corpse a nod of approval.

The Rageroar had told them all the weaknesses of the hold. Garrosh knew exactly where to direct his people. The first wave was doing well, surging up the paths to the courtyard areas, and Garrosh scrambled to a higher viewpoint to assess the situation.

To his left, the vessels sent by blood elves, goblins, and Forsaken were doing their jobs exactly as planned. Despite what sounded like continuous cannon fire from the Alliance, several dinghies had made it to the shore, their occupants scrambling toward their enemies and cutting them down without mercy.

To his right, the tauren and trolls were ruthlessly hammering at the walls. Even as Garrosh watched, one of them crumbled, and a wave of brown-furred and green- and blue-skinned bodies flowed over.

And straight ahead, the orcs—his orcs, his people, the true and original members of the Horde—slaughtered and whooped and laughed.

It would take perhaps an hour to finish the job, to penetrate so deeply into the hold that no clever ruse or strategy by Admiral Aubrey could ever win it back. Garrosh did not wish to wait that long. His gaze darted over the scene. The vast bulk of his people had plunged ahead. Only a few remained here, at the outskirts of the battle, picking off the guards who were attempting to keep the fighting outside of the hold. They would not need the makeshift bridges anymore.

It was time to deliver the final blow and bring the battle to a swift, decisive victory.

A few feet below Garrosh, Malkorok fought three guards: two humans, a male and a female, and one dwarf. Most orcs favored larger weapons—two-handed broadswords, massive axes or hammers. The Blackrock orc's weapons of choice for the battle were instead two small but exquisitely swift and sharp axes. As the three charged him, thinking to enclose him in a circle, Malkorok laughed with glee. "Death to the Alliance!" he shouted, crouching and grinning. Then he exploded into motion, moving much faster than the enemy had expected. The axes became a blur, two glittering slices of death. Before she could even realize what was happening, the hapless human female was nearly sliced in two. Malkorok did not slow, whirling around and following the arc of the first axe with the second. The dwarf got in a blow, but his sword clanged uselessly off of Malkorok's armor. Malkorok buried an axe deep into the space between neck and shoulder, and the dwarf crumpled. Snarling, the orc turned, again whirling the axes, his lack of two fingers not hampering him at all. The human male guard brought his sword up to parry, but he could only block one weapon. Uttering a cry, Malkorok lifted the second bloodied blade high and brought it plunging down into the man's chest.

He turned, eyes darting about for his next target, but immediately looked up as his name was called by his warchief.

"The shaman!" shouted Garrosh. "Send them in!"

Malkorok grinned and lifted a fist to show that he had heard. Garrosh nodded once, then grasped Gorehowl. Throwing back his head, he uttered a bellow and dropped down from his vantage point. He leaped onto a boulder in the water and sprang from that to several unevenly placed boards, and then to the shoreline. Garrosh Hellscream had uttered the last command he would need to in this battle, and Malkorok saw how happy he was to finally be standing shoulder to shoulder with his brethren and using his father's famous weapon to slaughter Alliance.

Malkorok reached out, grabbed the nearest Kor'kron, and repeated the order. The other orc nodded and raced back toward the north, where most of the shaman were waiting. They had been held in reserve for this moment.

Within minutes, several shaman were hurrying toward the battle front. Most of them were orcs. They wore not the simple white or earth-brown robes common to their ranks, but more ominous-looking garments that made them more akin to warlocks, and they moved with barely contained excitement.

Heavily armored warriors escorted them, forcing their way through clusters of frantically battling Horde and Alliance. The shaman made no effort to join the fight. They were focused on the boulders, covered with water and mud, several yards ahead.

As they approached, the shaman slowed, calming their breathing. They eyed one another, sharing secret smiles, then lifted their hands and uttered the commands that would cause the elements to obey.

Malkorok knew what was to come, but he paused a moment in the battle to watch, his heart swelling with orcish pride. There were at least two dozen boulders in the water. They had enabled the troops and the heavier weapons to cross, and now their second purpose was about to be fulfilled.

Before Malkorok's eager gaze, the boulders quivered. Their hue turned from the dark red and brown of simple stone to a redder shade, then a mottled orange one, and they began . . . to *melt*. But the water did not cool them or stop this change, turning the magma back into rock as nature usually would. Instead, the water boiled and steamed away, as if the element of water itself was recoiling in fear from what was now in its depths. The stones continued to shudder and pulse as they lost shape and became liquid, their heat so powerful that even the shaman who controlled them were forced to turn their heads away or take a step back.

A tendril shot out from one of the rocks. A second tendril followed, then another, and another. The other boulders followed suit, the tendrils shortening, becoming denser, sprouting fingers and toes. A head burst through the top part of a rock, and a mouth gaped open. Small, glowing eyes looked about, down at the rock body, at the shaman who controlled it. One of the creatures growled, turning slowly around, reaching out for a black-leather-clad orc, who raised a commanding hand. The molten giant, for such it was, cringed back, muttering, then began to move forward. It would obey.

Even the orcs, who knew to expect this, seemed awe-struck by the sight. *As well they should be*, thought Malkorok.

"Alliance!" he cried. "Behold the power that Garrosh Hellscream controls! Behold, and tremble, and die!"

Baine swung his mace, fighting off two soldiers with pikes. All around him, the air was full of sound: the crackle of gunfire, the booming of the cannons, the singing of arrows being loosed, and over and around it all, the cries of Horde and Alliance fighting, killing, and dying. One of the soldiers lunged toward him. Baine moved more swiftly than the man had bargained for, and the pike stabbed only empty air. Baine's mace slammed into him as he stumbled, and the human fell. The other Northwatch soldier thought he had an opening, but Baine's mace snapped the pike's shaft as if it were a twig and, on the backswing, crunched the soldier's skull as if it were an acorn.

Baine shook his head, regret filling him. At least he offered a swift death.

It was then that the sounds changed. A new one was added—a deep bellow of anger, as if the earth itself had been given voice. Baine's ears pricked up at once and his head turned to follow the sound. His eyes widened.

Before he could speak, though, another voice rose, loud and full of righteous anger.

"In the name of the Earth Mother!" cried Kador Cloud-song. "Garrosh! What have you done?"

"What are these—things?" Baine demanded.

Kador turned to him, his fur bristling with outrage. "They are molten giants," he said, "powerful fire elementals that do not work willingly with the shaman but must be forced to obey. The Earth Mother is angry that her children are so used. The Earthen Ring has forbidden such things. They fear it could cause further instability in the earth."

"Like the Cataclysm," Baine murmured.

The aptly named molten giants were seemingly reveling in destruction. They strode about, towering over both Horde and Alliance, swinging their arms and smashing whatever had the misfortune to be in their way.

Baine had seen enough. "Retreat!" he cried. "Retreat! Fall back, tauren of Mulgore!" He had honored his word and brought his braves into battle. They had fought with courage. He had fulfilled his obligation to Garrosh and would not stand by and watch a single one of his people fall to these monsters in the name of the warchief's foolish—and dangerous—arrogance.

"Behold and die!" The Horde took up the cry, their bloodlust renewed by something approaching giddy gleefulness.

The Alliance defenders, as Garrosh predicted, were defeated in that moment. They were terrified by nearly a dozen molten-rock monsters that were bearing down on them. Many fell beneath a simple footfall. Others died as, with an almost casual blow, the remaining walls were reduced to rubble.

"Stand firm, Alliance soldiers!" The cry came from one of the towers. Laughing softly, Malkorok glanced up to see the human, wearing an admiral's hat, desperately and futilely attempting to rally his troops. It was foolish, but Malkorok could not help but respect the doomed human. He, at least, would die with honor.

But most of those he commanded were fleeing. And Malkorok could not blame them. It was, after all, what Garrosh had counted on.

Terrified beyond thought, the majority had simply flung down their weapons and raced for the safety of the water or the hills. Anywhere but here, facing death from creatures made of liquid rock and hatred. The fleeing soldiers made easy prey for the Horde fighters who were waiting at all the exits. Almost too easy. If any survived, Malkorok mused, they would have to count themselves among the luckiest of beings.

Malkorok continued to charge at the Alliance soldiers seeking escape. They were too frightened to even fight well, and he cut them down swiftly. After a few moments, he realized there was no more activity in the immediate area. What Alliance members he could see lay very still. He looked around, eyes narrowed, for any pockets of fighting. There was none. Even so, the molten giants continued to march, bellowing and slamming at the remains of the walls, smashing the mighty cannons and other engines of war like so much kindling.

Malkorok spied Garrosh standing over the body of a worgen. Its head lay a yard away, its lupine features locked in a snarl but its eyes wide with fear. Garrosh turned to the Blackrock orc, his face and body spattered with blood, and smiled fiercely around his tusks.

"Well?" he demanded.

"We have won, my warchief!" said Malkorok. "I see no Alliance other than corpses."

Garrosh's grin widened and he threw back his head, spread his arms, and let forth a mighty howl of triumph. "Victory to the Horde! Victory to the Horde!"

The cry was picked up and repeated, sweeping like wildfire through the troops. Malkorok noticed that the molten giants slowed, then stopped, and he realized that the dark shaman who had summoned them had also heard the happy shouts of victory and were now sending the elementals back to whence they had come.

Or . . . attempting to.

The molten giants, it seemed, had no wish to lose this form. They turned slowly, small heads with glowing red eyes moving as they sought their "masters." Grunting, they began to surge forward.

Malkorok and Garrosh looked about for the dark-clad forms, who were gesticulating with a vigor that bordered on frantic. For a moment, elementals and shaman were locked in a struggle of wills. Then, as one, the molten giants opened their mouths to let out a chilling cry of both rage and defeat.

The earth itself replied.

Malkorok felt the ground beneath him tremble, slightly at first, then with more intensity. Alarmed, he glanced about, but there was no shelter, not here. There were only corpses, and weapons, and rubble where a hold had once stood. Shouts of warning filled the air as many lost their footing, falling hard on the earth and clinging to it even though it was now the enemy. Suddenly dark clouds gathered. Lightning flashed, and a nearly deafening crack of thunder followed immediately.

The mouths of the molten giants kept opening, wider, wider still, as their heads and shoulders started to melt and dissolve. The elemental beings lost cohesion, their limbs flowing back into a single mass. The color faded, cooled, becoming first dark red, then brown, as the elementals shrank back to their original forms—now merely boulders, nothing more.

A final buck and shudder from the earth, and then it was still. The silence pressed like cotton on Malkorok's ears, hot from the noise that had assaulted them. The Horde members who had fallen to the earth got to their feet, cautiously, and then cheers filled the air once again.

"We have not only defeated the Alliance," said Garrosh, stepping beside Malkorok and clapping him on the back, "we have shown our mastery over the very elements!"

"What you have shown," said a deep, rumbling voice that was rich and cold with fury, "is that you are reckless, Garrosh Hellscream!"

Both orcs whirled to see Baine Bloodhoof and one of his shaman. Baine was in full war regalia, his face decorated, but not with war paint. His armor, too, was spattered with blood. But he was not reveling in victory.

Baine continued. "Kador Cloudsong tells me that the Earthen Ring has specifically forbidden the sort of thing you have meddled with, Hellscream."

Malkorok frowned. "You will address him as 'warchief,'" the Blackrock orc said in a low voice.

"Very well. *Warchief*," said Baine, "your choice to use these—these molten giants is an offense to the Earth Mother and to the Horde you claim to lead! Do you not understand what you are doing? Did you not feel the angry wrath of the earth itself? You could bring about a second Cataclysm. By the ancestors, did you learn nothing from the first one?"

"*I have made the Cataclysm work in our favor!*" shouted Garrosh. "This"—and he stabbed a finger at the rubble that had once been Northwatch Hold—"is the first major step toward complete and utter conquest of this continent! Theramore falls next, and I will use whatever tool I need to in order to achieve these goals, tauren!"

"You will not endanger—"

Malkorok grabbed Baine's arm and shoved his face up toward the tauren's. "Silence! You serve at the warchief's whim, Baine Bloodhoof! Do you offer him insult? *Do you?* Because if you do, I challenge you to a mak'gora!"

He was seething and prayed that the tauren would accept the challenge. This Bloodhoof, like his father before him, had long been a thorn in the side of the orcs. The tauren as a whole were too soft, too pacifistic, and the Bloodhoof were the worst. Malkorok considered Cairne's death to be a good thing, regardless of how it had happened. He would deem it an honor to put Baine Bloodhoof out of Garrosh's misery.

Baine's eyes flickered with fury; then he growled low. "I have lost many braves today, obeying the warchief's word. I have no desire to lose any more Horde lives needlessly." He turned to Garrosh. "I speak only from concern for what may come. You know that, Warchief."

Garrosh nodded. "Your . . . *concern* is noted but unwarranted. I know what I am doing. I know what my shaman can handle. These are my methods, High Chieftain. My next step will be to march on Theramore. There, I will cut off the Alliance supply line to Kalimdor and destroy the Proudmoore bitch, who confuses diplomacy with meddling. I have plans for Feathermoon Stronghold, Teldrassil, the Moonglade, Lor'danel, too—all will fall. And then, you will see. You will see how things stand."

He laughed. "And when you do, I will accept your apology graciously. Until then"—Garrosh sobered—"I will hear no more word from you about any 'concerns.' Do we understand each other?"

Baine's ears flattened and his nostrils flared. "Yes, my warchief. You have made yourself quite clear."

Malkorok watched him go.

Baine felt as if his own core were molten with outrage. It was with the greatest of efforts that he had kept from exploding in anger when Malkorok had challenged him. He was not afraid Malkorok could defeat him—by all accounts, Cairne had been winning the battle against Garrosh, before Magatha's poison had claimed him. Baine bore his father's blood and he had youth on his side. No, he had declined because there was no way to truly win. Poison would be used again, but better hidden this time. Or even if he slew Malkorok, there would be an ambush waiting in the shadows. And then, what would happen to his people? There was no clear successor yet. Garrosh would somehow see to it that a tauren was appointed whose thinking was more in line with his own—or who could be persuaded to think so.

No. His people needed him alive. And so, Baine would live, and do what he was ordered to do. Exactly, and *only*, what he was ordered to do. And when all this exploded in Garrosh's tattooed face, as it certainly would, Baine, Vol'jin, and other cooler heads would be there to pick up the pieces and protect the Horde. What Garrosh had left of it, at least.

But Baine Bloodhoof was not helpless. The idea that had been forming as he began the march on Northwatch had solidified. Seeing Garrosh's thoughtless, heedless, selfish manipulation of the elements for personal power had merely confirmed in Baine's head what he knew in his heart to be the right path.

He had left orders to the tauren he commanded to attend to the bodies of the fallen. They would receive the proper death rituals. Too, he had ordered his people not to desecrate the bodies of the Alliance. Such disregard displeased the Earth Mother, who loved all her children. He did not stay for the ceremonies, leaving them in the capable hands of Kador.

He retired to his traveling teepee, to put his plan into motion. Before lifting the flap, he looked about carefully. There were no signs of any listening ears. To a young brave standing guard outside, he said, "Send me Perith Stormhoof. I have a very important task for him."

9

Wought to be able to figure this out," said Jaina, anger—a feeling she rarely experienced— creeping into her voice. "We've got a blue dragon, two extremely skilled magi, and a talented and insightful apprentice. Plus the Kirin Tor at our disposal." She ran a hand through her blond hair, forcing back the emotion that threatened to cloud her thoughts. She couldn't afford the luxury of anger or irritation now. She had to think.

"Lady, there simply is *no* record *anywhere* of a spell that can hide a magical object from being sensed by a superior mage," Kinndy said. "We've got to assume that Kalecgos here is superior to any mage of the shorter-lived Azerothian races. And begging your pardon, but it's hard to sit here and think and ponder and twiddle our thumbs while Northwatch may be falling to the Horde right this moment!"

"Not to make light of your concern, Kinndy," said Kalecgos, "but if I do not recover the Focusing Iris, the destruction that could be wrought on this world will make the fall of Northwatch look like a captured piece in a board game."

Kinndy frowned and looked away.

"We all are distracted," Jaina said, forcing calm upon her mind. "But Kalec's right. The sooner we can figure out how its abductors are hiding the Focusing Iris from Kalec's sensing, the safer we will all be."

Kinndy nodded. "I know, I know," she said. "But . . . it's hard."

Jaina regarded her apprentice and thought of the last time she had seen her own master, Antonidas. They had stood together in his happily disorganized study, and she had asked—begged—to stay and help him defend Dalaran against Arthas Menethil. Arthas had already arrived, was standing right outside, shouting taunts that wounded Jaina as much as if they had been physical arrows. How desperately she had wanted to protect the beautiful mage city—and how bitter it had been to know that Arthas, her Arthas, was the one responsible for the threat to it. But Antonidas had refused to permit her to linger. "You have other duties," he had said. "Keep safe those you have promised to take care of, Jaina Proudmoore. One more or one less here . . . will make no difference."

Jaina had no doubt that she and Kalec could make a difference at Northwatch—if they arrived in time. But even if they did, what then? Every minute counted now. They still didn't know who had the cursed artifact, or what his or her plans were. And so, just as leaving Antonidas to die and Dalaran to fall had been the right thing to do, wrenching though the choice had been, she had to believe that staying here and finding the Iris were the right things to do this time.

Jaina felt the tears in her eyes again, even after so long. She reached over and squeezed Kinndy's limp hand. "Part of becoming a mage, and having so much responsibility, is learning how to make the hard choices. I understand how you feel, Kinndy. But we are where we need to be."

Kinndy nodded. The gnome girl was tired, as were they all. Her pink hair was messily tied, and there were circles under her large eyes. Tervosh looked years older than his actual age. Even Kalec's lips were pressed together in a thin line, and Jaina didn't want to know what *she* looked like. She'd been avoiding mirrors.

Her brow furrowed as she examined yet another scroll. Then, abruptly, she put it down and looked at them all. "Kinndy is right about the fact that there is no known record of a spell that can do what is being done. But obviously, someone figured it out, because it's happening right now. Someone is hiding the artifact from Kalecgos. And I simply refuse to believe that we can't undo this!" She slammed her hand down on the table and they all looked at her, startled. Jaina never erupted in fits of temper. "If we know what spell was used, or even can make a guess at the type, we can determine how to counter it."

"But—" Kinndy said, then bit her lip as Jaina shot her a sharp look.

"No buts. No excuses."

No one knew how to respond. Kalecgos was regarding her curiously, a faint frown of worry on his lips. Once again, Jaina reached for calm. "I'm sorry I raised my voice. But surely, surely we will find a way to solve this!"

Kinndy rose and got them all fresh tea as they sat in silence. Finally, Kalecgos spoke in a halting, uncertain voice.

"Let's agree that there is no known spell that can hide so powerful an object from a mage as skilled as I am. Especially as I have a unique connection to the Focusing Iris," he said. Jaina took a sip of the tea, letting the familiar scent and taste steady her, and nodded that he should continue. "So the logical conclusion is either that there is a mage out there clever enough to create such a spell, or . . . that's not what's going on here."

"What do you mean, 'that's not what's going on here'?" yelped Kinndy. "That's *exactly* what's going on!"

Jaina lifted a hand. It trembled slightly . . . with renewed hope. "Hold on a moment," she said. "Kalec . . . I think I know what you're getting at."

He smiled, radiant and happy. "I knew you would."

"It's not actually being hidden," Jaina said, encouraged by his reaction. She worked it through step by step as she spoke, getting to her feet and pacing. "We just think it is because we can't sense it."

"And we can't sense it because it's not what we're looking for," Kalec said.

"Exactly!"

"Someone care to enlighten us poor mortals?" said Tervosh dryly. He was leaning his chair back, the front two legs off the floor. "I'm not following this at all."

Jaina turned to him. "What were you last Hallow's End?" she said. She fought back a pang as she recalled one Hallow's End in particular. Arthas had invited her to Lordaeron for the traditional lighting of the wicker man. The effigy was supposed to metaphorically "burn away" things those watching the event wished to be free of. Jaina had lit the wicker man on fire with a spell, to the delight of the onlookers. Later that night, Jaina felt that she and Arthas had cast a spell of their own. By the light of the flames of the wicker man, Jaina herself had taken Arthas's hand and led him to the bed where they would first become lovers.

"I . . . beg your pardon?" Tervosh looked at her as if

she had gone quite mad. Jaina firmly steered her thoughts back to the present—and the problem they might just be on the verge of solving.

"What did you become in order to attend the celebrations?" she asked the other mage.

And Tervosh's eyes widened as comprehension dawned. He leaned forward, and the chair came to the floor with a thump. "The silly little spell from that commonplace wand made me become a pirate," he said.

"I am trying to magically sense one thing, and it is manifesting as something else. That 'silly little spell' you speak of provides just enough misdirection so that I can't trace the Focusing Iris," said Kalecgos. His gaze grew distant, and then he grinned. "Or at least . . . I *couldn't!*"

"And you can now!" Kinndy crowed excitedly.

He nodded. "Yes—and no. It comes and goes."

"Because whoever put the silly little spell on the thing knows that he or she needs to change it from time to time because it wears off," said Jaina.

"Exactly!" Kalec, who had also risen during the conversation, now closed the distance between himself and Jaina in three long-legged strides. Jaina thought he was going to embrace her, but he merely clasped her hands, squeezing them tightly. His hands were warm and strong and comforting.

"Jaina, you're brilliant," he said.

She felt color rise to her face. "I just followed through on your idea," she said.

"I had a general idea," he said. "You figured out precisely what happened and how to see through the illusion. I have to go, now that I know where it is." He hesitated. "I realize you're concerned about Northwatch, but . . . please stay here. I can track the Focusing Iris, but I don't have it back yet. I may still need your help."

Jaina thought painfully of what might be transpiring—or what might have already transpired—at Northwatch Hold. She bit her lip for a moment, then nodded.

"I will stay," she said.

"Thank you. I know how difficult this must be."

"Good luck, Kalecgos," said Tervosh.

"I hope you find it quickly," said Kinndy.

"Thank you. I certainly have a better chance now. You have all been of such great help. I hope that I will have good news for you shortly."

As he started to stride out, Jaina followed him. They said nothing as they descended the winding stairway to the ground level, and neither felt the silence uncomfortable. Kalec stepped out into the sunlight and turned once again to Jaina.

"You will find it," Jaina said firmly.

Kalec smiled gently. "When you say it so confidently, I believe I will," he replied.

"Be safe," she said, then felt foolish. He was a *dragon*, and not just any dragon—a former Aspect. What on this continent could truly threaten him? And then she thought of the dragons that had been killed when the Focusing Iris had been abducted, and suddenly her concern didn't feel quite so foolish after all.

"I will," he said seriously. Then a grin got the better of him. "I'll be back for more of those delicious biscuits you serve with your tea."

Jaina laughed. He lingered a moment longer—why, she wasn't certain—then bowed and moved a distance away from her.

He changed so swiftly she gasped. Where before a handsome, half-elven male had stood, suddenly there was an enormous blue dragon, no less handsome in his own way, but also powerful and not a little frightening. To call him "blue" was to insult the vast palette of that color with which he had been painted. Azure, cobalt, cerulean, even the unique light blue shade of ice—Kalecgos the dragon bore them all. He flexed mighty wings, doubtless enjoying the sensation after staying so long in his half-elven form. Beautiful, deadly, dangerous, glorious—he was all these things, and Jaina suddenly paled when she recalled how sharply she had spoken to him on occasion.

He could not read her thoughts, but perhaps he didn't have to. Kalecgos switched a tail adorned with barbs that looked like icicles, turned his massive horned head on his long, sinuous neck, and caught Jaina's gaze. She couldn't look away.

He gave her a quick wink. He was Kalecgos, the mighty dragon, the former Aspect, yes. And he was Kalec, the humorous, insightful friend who had taught her the true beauty and magnificence inherent in the arcane.

The almost alarmed awe in which Jaina had held him a moment ago dissolved, like a snowflake in the sunlight, and the mage felt her whole body shed tension as if she were dropping a too-heavy cloak. She gave him a smile and a wave. He dipped his head in acknowledgment, then looked skyward. His massive feet moved beneath him as, like a giant cat, he gathered himself for the leap.

Then Kalecgos was airborne, the great wings creating a gentle wind as they beat. Upward he flew, swiftly and with purpose. Jaina shielded her eyes against the sun as he climbed higher, becoming a small dot against the sky, and then finally disappeared.

She stood there a moment longer, then turned and entered the keep, wondering why she felt oddly bereft.

Hallow's End costumes indeed.

Kalecgos snorted as he flew, trying and failing to keep from scolding himself for missing something so simple. But the similarity that had alerted Jaina to the spell's nature came from a celebration that was not of his culture. Hallow's End was not a dragon festival, nor were the great creatures accustomed to donning costumes . . . well, other than their bipedal forms, of course, but those were simply another manifestation of themselves. It was not intended as an illusion or trick.

Or was it? After all, some dragons *did* use this transformation of their appearance to mingle with the younger races, unnoticed. Therefore, one *could*, albeit uncharitably, call it a trick. But Kalecgos had never felt that he was in disguise. He was . . . himself. He just looked different.

It was all very confusing, this penchant of the younger races to use magic in so lighthearted a fashion. It had taken Jaina, who was familiar with such basic little magics, to put two and two together. It was yet another example of why, in this new world that had averted the Hour of Twilight, the dragons needed to listen to what they formerly dismissed as frivolousness.

Now that he knew what was going on, as he told Jaina, he could sense the Focusing Iris by magically "looking for" what it really was, not what its captors wanted it to be—focusing on the true arcane essence of the artifact and not the "costume" it "wore." Even so, Kalecgos still did not sense it as strongly as he had before it had vanished. But it was there, like a faint whiff of a scent in the mind. There were moments—long ones—when it seemed to disappear again. At such times, Kalecgos called on the patience of his race and simply hovered, trusting that the Focusing Iris would reappear to his now-awakened understanding of what to seek.

One issue both puzzled and worried him, and that was the speed at which the cursed thing was traveling. It seemed to be . . . *flying* at speeds he knew none of the younger races should be able to achieve. How was that possible? Who had the ability to do this? If he could figure that out, he would solve the mystery.

A thought, seductive and heartbreaking at the same time, crept into his mind: Would he have been able to find the Focusing Iris more quickly if he still had an Aspect's abilities?

He shook his head angrily. That was a dangerous path down which to travel, one that could only end in despair. There was no room for the enormous yet tiny word "if." That was the siren song of utter failure, disguised in its own costume of wishful thinking. What was, was, and he needed all the wisdom and clearheadedness and confidence he could muster if disaster was to be averted.

Jaina found, somewhat to her surprise, that she missed Kalec's presence. He was never inappropriately dismissive of the direness of their situation—indeed, he more than anyone bore the burden of locating the Focusing Iris, since it belonged to his flight—but he brought a certain lightness to an otherwise dark and frightening quest. His wit and mind were quick, his manner gentle and kind, his insight great. He seemed to know exactly when to suggest a break, or when to push for the breakthrough, the new place to look, or the new way of thinking that made all four of them want to continue despite the odds.

And, she had to admit, in his half-elven form, he was not at all unpleasant to look at. She realized with mild surprise that it had been a long time since she had allowed herself to enjoy simple things like male company and quiet conversation. Even longer since she had felt . . . well . . . *safe* enough to open up to work so fully and completely with another. Jaina had learned through bitter experience that part of being a good diplomat was never truly letting your guard down, nor showing all your cards. To do so was to expose yourself, to become vulnerable. And while a diplomat could certainly make gestures of trust, and honestly work for what was best for everyone, he or she should never become vulnerable. To become so was to lose all. Jaina had once thought she had lost all, when Arthas fell to darkness. She had learned that she had not, but nonetheless she had remained guarded—as a diplomat and as a person.

She realized she'd become vulnerable with Kalecgos. He seemed to coax it from her without her even being aware of it. *How odd,* she thought, the drollness of the situation curving her lips in a smile, *I feel* safe *with a dragon.* Then again, she had felt safe with Go'el, too—an orc, for Light's sake, the warchief of the Horde—but she had never allowed herself to be truly vulnerable.

Though they all hoped that Kalec would be able to locate the Focusing Iris now that he could once again properly identify it, there was still work to be done in case the trail went cold. Tervosh was investigating distance-confinement spells, and Kinndy had returned to Dalaran to rummage through a trunk of scrolls that had been tucked in the far back of the library. "You'd envy me," she had told Jaina when they spoke through the mirror. "There's dust *everywhere*."

On a less hopeful and more brutally practical note, Jaina, Tervosh, and Pained had begun to examine ways, both magical and mundane, to evacuate the major Alliance cities if the abductors chose to strike using the Focusing Iris. Jaina had wondered aloud about notifying the Horde, but Pained gave her a sharp look. "My lady," she said, "we cannot discount the possibility that it is members of the Horde who stole the thing in the first place."

"Nor can we discount that it might be members of the Alliance," Jaina said. "Magic is known to both, Pained. Kel'Thuzad used to be a member of the Kirin Tor. Or it could be some other race entirely. Kalimdor is a large continent."

"Then let us create some possibilities for the Horde, too," suggested Tervosh, long used to finding common ground between the two women. "It couldn't hurt."

"And if the Horde is attacked, then perhaps offering aid swiftly can help build trust," Jaina the diplomat said. Pained grimaced but said nothing.

After so long feeling as if she were wrestling with air, with no idea what to search for or where to turn, plotting something concrete like evacuation strategies for the major cities of Kalimdor was a relief. Jaina dropped easily, almost mechanically, into her logical, rational mind. Kalec had taught her what she already knew but did not realize she knew—that magic was mathematics. There was always some way for things to fit together correctly, and if there was not, well, you just hadn't found that way yet.

The afternoon wound down into evening. After so many late nights and early mornings, Jaina welcomed rest. She crawled into bed almost as soon as the sun had set. Certain that Kalec would locate the Iris now, and that their troubles at least from that quarter would shortly be resolved, she fell asleep quickly.

"My lady."

Jaina was so groggy that the urgent voice seemed part of her dream. She blinked awake to see a tall form with long ears silhouetted against the window. "Pained?" she murmured.

"A messenger has come. We have intercepted"—and Pained's voice conveyed her doubt—"a Horde member who insists he speak with you."

Now Jaina was fully awake. She slipped out of bed and grabbed a wrap, lighting the lamps with a quick gesture. Pained was dressed in her usual armor. "He claims to have been sent from Northwatch Hold, where the Alliance has fallen to the Horde."

Jaina's breath caught. Perhaps she should have gone to Northwatch after Kalecgos left. She sighed bitterly. "I am relieved that whoever found him didn't kill him on sight."

"He openly approached the guards," Pained said. "And he brought this as a token. He assured them you would recognize it and wish to speak with him. The guards thought they should at least confirm his story."

Pained held out a white, covered bundle. Jaina accepted it, noting that it was quite heavy. She gently removed the linen, and her eyes widened.

It was a mace, a thing of great beauty and clearly of dwarven craftsmanship. The head was silver, wrapped in intersecting bands of gold. Small gems were inlaid here and there, and it had runes etched upon it as well.

Jaina gazed at it raptly for a moment, then looked up at Pained. "Bring him to me," was all she said.

A few moments later, the Horde messenger—Jaina no longer thought of him as a spy—was escorted in.

He was a huge shape, his form concealed by an encompassing cloak, and towered over the guards. Jaina got the feeling that, had he wished to, he could easily have dispatched both of them in a moment. Instead, he permitted himself to be roughly led in.

"Leave us," Jaina said.

"My lady?" one of them asked. "Leave you alone with this . . . creature?"

She glanced at the guard sharply. "He has come to me in good faith, and you will not speak so of him."

The guard colored slightly. The two bowed to their mistress, then withdrew, closing the parlor doors behind them.

The huge shape straightened. One hand emerged from the depths of the cloak to shrug off the hood, and Jaina found herself gazing into the calm, proud visage of a tauren.

"Lady Jaina Proudmoore," he said, inclining his head. "My name is Perith Stormhoof. I come on orders from my high chieftain. He asked me to give you the mace. He said . . . it would help you to believe my words are truth."

Jaina clutched the mace. "I would never mistake Fearbreaker," she said. She recalled the time when she, Baine Bloodhoof, and Anduin Wrynn had sat together in this very chamber. Moved by Baine's loss and uncertainty at assuming the title of his slain father, the human prince had rushed to his room and returned with this mace. It had been given to Anduin by King Magni Bronzebeard, and Jaina was touched to see the boy offering it to Baine—the child of an Alliance king gifting the child of a Horde high chieftain with something precious and beautiful. When Baine had accepted the gift, Fearbreaker had shown its approval by glowing softly in the tauren's giant hand.

"He knew you would not. Lady Jaina—my high chieftain thinks gratefully and highly of you, and it is because of the memory of the night when he received Fearbreaker that he has sent me with this warning. Northwatch Hold has fallen to the Horde." He did not speak with pleasure; indeed, Perith seemed grim and sad. "It further wounds him that this victory was won with the usage of dark shamanic magic. He despises these actions, but to protect his people, Baine has agreed that the tauren will continue to serve the Horde as they are needed. He wishes me to emphasize that at times, this obligation brings him little joy."

Jaina nodded. "Well do I believe that. Still, he has participated in an act of violence against the Alliance. Northwatch Hold—"

"Is only a start," Perith said, interrupting her. "Hellscream would reach much farther than a simple hold."

"*What?*"

"His goal is nothing less than the conquest of the continent," said Perith, the words relentless and horrifying even when spoken by this calm tauren. "He will shortly be ordering the Horde to march on Theramore. And mark me well, their numbers are strong. As you are now, you will fall."

The statement was not delivered to intimidate. It was blunt and to the point—simple reality. Jaina swallowed.

"My high chieftain remembers the aid you gave him and asked me to warn you. He has no wish to see you caught unawares."

Jaina was overwhelmed at the gesture. "Your high

chieftain," she said, her heart full, "is a truly honorable tauren. I am proud to be so highly regarded by him. I thank him for this timely warning. Please tell him it will help save innocent lives."

"He regrets that a warning is all he can give you, my lady. And . . . he asks you to please take Fearbreaker, and return it to the one who so kindly gifted it to him. Baine feels that it is no longer his to keep."

Jaina nodded, though quick tears stung her eyes. She had hoped that that night would be the beginning of healing, of understanding, but it was not to be. Baine was telling her, in his typically gentle but firm fashion, that their friendship only went so far—he was not, and would never become, a member of the Alliance. He would stand and fight with the Horde. She understood. She was fully aware of how vulnerable the tauren people would be if they stood against Garrosh now, and she had no wish to see them come to harm.

"I will see to it that Fearbreaker is returned to its former owner," she said, with the few simple words conveying all the shades and complexities of what was in her heart.

Perith was a fine courier. He understood and bowed deeply. Jaina went to the small desk that was on the far end of the room. Locating parchment, ink, quill, and wax, she quickly wrote a brief note. She dusted powder on the ink to dry it, folded the missive, then sealed it with red wax and her own personal stamp. Rising, she handed it to the waiting tauren.

"This will ensure your safe passage through Alliance territory, if you are caught."

He chuckled. "I will not be, but your concern is appreciated."

"And tell your noble high chieftain there will be no rumors of a tauren Longwalker visiting me. To all who would ask, I will say that word reached me from an Alliance scout who managed to escape the battle. Take refreshment, then return safely."

"May the Earth Mother smile upon you, Lady," said Perith. "I understand my high chieftain's choice even better now that I have met you."

She gave him a sad smile. "One day, perhaps we will fight on the same side."

"One day, perhaps. But that day is not today."

Jaina acknowledged this truth with a nod. "Light be with you, Perith Stormhoof."

"And the Earth Mother's blessing be upon you."

She watched him go, fighting an irrational urge to call him back, to offer him, Baine, all the tauren people asylum. She did not want to have to face Baine in battle, to utter spells that would kill these gentle, wise beings. But the tauren were hunters, warriors, and would never shirk their duty. Baine had already done all he could—more, in fact, than Jaina had ever expected. Some would call this warning treason.

She hoped that Baine's gesture would not result in tragedy for the tauren high chieftain.

Jaina buried her face in her hands, gathering strength. Then, composing herself, she called for Pained.

"Rouse Tervosh and recall Kinndy. Have them meet me in the library."

"May I ask what is going on?"

Jaina turned a tired visage to her bodyguard and friend. "War," was all she said.

10

The Focusing Iris appeared to have sprouted wings, so swiftly was it traveling. Like a mastiff on the scent, Kalecgos had spent most of the day dutifully following where it led. It had been to the northwest of Theramore when he had departed that isle, and Kalecgos suspected it was now in Mulgore, perhaps near Thunder Bluff. When Kalecgos had made it to the Great Gate, the Iris stopped for a moment, then began moving northeast toward Orgrimmar. Kalec followed, flying as quickly as his wings would allow in an attempt to catch up. No sooner had he gotten to the Crossroads than the Focusing Iris shifted course yet again, this time heading almost directly south.

A realization struck him, as shocking as lightning, and his wing beats faltered.

"You are clever, my enemy," he said softly.

They were no fools. But he had been one, more than once on this journey. First he had failed to see through a simple spell. And then he had arrogantly assumed that the thieves who had absconded with the Focusing Iris hadn't counted on being followed.

Of course they had. One didn't steal a priceless magical

artifact from a dragonflight without being prepared for repercussions. They had known someone from the blue dragonflight, probably Kalecgos himself, would come in search of the Focusing Iris. They had not only disguised the object but were now ferrying it about somehow from place to place in an effort to exhaust him as he followed something he would never get close enough to find.

He believed the human phrase for such a useless pursuit was "a wild goose chase."

His temper got the better of him, and he bellowed in anger. Not even a dragon could fly ceaselessly. He could never hope to catch it. Even as he realized this, the artifact took a turn toward the southwest.

Kalecgos thrashed his tail and beat his wings, then calmed himself. It was true that as long as the thieves were toying with him like this, he would never get close enough to the Focusing Iris to retrieve it.

But they could not do this forever. As long as the Focusing Iris was flitting erratically from place to place, Azeroth was safe. It would have to come to a halt in order for any use to be made of it.

His path over the last several hours, during which he had been forced to pause and rest, had taken him over Silithus, the Un'Goro Crater, Feralas, Mulgore, the Barrens, and now to—

Northwatch Hold. Or rather, what remained of Northwatch Hold.

Once it had boasted towers, and walls to enclose its inhabitants safely. Once it had been a military stronghold that had sent out scouts and siege weapons, warriors and generals. The troops that had destroyed Camp Taurajo had been garrisoned there. Now it looked as if some giant hand had smashed it like a toy. The towers were reduced to just a pile of stones, as were the walls. The cannons were silent, and smoke wafted upward in a thin gray-black line from a large fire. And swarming around the ruins of a once-proud Alliance hold were hundreds of tiny figures.

Horde. From this height Kalec could not distinguish what races, but he could spot the basic colors of each banner. All were represented here. The wind shifted, and Kalec grimaced as his sharp nose caught an acrid scent. The victors were burning bodies—whether their own in a sober ceremony or those of their enemies, Kalec could not tell, and had no wish to.

The trail of the Focusing Iris continued blithely along. It turned yet again, heading back toward Mulgore, but Kalecgos was no longer following it. With one strong downward beat of his wings, Kalec repositioned his body and changed direction, flying now directly to the south. He knew what he needed to do.

He could track the Focusing Iris from Theramore. And he would. He would wait until it finally came to a stop, until the thieves had tired of the game, and then head directly for it. In the meantime, he would return to Jaina Proudmoore.

From what he had seen, she was going to need all the help she could get.

"How many did he say?" asked Pained. She, Tervosh, Kinndy, and Jaina were in the library, but the long table at which they had spent so many hours recently was no longer covered with books or scrolls. Instead, a large map of Kalimdor was spread out over it, the only books remaining on the table serving to anchor the parchment at each corner.

"He didn't," Jaina said. "At least not specifically. He said only that the Horde's numbers were strong, and as we are now, we would fall."

"Are you sure you can trust him?" asked Kinndy. "I mean, come on—he's a member of the Horde. This could be a trap of some sort. We end up calling in reinforcements and bracing Theramore, and then they attack Stormwind or something."

"For someone so young, Kinndy, you have quite a suspicious mind," said a voice.

Jaina whirled, her heart lightening as Kalec strode into the room. Her pleasure faded somewhat as she caught sight of his face. It was still handsome and smiling, but he was paler than she recalled, and there were furrows in his brow.

"You couldn't find it," she said quietly.

Kalec shook his head. "They're playing a little game with me," he said. "Whenever I get close to the Focusing Iris, they move it somewhere else."

"Trying to wear you out," said Pained. "It is a sound strategy."

"Sound or not, it's as frustrating as trying to haggle with a goblin," said Kalec. "I can sense it from here. I will wait until it slows and stops. Then I will go in search of it."

"Is it safe to wait?" asked Pained.

Jaina answered for him. "We don't know what they're planning, but attuning so ancient an artifact toward whatever it is they want to do will take time and effort. Especially as they aren't blue dragons, and therefore have no innate connection with the Focusing Iris. They cannot perform such complex work if they are traveling with it. Kalecgos is right. When the Iris ceases to move, then he can track it down."

"I hope you have enough time," said Kinndy.

"You would have me out there, flying around uselessly?"

"Well, when you put it that way—no."

He nodded, then turned to Jaina. "I came back for another reason," he said. "It sounds as if you have already heard, but Northwatch Hold has fallen to the Horde. I saw what was left of it."

"We have heard," she said. "From a very trusted source. But—you've seen it. I was also warned that from there, the Horde plans to march on Theramore."

Kalec paled even more. "Jaina—you're completely unprepared for them."

"We were told their numbers are strong," Jaina said. "And that, yes, right now, we aren't prepared for them. But thanks to the warning, I've had a chance to send out some requests for aid."

"I don't know if that will be enough," said Kalecgos. "Jaina, every race of the Horde was there. They have all but wiped Northwatch from the face of Azeroth. The only things that remain are rubble and—and pyres. They've not dispersed. The army—and it is an army—is still gathered. I wish I could truly show you what I saw. If your requests for aid are not met, and quickly, you're not going to survive the attack."

"And then Garrosh will summarily destroy the rest of the Alliance footholds," said Tervosh. Kalec nodded, his eyes somber.

Jaina looked at them, then at Pained and Kinndy. "You're all acting as if the Horde has already won. I won't accept that." She narrowed her eyes and jutted her chin out defiantly. "I believe Kalec when he says they have an army encamped at Northwatch. But if they are there now, then they're not marching. And if they're not marching, then they're not *ready* to march. That means we still have time."

She moved to the table, feeling Kalec's curious gaze upon her. "Look. Here's Northwatch." She tapped a slender finger on the map. "And here's Theramore." She drew her finger down and to the right. "Over here is Brackenwall Village. Some Horde live there, but it's not a military outpost. It does stand between Fort Triumph and us, however." Fort Triumph was a rather newly established military base. If there had been more time, Jaina thought, it would have sent reinforcements to Northwatch. It might be too late for Northwatch Hold, but she prayed it wasn't too late for Theramore.

"We'll have the soldiers from Fort Triumph march through Dustwallow Marsh. They can avoid Brackenwall if they're careful. We'll also send out runners to Forward Command."

"Any who are left," Kalec said. "When I passed over the area, it seemed deserted."

"Most of them probably went to help Northwatch," said Kinndy quietly.

Which, Jaina thought with a pang, meant most of them were dead. She shook her golden head, almost physically trying to clear the image from her mind's eye.

"Any who escaped the battle probably regrouped at Fort Triumph rather than Ratchet," she said. "It's the first place we should look for survivors."

Kalec stepped beside her, his focus on the map. She looked at him in query, expecting him to have a comment. He shook his head. "Go on," he said.

"Theramore is both uniquely vulnerable and highly defensible, depending on how fast reinforcements can get here. If we act quickly, Stormwind can send several ships, and any Horde vessels that attack will, hopefully, not even get close enough for their crews to come ashore." She placed a finger on the map and drew a half circle around Theramore.

"If the Horde reaches the harbor first," Pained said, "we will have no chance at all."

Jaina turned to look at her. "That is true," she said. "Perhaps we should all just lay down our arms and go to the dock so we can greet the Horde and thus save ourselves the trouble of a battle."

Pained's purple-pink cheeks flushed a darker hue. "You know I do not advocate that."

"Of course you don't. But we have to go into this battle thinking—no, *knowing*—we will succeed. I welcome all comments about flaws in my planning," she said, addressing this to Kalecgos. Pained, Kinndy, and Tervosh already knew Jaina was open to constructive criticism. "But comments like that, Pained, do nothing save drag us down. Theramore has defended itself well in the past. We will do so again."

"Whom have you sent letters to so far?" asked Kalec.

Jaina smiled a little. "Letters? None. Nor have I teleported. I have a way to instantly communicate with King Varian, young Anduin, and the Council of Three Hammers."

"That must be interesting," said Kalec. "From what I hear, the three dwarves seem inclined to agree on very little."

Not so long ago, Ironforge's leader had been Magni Bronzebeard. In an attempt to better understand the unease of the earth prior to the Cataclysm, Magni had performed a rite to make him "one with the earth." It had succeeded, after a fashion. Magni had been turned into diamond, indeed becoming one with the earth. After a brief time of chaos—during which Magni's daughter, Moira, attempted to claim the Ironforge throne and rule with the Dark Iron dwarves—order was restored when a council was formed instead of continuing the tradition of a single ruler. Each clan of dwarves—Bronzebeard, Wild-hammer, and Dark Iron—now had a representative. The ruling body was called the Council of Three Hammers, and while its members cooperated, getting unanimity on anything was a challenge.

"It would seem that no one likes the idea of the Horde running Kalimdor," Jaina said. "While they might argue some of the details, all three were in agreement about that."

Kalecgos suddenly looked uneasy. Jaina thought she knew why. Gently, she placed a hand on his arm. "You are a dragon, Kalecgos," she said. "You don't need to be involved in this. Especially since you are a former Aspect who is already preoccupied with tracking down a stolen artifact."

He smiled gratefully. "Thank you for understanding, Jaina. But . . . I would see none of you come to harm."

"Lady Jaina knows what she's doing," said Kinndy. "The Alliance will come to protect its own."

Kalecgos shook his head. "This is more than a scuffle or a raid on a small village. If the Horde succeeds, Garrosh would not be overconfident to assume that he could indeed control Kalimdor. I . . . will need to think on this before offering my aid. I'm sorry, Jaina."

He looked into her eyes, and she knew with perfect understanding how much this was tormenting him. Their hands, seemingly of their own volition, met and clasped. Jaina found herself reluctant to let go, but she had time only for the defense of Theramore right now.

"We need to take steps immediately," she said. "I'll go contact Varian. Pained, you go among the soldiers, both here in Theramore proper and those stationed along the roads. If Sentry Point is without at least one horse, get them one. They need to be able to ride swiftly to inform us if the Horde approaches."

The night elf nodded, saluted, and left at a running trot. "What about the civilians?" asked Kinndy. "Should we tell them?"

Jaina considered, her brow furrowing in thought. "Yes," she said finally. "Theramore was originally a martial city. Those who choose to dwell here know its strategic position. We've been fortunate ere now. They will understand and obey our orders."

She turned to Tervosh. "You and Kinndy start going door-to-door informing the citizens. No more ships are to set sail from this port. We need every single vessel we can muster. Those civilians who wish to leave may, though I believe they'll be safer here than in the marsh with the Horde approaching. The gates will be open until sundown, at which time they will be closed and not reopened until the danger has passed. I'm also putting a curfew into effect at two bells beyond sundown."

"Why not at sunset?" Kalec queried.

"Because they are people, and they need to feel like people, not trapped animals. Two hours past sundown will give everyone the chance to have a meal at an inn with their family, or a drink or two with friends by the fire. Such simple things will remind them, when the fighting does come, what they are fighting for: not just an ideal or even their own survival, but also their homes, their families, their way of life."

Kalecgos looked surprised. "That . . . had not occurred to me."

"And two hours isn't really enough for anyone to get into trouble," said Kinndy. "Good idea." Jaina gave her a bemused glance and wondered how she knew about such things.

"Thank you, world-weary one," Jaina said, smiling as the gnome rolled her eyes. "Any questions?"

"Nope," said Kinndy. "Come on, Tervosh. I'll go down to the harbor; you go talk to the soldiers at Foothold Citadel. While you're there, find out what supplies Dr. Van-Howzen is going to need to treat the injured. I'm sure there are many civilians here with first aid training who will be glad to help."

Tervosh suppressed a grin. "Yes, boss," he said as Kinndy waved absently at Jaina and Kalec and started descending the stairs at a brisk pace. Shrugging, Tervosh followed her.

"Your apprentice is most self-assured," Kalecgos said.

"A quality I have no desire to see her lose," said Jaina. "Few things are more dangerous than an insecure mage. Indecision at a crucial moment can cost lives."

He nodded. "Very true. Now . . . what can I be doing to help?"

"I will let you know. First, I need to contact King Varian," she said, adding apologetically, "I'm not sure he'd be particularly glad to know there is a blue dragon here."

"Ah, yes, I can quite understand that," said Kalec. "I will return to my quarters until you send for me."

"No, you can come," Jaina said. "Just don't stand in front of the mirror."

He looked at her, baffled, and she smiled.

• • •

Kalecgos followed Jaina as they went from the library, which of course housed hundreds of books, to her parlor, which probably only housed dozens. Jaina stepped up to one shelf and touched three books in what struck Kalec as a very precise order. He was not altogether surprised when the bookshelf slid aside to reveal a mirror, oval and not elaborately framed, hidden behind the books. Kalec blinked. In the mirror, he saw Jaina's reflection and his own.

"You did mention a mirror. I assume there is more to this than a way to discreetly tell me I need to shave?" he joked.

"Much more," she said. "It operates using the same methodology, the same math"—she bowed slightly—"that a portal does. Except it's much simpler and more basic. Portals actually have to be able to physically transport someone somewhere. The mirror just allows viewing of a different place and, if the timing is right, other people. I'm going to use this to contact Varian. Let's hope he's nearby, or we will have to try again."

Kalec shook his head, again marveling at the wonderful lack of complexity of the younger races and their spells. "I know of this sort of spell. Very old, and very simple. Just like the 'costume' spell the thieves utilized to hide the Focusing Iris from my detection."

"Yet your flight doesn't use such things?"

"Most would think it beneath them to use a garden-variety spell like this one," he said, adding quickly, "but I think it's brilliant."

"I'm trying not to be insulted," said Jaina. She said the words lightly, but her brow had furrowed again.

"I," said Kalec, reaching for her hands, "am both clumsy

and rude. I *do* think it's brilliant. We dragons . . ." He struggled to explain the mentality of dragonflights, especially that of the blues. "Dragons seem to think that the more complicated a thing is—the longer it takes to perform, the more ingredients it has, and the more people it requires to participate—the better it is. That goes for clothing, meals, magic, art—everything. They would rather sit down for days and design a laborious spell to teleport a thing directly to their hands than simply get up and fetch the saltcellar."

That got a smile out of her, and Kalec was glad. "So, you like that I'm simple and uncomplicated?" Jaina queried.

All the humor fled him. "I like *you*," was all he could say. "I've seen you be simple, and I've seen you be complex, and it all suits you. You're Jaina. And . . . I like Jaina."

She did not let go of his hands; instead she looked down at them. "That is high praise, coming from a dragon," she said.

He placed a finger beneath her chin and tilted it up so that she looked into his eyes. "If that is praise, then you have earned it."

Color suffused her cheeks and she stepped back, releasing his hands and smoothing her robe unnecessarily. "Well . . . thank you. Now, please, move all the way over into that corner. You should be out of Varian's line of sight there."

"I obey, my lady," he said, bowing and retreating to the corner she had indicated.

Jaina turned to face the mirror. She paused for a moment to tidy a stray lock of hair and inhaled a deep, steadying breath. Composed, she murmured an incantation and waved her hands. As Kalec watched, her face was bathed not in the ordinary hues of lamp or sunlight, but in a soft blue tint.

"Jaina!" said Varian. "It is good to see you."

"And you, Varian. Although I wish I were contacting you to ask how Anduin's studies are going."

"It sounds as if I should be wishing that too. What's happening?"

Succinctly she informed him of the situation. Word had not yet reached him about the fall of Northwatch Hold. Varian remained silent as Jaina spoke, interrupting only occasionally for clarification. She told him she had received a warning that the Horde's reach far exceeded its current grasp of Northwatch.

"Garrosh wants nothing less than the entirety of Kalimdor," Jaina said quietly. "He will take Theramore and then launch his forces across the continent all the way to Teldrassil."

"If Theramore falls, he could do it, too," growled Varian. "Damn it, Jaina, I always warned you that this Horde you are so fond of would turn on you like a tamed wild beast!"

Kalec raised an eyebrow, but Jaina remained calm. "It is clear to me that Garrosh is the driving force behind all this. The Horde would never have done anything like this under Thrall's leadership."

"But Thrall is *not* leading the Horde, and now Theramore—indeed, all of Kalimdor—might pay the price!"

She didn't rise to the bait. "It is clear, then, that you realize the severity of the situation."

A sigh. "I do," he said, "and in answer to your unasked question, yes, Stormwind will stand with Theramore. I'll divert the 7th Legion's naval fleet toward Theramore immediately." There was a pause. "And, as things seem to be quiet for once in at least a few parts of this world, I'll notify several of my finest generals to report to you as well. They'll give you a hand with the city's defense, and together you can hammer out a strategy that will send those Horde dogs home with their tails between their legs."

She smiled gratefully. "Varian—thank you."

"Don't thank me yet," the king of Stormwind said. "It's going to take a few days. You'll want a good-sized force to greet the Horde, and some of the generals I want to send to you are stationed in rather distant places."

Kalec's heart sank. The Horde was only a day's march, perhaps two, and its forces were already gathered at Northwatch. Varian's strategy was a good one, so far as it went. But all the king's generals and all the king's ships could not save Theramore if they arrived an hour too late. He wished he could speak but had to content himself with clenching his fists in frustration. What was worse than his own dismay was seeing Jaina looking stunned and worried.

"Are you sure? Varian, Ka—one of my scouts said he saw the Horde still assembled in full numbers at Northwatch."

"If they are still gathered and not yet marching," said Varian, "they obviously are not interested in a swift conquest. They have their own plots. I will move as fast as I may, Jaina, but nothing can change the fact that it will take time to assemble any kind of a fleet that would make a difference. I'm sorry. It's the best I can do."

Jaina nodded. "Of course I know that, Varian. And you raise a good point. I'll be contacting the other Alliance leaders as well. The kaldorei may be able to send both ships and warriors; the dwarves, warriors and perhaps gryphons. I think even the draenei would be willing to help."

"I will speak with Greymane," said Varian. "I know well a few worgen on the battlefield will strike fear even into the hearts of the more bestial members of the Horde."

"Thank you," Jaina said. "Sometimes it's easy to feel a bit deserted here on this island."

"Well, don't," said Varian, but his voice was kind. "Contact me again in a few hours, and we will share our information. Take care, Jaina. We will win this yet."

"I know we will," said Jaina.

And as the soft blue light of the magic mirror faded and her features returned to normal hues, Kalecgos resolved that whatever happened, he would do all he could to make sure Jaina's faith was justified.

11

Four days. Four full days had the massed army of the Horde waited for the order to march on Theramore. Garrosh had stayed in his warchief's battle tent, and no request for an audience had been granted.

Loyal the Horde might have been to its warchief, but patient its members were not. There had been muttered complaints, quietly voiced questions. Baine, who had complaints and questions aplenty, had kept his sharp ears tuned to the murmurs and had discreetly spoken with those who, like he, were concerned about this inexplicable delay.

He and Hamuul Runetotem set up a meeting some distance away from the ruin, near a giant tree that had been on the right side of the Great Divide when the land had bucked and heaved during the Cataclysm, and were the first to arrive. They all came one by one: Captain Frandis Farley and a few companions from the Forsaken; Kelantir Bloodblade; Captain Zixx Grindergear, who commanded one of the zeppelins, and his first mate, Blar Xyzzik; Margolag, who represented Eitrigg; and more than a few of his own tauren. The last ones to come were Vol'jin and two of his people. Baine was both pleased and worried to see his friend present for this meeting.

For a moment, they all simply stood and regarded Baine. He looked at them each in turn. "No one here is a traitor to the Horde," he said in his deep, rumbling voice. "It is possible to be loyal and yet question the wisdom of certain behavior. But all of us gathered here tonight know well that treason is in the eye of the beholder and that Malkorok views us with a very unkind eye indeed."

Silence, save the soft sound of weight being shifted from one foot to another. Baine continued.

"It is for love of the Horde that I have asked you to attend. And now, before anyone can be accused of treasonous behavior, I invite those who do not wish to be here to leave. No one will condemn you for withdrawing. But if you so choose, as we will forget your involvement up to this point if we are captured and interrogated, I would ask you to forget ours. Leave freely, and go in peace."

A tauren, nothing more than a large shape to Baine's eyes as he stood far from the small campfire, turned to go. One or two of the undead left as well. The rest remained.

"You are courageous," Baine told them, indicating that they might sit.

"We're scared witless, is what we is," said Zixx's first mate. "Anybody got any booze?" Wordlessly a troll handed him a wineskin, and the goblin took a huge swallow.

"Blar speaks truly, if somewhat inelegantly," said Kelantir. "We have heard what happens to those who speak out against Garrosh. Thrall at least would have listened! And he never would have led us down this path! The Alliance will—"

Baine held up a hand. "Peace, my friend. You are

right about such things, but Thrall is no longer our war-chief. Garrosh Hellscream is. And our purpose here to-night is not to lead an insurrection, but to discuss what he has done up until this point and the wisdom—or lack thereof—of his choices." He nodded to Hamuul, who handed him a branch around which feathers, beads, and bits of bone were tied. "This is the speaking stick. Only he or she who holds it may speak." He held it out in front of him. "Who wishes to speak first?"

"I would speak, High Chieftain Bloodhoof." It was Frandis Farley. Baine inclined his head, and the stick was passed to the leader of Garrosh's Forsaken forces. "I serve the Horde. But it seems the Horde does not serve me, or my lady. We were once human; I myself once lived in the very city of Stormwind, which is certain to come bearing down on us at any moment. The Alliance is surely aware of what has happened by now, and I think Lady Jaina too wise a leader not to know that Theramore could be next in line to fall."

His supposition was truer than he knew. Baine did not reveal anything by a change of expression; he merely listened.

"Yet knowing all this, Lady Sylvanas agreed to send aid to the endeavor. But to what end? We are gathered! The Horde has food, supplies, and for those of you whose blood still flows in your veins, I know that blood burns hot for battle. Why is he waiting? Each day that passes, his troops become more uncertain. This is not wisdom. This is simply . . ." He groped for words. "Irresponsibility."

Bloodblade extended her hand for the speaking stick. "I agree with Captain Farley. His lands and ours are vulnerable if the humans decide to retaliate there instead of sending ships to Theramore. The swifter the strike, the swifter the reward. I cannot comprehend why Garrosh delays. More time serves our enemies and harms us."

"I don't know why he—" began the goblin first mate.

"Wait for the stick, friend," rumbled Baine. Blar looked a little embarrassed. He cleared his throat and began again, clutching the stick with both hands.

"What I was going to say is, I don't know why he did this in the first place. Trade Prince Gallywix might see coffers overflowing with gold, but all I see are goblins being used as cannon fodder for no real profit."

Vol'jin gestured for the stick. "Thank you, mah little green friend," he said. "You all know da trolls be a proud and ancient people. We joined da Horde because Sen'jin had a vision dat Thrall would help us. Lead us to safety. And he did. He was a good leader. Now Thrall be gone, and Garrosh be in his place. Thrall, he understand da elements, da spirits. He be da first new shaman his people had seen in a long, long time. We understand da elements, da spirits too, and I tell you true now, what dat Garrosh did wit' his dark shaman—it make da spirits angry. I doan know how long he be able to control dose molten giants, and if he don't . . ." He cackled. "Well, we all saw da Cataclysm. Dat was da world in pain from Deat'wing. How much worse is it gonna be if de elements be in pain from da Horde? Who you tink dey gonna attack? It be us, mon."

"Yes, it be you who will suffer, *mon*, but not from the elements!"

The deep, rough voice came from nowhere. At once Baine leaped to his hooves. The others assembled did likewise, many of them drawing weapons. But Baine recognized that voice and shouted, "Lay down your weapons! *Lay them down!*"

"The bull speaks wisely," said Malkorok, stepping

forward so he could be seen by the campfire's light. "If I see any weapons in the next three heartbeats, I will slay their owners."

The threat was not bellowed, but it did not need to be to chill the blood of everyone who heard it. Slowly, those Horde members who had drawn daggers or swords or who had nocked their arrows complied.

"I did not believe it," said another voice. This one was not calm but angry. And, Baine realized, wounded.

Garrosh Hellscream strode forward, regarding the gathering with disgust. Baine could now see the two had not come alone; shapes were shifting about in the darkness. Kor'kron.

"I had word of your little meeting," said Garrosh. His gaze fell upon Captain Zixx, and he beckoned. At once, the goblin scurried to Garrosh, trying to look calm and merely looking as though he was hiding behind the orc's massive bulk. "I came to observe, with my own eyes and ears, if what Malkorok said was true."

Baine turned toward him. "If you saw and heard it all," he said, "then you know that this is not treachery. No one here sought to overthrow you. No one here chanted 'Death to Garrosh.' What was said here was said out of concern for the Horde, which we *all* are devoted to."

"To question the Horde's warchief is to question the Horde," growled Malkorok.

"It does so only if in your mind, two plus two equals five," retorted Baine. "Our concerns are valid, Warchief. Many of us have sought audience with you so that we might say things to your face, so that we might have answers or explanations. The only reason we are gathered here tonight is because you would not see us!"

"I do not need to answer to you, tauren," spat Garrosh.

"Or you, troll," he said to Vol'jin. "You are not my keepers, nor are you puppet masters to make me dance to your tunes. You serve as the blade of the Horde. I am the wielder of that blade. I know things that you do not, and I tell you, you will *wait*. And you will continue to wait until I deem the time is right."

"Thrall would have seen us," Hamuul said angrily. "Thrall listened to advice when it was sound. And he did not keep his methods or plans overly secret. He knew that while he was the leader of the Horde, it was the Horde as a whole that mattered."

Garrosh strode up to the elderly tauren, pointing to his brown face with its black tattoos. "Does *this* look like the green skin of Thrall?"

"No, Warchief," said Hamuul. "No one would *ever* mistake you for Thrall."

It was almost respectful, and Baine saw Malkorok's eyes narrow at the comment. Garrosh, however, appeared mollified.

"The inexplicable love some of you have for that peace-hungry shaman astounds me," he said. He moved as he spoke, looking from face to face. "You would do well to remember it is because of Thrall that we are in this position to begin with! It was Thrall, not Garrosh, who let the Alliance encroach. Thrall, who held secret meetings with the human mage Jaina Proudmoore and all but sat like a dog at her feet. Thrall, whose mistakes I must now correct!"

Bloodblade began to speak. "But, Warchief—"

Garrosh whirled on the blood elf, striking her hard across the face. There was an angry murmur and a slight surge of the crowd. At once, Garrosh had Gorehowl in his hands, and the Kor'kron had swords and maces in theirs.

"Your warchief is merciful," Garrosh snarled. "You live, so that you may obey me, blood elf!"

Bloodblade nodded slowly; the gesture was clearly painful.

"Yes," said Garrosh, eyeing Baine and Vol'jin. "Your warchief is indeed merciful. In your own tauren fashion, Baine, you are right. Your concern is for the Horde. I cannot be your leader and not value that, even if your way of showing concern could be viewed as treasonous by a lesser leader. I need you—all of you. We will work together, for the glory of the Horde. And when the time is right, trust me—you will have no lack of Alliance scum to slaughter. Now it is time to return to your encampments . . . and await your warchief's order."

Baine, Vol'jin, and the others bowed as Garrosh passed. Like shadows, the Kor'kron followed behind him.

Baine breathed a sigh of relief. Word must not have reached the ears of Garrosh—or, more important, Malkorok—about Perith Stormhoof's mission, or else Baine Bloodhoof would no longer be alive. Baine realized that in his own way, Garrosh needed Baine's goodwill as much as Baine needed Garrosh's. Garrosh had to know that there were many who did not follow willingly, and Baine was a known moderate. As Baine went, so went a large number of Horde. For a moment, Baine stood silently contemplating this revelation; then he retired to his tent. After tonight's events, he badly needed to purify himself with the clean scent of sage smoke. He always felt sullied every time he acquiesced to anything Garrosh Hellscream demanded.

• • •

"You should have let me kill a few," grumbled Malkorok. "Or at least punish them in some fashion."

"They are all fine soldiers, and we will need them," Garrosh replied. "They are afraid. That will suffice. For now."

A younger orc ran up to Malkorok and whispered something in his ear. The Blackrock orc smiled.

"On the heels of such an unpleasant encounter," he said, "I have good news for my warchief. Phase two of your campaign has begun."

Captain Gharga squinted one eye against the bright sunlight and peered through a spyglass with the other. The waves were cooperating—the sailing was smooth. His lips curved around his tusks as he grinned at what he saw, and then he lowered the spyglass. He looked aft to see the other ships of the warchief's navy sailing steadily behind.

The *Blood and Thunder* and the other vessels, all crowded with cannons and crewed by orcs eager for the battle that was yet to come, moved closer to their destination.

Initially Gharga had been insulted when the *Blood and Thunder* and the other orc vessels had not been asked to participate in the Razing of Northwatch Hold, as it was coming to be known. He was mollified when Garrosh had told him that while Northwatch was being taken by the goblins, Forsaken, and blood elves, he was saving his orcs for another, more glorious battle. Garrosh had informed him, "You, Captain Gharga, will lead the fleet against Theramore!"

Gharga's barrel chest had swelled with pride. It was not the first time Garrosh had shown the *Blood and Thunder* favor. Well did Gharga recall when, as first mate, he had assisted in ferrying several magnataur from Northrend to unleash upon the Alliance. Briln, the captain, had taken full responsibility for the loss of two magnataur during a terrible storm. Briln had fully expected to be executed for the setback. Instead, Garrosh had held the captain blameless and had actually promoted him—and, with that gesture, promoted Gharga to captain.

The *Blood and Thunder* was a lucky ship, it would seem. Everyone wanted to transfer to her, so Gharga had had his pick of sea dogs from which to choose. It boded well for the battle.

While the blood elf, goblin, and Forsaken ships had assembled in Ratchet, the orc ships had set sail for Theramore. They had waited in Horde waters, safely out of sight. Waited . . . and waited . . . for further instructions, which had come in the form of a hawk with a message tied to its leg:

> Move into position. Take care you do not cross into Alliance territory. Do not flush the quarry too soon. Await my order.

So it was that now, eagerly, they moved close enough to see the towers of Theramore through a spyglass. Satisfied that they were still technically in Horde waters, Gharga barked the order that the anchor be dropped. With much grunting, two crewmen wrestled the giant iron hook into the water. It splashed loudly, then sank to the ocean bottom.

Gharga noticed his first mate looking both sad and sullen. He smacked the young orc gently on the head. "An expression like that will spoil the rum," he said.

The young orc snapped to attention, saluting. "Pardon, Captain, sir! I was just . . ."

"Just what?"

"Sir! Wondering why we moved at all, sir, if we're not going to attack."

"A fair question, but a foolish one," Gharga replied. "We are now close enough so that when the order to attack does come, we will be able to respond at once. And yet, we are not in Alliance waters. They will see us, and wring their hands, and worry, but they can do nothing unless we violate their waters. Even here, so far from shore, the Horde causes the Alliance to quake with fear. Our duty is to hold position, Lokhor. Garrosh knows more than we do. We will stay put until the moment he tells us the time is right to strike. Do not worry," he said, gentling his voice. "Alliance blood will flow, and you will be one who sheds it. All of you!"

Lokhor smiled, and the crew of the *Blood and Thunder* cheered.

Jaina had hoped that what the dockmaster had told her wasn't true. Prayed, even. But when she looked through the spyglass herself in the topmost part of the tower, her heart sank.

"So many," she murmured.

Kalec, Kinndy, Pained, and Tervosh peered through the spyglass, and all looked solemn.

"It seems as though your information was correct," said Tervosh.

"And you said Varian's fleet isn't due to arrive for at least another day, probably two," said Kinndy somberly. "I counted at least eight warships. If they decide to attack before the 7th gets here, we all might as well start getting used to eating cactus apple surprise."

Jaina placed a hand on Kinndy's shoulder. "I wouldn't be sure that Garrosh even takes prisoners, Kinndy."

"My lady," said Pained, "let us strike now! Surely Garrosh is not sending only a few ships. Remember the numbers gathered, waiting, at Northwatch! It will cost lives, but at least—"

"No," Jaina said firmly. "They are not in Alliance waters. I will defend Theramore, but I cannot condone being the aggressor. We'll just have to wait."

"And hope," muttered Tervosh.

Kalecgos had remained silent through the conversation, no doubt because he wished to remain neutral. Just as he opened his mouth to speak, Kinndy piped up.

"Lady . . . I think you should go to Dalaran."

Jaina's brow furrowed. "What do you mean?"

"You have friends there, and admirers."

"That's so, but the Kirin Tor is composed of both Horde and Alliance magi. They cannot side with us; they would betray that neutrality."

"Maybe they would, and maybe they wouldn't," Kinndy said. "I mean—they don't want to see the kind of bloodshed Garrosh is after. And we know there are even some Horde members who were willing to risk everything to warn us. It's worth asking."

"Indeed it is," said Kalec, looking pleased. "There is such a thing as the greater good."

Jaina looked at Tervosh. "I agree with Kinndy," he said.

"Quite rightly," said the gnome. Pained was nodding as well.

Jaina sighed. "Very well, let's see what Master Rhonin has to say. Please—do not get your hopes up. Pained, start talking with the soldiers. We should be ready in case the captains of those ships decide that now is a fine time to attack."

She met Kalec's eyes. He gave her a reassuring smile. She returned it with one that did not feel reassured, and went to her parlor.

She touched the three books, and the bookshelf slid aside, revealing the mirror.

Chanting the spell and moving her hands, Jaina stood before the mirror, gazing into her own eyes for a moment before the blue swirl obscured its reflective surface. For several tense heartbeats, she worried that Rhonin was too far away, but then his face came into view, tinted in hues of blue. His strong features looked weary until he recognized Jaina. Then he brightened.

"Lady," he said. "Please tell me you are contacting me because Kalecgos has recovered the Focusing Iris."

"Unfortunately, no. We were able to find a way for him to detect it again, but it seems whoever has it is ferrying it about to distract him. He is waiting—they must stop at some point if they are to use it."

Rhonin nodded his red head and rubbed his eyes. "That assumes he'll be able to get to it in time before they do—whatever it is they intend to do with it."

"He is well aware of that," said Jaina. "But there seems to be no other option."

"Even dragons tire," said Rhonin. "Well, if that isn't what you wish to talk about, what is?"

Rhonin's no-nonsense attitude often irritated others, but not Jaina. She found it refreshing. He had been a seemingly strange choice to lead the Kirin Tor, and no one knew that better than he. He was well aware that he was chosen because he had a history of looking at things in a different way from past leaders. And he was also a damned fine mage.

"Have you heard about Northwatch?" she asked.

"No," he said. "It's a rather small outpost, isn't it?"

"It is—it *was* a respectably sized garrison, designed to keep an eye on the Horde activity in the Southern Barrens." Rhonin had gone instantly alert at the usage of the past tense. "Four days ago, the Horde destroyed it utterly. It is reported that they used elemental magic of a very dark kind to do so. I received a warning from someone who was at that battle that the Horde's plan is to march on Theramore."

Rhonin narrowed his eyes. "And you will not name the source?"

"I cannot," she said. "He came in good faith. I will not dishonor him."

"Hmm," Rhonin said, and pulled on his red beard thoughtfully for a moment. "But . . . you said this was four days ago. Why didn't the Horde march straight south and wipe Theramore off the map?"

"We don't know," said Jaina. "But we do know there is a fleet of Horde battleships sitting right at the very outskirts of Alliance waters."

Rhonin didn't reply at once. Then he said, very carefully, "This is all very troubling for the Alliance and Theramore, of course. But what does it have to do with me?"

"Garrosh doesn't plan to stop there," Jaina said. "It's just a jumping-off point to conquer the whole continent. You know Garrosh; he's a hothead."

"So am I," said Rhonin.

Not bothering with tact, Jaina said, "You once were, perhaps, but since you became a husband and father and leader of the Kirin Tor, you've calmed quite a bit."

He shrugged and smiled a little, acknowledging the comment.

"Thousands will die," Jaina said, pressing him. "The Alliance will be driven from the shores of Kalimdor. Those who survive will be refugees. We already have too many without food and shelter still from the Cataclysm. The Eastern Kingdoms will not be able to care for the population of half an entire continent!"

"I ask you again, Jaina Proudmoore," Rhonin said quietly, "what does this have to do with me?"

"The Kirin Tor does not take sides; I know that," Jaina said. "But even Kalecgos thought you might be willing to come to our aid."

"Protect an Alliance city from an attack by the Horde?"

She nodded mutely. He looked off to the side for a long moment, his eyes not focused, then said, "I cannot make such a decision alone. You're going to have to convince others besides me. Dalaran is lovely this time of year."

12

Every time Jaina traveled to Dalaran, she was reminded anew of just how beautiful it was. The rich purple-hued spires of the city reached skyward, even as Dalaran hovered in the sky itself, untouched and untroubled by the concerns of Northrend below it. The streets gleamed, their red cobblestones clean, and its citizens, most of them as untouched and untroubled as the city itself, wandered freely. Here and nowhere else could be found remarkable items from vendors of all things rare and curious; here could be learned spells and history, whispered in hushed voices in quiet, peaceful halls.

Once, Dalaran had been a firm part of another continent altogether. Jaina remembered it best from those days, remembered strolling in the gardens, plucking golden-bark apples warm from the kiss of the sun.

Then Arthas had come.

Dalaran had been destroyed but not vanquished. The Kirin Tor had returned and rebuilt the mage capital, protecting it with a dome of violet magic, until the time had come for Dalaran to flourish anew as a hovering city. From here, the city-state had been the central focus of the Nexus War against Malygos, and, later, the fight against the Lich King. Yet one would find little here that was martial. Dalaran was at its best, and its populace happiest, when knowledge and learning were its greatest concerns.

Jaina herself had erected a monument to Antonidas. Usually when she traveled here, she paid "him" a visit, sometimes speaking her thoughts aloud as she sat in the shadow of the man's statue. But now her mission was of utmost importance.

She materialized inside the Violet Citadel itself, and the first face she saw was Rhonin's. He smiled in welcome, but his eyes were troubled.

"Welcome, Lady Jaina," he said. "You know everyone here."

"Indeed I do," said Jaina. Standing next to her husband was the white-haired, beautiful Vereesa Windrunner. She was the founder of the Silver Covenant and sister to Sylvanas, leader of the Forsaken, and Alleria, lost in Outland. Though the Windrunner family had suffered more than its share of tragedies, Vereesa, it seemed, had found happiness as the wife of a great mage and the proud mother of two beautiful children. Such domestic achievements, though, did not mean the high elf was content to stay in the shadows. As leader of the Silver Covenant, Jaina knew, Vereesa had publicly and staunchly opposed the admission of blood elves into the Kirin Tor.

She was, however, destined to be doomed in that pursuit, as the mage on Rhonin's left proved. This was Archmage Aethas Sunreaver, the blood elf who had struggled as hard to gain admittance into the Kirin Tor as Vereesa had struggled to forbid it. The fourth present was a human female who, though her hair was snowy white, looked as though she could take—and best—anyone in a fight. Archmage Modera had the distinction of serving the longest in the high council of magi, the Council of Six, having been a member since the Second War.

Jaina nodded respectful greetings to them all, then turned to Rhonin. He stepped back a pace and moved his hands with the ease of one long used to working magic. A portal appeared. Jaina frowned slightly. Usually one could get a good glimpse of the place one was traveling to, but this portal seemed to lead not into a room, or even a place on land, but into open air. She gave Rhonin a quizzical glance.

"The rest of the Six are assembled there," Rhonin said, not bothering to answer her unasked question. "Let's not keep them waiting, shall we?"

Trusting him completely, Jaina stepped through.

The floor, simple gray and thankfully solid stone inlaid with a diamond pattern, was all that seemed stable. Above and on every side was a shifting sky. Now it was bright blue with lazily drifting clouds, but a heartbeat later stars appeared and a rich blackness seemed to seep over the blue like spilled ink.

"Welcome, Lady Jaina, to the Chamber of the Air," said a voice. Or was it several voices all speaking at once? Dazzled by the room's endless and constantly changing vista, Jaina couldn't be sure. She tore her gaze away from the compelling, almost hypnotic sky-wall and looked at the Six, who formed a circle with Jaina in the center.

In bygone days, she knew, they had concealed their identities, even from other members of the Kirin Tor. But that tradition had recently fallen by the wayside. She could plainly identify each member. In addition to Modera, Aethas, and Rhonin, she beheld Ansirem Runeweaver. He was not often in Dalaran; recent tasks had necessitated his traveling extensively. On what mission, of course, Jaina did not know. Runeweaver Square was named in homage to this sharp-eyed, decisive man. Present too was Karlain, alchemist and mage both. Once at the mercy of his emotions, Karlain had learned to master them. Few were as controlled and thoughtful as he.

Last but most assuredly not least, Jaina recognized the aged visage of a young man—Khadgar, one of the most powerful magi in Azerothian history. Though he looked to be thrice Jaina's age, she knew the mage was only a decade older than she. Apprentice to Medivh, observer for the Kirin Tor, the closer of the Dark Portal, he dwelt in Outland, working with the naaru A'dal. That he was here, willing to discuss the matter of the protection of Theramore, gave her hope.

"Don't just stand there gawking," he said chidingly, but with a twinkle in his eye. "I'm not getting any younger."

Jaina inclined her head respectfully. "First, let me say that you do me great honor by listening to my plea. I shall be brief. You all know me as a moderate, a diplomat. For years, I have ceaselessly worked toward peace in Azeroth between the Alliance and the Horde. That I am here now, asking the aid of the Kirin Tor to defend an Alliance city against the Horde, must convey to you how dire and one-sided the situation truly is."

She moved slowly as she spoke, catching the eye of each mage in turn, letting them see her earnestness. Khadgar, she suspected, was inclined to agree. Karlain was harder to read, as was Ansirem, and they both regarded her with folded arms and blank expressions.

"The Horde has destroyed Northwatch Hold. Not only did Garrosh Hellscream amass an army of all Horde races, but his shaman used dark magic to control and direct molten giants—unpredictable and violent fire elementals.

The use of such coercion could trigger an event similar to the Cataclysm, if the elements grow sufficiently angry."

On to Modera, who gave her the slightest of smiles, and the helmeted Aethas, who stood as still as if he had been carved out of stone.

"They have set their sights on Theramore. We have a strong defense, and King Varian Wrynn has agreed to send us support in the form of the 7th Legion's naval fleet."

"Then why," asked Karlain, "do you need our aid? Theramore is a military city of no little reputation. And surely with the fleet, you will be able to send the Horde back to their lands, blushing with shame." Aethas's head turned at the comment, but the blood elf archmage did not speak.

"Because the Horde is amassed and ready to march," Jaina said. "And His Majesty's fleet is yet a few days away." She turned and spoke directly to Aethas. "I would prefer a meeting of minds to a clash of swords, but I must defend my people, who trust me to protect them. I would not fight the Horde, but I will if I must. It is my most sincere hope that if the Kirin Tor agrees to aid Theramore at this time when it is so very vulnerable, we can turn this potential attack into an opportunity to create peace."

"For all your years of diplomatic service, Jaina Proudmoore," said Aethas in a silky voice, "you know little of the Horde if you think they will stop when they see victory."

"Perhaps they will stop if they see magi from the Kirin Tor," Jaina retorted. "Please . . . there are families in Theramore. I will defend them with my life, as will the soldiers quartered there. But we might not be enough. And if Theramore falls, so well might Kalimdor. Nothing would then stop the Horde from attacking Ashenvale or Teldrassil, and driving the night elves out of their ancient lands. Garrosh wishes the entire continent—and, with respect, that cannot possibly be what the Kirin Tor wishes as a whole. Not if it truly believes in neutrality."

"We understand the situation," said Karlain. "You do not need to tell us our business."

"I do not seek to," Jaina said. "But I am counting on your wisdom to see that this is not asking you to take sides. This is asking you to save innocent lives—and keep a balance that is already too tentative."

An unseen signal must have passed between the other magi, for as one all of them stepped back a pace. "Thank you, Lady Jaina," said Rhonin in a voice that was clearly a dismissal. "We will speak and ask the opinions of others ere we decide. I will notify you when we reach an agreement."

There was the hum of another portal opening, and Jaina stepped through it onto the almost too-clean cobblestone streets of Dalaran, feeling like a little girl who had been told to go tidy her room if she wished to have supper. She was unused to being dismissed but reasoned that if anyone had the right to do so, it was the Council of Six.

She started to cast a teleportation spell back to Theramore but paused in mid-motion. There were two people she should see while she was here.

After Jaina had departed, the other five members turned expectantly to Rhonin. Before any of them could speak, he lifted a hand. "We will reconvene in an hour," he said.

"But we're all already here," said Modera, slightly puzzled.

"I—have some precedents I'd like to check out," said Rhonin. "I might suggest the rest of you do the same. Whichever way we decide—to aid Theramore or stand back and let the Horde come—it's a big choice. I'd like more than my own opinion before I cast my vote."

There were a few sour faces, but they nodded. Rhonin teleported himself back to his chamber and stood there for a moment, his red brows knitting together. Then he strode over to his desk—nearly every inch of it covered in blank parchment, scrolls, or books—and waved a hand.

The messy pile floated upward and remained about three feet off the desk. The desk's top flipped open to reveal a small, simple box. What was inside, however, was anything but simple.

Rhonin removed the box, closed the desk's top, and allowed the parchment, books, and scrolls to return to their various positions. He took the box to a chair and sat down with it. "Old friend, it is at times like this that I miss you more than I can say," he said. "But I must admit, it's comforting to hear you speak to me beyond death—even if you have to do it in riddles."

He unlocked the box with a small key he kept around his neck and thoughtfully regarded the small pile of scrolls. Each one was a prophecy from Korialstrasz, the late consort of Alexstrasza the Life-Binder. The visions had come to him over the years, and when he had bequeathed them to Rhonin, saying with a grin, "This may help explain how at times I appear so damned clever," Rhonin had been humbled. He had asked Rhonin to keep the knowledge of the prophecies hidden, and upon Rhonin's death he was to leave the key to one person he trusted. "They must not fall into the wrong hands," Krasus had warned him.

That night, Rhonin had stayed up until the small hours of the morning reading through all the prophecies. And there was one in particular he wished to consult now.

"I take it back," he said aloud. "Why did you have to write these in riddles, Krasus?"

He was sure that, somewhere, the great red dragon was laughing.

It was only the second visit Jaina had paid the Sparkshine family. The first time, she had come to take their daughter to a faraway land. They had been fairly bursting with pride for Kinndy, but Jaina could easily see that the family was tightly knit, perhaps because it consisted only of the three of them. The parting had been hard, but Jaina had been welcomed not as an intruder depriving them of their daughter, but as a long-lost relative to be received with open arms. Even so, she now hesitated at the door. Coming here had been an impulsive decision. Jaina felt that she owed it to her apprentice's parents to let them know, first and foremost, how impressed she was with Kinndy's abilities. And second, to inform them that that impressive, beloved girl was about to be put in harm's way.

Steeling herself for the encounter, she knocked on the door. As she remembered would happen, a smaller door, inlaid into the main one, squeaked open. An elderly, purple-clad mage peered out, around, and then up.

"Good afternoon, mage Sparkshine," Jaina said, smiling.

At once he whipped off his pointed hat and bowed deeply. "Lady Proudmoore!" he exclaimed. "What brings you to—" His eyes widened slightly. "Our little Kinndy is well, I trust?"

"Quite well, and performing her apprenticeship duties admirably," Jaina said. Both comments, at this moment, were utterly true. "Might I come in?"

"Oh, certainly, certainly!" Windle Sparkshine ducked back inside and closed the door, and then the main door opened to admit Jaina.

The tidy little apartment was, as far as Jaina was concerned, decorated in perfect miniature. The ceiling was high enough for her to stand erect, but it would have been impossible for her to sit in the tiny chairs. Fortunately, Windle was already pulling out what he referred to as the "Tall Folk chair."

"There you are. Sit yourself right down by the fire here." Jaina looked at the hearth but said nothing. There were logs arranged, but they remained unlit. She smothered a smile. It was an old joke with the Sparkshine family, and she had no intention of spoiling it.

Windle pretended to gasp. "Why, that fire's not lit!" he exclaimed. He withdrew a wand, muttered something softly, then flicked the tip of the magical tool toward the hearth. At once, a bright blaze sprang up, adding even more cheer to the already pleasant scene.

A lovely smell wafted from the kitchen, and a gray-haired female gnome, her face smudged with flour, peered out. "Windle, who was it at—why, Lady," she said, "what a surprise! Give me just a moment to get these pies into the oven, and I'll be right with you."

"Take your time, Mrs. Sparkshine."

"I told you when we met, it's Jaxi, or no apple tarts," was the gentle reproof. For the first time in what felt like years, Jaina laughed.

She sat in the comfortable and appropriately sized chair and appreciatively accepted some tea and pastries.

Windle and Jaxi sat in their own appropriately sized chairs and made idle chitchat for a while.

Finally, Jaina put down her cup and looked at them. "Your daughter," she said, "is doing a fine job. No," she said, amending that, "a tremendous job. She impresses me more every day. I'm sure once her training is completed, she'll impress everyone else. Many apprentices have potential. Not all of them live up to it."

The couple beamed and turned to each other, clasping hands. "She's our only one, you know," Windle said. "I'm sure you haven't noticed, but I'm getting up in years." It was said with a twinkle in his eye; the long white beard gave him away. "Jaxi and I had all but given up hope of having a child. Kinndy's our little miracle."

"We do worry about her, all the way over there in Theramore," Jaxi said, "but we appreciate that you let her come visit us so often."

"You must be teasing me," Jaina said, "considering that every time she comes back, she brings us all some of your pastries! I'd send her to you daily if I could spare her!"

They all chuckled. It was so serene, sitting in this cozy, old-fashioned room next to a blazing fire. Jaina wished with all her heart that it could remain so simple and so untroubled by thoughts of the danger Theramore was facing.

"Oh, Lady Jaina," said Jaxi, "what unhappy thought makes you so sad?"

Jaina sighed. Much as she might wish otherwise, these good people had a right to know that their daughter was in danger.

"Theramore is in need of aid from the Kirin Tor," Jaina said quietly. "It was actually Kinndy's idea that I come here and ask for help. More I cannot tell you, but I fear I am going to go home empty-handed."

"What kind of—" Jaxi began to say, but Windle laid a wrinkled hand over hers and squeezed it.

"Now, now, Lady Jaina has an awful lot going on," he said. "If she can't tell us, well, that's good enough for me."

"And me, of course," said Jaxi. Her other hand crept over to hold her husband's. "I just . . . Is Kinndy . . ."

"Kinndy has been working tirelessly, and her aid is invaluable," Jaina said. "I give you my word, I will keep her as safe as I possibly can. After all"—and she tried to keep her voice light—"I've invested a great deal of time into training her. I'd hate to have to start all over again with a new apprentice all wet behind the ears!"

"Don't you fret about the Kirin Tor," Windle said, trying to reassure her. "They wouldn't just leave you hanging out there alone in Theramore. They'll do the right thing. You'll see!"

They loaded her down with hugs, the fondest of wishes, and a bag of various boxed pastries. So confident and cheerful were they that Jaina began to think that maybe, just maybe, this particular trip to Dalaran would yield fruit.

13

I suspect, little miss apprentice," Kalec said as he stared at the small pieces on the table, "that you are intimately familiar with the nuances of this game."

Kinndy's large eyes grew even larger in feigned innocence. "Me? Oh, hardly! Tervosh only taught it to me last week." The dragon lifted his blue gaze from the game pieces on the board and quirked an indigo eyebrow. Her expression dissolved into a grin. "Well," she said, "there might be a reason no one else will play with me anymore."

"So I'm simply fresh blood?"

"Mmmm," Kinndy said noncommittally. Kalec was just about to move the knight when he heard the familiar sound of a teleportation spell. He turned, the game forgotten, as Jaina materialized in her parlor. She was smiling, an expression Kalec had not often seen on her face, and he said a silent thanks to whoever or whatever had caused it.

"Your parents," Jaina said to Kinndy, "are the nicest people in Azeroth. And the most generous." She handed Kinndy a box of pastries from the bag. Kinndy opened it to reveal a staggering variety—small cakes, individual pies, éclairs, puffs, all manner of delicious-appearing delights.

"So, how did it go?" asked Kinndy, taking a bite of something frosted and divine-smelling.

Jaina's expression sobered. She slipped into her own chair and poured some tea. "Not well," she confessed. "But I think I did manage to change a few minds. Don't look so downcast," she added as Kinndy slumped a bit in her seat. "They haven't given me their decision on it yet. Which means there's going to be more debate and discussion. The tide may yet turn. Regardless, it was a good idea, Kinndy."

"It would be a better idea if a whole bunch of the Kirin Tor had come back with you," Kinndy said.

"I cannot argue that point," Jaina replied, "but I will take what I can get. And what I can get are berry pastries."

"I am glad to see that you do not feel that all of the sweetness has gone out of the world," Kalec said, helping himself to one. "But I regret that the meeting was not more positive."

Jaina waved a sugared hand. "I will not worry until I hear one way or the other," she said. "But I would not object if you had some good news about the situation here."

"If only I did," Kalec said, meaning the words with his whole heart. "The Horde continues to wait on our doorstep, careful not to advance. And unfortunately the Focusing Iris is still on its tour of Kalimdor at speeds that astonish me."

Kinndy was watching them both as she ate her pastry, and her eyes narrowed thoughtfully. "I think I'll go finish this upstairs in my room," she said. "There's a book there I've been meaning to get to. I might learn something that could help."

She placed her tea and pastry on a tray and with no further word trundled off. Jaina raised a golden eyebrow, and her forehead furrowed in confusion.

"What do you think that was all about?" she asked.

"I've no idea," responded Kalec. It was not entirely the truth. He did have a suspicion as to why the gnome wished to leave the two of them alone . . . but he had no desire to dwell on it.

She turned to him, eyeing him curiously. "Why are you here, Kalecgos of the blue dragonflight?"

For no reason he could understand, the question made him uncomfortable. "I'm looking for—"

"The Focusing Iris, I know. That may be what brought you here, but . . . why do you stay? You could pick any place in the continent to wait for the Focusing Iris to slow and stabilize, yet you linger here."

Kalec felt heat rise in his cheeks. It was a simple question: Why *did* he linger here, rather than seek silence in the wilderness? He could sense the magical object he had come in search of easily enough elsewhere. Yet here he stayed, learning to play chess with a gnome, discussing military tactics with a night elf, the nature of the arcane with Tervosh and—

Jaina.

He stayed because of Jaina.

She was looking at him expectantly, one slender hand tucking a stray lock of golden hair behind her ear, her head tilted in a quizzical expression, that distinctive furrow of curiosity creasing a brow that was otherwise remarkably unmarred for a human of her age.

She wanted an answer, and he could not give her one. At least, not one that was true. And as he opened his mouth for a glib fabrication, he found he did not wish to lie to her.

"There are several reasons," he said, looking away.

Jaina leaned forward. "Oh?"

"Well . . . you are a master of magic among your people, Jaina. I feel comfortable with you. Maybe I want to stay with the younger races because my people persecuted yours. With no real right to do so other than a vaguely worded statement about being the minders of magic. So very many died in the Nexus War, among both dragonkind and the younger races. They died needlessly and brutally." His blue eyes met hers, and this time it was she who had to look away. "I suppose I feel I owe it to you to help. And . . ." He smiled a little, knowing that this much, at least, was true. "You're good company."

"Oh, I doubt that," Jaina said.

"I don't." His voice was soft, and he realized it trembled. He wanted to place his hand over hers but did not dare. Kalecgos was himself unsure of what drove this interest in Lady Jaina Proudmoore, mage. He needed to know exactly what he did feel, and why, before he even ventured to inquire if she felt the same way.

Probably not, he thought. Malygos had been responsible for starting the Nexus War. His goal had been to direct arcane energy away from everywhere but his own realm. It was good-hearted enough of her to seem to want to be his friend. He didn't want to risk asking for anything more, especially now, with an attack poised to happen right on her doorstep.

"Well, there's no accounting for taste," Jaina said flippantly. Kalec felt a surge of anger at whoever or whatever had made her think so disparagingly of herself. Was it Kael'thas? Arthas? Her father, whom she had so bravely stood against when all logic and all emotion doubtless cried out that she should not? There was a sorrow in her eyes, one that had not come from news of imminent battle—a sorrow that had been there since the moment he arrived. A sorrow he longed to chase away.

She needed him right now. The Kirin Tor would likely turn their backs on her, abandon Theramore to fall beneath the wave of orc, troll, tauren, Forsaken, goblin, and blood elf. In his mind's eye, he saw Jaina standing alone, wielding startlingly powerful magic, her strong face all the more beautiful in her fierce determination to defend her city.

But all the skill in the world, if wielded only by a single person, could not stand against such odds. Theramore would fall, and Jaina with it.

He opened his mouth to speak, but at that moment, he sensed a slight tingling of magic in the air. Jaina's eyes widened and she leaped to her feet, hurrying to tap the three books in their special order. The bookcase slid back to reveal the mirror pulsing with mist.

"Speak," Jaina said in a voice tremulous with hope.

At the command, the mist in the mirror took on the shape of a human male face.

Archmage Rhonin.

"You are a very persuasive woman, Lady," said Rhonin. "While the Kirin Tor feels very strongly that we should remain impartial, your plea moved us to action. Even Aethas Sunreaver voted in favor of rendering aid. It seems that to not assist you against such tremendous opposition would be to tacitly support the Horde. At least, that's the logic he used."

"Please tell Archmage Aethas that his logic is deeply appreciated," Jaina said. Her slim body was quivering as she forcibly kept her composure. She looked as though she was struggling not to leap for joy. Kalec knew he wanted to.

"I and several others will be arriving shortly to lend our assistance in the defense of Theramore. I stress the word 'defense.' We will protect, but we will make no offensive moves. Our greatest hope is that our presence will serve as a deterrent. Is this fully understood?"

"Quite fully, Archmage. It is my hope as well that somehow we can find a peaceful solution."

Rhonin sighed, dropping his formerly stern mien. "I suspect we're all just whistling in the dark, but we'll be damned if we sit by and twiddle our thumbs. Expect us shortly."

The image faded. There was a final swirl of magical blue mist, and then the mirror placidly reflected only Jaina and Kalecgos.

Jaina sagged with relief. "Thank the Light," she murmured. "They will get here in time, even if—" She shook her head, as if to chase away the negative thought that Varian's fleet might *not* arrive in time. She smiled radiantly, and Kalec's heart jumped in his chest.

He wanted to speak. But he couldn't. The inner voice—of wisdom or fear, he knew not which—spoke and said, *No. Not now. Perhaps not ever.* Kalec was aware of what he had to do—for both of them. And the knowing was like a knife in his gut.

"I am very glad indeed," he said. "They will protect Theramore as well as I could, perhaps better."

Some of her exuberance subsided. "Could?" she asked.

He nodded. "Yes," he said. "You have reminded me of a duty I must perform. Now that I know you have allies, I am going to do another sweep of the continent, to see if perhaps I can close in on the Focusing Iris."

"I see. Of course, that's an excellent idea." She smiled briskly, and the sorrow returned to her eyes. Doubtless because she felt that he was abandoning her.

Which I am, he thought sickly. *But it is for her own good.* He knew if he stayed, he would be unable to refrain from speaking his heart. And that would be a burden Lady Jaina Proudmoore most certainly did not need as she faced what could be Theramore's darkest hour.

As he had told Jaina, Archmage Rhonin and others of the Kirin Tor would protect her as well as he could, and none of them was in danger of distracting Jaina from what needed to be her pure, focused purpose.

"I suppose this is good-bye, then," Jaina said. She smiled, the sincere yet practiced smile of the diplomat, and extended her hand. Kalecgos took it, closing his fingers around her slender ones, savoring the simple handshake for what it surely must have been—the last time he would be able to touch her.

"You are in good hands," he said.

"The finest in Azeroth," Jaina said cheerfully. "I wish you every success, Kalecgos. I know you will find what you are seeking. For your flight, and for the whole world. Perhaps . . . after the battle, if you do not find it, I can be of further help?"

He swallowed hard, then let her hand fall. "After the battle, if I do not find it, you shall be the first to know," he said sincerely.

Kalecgos strode with more energy than was warranted out of the tower and into an area clear enough for him to transform. He leaped into the sky, extending his senses, willing the cursed Focusing Iris to slow, to stop, so that he could recover it and return to Jaina. But it would not cooperate, and its rapid speed taunted him as he flapped his wings and sped off in what was probably futile pursuit.

• • •

Jaina was surprised at Kalec's rather abrupt departure and realized that she had assumed he would stay and help. But it was not his battle, she reasoned; he probably had already intervened much more than he had originally intended. Charming as he was in his half-elven form, he was, in the end, a dragon. And the dragons did not take sides in the affairs of the younger races. Still, she felt an odd sense of loss. He had become a friend during these tense few days, and she would miss him more than she had expected.

She did not have time to brood on his absence, however, as Rhonin, true to his word, materialized outside Jaina's tower a scant half hour after he had contacted her. And also true to his word, he did not come alone.

With him were nearly a dozen others, four of whom Jaina knew to be prominent members of the Kirin Tor, if not members of the council. The rest of the magi she did not know, but she certainly recognized Vereesa Windrunner. Clearly, she was not going to let her husband be put in harm's way without standing beside him. Jaina gave her a welcoming smile and turned to the magi.

The four premier magi Rhonin had selected were Tari Cogg, one of the foremost gnome magi in Dalaran; Amara Leeson, a human mage with long black hair and a pinched-looking face whose cross expression belied a kind heart; Thoder Windermere, whose massive physical build and roughed-up features would make one think he was a warrior rather than one of the deftest spellcasters Jaina had ever met; and, to her surprise, Thalen Songweaver, a Sunreaver, slender, sharp-featured, and with hair the color of moonlight.

"I know many of you and look forward to getting to know the rest," Jaina said warmly, "and I thank you from my heart for answering my call for aid. Mage Songweaver,

I especially thank you for being here. The choice must have been difficult, for you and for Archmage Aethas."

"Not as much as you would think," said Songweaver in a husky, pleasant voice. "It was my lord Aethas who cast the deciding vote."

"Even after being married to an elf, their logic still confounds me," said Rhonin. Vereesa gave him a mock glare. Rhonin winked at his wife, then turned back to Jaina. "Well, here we are. I need to speak with you privately, Lady Proudmoore, but my colleagues here await instruction."

"Let us say rather requests," Jaina said, turning to Tervosh. "Tervosh, Kinndy, Pained? Will you acquaint our guests with the layout of the city and introduce them to Captain Vimes and Captain Evencane?"

Pained merely nodded. Tervosh said, "It would be an honor. We are most grateful for your aid." Kinndy looked a little stunned and, for once, seemed to have nothing to say. Jaina watched the group go, then turned to Rhonin.

"You realize you've irritated a lot of magi," Rhonin said without preamble.

"I?" Jaina was confused.

"I know, I know, that's usually my area of expertise," the red-haired archmage said with a self-deprecating grin. "Some people like to hold grudges. I won't go so far as to say you made enemies during the Third War, but your choices didn't endear you to very many."

"What did I do?"

"It's more what you *didn't* do. Some in Dalaran feel you abandoned them. When you chose not to work with the Kirin Tor but struck off on your own."

"I wasn't needed there," Jaina replied. "I had a different—well, calling. I went where I felt I could best serve. I had no idea other magi felt insulted by that choice."

"It's old grumbling, nothing more," Rhonin told her. "Some people just like to be cranky. And the main reason it still doesn't sit right with some of them is because there were more than a few magi who thought that you should have been the future of the council, not a smart-mouthed redhead." At her shocked expression he added, "Come now, Jaina, I've heard you say often enough that it's as much a mistake to downplay one's talents as it is to inflate them. I'm good. Damn good. And so are many others in the Kirin Tor. Some of those are here today. But you . . ." He shook his head admiringly. "You're a fine diplomat, no question. Azeroth owes a lot to you. But even I think you may be squandering your gifts, staying here in Theramore."

"Theramore is a nation. One I founded to shine out as a beacon of hope for peace in this world. One I have promised to take care of and protect. I would be but one of many in the Kirin Tor. Here . . ." Jaina gestured at the activity all around them. "I can't leave, not now and probably not ever, Rhonin. You know that. Theramore needs me. And whatever you say, I cannot believe that I could better serve Azeroth as one of many magi in the Kirin Tor than I have as a diplomat."

He nodded, a bit mournfully, it seemed to her. "You *are* Theramore," he said in agreement. "More than I or anyone can be the Kirin Tor. This world is in a sad, sad state, Jaina. It's not been allowed to recover. First the war against Malygos and the blues. Then fighting that bas—forgive me, the Lich King—cost so many lives. And then Azeroth itself practically cracks in half. No disrespect to your efforts, but I don't think that either the Horde or the Alliance would know what to do with peace if it bit them."

Jaina knew that Rhonin did not mean his comments as a criticism. He was merely lamenting, as did she, the fact that Azeroth and its denizens had been forced to endure so many catastrophes, so much violence. And yet, what he said galvanized her, as it struck far too close. *Was* she wasting her time? Hadn't she said as much to Go'el not so long ago, that she feared her words were falling on deaf ears? What she said came back to her: *It seems as if I am struggling through mud simply to be heard, let alone actually listened to. It's . . . difficult to try to be a diplomat and work for real, solid results when the other side won't acknowledge reason anymore. I feel like a crow cawing in the field. I wonder if it's just wasted breath.*

Kalecgos, too, had expressed the same thing. *Why are you not in Dalaran?* he had asked her. *Why are you here, standing between swamp and ocean, between Horde and Alliance?*

Because someone has to, she had answered. And because she believed she had the ability to succeed as a diplomat.

If you believe that—and I am not saying you are wrong—why are you trying so very hard to convince yourself?

Had she been doing the wrong thing, in the wrong place?

Jaina forced the thought back. Now was not the time to get lost in regrets. Now was the time to act, to defend her people from the battle that was quite literally on the horizon. "I must see my people safe first," she said to Rhonin. "Not even I can talk of peace while they are in harm's way. Let's go."

14

The sun set, red and swollen. The troll and the tauren, fur and skin seemingly bloodied by the hue, made their silent, steady way up the hill to the ruins of Northwatch Hold. There was no Alliance there anymore, not even corpses. Garrosh Hellscream now slept in a tower once occupied by an admiral, and it was he whom the troll and tauren sought.

Garrosh was in a good mood. The evening campfires for cooking, warmth, and light were already lit. Garrosh was happy for any Alliance spies to see how many of the Horde they would be facing, and put no limits on how large the fires blazed or how numerous they were. A haunch of zhevra roasted over one such fire now, turning on a spit and rendering both fat that sizzled as it dripped and a mouthwatering scent as it cooked.

"Let them come forward," Garrosh said expansively to Malkorok. "They are the leaders of their people. Vol'jin, Baine, come join me. Tear off some of this delicious meat for yourselves!"

The tauren and the troll glanced at each other, then stepped forward. Each had a knife and sliced off and speared a chunk of the dripping flesh. A cask of cherry grog was passed around, and they drank politely.

"Now," said Garrosh, "to what do I owe the pleasure?"

"Warchief," said Baine, "your people sit and await your orders. Their blood burns with the fire for battle. You know our feelings on this matter. We come, openly, imploringly, to tell you that you must strike soon, or the Alliance will have time to prepare a defense!"

"I thought you liked the Alliance, Baine Bloodhoof," drawled Garrosh. His small dark eyes were sharp and alert, contradicting his languorous pose.

"You know where my loyalties lie," said Baine, his voice dropping almost to a growl. "I have no wish to lead my braves into a battle where they will be slaughtered— not when I can lead them into one in which they will be the victors."

"You share this opinion," stated Garrosh, turning to Vol'jin.

The troll spread his arms. "You heard us before on dis, Wahchief. My people be ready to taste Alliance blood. Dey get impatient if you keep holdin' dem back. Da Forsaken might be fine wit' patience an' all, but I gotta ask you—what you be tinkin'? You be a great warrior! You not be afraid of dem Alliance. So why we not be strikin' now?"

"You are right. I am a great warrior. And I know more than a little of strategy," Garrosh replied. "I am growing very weary of your questioning my wisdom in this matter." Gone was the cheerful, relaxed pose. Garrosh had neither drunk too much nor feasted too much. His eyes were fixed upon them intently.

"We do not question," said Baine carefully. "We too are warriors of no little repute. We too understand the need for tactics. We are offering our advice, dearly bought with the blood of our people, in an effort to prevent unnecessary bloodshed. And we urge you to listen to us."

Baine took a deep breath, rose, strode to Garrosh, and knelt before him. The gesture of obeisance rankled, but it was genuine. He *needed* Garrosh to listen. His people—nay, the entire Horde—needed it.

"The tauren and the trolls have ever been friends to the orcs," he said. "We admire and respect your race. You are warchief of the Horde, Garrosh Hellscream, not just warchief of the orcs." He let his gaze move to the imposing figure of Malkorok standing beside Garrosh, his arms folded across his massive gray chest as he stared balefully at Baine. "You lead us—all of us. You are too smart to be ignoring our advice on this. We do not understand why you seem to wish to listen only to this Blackrock orc."

Malkorok growled low and took a step forward. Garrosh raised a hand, and the other orc paused in midstride. "I need you to get a message to the *Blood and Thunder* and the other vessels gathered just outside of Theramore Harbor," he said, his eyes not on Malkorok but on Baine. "Tell them that I have new orders for them."

Baine and Vol'jin exchanged hopeful glances. Perhaps Garrosh was finally listening to them.

Garrosh smiled around his tusks, and when he spoke, his voice was hard. "Tell the fleet to pull back even farther from Theramore. Far enough away that the most sophisticated Alliance contraption can no longer see them. Their presence isn't needed anymore."

"*What?*" Vol'jin's question was a strangled cry of disbelief.

"My goal has been accomplished. I wanted the Alliance to be aware of the possible threat to their shores."

Slowly, Baine got to his hooves. "You . . . plan to withdraw the fleet," he said, his voice hollow.

"I do," Garrosh said, also rising. The two stared at each other.

"Instead of pressing the attack before Theramore can call in aid . . . you are withdrawing."

"Yes. And here we have it, tauren. Those are my orders. Are you questioning them?"

The moment strung out, tense and silent save for the sizzle of meat juices dripping into the fire. No one moved, though everyone watching was prepared to.

"You are the warchief of the Horde, Garrosh Hellscream," Baine said finally. "You will do as you wish. I only pray to the Earth Mother that when this debacle is all over, there is a Horde left."

Before Garrosh could taunt him further, Baine turned and left. Vol'jin was right beside him. As they headed back toward their encampments, they could hear harsh orcish laughter behind them.

The attitude in Theramore was determined and grim. The martial aspect of the city, always present, surged to the forefront. The inn was no longer a place to sit by a fire, enjoying a brew and conversation, but a place where soldiers were quartered, sometimes eight to a room. Cots even covered the floor of the public areas. Dried beans, grains, smoked meats, and containers of fresh water were stockpiled deep in the heart of Foothold Citadel.

A sliver of hope energized the city briefly when the sails of the 7th's fleet were spotted on the horizon. The ships, twenty in all, carried not just Stormwind's finest sailors but also several generals of no small repute. The air grew almost celebratory when the flagship, the *Spirit of Tiffin*, docked in Theramore Harbor, followed by the rest of the fleet. Despite the urgency, the marines of the flagship disembarked with an abbreviated but precise ceremony, moving to the martial rat-a-tat of a drum so they were lining up facing Jaina, Pained, Tervosh, Kinndy, Vereesa, and the members of the Kirin Tor. Gathered behind them were the citizens of Theramore, their weary, wary faces relaxing as they cheered the men and women who had come to help defend them.

Varian had told Jaina he would send as many as he could, but he had named no names, as he himself was uncertain as to whom he could reach in time. Jaina shielded her eyes from the sun, watching eagerly as ramrod-straight males and females from nearly all the races of the Alliance strode down the gangplank.

"Marcus Jonathan, general of Stormwind, high commander of Stormwind Defense," one of the marines announced. A large, imposing man wearing heavy plate mail moved with surprising lightness from the plank to the dock. His beard and mustache were full, but his red-brown hair was cropped fairly short. He looked simultaneously relaxed and ready to spring into action in a heartbeat. Jaina was not a particularly short woman, but as he stood and extended a hand to her, she felt very small indeed.

"I was the first King Varian asked, and the first to accept," he said. "You have done so much for the Alliance, Lady Proudmoore, that it is an honor to be able to assist you."

"Thank you, General," she said. "You bring hope with you."

The next two were dwarves. Jaina had never met them,

but she knew who they were, and the tragic reason these two particular dwarves were here and not two others.

"Thaddus Stoutblow o' the Wildhammer," the first one said gruffly, saluting her with his hammer rather than shaking her hand.

"Horran Redmane o' the 7th Legion Base Camp," the second said.

"You are both most welcome," Jaina said. "And let me extend my sympathies for the deaths of General Thunderclash and General Marstone."

Thaddus Stoutblow nodded brusquely. "Aye, the deaths o' our superiors were nae the ways we wanted tae get our commands, that's fer sure."

"But we'll avenge them," put in Redmane. "Happy tae come help, Lady. Killin' Horde is killin' Horde, nae matter where we do it."

Even with the Horde all but camped on her doorstep, she regretted the necessity to fight, and such bloodthirst as the two dwarves displayed pained Jaina. However, she merely nodded and turned her attention to the next general.

His hooves clopping gently on the wood of the gangplank, draenei general Tiras'alan strode toward her. She was surprised but pleased to see him, especially after the open, if understandable, hostility displayed by the dwarves toward the Horde. Tiras'alan had been present at the historic moment when Lady Liadrin of the Blood Knights had spoken with the naaru A'dal, renouncing Kael'thas and choosing to serve the Shattered Sun Offensive. He had initially been furious that she would dare approach, after all her people had done. Yet A'dal had shown forgiveness and compassion, and it had been Tiras'alan who had given Lady Liadrin the tabard of the Shattered Sun.

Jaina welcomed the draenei warmly. Strength and gentleness radiated from him, just as golden light seemed to radiate from his armor as he bowed to her.

"I come to protect and defend," he said. "Word of your great deeds and efforts for peace has reached even Shattrath City, Lady." His voice was musical and deep. "Theramore must stand. The Horde will not triumph."

No talk of "killin' Horde" from the draenei, but his was as firm and earnest a pledge of support as the dwarves had given.

"Your wisdom will be most welcome," Jaina said. "It will be good to have a paladin's Light in the battle to come."

A purple-skinned, blue-haired night elf stepped out, blinking at the sun. Jaina's eyes widened and she smiled, welcoming this particular ally—Shandris Feathermoon, general of the night elf Sentinels—as a friend.

"Battle sister," Shandris said, returning the smile gently. "The archdruid and the high priestess send me to you with joy, and it is with joy that I and my Sentinels come to aid you."

"You and they are most welcome," said Jaina, realizing that if Shandris had brought some of her people, it was likely that the other generals had brought what could be spared of their finest as well. Garrosh was bringing all the races of the Horde to bear on Theramore; they would be greeted in kind.

The last to stride onto the dock of Theramore Harbor was no general, but a familiar figure nonetheless. Jaina had learned only a short time ago that he had survived the Razing of Northwatch Hold. He had been badly injured and fallen unconscious, and the Horde had left him for dead. Her pleasure at seeing him was followed instantly by shock and grief at his appearance. He had not come through the battle for Northwatch Hold unscathed; he had lost an eye and had a jagged scar marring what had once been a handsome visage. As he walked toward her, she noticed that one leg dragged slightly. He saw where her gaze went and her sympathetic expression, and smiled as much as he could with his damaged face.

"Admiral Aubrey," Jaina said warmly, hurrying up to him with her hands outstretched in welcome.

"Lady Proudmoore," he said. "I'm alive, and the Horde didn't take my wits. That's all that matters. I'll serve you as best I can."

"As best you can is better than most could serve. I am so pleased to see you. The Alliance is going to be very glad of those wits. And a firsthand account of the Horde's tactics will be helpful as well." She squeezed his hands and inquired, "Are there any others with . . . ?" Her voice trailed off as his expression grew solemn.

"About half a dozen survived with enough of their body parts left to join me," he said. "And I've news of the Horde fleet as well, which I need to share as quickly as possible."

"Aye, Admiral Aubrey's right," said Thaddus Stoutblow. "This is nae the time fer a cup o' tea an' idle chatter."

"Agreed," Jaina said at once. "Would that we had time for proper ceremony. Captain Vimes will help familiarize your crews and soldiers with the city and its defenses. Generals—and Admiral—please come into the keep. We have a great deal to discuss."

A few moments later saw Jaina, the five generals, the five members of the Kirin Tor, Ranger-General Vereesa, and the single admiral seated around a large table. Ink, quills, and paper were on hand, as were glasses of fresh water. Not even the dwarves asked for alcohol; all knew that their wits needed to be clear and sharp.

"I bid all of you welcome once again," Jaina said before anyone else could speak. "Generals, Admiral, the magi you see before you are respected members of the Kirin Tor—including the respected mage Thalen Songweaver. They have come to offer their insight and expertise in defense of Theramore."

Marcus Jonathan peered at Rhonin. "In defense," he repeated. "I take it you are still not choosing sides in the coming battle?"

"It is my hope, unrealized as it is likely to be, that there might not be a battle at all," said Rhonin with a placidness unusual for him. As muttering began to make its way around the table, he lifted a hand. "If our presence is an insufficient deterrent to violence, then we will act to defend the city in order to prevent as much loss of life as possible. In the meantime"—he smiled—"a few of us have gotten our hands dirty before. Perhaps we can help in the planning."

"The Light sends aid in all manner of ways, and in all manner of beings," said Tiras'alan calmly, directing the words to the Sunreaver. "I for one welcome your cumulative wisdom."

There were nods, some more blatantly reluctant than others. "I am relieved that we all realize that we have a common foe," Jaina said. "There are so many years of experience gathered here around this table. I am glad every one of you is here."

Aubrey leaned forward. "Before we start talking strategies and planning, Lady Jaina, I need to tell you what we saw as we sailed toward the harbor."

Jaina felt the blood drain from her face. "Let me guess," she said. "Several Horde battleships."

Jonathan frowned slightly. "You cannot see them from the harbor," he said, "and Theramore's ships stayed close to home, or so we were informed. How did you know?"

"They were here a few days ago, being very careful to stay just inside Horde territory," said Pained. "It appears they never truly left."

"We were more than ready to engage if they had given us even a whiff of provocation," said Jonathan. "But they sat there quite calmly, as if out for a scenic boat ride. They didn't budge."

Stoutblow glowered. "Which I, fer one, am verra sorry fer."

"We had no desire to start this war," Jonathan said, though Jaina didn't miss that he, too, looked as if he wished that the Horde had fired on them so that the tension, at least, would be broken. "But we *will* be the ones to end it. They're there, they're armed, and they're just . . . waiting."

Tiras'alan cleared his throat. "If I may? Lady Jaina, word reached us that you were . . . warned about the attack. Do you believe that it might have been a trick? That perhaps Garrosh wants you to think the target is Theramore, when in reality it is elsewhere?"

"There's nae other decent target reachable by land," said Redmane, scoffing. "Seems a wee bit silly tae have all them Hordies squattin' there fer nae reason. Th' Horde's big, true, but nae that big."

"The thought did occur to us," said Shandris. "We have seen no evidence that there are plans to attack anywhere other than Theramore."

Jaina pondered, then shook her golden head. "No. I am

certain it was no ruse. My . . . contact risked a great deal to warn me, and I trust him completely." She had sat with Baine while he grieved a father slain by treachery, had seen a weapon sacred to the Light glow approvingly in his mighty fist. He would not betray her.

The draenei regarded her, then nodded. "Then we will take this unknown contact at his word. The evidence does appear to support it."

Shandris leaned forward. "Admiral Aubrey," she said, "we have had the honor to speak with you during our journey here. Lady Jaina and the others have not. Why do you not tell them what you have shared with us?" She smiled. It was not a pleasant smile. Shandris Feathermoon was a predator, and it was clear that she was ready to begin the hunt. "Then we shall make our strategies."

Jaina took a moment to be grateful to the Light—and to Varian Wrynn, A'dal, High Priestess Tyrande, Archdruid Malfurion, Rhonin, and the Council of Three Hammers—for the collective wisdom of these battle-hardened men and women. With luck, not only would they withstand the Horde attack, but they would do so with the fewest number of casualties on both sides.

Then, when Garrosh Hellscream realized that even his best efforts at violence would not prevail, maybe he would be willing to talk peace.

Earth Mother, give me guidance, Baine prayed silently. He had come to the little remembrance site—the tauren equivalent of a graveyard—close to the encampment that the tauren had passed on their path to Northwatch. He found comfort here, where the benevolent spirits of those who had died might yet linger.

The days crawled by as the Horde waited . . . and waited, and the Alliance defenses at Theramore grew stronger by the moment. Baine had heard from Perith and knew that Jaina had received his message with the graciousness and appreciation he had come to expect from the lady of Theramore. Even so, the warning had been given to prevent a massacre of the Alliance, not so that the Alliance would have a chance to massacre the Horde. Which it was shaping up to be. Still, this could not be laid at Jaina's feet; Garrosh, for some unfathomable and alarming reason, seemed content to stay holed up with his Kor'kron and that Blackrock orc while precious moments passed.

Word had come that the 7th Legion's famous fleet had arrived and that the decks of the flagship were crawling with Alliance generals whose names ought to have been striking terror into Garrosh's heart. Instead, Baine had heard laughter and bold comments coming from the warchief's encampment while the dire news was being whispered among the Horde's foot soldiers, who sat awaiting orders.

Baine no longer had the heart to even protest Garrosh's delay. At best, he would be taunted and pushed to his limits, then dismissed. At worst, he could be accused of treason and perhaps executed.

Baine was a warrior. He was no stranger to tactics and strategy and knew that what seemed like foolishness *sometimes* was wisdom. But he could see nothing here that resembled wisdom. Garrosh had attacked Northwatch, and the victory was overwhelming. Had they pushed on to Theramore even a day or two later, a similar victory would have been assured. But instead, Grom's son had waited and let Jaina learn about the planned attack, had let her stockpile food and weapons, had let her receive outside assistance.

"Why?" Baine said aloud. He thought of his people, steady and solid, and his oath of loyalty to Garrosh as leader of the Horde. And he thought of them lying as stiffening corpses, slain more truly by Garrosh's foolishness and utterly inexplicable decisions than by Alliance weapons. He lifted his muzzle to the sky, sharp, stinging tears filling his eyes, and, alone with his ancestors, shook his fists furiously and cried with all his confused and aching and angry heart, *"Why?"*

15

Nothing. No luck. The Focusing Iris continued to zig and zag around Kalimdor as if it was on a tour of the continent directed by madmen. Emotions buffeted Kalecgos—worry, fear, frustration, anger, and worst of all, a dreadful, gnawing sense of impotent helplessness.

He was not usually given to the arrogance displayed by many dragons, his own flight in particular. But he was a blue dragon, once the blues' Aspect, and the Focusing Iris belonged to them. How was it that so powerful a thing not only could be stolen, but could keep eluding him?

And why did he feel more driven to return to Theramore and protect it against the coming onslaught than to continue his search? The answer to that was simple, but he refused to acknowledge it. He snapped his tail in frustration, dove, wheeled, and turned again toward the east.

The Horde continued to stay where it was: a massive sprawl of small, stationary forms, tiny tents, miniature engines of war. Even during the day, Kalec saw the minuscule glowing dots that indicated campfires.

Was the army . . . larger than before? Was that why Garrosh was playing a waiting game—to gather more reinforcements? Or was it merely spread out?

Clarity came upon him like a thunderclap, and with it a sense of peace at finally knowing his path. He flapped his massive wings, once, twice, thrice, tilting his sinuous azure form and wheeling back the way he had come.

The Focusing Iris was, of course and still, the most important thing. The damage to this world could be staggering if its abductors chose to use it for destruction. But the Focusing Iris would not be obtained, not as long as it was being moved so erratically. It was a great danger, but not an immediate one.

The Horde was.

It was not the decision he should have made, he knew. Not the decision another blue dragon would have made.

But another blue dragon was not Kalecgos. And the heart of Kalecgos lifted with every beat of his powerful wings.

The planning session, complete with maps, miniatures, sandwiches, and often heated debate, had gone on for four and a half hours when Marcus Jonathan finally called for a break.

Jaina had made certain that she would have a chance to spend those precious minutes of recovery alone. For too long, it seemed, she had lurched from crisis to crisis where everyone needed her attention, her wisdom, her advice, her skills. Most recently it had been the search for the Focusing Iris—a search that she did not dare think of overmuch, as she was fighting a growing fear that it would prove futile, even for the former blue Dragon Aspect. And then this—the Horde destroying Northwatch and now turning its eyes toward her own city.

Jaina had never been a particularly social young woman, preferring the solitary delights of books and scrolls to the more cacophonous and energetic diversions of balls or parties. Nor had she been such as an adult woman, though as a diplomat of note she had attended more than her share of formal functions. She liked to negotiate personally, one-on-one if possible. And when the negotiations were done, and the treaty signed, and the toasts raised to it, she returned home, to Theramore, eager for its comparative isolation and slower pace. Now Theramore was filled with more activity than Jaina ever remembered encountering at Lordaeron. It was crowded with men and women who exuded power and authority and decisiveness. Jaina's solitude had been shattered like a broken mirror, reflecting only sharp shards of chaos and urgency.

Not everyone in Theramore appreciated the pungency of the nearby swamp, but as she stepped outside and took a deep breath, Jaina found herself smiling. It was hardly the exquisite scent of apple blossoms and flowers of the Dalaran of her childhood, nor was it the clean, piney fragrance of Lordaeron. But for her, it was the smell of home.

A large shadow fell over her. She looked up, shielding her eyes, and saw a small shape blocking the sun. It circled, growing larger and larger as it descended, and Jaina felt a smile curve her lips as she waved to Kalecgos.

There were fewer areas for him to land since the arrival of so many troops, and she saw him veer off toward the sandy beaches of Dreadmurk Shore. Jaina began to walk toward the gates—closed and guarded constantly now—and impatiently waved for them to be opened. She hurried over the hills to the shore, dodging the many large, slow-moving turtles that trundled in and out of the ocean.

The sandy spit was not a true beach but a narrow area upon which Kalecgos landed very carefully. He transformed into his half-elven form as Jaina hastened up. Jaina slowed as she approached him, suddenly aware that her impulsive, rather girlish decision to quicken her pace was quite unseemly in a woman of her age and position. Her cheeks were hot, whether from embarrassment or exertion, she couldn't tell.

His smile at the sight of her lit up his handsome face, and she felt hope rise in her as she clasped his outstretched hands. "You found it?"

Kalec's smile faltered. "Unfortunately, no. It's still behaving far too erratically for me to properly trace."

She winced in sympathy. "I'm sorry," she said, "for all of us."

"As am I. But tell me . . . you seem distressed. Are the talks not going well? I would think with so many wise advisors, you would have figured out how to beat the Horde, send them home to their mothers, and convince them to take up knitting and adopting kittens."

She had to laugh at that. "We are indeed fortunate to have so many who are so experienced. But . . . that might be the problem."

Kalec glanced back toward the gates of Theramore. "Must you hasten to return?"

"I have a little time."

He squeezed her hands and dropped one, still holding the other, and indicated that they should walk down the beach a ways. "Tell me," was all he said.

"They are . . . very warlike."

"They *are* generals."

Jaina waved a hand in frustration, wondering as she did so why she continued to hold on to Kalec's hand as they walked. "Of course, but—there is not just the grim necessity of war. For many of them, it's personal. And I know I should have expected that too. But . . . you know my history, Kalec. I lost my father and my brother to the Horde. I chose not to follow his path, but to strive for peace. If anyone should be bitter and hateful, it should be me. Yet I hear the things some of them call the Horde—insulting, cruel terms—and I feel so much regret. I want to defend my home, yes. I want to drive the Horde back, so that they aren't an immediate threat. But I don't want to—to gut them, or mount their heads on pikes!"

"No one could blame you overmuch if you did," Kalec said.

"But I don't! I don't . . ." She fell silent, searching for the right words. "My father didn't just want to win. He hated the orcs. He wanted to crush them. Wipe them off the face of Azeroth. And so do some of these generals." She looked up at Kalecgos. His face was in profile to hers, his features clean and straight as if they had been drawn by a few perfect strokes of an artist's pen, his brow furrowed as he listened with deep attention even as his gaze stayed on the ground to avoid missteps for either of them. Feeling her regarding him, he turned to look at her. She hadn't realized just how intensely *blue* his eyes were.

"You loved them very much," Kalec said gently. "Your father, Daelin, and your brother, Derek."

"Of course I did," Jaina said. She suddenly couldn't look into those kind blue eyes and instead glanced down at her booted feet, moving slowly across the sand and driftwood. "I felt . . . very guilty when they died."

"Your father perished at the hand of an orc, and you later became great friends with Thrall. And your brother," he said, his voice even softer and turning sad, "was slain by one of the red dragons the orcs rode."

"And now I am friends with a dragon," Jaina said, attempting to lighten the moment. Kalec smiled a little, though it didn't reach his eyes.

"And you wonder what your father would think of your choices now," Kalec said. Jaina nodded, stunned by how well he seemed to understand. "Do you think there was any merit to his beliefs?"

"No," Jaina said, shaking her blond head. "But it is difficult—hearing the same hate-filled rhetoric now. It's . . . like an echo of the past. And I don't think I was expecting or prepared to hear it. But how can I tell them that their anger and pain are wrong, when they have seen so much and lost so many?"

"It is not their anger or pain that distresses you," Kalec replied. "No one can say that you have not had more than your fair share of both. You do not agree with the conclusion they have drawn from their experiences. There is nothing wrong with disagreeing. But do you think their hatred will make them unreliable commanders in battle?"

Jaina considered the question, then said, "No."

"Then I believe it likely that they do not think your propensity toward peace would affect your ability to fight and defend your city."

"So—it doesn't matter. How they feel, how I feel?"

"It matters a great deal. But you are all in agreement that the city must not fall. And for the moment, that is what matters most."

There was something about the way he said this, an urgency that seemed quite separate from the topic of conversation, that made her pause and look up at him quizzically. "Kalec . . . I know it's vital that you locate the Focusing Iris. I didn't expect you to return if you did so—indeed, that you'd even return at all. Why *did* you come back?"

The question, which she had thought would be simple, seemed to rattle him. He didn't answer at once, nor did he meet her gaze, looking away as if at something she couldn't see. She waited patiently. At length, he turned to face her, taking both of her hands in his.

"I had a choice as well. I could continue to follow the Focusing Iris, hoping, likely futilely, that it would come to a stop. Or I could return here and tell you that I stand ready to help you defend Theramore."

Her lips parted, but no words came out for a moment. "Kalec . . . that is very kind of you, but—this should not be any of your concern. You need to find the Focusing Iris."

"Do not think I have forgotten the duty to my flight," he told her. "I will keep searching until the last possible moment. But then, Jaina Proudmoore—if you, mage that you are, will have a blue dragon as your ally in this coming battle . . . have one you shall."

Gratitude and fresh hope made Jaina feel a little weak. She clung tightly to Kalec's hands as he gazed down at her. She couldn't even think of the words to thank him. Her heart felt full and happy in a way that seemed as though it should be familiar. She dismissed that at once. Kalecgos was the leader of the blue dragonflight. She knew from their talks that he was an "odd one," as he had often phrased it. This was no more than his quirky interest in the younger races' affairs. She did not permit herself to think it could possibly be anything else. Light knew, she had never been a good judge of men. Yet . . . why then did he continue to hold her hands, his fingers warm and strong as they closed protectively over hers?

"Theramore and the Alliance will be forever grateful," she managed to say, unable to meet his eyes.

He placed a forefinger under her sharp chin, tilting her face up so she was forced to look at him.

"I do not do this for the Alliance, or for Theramore," Kalec said gently. "I do this for Theramore's lady." Then, as if he felt he had said too much, he stepped back quickly. "I must resume my search, but I will not be far," he said, sobering. "I will return before the Horde arrives. This, I swear."

He pressed a kiss into the palm of her hand, then retreated several paces in order to shift into his mighty dragon form. The great blue lowered his massive head almost to the ground, a few feet from Jaina, in a courtly draconic bow. Then Kalecgos leaped skyward.

Jaina watched him go, slowly curling trembling fingers closed over her palm, as if to protect the kiss that still lingered there.

At long last, the orders came down.

The Horde was on the march.

Campsites, inhabited by impatient soldiers for too long, were eagerly and swiftly struck. Weapons, refletched or sharpened in an effort to while away the boredom and restlessness of enforced inactivity, were loaded into quivers, sheathed, or otherwise prepared to taste Alliance blood. Armor, glinting in the red light of dawn or rendered supple with oil, was donned, and the Horde began to move.

Like beasts straining at the lead, at first the separate

divisions seemed to jockey for position, but Garrosh appeared to have expected such a desire. The Kor'kron, led by Malkorok, rode their great black wolves in between each section. Accompanying the orcs were drummers, who pounded out a steady marching rhythm. Gradually the anticipatory chaos calmed and each group—orcs in the forefront, followed by tauren, trolls, Forsaken, and blood elves, with goblins and their various nefarious contraptions interspersed throughout—began to fall into step.

The very earth seemed to tremble beneath so many marching to the thrumming sounds of the war drums— drums that had, in battles past, unsettled the enemy long before the mighty Horde was even glimpsed. The Alliance liked to think of the members of the Horde as "primitive," so that they might think of themselves as "civilized" and, thus, superior. But what dwarf, safe in his halls of stone, knew what it was like to feast upon the fallen foe as a Forsaken did? What human, in his complacency, could be so lost in battle lust that, minutes later, he would find himself blinking blood out of his eyes, his voice hoarse with screams as he stood over the corpse of his enemy? What little gnome had tasted the joy of seeing the spirits of her ancestors fight alongside her in a spectral echo of the very real battle?

None.

This was the Horde. This was its glory. Beneath feet bare and shod and hoofed and two-toed, the ground yielded to them as they marched. Muscles moved beneath taut green or blue or brown or pale pink skin or fur; throats were opened in song. Spear and sword, bow and blade, were already out and ready to strike.

The vast wave flowed south toward Theramore, thousands strong, with a single purpose.

To fight, and perhaps to die, with all honor and glory.
For the Horde.

It made no logical sense, and Kalecgos was too wise not
to know it, but nonetheless, his parting from Jaina filled
the dragon with new hope. The surprise and happiness
on her face as he kissed her hand—not daring anything
more, not yet—made him see the world with new eyes.
He had spoken of the joy of the humans; now he truly felt
that he could taste it himself.

Theramore would stand against the Horde; he knew
it. The arrogance that was Garrosh would be exposed for
the Horde to see. Wiser heads would come to the nego-
tiating table—Baine, perhaps, or Vol'jin—and a new era
could begin.

All things were possible, if Jaina Proudmoore felt as he
did. And Kalec dared hope it was so.

As if his very ebullience had willed it into being,
the hitherto random motions of the Focusing Iris
slowed and all but ceased. Kalecgos paused, beating his
wings strongly as he hovered, extending his magical
senses.

It had slowed . . . and it was *close*. Closer than he had
ever sensed it. There—it was coming from the north.
Swiftly he dropped, veered, and headed with a renewed
sense of purpose in that direction, following the trail.
His eyes were fastened on the ground, and Kalec realized
with a sudden, sickening jolt that his joyful anticipation of
victory was terrifyingly premature.

The Horde was on the move.

• • •

"They are appeased," said Malkorok as he rode beside his warchief.

"Of course they are," Garrosh replied, looking proudly at the vast numbers steadily marching on Theramore. "They are warriors. They crave Alliance blood. I have held them in check. Now their thirst is even greater—and my plan is even more secure." He thought of Baine and Vol'jin. Garrosh had learned his lesson with Cairne's death, and while the troll and tauren leaders irritated him to no end, he knew it would be foolishness to challenge either of them to ritual combat. They were loved and respected by their people, and both did have true loyalty to the Horde, if not to Garrosh individually. Soon, they would come to heel and acknowledge that his tactics had been beyond brilliant—indeed, that he had achieved more for the Horde than any leader, including the adored Thrall, had ever done.

Then they would honor him as well as the Horde, and he would show his magnanimity to them as he had with Captain Briln. Garrosh permitted a pleased, rather smug smile to curve his lips.

Suddenly there was a great hue and cry. Everyone was pointing skyward and shouting. Garrosh squinted against the already-bright sunlight and saw a black silhouette. It was long and sleek and—

"Dragon!" he roared. "Bring it down!"

Even as he shouted, the wind riders were attacking. The Horde had an aerial front as well, composed not only of the beloved wyverns of the orcs, but bats, dragonhawks, and other creatures domesticated and used for their unique abilities. The dragon dove as it came under attack, flying irregularly to avoid huge pole-arms, thrown spears, and the sting of dozens of arrows, all doubtless targeting the leviathan's sensitive eyes. It opened its mouth. A wyvern and his rider halted, encased in a sudden sheet of—

"Ice!" cried Garrosh. He threw back his head and laughed, even as the unfortunate wind rider and mount plummeted like a stone to the earth. He clapped Malkorok on the back. "Ice!" he repeated. "Behold, Malkorok, it is a *blue* dragon who attacks us!"

The Horde members who surrounded him did not know why he laughed, but it fueled them nonetheless. Those on the ground cheered on their embattled comrades in the sky, who harried the dragon as sparrows harry a hawk, while they set up ballistae and catapults and loaded cannons. All were now pointing skyward.

Garrosh, giddy with pleasure, raced among his people, shouting encouragement. It was he who gave the order to fire a flaming, pointed bolt almost vertically, and he who led the cheers when it was clear from the blue's erratic movements that the bolt had struck home.

Agony ripped through Kalecgos. He had been so engrossed in following the emanations of the Focusing Iris that he had flown right into peril. The Horde had reacted swiftly and in a manner that reminded Kalec alarmingly of the battle at Wyrmrest Temple not so long ago.

The fiery bolt had seared a black groove in his side. It was not a lethal blow, not even one that had knocked him out of the sky, but it brought home that although he was a dragon, he was one, and they were many. He would not be able to help Jaina at all if he were killed now, foolishly staying to try to fight. The Focusing Iris, though close, was still heading northward as the Horde troops marched south. His worst fear—that the Horde had captured it—seemed to have been a false one. For surely if so powerful an item were in their possession, they would be bearing it south with them to use against the hated Alliance in the upcoming battle.

He steeled himself against the aching pain in his side and lashed out with his tail, sending a bat hurtling end over end while it flapped frantically, and its rider fell to a doom certain enough even for a Forsaken.

Kalec's mighty wing beats carried him higher, safely out of range of the earthbound weapons and too swiftly for the wyverns, bats, or dragonhawks to follow. Once out of immediate danger, Kalec stretched out his long, sinuous neck and tucked in his paws, making himself as aerodynamic as possible. He headed due south, determined to give Theramore—and its lady—as much warning as possible that the Horde would soon be beating down the door.

16

"We will be facing a battle on three fronts," Jonathan said. He stood, pointing to the map of Theramore on the table. Everyone was standing now, the shorter dwarves craning their necks to see. "From the harbor, of course. We have a good idea of how many ships are there already."

"And if I were Garrosh, I would be holding a few in reserve and then sending them off within about four hours of the battle," added Aubrey.

Jonathan nodded. "We should plan on that. When is the *Starsword* due to return?"

Shortly after the arrival of the 7th's fleet, Jaina had insisted that one ship, the *Starsword*, be dispatched to bear the civilians of the city who wished to leave to safety. All of the children went aboard, and many of their families. Others chose to stay. It was their home; they loved it as Jaina did and wanted to defend it. Ratchet would have been the first choice, and from there the ship would have traveled to Stranglethorn. Unfortunately, while the goblins who ran Ratchet were neutral, considering the flood of Horde that had recently passed through that town,

Ratchet was deemed far too unsafe for Alliance refugees. So instead, the *Starsword* had sailed for Gadgetzan.

"The draenei shaman have assured me that with the cooperation of the air and water elementals, the trip will go much more quickly," Jaina said.

"Perhaps," said Stoutblow. "But the ship just sailed a few hours ago. We canna hope tae see it back afore tomorrow at the earliest."

"Children never belong in battle," said Tiras'alan quietly. "Even if it means we do not have a battleship available, transporting them to safety was the right choice."

"The young are indeed too precious to risk," said Shandris. "And also . . . civilians only get in the way."

It was a harsh assessment, but Jaina and all the others knew it to be true. A battle demanded everything from those who would fight it. Worrying if children might come in harm's way was not an option. Removing them from the equation was more than the morally right thing to do—it was a necessary and intelligent thing to do.

"The road north troubles me more than the road west," said Jonathan, bringing them all back to the subject at hand. "We have seen no buildup at Brackenwall Village."

"Yet," growled Rhonin.

"Yet," said Jonathan. "But it is likely that Garrosh's army will march through there and either gather reinforcements or leave a portion of his troops behind to send in later if they prove to be needed. It would also be a safe place to retreat and regroup—a luxury we don't have."

"What about the siege weapons that are currently stationed along the western road?" said Pained. "We could bring those in closer to the city and position them at both gates."

"What about the Grimtotem?" asked Kinndy.

"I doubt we need to worry about them," Jaina said. "We are battling the Horde now, and even if they offered their services to Garrosh, I do not believe Baine would stand for it. Or even Garrosh. Not after what Magatha did to Cairne."

"They could try to use the distraction of battle to their advantage," said Vereesa. "Take the opportunity to enter the city in an attempt to loot or simply kill."

"Only if we fall," said Pained bluntly. "They would not dare otherwise."

"It's settled then," said Jonathan. "We pull back the siege engines and—"

The doors to the hall were flung open. Kalecgos stood in the doorway, swaying slightly, one hand clasped to his side. Behind him were two guards, who looked more worried about the blue dragon than the fact that he had entered the meeting room unannounced.

Jaina saw blood pooling beneath Kalec's fingers. She rose and hurried toward him, even as he spoke quickly.

"The Horde is on the move," he said. "They are heading south and will be here in only a few hours." As Jaina slipped an arm around him, looking up at him worriedly, he said, more for her ears than anyone else's, "It's not a serious wound. I came back to warn you. To help."

"I don't know that any of this is a concern of the blue dragonflight," Rhonin said. Others who did not recognize Kalecgos on sight frowned slightly as the realization struck.

"Kalec—let the guards take you to our doctor and healers before you do anything else. You can brief us when you return." To the others, Jaina said, "We may recently have been at war with the blue dragonflight, but everyone here, including the Kirin Tor members, must know that

Kalecgos has never sought to quarrel with the younger races. He was key in the defeat of Deathwing, and we are honored and frankly lucky that he is willing to help defend Theramore."

Rhonin's gaze flickered from Kalec to Jaina, and then he nodded. "We could use it," was all he said, but it was enough. The other members of the Kirin Tor ceased their muttering, and even some of the generals were nodding.

"Let's be honest," said Redmane, chuckling. "A great blue beastie up in the sky in addition tae all o' the rest o' us might rattle Garrosh more than a wee bit."

It was settled, then. Jaina turned to Kalec. His wound was obviously more serious than he wanted her to know, but there were many gifted healers stationed here in anticipation of the battle. He would soon be well enough to join the fight.

"It's going to be all right, Jaina," he said. He smiled gently and spoke quietly. "Don't be afraid."

Jaina gave him a smile of her own. "I'd be foolish not to be afraid, Kalec," she said, speaking just as quietly. "But I've been through battles before, battles that were a lot . . . harder, personally, than this one for me to bear. Do not worry. I will protect Theramore without shying from what must be done."

Admiration lit his blue eyes. "Forgive me," he said. "You are perhaps more battle-hardened than I, Lady Jaina."

Her smile ebbed a little. "I pray I will never be hardened," she said, "but I am no stranger to it, either. Now go. We'll fill each other in upon your return." As one guard escorted Kalec to the priests, Jaina turned to the other. "Send a missive to Stormwind immediately. Varian must know that the attack is about to begin."

• • •

The sense of urgency that had been present since before the arrival of the generals and the fleet was now even greater. As Jaina predicted, Kalecgos, though drained from his ordeal, was quickly healed, and he briefed everyone on what he had seen. Thanks to him, they now knew which route the Horde had chosen. Fort Triumph, which lay northwest of Theramore, had been notified as soon as Theramore had known of the planned attack. They would put up a good fight, and it was likely that the Horde would not want to waste its resources, troops, and energy attacking a site that was not its intended goal. Hopes were high that the brave men and women at Fort Triumph would be able to inflict damage and slow the approach of the Horde while not being utterly devastated themselves. It was a risk that was unavoidable.

Plans were translated nearly instantly into orders. The ballistae and other siege weaponry were moved east toward the gates of Theramore. Riders were dispatched to Sentry Point, slightly north of the city, with instructions that when the Horde was spotted, they were to send warning immediately. Captain Wymor and his soldiers were ordered to hold back the Horde if they could—and retreat to the city if they couldn't, where others would join them.

The gates would remain closed unless the Horde beat them down. Wymor understood.

Sixteen battleships turned and sailed out of the harbor. The *Starsword* would likely return too late from its mission of mercy to be of any help. Like the Horde fleet, they stayed in their own waters—barely. There they waited, the plan being to destroy the Horde fleet once the battle began so that the threat would be completely removed.

Three remained in the harbor, a last line of defense against encroachment from the sea. Everyone hoped they would not be necessary.

It was midday when the first rider came.

He wore no armor, only ordinary clothes spattered with mud and blood, no doubt to spare the horse upon which he galloped. Even so, the steed heaved and foamed as it clattered up to the northern gate. The guards stationed there assisted the shaking man as he all but slid off the animal, which seemed on the verge of collapse itself. As they caught him with as much gentleness as they could muster, his cloak fell aside. They realized that the blood belonged almost entirely to the dark-haired, bearded rider, who struggled to speak.

"F-Fort Triumph h-has fallen," said the rider, and then said no more.

And so it began.

The Horde army was now augmented with blade throwers, ballistae, and catapults carved in the likeness of mighty eagles. Alliance weapons, to be used on the Alliance. Many of those who marched also bore other, more gruesome trophies to remember the battle. The trolls, in particular, seemed delighted to decorate themselves with fingers and ears.

Doubtless the poorly named Fort Triumph had thought to make a stand that would cripple the wave of Horde flowing south toward Theramore. They had grossly overestimated their own abilities and underestimated those of their enemy.

War songs were sung. The drums were beaten, and the

creaking of the massive engines of war—some of Horde design, others Alliance—provided its own unique music.

The Horde had surprised Northwatch Hold and had taken it thanks to that. Now they came to their next target, proud of their numbers and their power, fairly shouting their presence as they marched southward. Theramore had had days to prepare for the attack; its residents had also had nights likely spent sleeplessly, fraught with nightmares about the Horde pouring through their gates.

Fear, too, was a weapon.

The beasts of the Barrens gave them a wide berth, and those zhevra and gazelles that ventured too close were slain to feed the hungry troops. Their numbers formed into a thinner line to navigate the narrower road through Dustwallow Marsh, and the hot sun now filtered through the tall, mossy trees. Past the ruins of the Shady Rest Inn, they halted at a crossroads with paths that led to Theramore Isle, Mudsprocket, and Brackenwall Village. Here, Garrosh divided the army in half. He would take command of the forces that would head north, to be reinforced by new recruits from the village—more orcs and even ogres, who would bear down on Theramore from the north. Malkorok would lead the remaining troops along the road toward the east.

The two arms of attack would meet at Theramore; they would meet for victory and crush the city between them.

Malkorok and his soldiers marched deep into the heart of Dustwallow Marsh and into the Quagmire, ripping down the banners of the Alliance and grinding them into the mud with laughter. Their path, once blocked by Theramore soldiers and weapons of war, was open, as they had expected.

Nor was there sign of the Grimtotem, also expected. Word had likely spread of the approaching troops, and those cowardly tauren—despised by Alliance and Horde alike—were lying low.

"Our approach has doubtless been heralded," said Malkorok. "I will send some runners ahead and we will proceed with—"

He was interrupted by the sound of furious growls. No fewer than ten beasts suddenly charged out of the marsh, where they had been concealed by the many rounded hillocks and low-hanging branches of trees. Two warlocks, a mage, and a shaman went down, barely able to speak two words of a spell. The rest were locked in close-quarters combat as claws shredded flesh and massive jaws crunched down on windpipes. Before the attack of the shapeshifted Alliance druids could even register, more than a dozen Horde fighters dropped stone dead in their tracks, felled by knives in the back wielded by unglimpsed foes. Other animals now rushed from the concealment of the swamp, creatures of the arctic or of the desert, which should never have known this dank climate yet were here and harrowing the Horde.

The battle had only lasted a few seconds, and already more than two dozen were dead or dying.

"Ambush! Attack!" cried Malkorok. He suited action to word, charging at a huge brown bear with painted markings ripping into an undead warlock who was frantically trying to drain the druid's life to power his own magical abilities. The twin axes whirred, biting through the bear's protective throat ruff at such an angle that the blades met and the druid's head was nearly severed.

The cries of pain and rage and bloodlust were augmented by other sounds—the singing of arrows being

loosed and the echoing boom of gunfire. The hunters—
who were directing the spiders and scorpids, the wolves
and the crocolisks and the raptors—were now entering
the fight themselves. Malkorok swore beneath his breath
as he leaped over the fallen bodies of a goblin and a hyena
locked in a fatal embrace, the goblin's blade in the creature's eye and the beast's jaws about the green throat. His
eyes were on the cluster of several Horde fighting a single
opponent. As Malkorok approached, shouting his battle
cry, the crowd about the Alliance warrior parted for a
moment. A strong night elf female was at the center. She
wielded an almost blindingly radiant sword and moved so
swiftly she was a blur. A long blue braid whipped around,
looking almost like an azure serpent. Two slender bodies
were already at her feet, and a third blood elf clutched his
side and crumpled to join them.

For just an instant, she paused and her eyes locked
with Malkorok's. She saw his gray skin and grinned as,
with a shout, he sprang toward her.

There was plenty of warning. This was no surprise attack. So when the runner arrived, breathless, with a solid
estimate of the numbers about to descend upon first Sentry Point and then the north gate of Theramore, Captain
Wymor merely nodded.

"Take your positions," he said. Then he added, "I am
proud that I am fighting with you, on this day that will be
long remembered." The guards, some of them seeming
so young to him, saluted. Few of them had ever engaged
in anything other than a brief skirmish with a Horde
member before. Most of their fighting was with the
Grimtotem or the swamp beasts. Now they could hear

the drums in the distance and prepared themselves for true battle.

General Marcus Jonathan personally had come out to Sentry Point to discuss tactics. The term "Sentry Point" itself implied that it was a lookout, not a bastion of defense for Theramore. Yet it was destined to become one if Garrosh's forces decided to approach from the north.

"And they will," Jonathan had said. "They will attack from the north, the west, and the harbor. You cannot outfight them. You must outsmart them."

The runner was given a gulp of water, a moment to catch her breath, then remounted her horse and galloped for Theramore. The rest of the guards under Wymor took their positions and waited.

They did not have to wait long. The lone sentry up at the top of the tower gestured, raising his right arm and bringing it down sharply. The gnome standing next to Wymor, by the name of Adolphus Blastwidget, held a small device in his hands. At the signal from the tower, Blastwidget grinned and pressed a button. The sound of drumbeats was suddenly overwhelmed by a colossal boom. Black smoke curled upward, and the Alliance soldiers cheered. When the noise died down, the drums had fallen silent.

The bombs that had been carefully planted had no doubt eliminated many of the enemy, but the threat remained.

"Draw weapons," Wymor said. In the eerie silence, the scrape of swords being drawn sounded overly loud. The soldiers stood, taut and ready. The minutes ticked by. All that could be heard were the ceaseless hum of insects, the cry of seabirds, the wash of waves on the shore nearby, and the creaking of their own armor as they shifted uneasily.

And then came the cries of battle, chilling the blood and lifting the hair of the guards. The drums started again, closer this time, their rhythm faster, more urgent. From out of the shadows of the murky swamp, dozens, perhaps hundreds, charged, all of them screaming, all of them carrying weapons that looked as if they weighed more than an armored human.

"Run, Adolphus!" shouted Wymor to the gnome, who was standing transfixed with horror. Blastwidget started, stared wildly up at Wymor, and then took off as fast as his legs could carry him toward Theramore. He still clutched the detonator. Wymor lifted his sword and stood ready.

An orc, bristling with armor and swinging a great axe that seemed to howl with its own lust for blood, led the wave of orc, troll, tauren, Forsaken, blood elf, and goblin. He charged straight for Wymor. His shoulder armor appeared to be made of giant tusks, and between the shoulders and the gloves covering his hands was an expanse of brown, tattooed skin.

Wymor's golden beard parted in a smile.

Garrosh Hellscream.

The blade of Wymor's sword met the shaft of Gorehowl with a clash. Garrosh, vastly stronger than the human, shoved, and Wymor staggered back. He got his blade up just in time to parry a swift downstroke from the axe and darted beneath the warchief's bulk, pulling the sword with him. Garrosh grunted in surprised pain as the sword sliced across his inner arm.

"My first blood in this battle," the orc said in Common. "Well done, human. You will die with honor."

Wymor retreated several steps, brandishing the sword. "You won't," he said, taunting the orc. Garrosh growled beneath his breath and charged.

Exactly as Wymor wanted him to.

"Now, Blastwidget!" shouted Wymor. He heard a roaring sound, felt himself being hurled into the air, and then knew no more.

17

The elf was good—Malkorok had to give her that. That she had survived battles before was evident by the single great scar that marred her face. Seeing that their leader wanted her for his own kill, the other Horde members had scattered to take on other foes. Ancestors knew there were plenty of them.

The blue-haired night elf was uncannily fast, even though the sword she wielded had to be slowing her down. Malkorok was swift for an orc, and his weapons were much lighter, but even so the two small axes seemed only to bite thin air. Blue-Hair was there one minute, then gone the next, darting in under his defenses. More than once, it was only his heavy armor that saved him as the blade clanged against his midsection. If the glowing sword tip found the unprotected junction between torso and arm—

He brought one axe down while whirling the other over his head. She dove aside, but not before the blade bit into her thigh. She grunted.

"Ha!" snorted Malkorok. "If you can bleed, you can die."

Impossibly, she sprang toward him, her mouth open

in a snarl that would have done a worgen credit. He lifted the axes and crossed them in front of himself defensively. To his shock, Blue-Hair ignored her wound and *climbed up* the axes, moving as easily as if he had linked his hands together to provide a foothold. The point of her blade drove down toward his neck.

He twisted away at the last second, nearly falling, swinging his left axe around. Now she was behind him, and Malkorok turned, ready to begin the fight again.

A horn sounded. It was not one of the Horde's—this was light and musical and sweet. An elven horn. Instantly those Alliance members who had been fighting the Horde began to run for the still-opened gate. Blue-Hair grinned fiercely at Malkorok, and when he swung again at the place she had been, she was not there.

Malkorok roared his frustration and gave chase.

Though it looked like utter chaos, everything was going according to plan. The Horde was, as Jonathan had predicted, attacking on all three fronts. The sounds were deafening and frightening—the nearly constant boom of cannon fire, explosions to the north, and the clash of swords and the shrieking of battle cries to the west.

Jaina and Kinndy were at the top of one of the walkways facing the west. Jaina had struggled with her desire to keep Kinndy shut up safely away from harm but realized that would do the girl a disservice. Kinndy had come to her to learn, and there was no better way to learn about the horrors of war than to experience them firsthand. She kept the gnome close to her, but Kinndy had a front-row seat to the battle that raged below them.

When the horn sounded, Jaina told her apprentice, "Be

ready. Do what we talked about, and strike when I do."
Kinndy nodded, swallowing hard. Jaina lifted her hands,
waiting for the right moment. Dozens of Alliance fighters
were running as fast as they could for the safety of Theramore. The abruptness and speed of the retreat had gained
them a precious second or two, but now the Horde was
coming after them.

And waiting for the Horde were more than two dozen
engines of war.

"Now!" cried Jaina. She, Kinndy, and others who
fought with spells instead of swords all attacked at once.
Guttural cries filled the air as tauren and orc, goblin and
blood elf, Forsaken and troll were set on fire or frozen or
peppered with arrows.

"Well done!" Jaina cried. "The war engines will hold
them back for a bit, and then we'll return up here. Come on!"

Quickly they ran down the steps to the door. Almost
all the Alliance defenders were safely inside. There were
a few stragglers, slowed by their wounds or by carrying
others who were wounded.

"They're not going to make it!" yelped Kinndy, her
eyes wide and round.

"Yes, they will," Jaina said. She prayed she was right.
The gates would have to be closed any second now. *Come
on, come on . . .*

The last ones stumbled inside, and the gates slammed
shut with an echoing boom. Kinndy and Jaina rushed forward, casting protective wards on the gates. They were
joined by Thoder Windermere, and as they worked, the
air around the gates seemed to shimmer and turn pale
blue for a moment.

"Mage Thoder, you and Kinndy stay here. Keep an eye
on the gate. Reinforce if it starts to weaken."

"But—" Kinndy tried to protest. Jaina turned to her and spoke quickly but urgently.

"Kinndy, if that gate comes down, dozens—hundreds—of Horde will pour through. We've got to keep it as secure as possible. This might be the single most important thing anyone can do. You could save all our lives." It was true. If the gates fell, the losses could be staggering.

Kinndy nodded her pink head and turned to look at the gates. She set her mouth determinedly and extended her hands, adding her skills to those of the member of the Kirin Tor.

Jaina realized that the magi were turning out to be very important in perhaps unexpected ways. Not just in the seemingly passive act of reinforcing the gates, but every Alliance vessel in the harbor had at least one mage who had great skill with fire. As Aubrey had pointed out, a single well-placed bolt of flame, on the sails or on the wooden deck, could be enough to sink an entire ship. And it seemed to be doing exactly that.

She turned and hastened to Pained, who had been one of the last to retreat. Pained was permitting a priestess to tend to a gaping wound in her thigh as Jaina ran up to her.

"Report?" Jaina asked.

"Took them utterly by surprise," Pained said, her smile genuine but cruel. "Just as Jonathan predicted. We dropped at least a few dozen and only lost a handful. Now they are getting cannons in their faces. That should hold them for a while."

For a while, Jaina thought, *but not forever.*

Pained continued, nodding her thanks to the healer and rising to put her armor back on. "There is a Blackrock orc with them. He has the livery that marks him as a member of the Kor'kron. He fights very well."

"A *Blackrock* orc? Has Garrosh truly fallen so low?"

Pained shrugged. "I do not care if they are green, brown, gray, or orange; as long as they are attacking my lady's home, I shall slay them."

"Not this moment, but I fear soon," Jaina said. "I cannot imagine there will not be more hand-to-hand combat. For now, please go and help with the wounded, Pained."

"Yes, my lady."

Jaina turned her attention to the north gate. Blastwidget, the gnome demolitions expert who had detonated so many well-placed bombs, was standing a few feet back from the gate. Jaina went to him and smiled.

"Your work has paid off, Blastwidget," she said.

He turned a sorrowful face up to her. "It has," he said, "but it was Captain Wymor and the others who made sure the Horde was standing in the right spot."

Jaina's heart sank. "They—they were supposed to retreat! They knew the safe path!"

The white-haired Sunreaver paused in his strengthening of the gate to look at them both. "Wymor and his soldiers stayed," he said quietly. "It was a truly heroic gesture. Many of our enemies were slain. But still they come."

"My lady," a sentry called from the walkway, "mage Songweaver is right. They're running right over the bodies of their dead!"

"Keep warding the gate!" Jaina cried, and she raced to the top of the nearest walkway. Like a dark wave, the Horde kept coming. The bridge had exploded, and chunks of debris and bodies floated in the water. Some of the Horde swam. Others, as the sentry had grimly reported, crawled over their comrades. Jaina lifted her hands and murmured a spell.

Ice shards rained down, some of them killing on impact, others wounding. Another quick flick of her wrist, and several Horde fighters were frozen where they stood. A fireball shattered the frozen forms as if they were statues. The wave retreated. She repeated the actions in a steady rhythm, killing at least a dozen with every methodical and debilitating strike. She could see a figure lingering just out of range, shouting orders, and recognized the distinctive demon tusks that formed the orc's shoulder armor.

"Garrosh," she whispered. He shouldn't have survived the blast that had killed Wymor—but somehow he had. He could not have heard the soft sound, but at that moment he looked up and their eyes met. A sneer curled his lips, and he lifted Gorehowl and pointed at her.

Malkorok was angry—with himself, for not expecting the ambush; with the scouts, who should have discovered it; with the Alliance generals, who were too cursed clever and who had come up with the plan in the first place. The wave of stealthy rogues, druids, and hunter beasts had claimed many Horde lives. The close-quarters battle had claimed still more. Now they were being fired on by cannons and ballistae, and getting mowed down as they tried to approach.

He needed another tactic. He blew the horn of retreat and they fell back. Healers frantically tried to tend to the wounded while Malkorok shouted his orders.

"We are no match for their engines of war," he said, holding up a hand to stop any angry protests. "So we must eliminate those weapons—or else take them for our own. Those of you who are clever at stalking and murder—go now. We will draw their fire. Creep up on those Alliance worms who hide safely behind their technology, and put a knife in their ribs. Then take the equipment and turn it on Theramore itself!"

The angry protests became cheers. Malkorok grunted, pleased. The strategy could not fail to work. The Alliance generals were clever, yes.

But so was he.

"For the Horde!" he shouted, and they took up the cry: "For the Horde! For the Horde! *For the Horde!*"

Kalec flew over the ships in the harbor. From this distance, they looked like toys—toys that were firing cannons, bursting into flames, and sinking. There was damage on both sides; the Horde, too, had determined the wisdom of positioning magi to incinerate the enemy's vessels, and more than one of the famous 7th Legion's battleships bore blossoms of orange-and-gold fire. He dove low, sending a chilling breath to extinguish the flames where he could, and hearing the cheers of the relieved crews as he did so. He angled his body to wheel about, turning his attention to the Horde vessels and the more somber task of attacking rather than protecting. Kalec flew until he was directly over a cluster of three of them, then tucked his wings and dropped. So swift was he that the cannoneers didn't see him in time to redirect their fire. At the last second, the blue dragon opened his wings and lashed out with his tail. The mast of the ship in the center snapped like a twig. As Kalec gained height, he conjured a spell, and ice shards rained down, plunging toward the decks and punching massive holes in them.

Now the cannons did roar, but by then Kalec was well out of range.

He flew back over the city, aware of how many were engaged in aerial combat. Kalec swerved toward a group of several Horde fighters against only a few embattled gryphons and joined in the fray.

The Horde had reached the north gate, and the terrifying, rhythmic thud of a battering ram was added to the sounds of conflict. How they had gotten it over the swamp when the bridge was destroyed was a mystery—probably, thought Jaina as she hurried to the gate, several tauren had simply borne the massive thing on their shoulders as they waded across.

She had intended to race up the steps to the walkway again, to lend her aid to those who were already there and try to attack as many at once as possible. But something stopped her.

The gates were shuddering under the pounding.

And they shouldn't have been.

Not with a member of the Kirin Tor shoring them up with powerful magics. A terrible thought occurred to her.

Boom. Boom. Boom.

The timbers were bulging from the impact. And the hinges and metal bands—

They were curling in on themselves.

Jaina whirled and, with all her might, sent a massive blast of arcane energy directly at Thalen Songweaver.

In his arrogance, he was not expecting it. He stumbled back but recovered quickly. The blood elf stared at Jaina. For an instant, it appeared as if Thalen would protest his innocence, but then his white brows drew together as he sneered and lifted his hands.

He dropped like a stone. Pained stood behind him, still holding the sword whose hilt had so inelegantly yet efficiently disabled the foe.

"I'm surprised you didn't just kill him," Jaina said as two others rushed up and prepared to bind the mage hand and foot.

"A traitor is a useful thing to have on hand," Pained said. "With luck, we will . . . persuade him to talk."

"We're not the Scarlet Onslaught, Pained," Jaina said. She turned to redirect her attention to the gate, but two other magi had already stepped in to protect it. A human and a gnome.

"I hope you are not suggesting you will invite him to tea," Pained said.

"No. I will hand him over to Captain Evencane. He and others will interrogate him when we have a moment to spare." She nodded to the soldiers, who carted off the unconscious blood elf, and realized that Rhonin had stepped beside her.

"I can't believe it," he muttered. "I personally vouched for him to come."

"I am certain he fooled many others than you," Jaina said.

"Indeed," Rhonin said bitterly. "This will be a blow to Aethas and his cause."

"Do you think Thalen acted alone?"

"I do," Rhonin said. "Because if I don't—"

The gate splintered, caught fire, and the Horde rushed through.

• • •

Kinndy found herself trembling from the strain, and she had the help of a Kirin Tor mage! Thoder smiled down at her reassuringly, his rough face kind. "You're doing very well," he said. "Lady Jaina has chosen a fine apprentice."

"I'd be better if I didn't feel like I was going to fall over," Kinndy muttered.

"Take a rest," Thoder said. "Eat something. You'll be stronger for it in just a few moments, and I can hold it until then."

Kinndy nodded gratefully and staggered off, leaning against the stone wall as she gobbled down bread and water. She wondered if she'd ever be anywhere near as good as Thoder or Lady Jaina. They made it seem so effortless. Especially Lady Jaina. Kinndy had been in awe as Jaina had blasted wave after wave of the encroaching Horde with apparent ease. As she ate, Kinndy found her mind drifting toward the sounds of battle raging right on the other side of the wall, and felt herself drawing inward. Focusing on keeping the gate closed had helped distract her more than she had realized. Uneasy with the revelation, she straightened, brushed crumbs from her mouth, and ran over to rejoin Thoder.

As she approached, she saw the gate timbers strain, and the blood drained from her face. Outside, the battle was escalating.

Kinndy, if that gate comes down, dozens—hundreds—of Horde will pour through. We've got to keep it as secure as possible. This might be the single most important thing anyone can do. You could save all our lives.

She quickened her pace the rest of the way, extending her hands and muttering a spell as she did. And to her pride and relief, she saw the buckling of the wood subside.

"Horde have breached the gates! Horde have breached the gates!"

For a wild second, all Kinndy thought was, *No, the gates are holding just fine!* And then she understood. Apparently, the magi at the north gate had not been so fortunate.

Seldom had Theramore witnessed such violence. The Horde was pouring forward like a wave through a break in the dike.

That the Horde would somehow enter the city, by finally destroying the wards or by scrambling over the walls or by aerial assault, had been anticipated and prepared for. Treason from within the very ranks of the Kirin Tor had not. The battle inside Theramore had come too soon, and the Alliance defenders who had been expected to fight hand-to-hand were still recovering from their earlier injuries.

It was a saying that generals stood back and planned wars while others fought and died in them. Such was not the case with these. Fully armored and armed, Jonathan, Redmane, Stoutblow, Shandris, and Tiras'alan charged into the fray without hesitation, so that the Horde met not fresh-faced recruits but some of the very best fighters the Alliance had to offer.

Kalecgos flew over Theramore, doing reconnaissance to see how the battle was progressing and where he was needed. He saw the Horde flood into the city and immediately began pressing the attack. He breathed a cloud of frost on them, slowing their movements, then rose, wheeled, and attacked a second time.

He dove, caught Jaina up in his forepaw, and bore her upward—not taking her out of her battle, no, but giving her a dragon's-eye view.

"Where do you most need me?" he asked. "And where should you be?"

She was completely relaxed in the grasp of his huge forepaw. Her hands rested on a great talon, and she peered down, the wind from his wings whipping her hair about her face.

"The north gate!" she cried. "There are so many still out there—we must stop any more coming in! Kalec—can you bring some trees and boulders to block the entrance and then focus on the Horde remaining outside? Drive them back?"

"I will," Kalec promised. "And you?"

"Put me on the top of the citadel roof," she said. "I can see nearly everything from there and can attack without being a target myself."

"Save for those who take to the air," Kalec said, warning her.

"I know it's a risk, but it can't be helped. Hurry, please!"

At once Kalec veered toward the citadel and placed Jaina on its roof with exquisite gentleness. She gave him a heartfelt smile of gratitude. Kalec started to rise, but she held a hand out to him, imploring him to stop.

"Kalec, wait! You should know—Garrosh is with the forces at the north gate! If we can capture him—"

"Then we can end this war right now," he replied. "I understand."

"Stop the flow through the gate—then try to find Garrosh!"

He nodded, rose, turned, breathed frost once more

upon the Horde combatants still pouring in from the north gate, then headed toward the swamp.

From her position, Jaina had an excellent view. She looked to the harbor. It seemed as though the two sides were evenly matched; there were Horde ships and Alliance both aflame, and she could see the banners of each fluttering plaintively aboard half-sunken wreckage. The west gate held, and she felt a fierce swell of pride in Kinndy. Several hunters, magi, warlocks, and others who could fight well from a distance were lined along the walkways.

She turned to the north, and she felt both sadness and resolution. With so many in close quarters, she needed to target cleanly, so as to wound or kill the enemy without harming a fellow member of the Alliance.

Her eyes fell first upon Baine, and she felt a pang. Baine was locked in combat with Pained, and she realized that as long as there were other enemies to fight, she could not bring herself to attack the tauren high chieftain. And Light knew, there were plenty of other targets—undead wielding swords with arms that were half-rotting; massive orcs; small, swift goblins; beautiful sin'dorei who moved like dancers.

She focused on an orc shaman whose dark-hued garb seemed to more resemble that of a warlock than the pleasant natural hues Go'el had worn. Jaina murmured a spell, and shards of ice went flying toward the shaman. They pierced his black robes like so many daggers, and he arched in pain. He dropped, and Jaina, regretfully but efficiently, sought another target.

• • •

It was the first crashing sound of a boulder being dropped in front of the ruined gate that alerted Vol'jin that perhaps Garrosh's plan had a flaw. A big one.

He was in the courtyard with many others, using his connections with the loa to help his brothers and sisters. An undulating, hissing serpent ward kept several Alliance soldiers from attacking Horde members. He whirled, momentarily distracted as the boulder slammed down.

He swore in his native tongue, glancing about. Baine was battling beside Garrosh. The blue-haired night elf seemed to be giving Baine a good fight. Several Alliance defenders, including two dwarves dressed in very formal armor, were attacking Garrosh. A few moments earlier, the blue dragon had passed over them, slowing their movements. And now, that same creature was determined to shore up the gate.

Vol'jin fought his way up to Garrosh and Baine. Shouting to be heard over the din, he cried in Orcish, "Dat dragon be tryin' to trap us!"

Baine's long ears swiveled forward, and then the high chieftain skillfully maneuvered himself and the elf he was fighting so he could see. His eyes widened. The elf leaped on him, but Baine got his mace up and slammed her away. She turned the fall into a roll and started to come at him again. Swiftly Vol'jin set the serpent ward upon her, buying the tauren a brief respite.

"Garrosh!" bellowed Baine. "We will be sealed inside!"

Garrosh grunted and risked a quick glance. Strangely, he did not seem too concerned. "Agreed. Fall back, my Horde! Fall back to your brothers!"

A horn sounded the retreat. The boulder was joined by a large tree. A shaman called out for aid from the elements, and the boulder rolled away slightly, widening the gap. The Horde, once so keen to enter Theramore, now hastened to leave it. The Alliance, however, did all they could to stop the escape, renewing their efforts in hand-to-hand combat and shoring up the broken gate as fast as the Horde could tear it down.

Baine hung back, trying to fend off the persistent night elf, buying time for his people to escape. Vol'jin called to his trolls, though it was clear the bloodlust was high in them and they did not wish to stop fighting. Garrosh, strangely, hurried out, pausing to call back to those who did not follow at once.

"Baine!" he shouted. "Retreat now! I have no wish to mount a rescue party to save your furry hide!"

With a growl, Baine forced the night elf to dodge, slammed her once more with his mace, and raced through the ever-narrowing crack in the gate.

They were retreating! Again the deep song of the Horde war horn cut through the air. Not only were the attackers from the north fleeing back through the swamp, but those on the west were also hastening to safety.

Jaina turned, trying to see if the same order had been given to the ships in the harbor. It seemed so—as she watched, shaking a little with released tension, the Horde vessels that remained were sailing for open water. The 7th's fleet did not pursue, doubtless on Admiral Aubrey's orders.

Jaina let out a long breath. A large shadow blocked the sun for a moment. Peering up, she saw Kalecgos hovering. He dropped lower, reaching out a forepaw to her, and she happily climbed into it.

"We won, Kalec!" Jaina cried. "We won!"

18

"He is gone!" snapped Pained. "That cursed traitor Songweaver—he is gone! I am getting reports that a small group of Horde came in and freed him!"

"I will take some Sentinels and try to find them," Shandris stated. "They must not be allowed to escape."

"Indeed, they cannot," said Vereesa. "I will not let a blood elf reveal how we stand now. If you search the north road, I and a few others will see to the west." She turned to Rhonin. "I anticipate we will be back soon."

"I would tell you to be safe, my love, but that would be redundant," said Rhonin. Both appeared exhausted. Vereesa was spattered with blood that was, thankfully, not her own, and Rhonin looked as if a good stiff breeze would blow him over. Still, they knew their duties and would never shirk them.

She slipped into his arms and they kissed with the familiarity of lovers and companions who knew each other's body well. The kiss was sweet, but they did not linger.

"Rest, if you can," Vereesa urged. Rhonin snorted. She grinned. "I said, *if you can*."

"I'll try. But there are many wounded, and even those

of us who can't conjure a healing spell to save our souls can wrap bandages."

"This is why I love you so," she murmured. "I will be back soon, my love." Shandris and her Sentinels had already departed through the north gate. Vereesa's warriors were mounted and waiting as she hastened to a fresh horse, leaping atop it with lithe grace. She did not look back as they rode out the west gate. Rhonin didn't expect her to. His wife had made her farewells and was on to her duty, as he should be on to his.

Jaina's first duty in those early moments, when it sank in that, yes, they had won, was to care for her people. Such was always her first responsibility. She spoke briefly to Jonathan, who updated her on the status of their defenses. He assured her that the marines of the entire fleet would be coming ashore and offering their aid to the injured, and that it was the gryphon roosts and other aerial defenses that had taken the most damage.

"Do you think they will return?" she asked.

"Doubtful. They suffered many casualties and will need time to regroup. Besides, we've got a dragon if they send more than ground troops."

Jaina had to smile at that. "Then let's get to helping those who need it," she said. A quick look around assured her that the other generals were taking charge of the injured as well. Hunters set their pets to sniffing out still-living bodies in the rubble, and even as Jaina watched, two people were pulled out from beneath piles of stone and wood. They were wounded but smiling—and alive.

Dr. VanHowzen looked up as she entered the infirmary.

"Lady Jaina," he said, "please move back about three steps."

She quickly did as she was told, and two soldiers carrying a third on a stretcher ran past her. The infirmary was filled to overflowing. Blue sky could be glimpsed from a hole in the roof, but it appeared as though the building would hold. "What do you need, Doctor?" Jaina asked.

"We need to spread out into the courtyard area," he said. "And tell the most experienced healers to come meet me here. We can use their help. Anyone else will just get in the way right now."

Jaina nodded briskly. VanHowzen stabbed a bloody finger at her. "And you and the rest of your magi, get something to eat. I don't want to have to be treating you too. These soldiers need me more."

Jaina smiled wanly. "Message received." She turned and went back outside, mindful of those hurrying in with the wounded. She conjured bread and water, an easy spell, enough to fuel her for a little while, and forced herself to eat, although she was far from hungry.

They had won, Jaina thought sadly as she looked around, but not without cost. All the gryphons and hippogryphs, along with their riders, had been slain. Their furry, feathered bodies lay where they had fallen, pierced by arrows or blasted by spells, their roosts destroyed by the Horde intruders who had spirited away the traitor Songweaver. The beasts had not died alone, however; the bodies of giant bats, dragonhawks, and lionlike wyverns also sprawled on the ground of Theramore.

She spied a small figure wandering aimlessly where the inn had once stood. Jaina hurried up to Kinndy, relieved that her apprentice had survived. The face that Kinndy turned up to her, though, made her heart ache.

Kinndy was pale. Even her lips were bloodless. Her

eyes were enormous but dry, and Jaina reached down and stroked her messy pink hair comfortingly.

"I thought I knew . . . what it would be like," the gnome said quietly. Jaina found it hard to believe that this sweet, soft voice had once exchanged ribald jokes with Tervosh or had challenged a dragon.

"You can read all the books in the world, Kinndy, but no one ever knows what battle will be like until she's in it," Jaina said.

"You . . . had the same experience?"

Jaina thought back to her first encounter with the risen dead in the lands that would later be known as the Plaguelands. More vividly than she wished, she recalled walking into one of the farmhouses, breathing in the sickly sweet reek of carrion; the cries of the shambling thing that had once been a living human being, attacking her; and her own attack with a fireball, adding the smell of incinerated flesh to the miasma. She had burned the farmhouse down, consigning more of the walking corpses to true death. This battle had been different but in many ways the same. Anything that involved violence and killing or being killed was the same, as far as it affected her. Even now, she felt a chill touch her like the brush of a bony hand, and she shivered.

"Yes," she said, "I had the same experience."

"Do you . . . get used to seeing this?" Kinndy spread her short arms to indicate the bodies still strewn about. "Seeing people who were alive and well only a few hours ago now . . . like *this*?"

Her voice broke on the last word, and Jaina was relieved to see tears, finally, in the girl's eyes. Being able to grieve was the first step in healing from such horror.

"No, you don't," Jaina said. "It hurts, every time. But

the . . . unfamiliarity of it goes away, and you learn that you can go on. That those you've lost would *want* you to go on. You'll remember how to laugh and be thankful and enjoy life. But you won't ever forget."

"I don't think I'll ever be able to laugh again," said the girl. Jaina almost believed her. "Why me, Lady? Why did I survive and all of them didn't?"

"We will never know the answer to that. All we can do is honor those who aren't here by living our own lives to the fullest. Making sure their deaths meant something. Think of how much your parents love you and how grateful they will be that you weren't killed." Jaina smiled a little, though it was tinged with melancholy. "Think of how grateful *I* am that you weren't killed."

Kinndy looked up at her searchingly, and then the faintest ghost of a smile touched her pale lips. Jaina felt another knot in her stomach untie. Kinndy was made of strong stuff. She would be all right.

Jaina broke off a chunk of bread and gave it to the girl. "You handled yourself very well, Kinndy. You did me and your family proud."

Jaina wasn't sure what to expect. It wasn't what happened next. Kinndy, smart-mouthed, independent Kinndy, dropped the piece of bread to the bloodied earth, turned to Jaina, wrapped her arms around her mentor, and sobbed as though her heart would break.

Her own blue eyes sorrowful, Jaina gazed at the aftermath of battle, knelt down, and held her apprentice tight.

Of all the races that had given their allegiance to the Horde, there was no question that the tauren were among the most peaceable. Slow to anger, quick to forgive, stalwart and steadfast. But when a tauren did find a reason for fury and outrage, it was usually wisdom to move out of his way.

The throngs of Horde soldiers scurried to one side when Baine came through.

He strode heavily, angrily, his tail lashing, his ears flat. He did not request an audience with the warchief. He bellowed his demand for it, as his father before him had.

"Garrosh!" The roar of the normally calm bull silenced any other conversation and caused heads to whip around. Followed by Hamuul Runetotem and, hanging back slightly, Vol'jin, Baine marched up to where the warchief stood on the far west side of the bridge over Dustwallow Bay, arms folded, gazing at Theramore. He did not turn when Baine called his name. Heedless of any repercussions to himself, Baine grabbed Garrosh's arm and whirled the orc about to face him. At that moment the Kor'kron surged forward, Malkorok in the forefront, but Garrosh shook his head before they could move to slice the angry tauren into so much meat.

Baine shoved a bloody piece of cloth into Garrosh's face, growling furiously. This did get a reaction out of Garrosh, who snatched away the cloth and snarled at Baine.

"That, Garrosh, is the blood of a young tauren who died obeying *your* orders! *Your* commands! The commands that have left far too many stiffening in these muddy waters for no purpose!" shouted Baine. "It is a more fitting decoration than your tattoos, Garrosh!"

Malkorok was there, shoving the mighty bull so hard that Baine actually stumbled backward a step. Malkorok seized Baine's wrists in his powerful warrior's hands and started to twist, his missing fingers not hampering the strength of his grip. Garrosh had wiped his face clean of the bloody smears and now said, "Let him go, Malkorok."

For a moment, it seemed as though the Blackrock orc would refuse the direct command. Then, his body visibly straining against it, he released Baine, spat on the ground, and stepped back.

Garrosh regarded Baine and then, to the tauren's utter disbelief, began to laugh. It was a slow, deep rumble of mirth, building to a loud guffaw that seemed to echo across the water. "You stupid beast," said Garrosh, still chuckling. Facing Baine, he extended a hand and pointed back toward Theramore. "The moment of our victory has finally come!"

Baine gaped. Behind him, Vol'jin recovered first. "What in da name of da spirits you be tinkin', mon? We just lost! Not just lost—it was a disastah!"

"Disaster," repeated Garrosh, rolling the word around in his mouth as if tasting it. "No, I do not think so. You were all so very angry with me for waiting. You had secret meetings; you complained to me again, and again, and again. You did not trust my wisdom. My plans. And now, can you tell me what my decision to wait has bought us?"

"Defeat?" said Runetotem, spitting the word like acid.

Again Garrosh laughed, that inexplicable and inappropriate laughter that only threw fuel on the fire of Baine's grief and fury. He thought again of those he had lost, to no real purpose other than to satisfy Garrosh's ego. But before Baine could speak, Garrosh dropped the amused expression and drew himself up to his full height.

"Behold what happens to those who dare stand against the will of the warchief of the Horde!"

To Baine's confusion, he pointed again, but not toward Theramore or the harbor in which the ruins of Horde ships were sinking. Garrosh Hellscream pointed up.

So engrossed in his pain and anger had Baine been that he hadn't even noticed that they had had to shout to be heard above a whirring, buzzing noise. It was coming closer, and Baine could feel it shaking his very bones. Far off, now a fair distance from the docks but drawing nearer with each moment, flew not a dragon—as might have been an expected sight in a previous war—but a giant goblin sky galleon. Beneath it, fastened securely to the hull, was a large spherical object. So shocking was the sight that for an instant, Baine didn't even know what he was looking at.

And then his eyes widened in horrified comprehension.

Garrosh continued to rant, almost screaming to be heard. "We waited. On my orders, we waited. We waited until the 7th Legion's fleet, almost in its entirety, came to Theramore Harbor. We waited until the greatest generals of the Alliance—Marcus Jonathan and Shandris Feathermoon among them—came to the aid of poor Lady Jaina to offer their best soldiers and their brilliant strategies. We waited until Kalecgos of the blue dragonflight came, until five members of the Kirin Tor, including their leader, Rhonin, came. Ships and soldiers, magi and generals, all at Theramore. We threw ourselves at the gates, which our friend Thalen Songweaver weakened for us—and his loyalty was rewarded. While the Alliance focused on us, a small team infiltrated Theramore. Their accomplishments were twofold—they rescued Thalen and were able to cripple the Alliance aerial defenses. And now—we shall wait no longer!"

• • •

Each of the races, it seemed to Kalec, had its own way of honoring the slain. Sometimes grim necessity, in which the needs of the living came before those of the dead, dictated that these healing rituals be delayed and that the corpses of the fallen be dealt with in a more perfunctory manner than grieving hearts would wish. But here there was no need for a mass grave, or a bonfire for expediency. There was both time and a place to care for the dead. Kalec joined the survivors of the Battle of Theramore in lifting the broken bodies, identifying them, and gently placing them in wagons. The honored dead would be bathed and clad in clean clothing that did what it could to hide the hideous rents in the flesh. There would be a formal ceremony, and the fallen would be laid to rest in the cemetery outside the city.

He was engrossed both in melancholy and in a sort of solemn joy. They had rebuffed the Horde's attack. He had survived, and Jaina had survived. There would be—

His heart spasmed in his chest. Kalec stumbled to a sudden stop and had to catch himself in order to not drop the body of the slain soldier he was bearing in his arms.

It had been flitting on the edge of his consciousness during the battle: the essence of the Focusing Iris. He had feared that it had fallen into the hands of the Horde, but it had stayed stationary a ways to the south, and so Kalec had ceased to give it more thought and instead placed his attention on the immediate battle.

Now it was moving. Fast.

And it was moving northwest. Toward Theramore.

Quickly and carefully he placed the body he bore on the wagon and hastened to find Jaina.

• • •

Jaina was tending to those still injured. Kalecgos found her standing outside Foothold Citadel. There was a sea of wounded lying on the square where once they had trained with combat masters. Jaina walked among them, portaling them to safety. Several who were clearly not Theramore guards had come to help her with her task. Where the wounded would arrive, Kalec didn't know—perhaps at Stormwind, or Ironforge, but any major city deep in Alliance territory would be safer than here.

But even as he approached, something went wrong. The portal opened, then collapsed. Jaina frowned, that little furrow that was so uniquely hers appearing between her brows. "Something is preventing the portals from stabilizing," he heard her say to her assistants.

Jaina turned a weary but smiling face to Kalec and extended a hand. "Kalec, I—" The words died as she saw his expression. "Kalec, what is it? What's wrong?"

"The Focusing Iris," he said. "It's heading here. Now." Kalec felt fear clawing at the back of his throat and forced it down.

"But how? From the Horde? Kalec, that doesn't make sense. If they were the ones who stole it, why did they not use it immediately?"

He shook his head, his blue-black locks flying wildly. "I don't know," he said. And he realized that was the source of his fear. The not knowing, the not comprehending the *why*.

The frown deepened. "Perhaps that's why the portals aren't working," she said. She turned to her friends. "Maybe the Focusing Iris is causing interference—or maybe the Horde has figured out some kind of trick we don't know about. Please . . . go find Rhonin and bring him here. Between the two of us, he and I just might be able to keep a portal open despite this nullifying field."

They nodded and raced off. Jaina turned back to Kalecgos. "Where is it?"

"I can't pinpoint it. But it's coming. I have to find it. If the Horde is using it as a weapon . . ." He couldn't bear to speak it. He wanted more than anything to pull Jaina into his arms and kiss her, but he refused to let himself.

He refused to kiss her good-bye.

Jaina was familiar enough with what was about to happen to hasten a few steps back. Swiftly, but mindful of the injured littering the ground, Kalecgos changed into his dragon form and sprang upward, flying straight up, then toward the harbor—and the Focusing Iris.

He could only hope that he wasn't too late.

Rhonin was helping search amid the rubble that had been the keep, where he, Jaina, and the others had strategized for battle. He listened with half an ear to the pleas of the five Jaina had sent, putting the pieces together as they spoke with rising apprehension. If Kalec had sensed the approach of the Focusing Iris, they were in more danger than they realized. Rhonin was certain that Garrosh and the Horde had somehow tricked all of them—including Kalecgos, including himself—and were indeed the ones who had absconded with the artifact. The ways they could harness so much magic once it was in their firm possession were almost quite literally infinite.

A noise distracted him from his pondering. It was faint at first, then grew louder—a whirring, chopping, mechanical sound. Rhonin glanced up, and for an instant, his heart stopped.

A goblin sky galleon was making its way toward them from the southeast. Its distinctive silhouette gave it away, but it seemed to have something strapped to its hull, hidden at first by the galleon's shadow. Then the airship altered course slightly, and Rhonin saw a reflective glint of late afternoon sunlight.

It was a mana bomb.

Blood elves had created the cursed things—bombs fueled by pure arcane energy. Death was immediate. The size varied, but the bombs with which Rhonin was familiar were as large as a human male. This bomb, looking like delicate spun glass, ran the entire length of the galleon. And if it was being fueled by the Focusing Iris—

Vereesa—

He felt a sudden shudder of relief through the horror that gripped him. Vereesa was already well on her way west. There had been no report that she was heading back to Theramore. She would be out of the blast radius. His wife would be safe.

Depending on where the bomb would be deployed.

He turned to those who were awaiting his response. "Yes, please tell Lady Jaina that I've detected a sort of dampening field in operation. That's why the portals aren't working. Tell her to meet me in the top rooms of her tower. And tell her to hurry."

They left to deliver his message. Rhonin didn't hesitate. He ran for the appointed meeting place, his mind racing. The tower had been warded with all kinds of protective magics. It was a solid fortress against such attacks. It could work—but so many things had to go exactly right.

Well. Rhonin would just have to make sure they did, wouldn't he?

• • •

Mana bomb!

Kalec's mind reeled as he recognized the sphere that looked so deceptively lovely. So *this* was what the Horde thieves had planned! He had never conceived that one this large could be built. Theramore would be practically obliterated.

Unless it was detonated in the air . . .

It was a suicide venture. For a brief moment, Kalec felt a sharp, keen pain that he would never again see his fellow blues, especially dear Kirygosa; that he would never again see Jaina Proudmoore. But it was for Jaina and her people that he was doing this. If her life could be bought with his, it was an easy choice. He had been forced to watch Anveena sacrifice herself; he could not bear to see anyone else he loved die if he could help it.

He was a dragon, but the goblin aircraft would be armed, both magically and physically. He would have to attack not merely ferociously but cleverly. He hovered for a few precious moments, trying to make an assessment of what he would be fighting. The moments were abruptly cut short when three cannons opened fire on him.

Jaina was confused and more than a little irritated that Rhonin insisted she come to him. The wounded who needed to be portaled to care were here, not inside the tower! Nonetheless she and her assistants hurried as she was bidden. Rhonin was waiting for them at the top of the tower. He threw open one of the stained-glass windows and pointed skyward. Jaina gasped.

"Is it the Focusing Iris?"

"Yes," said Rhonin. "It's powering the biggest mana

bomb that's ever been made. And putting out a dampening field so that no one can get away." He whirled on
her. "I can divert it. But first, help me—I can hold back
the dampening field long enough to get these people to
safety."

Jaina glanced at her stalwart companions. "Of course!"

Rhonin muttered an incantation, his fingers fluttering as he concentrated, then nodded to Jaina. She began
to cast the portal-opening spell, but didn't understand
what she saw. She intended to send the injured directly
to Stormwind, but instead caught a glimpse not of that
great stone city but an island, little more than a rock, one
of many that dotted the Great Sea. She turned to Rhonin,
confused.

"Why are you redirecting my portal?"

"Takes . . . less energy," grunted Rhonin. Sweat was
dotting his brow, matting wisps of red hair to his forehead.

The reasoning made no sense. She opened her mouth,
and he snapped, "Don't argue. Just—go through, all of
you!"

Jaina's companions obeyed, racing into the swirling
portal. Jaina hung back. Something wasn't right. Why
was he—

And then she understood. "You can't defuse it! You're
planning on dying here!"

"Shut. Up. Just go through! I have to pull it here, *right
here*, to save Vereesa and Shandris and as . . . as many as I
can. The walls of this tower are steeped in magic. I should
be able to localize the detonation. Don't be a foolish little
girl, Jaina. Go!"

She stared at him, horrified. "No! I can't let you do this!
You have a family. You're the leader of the Kirin Tor!"

His eyes, closed in concentration, snapped open, and his gaze was both furious and pleading. His body trembled with the strain of holding open the portal and blocking the dampening field.

"And you're the *future* of it!"

"No! I'm not! Theramore is my city. I need to stay and defend it!"

"Jaina, if you don't go soon, we will both die, and my efforts to drag the cursed bomb here instead of letting it strike the heart of the city will be for nothing. Is that what you want? *Is it?*"

Of course not. But she couldn't stand by and let him sacrifice himself for her. "I won't abandon you!" Jaina cried, turning to look up at the bomb. "Maybe together we can divert it!" She was shouting to be heard over the noise of the sky galleon. It was coming closer now, and she saw, dipping and diving about it, several small flying figures.

And one large one.

Kalec!

Kalec folded his wings and dropped like a stone, the cannonballs narrowly missing him. He beat his wings powerfully, coming up beneath the galleon, his eyes glued to the mana bomb. He opened his jaws, intending to freeze the thing and then shatter it. The resulting explosion would destroy him, of course, and the goblins ferrying the bomb as well. But the residue that would fall upon Theramore would be only mildly damaging. The city—and Jaina—would survive.

A sudden sharp pain pierced him. He faltered, whirling to challenge his opponent—a Forsaken mounted atop a huge bat. The Forsaken's polearm had struck Kalec where

his forearm joined his body—one of the few places without protective scales—and had gone deep. Kalec's abrupt
movement ripped the polearm out of the Forsaken's bony
hand, and the blue dragon's retaliatory and instinctive tail
swipe knocked both bat and rider from the sky.

The galleon had dropped now, and the cannons were
aimed upward at him. Kalec tried to dodge out of the way
but came under the sudden attack of dozens of wind riders. A huge boom echoed, and this time, Kalec wasn't able
to dodge the cannonballs.

Jaina cried out as she saw Kalecgos start to fall. At that
precise moment, the sky galleon released its cargo.

She would never remember exactly what happened
next. She felt herself being both pushed and pulled toward
the still-whirling portal entrance. She shouted in protest,
trying to tug herself free, and craned her neck to look
back just in time to see hell.

The world went absolutely white. The tower shattered. Rhonin's body, standing tall, arms outstretched as
he glared defiantly at his fate, turned suddenly purple. He
was frozen in time for a fraction of a heartbeat; then he
exploded in a cloud of lavender ash. As the portal whirled
closed and Jaina was dragged farther and farther away,
she saw a violet ocean of arcane energy wash over Theramore. Cries of utter, absolute, depthless terror assaulted
her ears, and then she knew no more.

King Bentimerand: Tides of War

19

Baine was a warrior. His eyes had seen almost more than he could bear of the horrors of war. He had beheld towns and forts and even his own city of Thunder Bluff ablaze. He had witnessed battles of magic as well as those of blade and fire and fist, and knew that spells killed as surely and as brutally as steel. His voice had shouted orders to attack, and his two hands had taken lives.

But *this* . . .

The night sky was not a black background lit with the dull orange-red of flames consuming buildings and flesh, although some buildings had indeed caught fire earlier in the battle. Instead, there was a violet glow, almost pretty, like moonlight on snow, emanating from the city. And above that deceptively pleasant radiance, the sky was putting on a show. Bright spikes of lightning slashed through the blackness in all colors of the rainbow. Here and there, the jagged illumination lingered, moving and turning only to wink out and reappear elsewhere. They were close enough to hear booming and cracking sounds as the very fabric of the world was again and again rent asunder and knitted together. As the colorful lights paraded themselves in the sky,

Baine thought incongruously of a phenomenon known as the northern lights his father had seen in Northrend. Cairne had spoken of being filled with awe at the sight, and as Baine beheld the glow, awe mixed with stunned, sick revulsion filled him.

The soft purple glow heralded the blanket of arcane energy that enveloped Theramore. The mana bomb, so thoughtfully provided by the blood elves—who stood cheering with other Horde members who somehow felt that what Garrosh had wrought was a good thing—had exploded over an entire city and had not just harmed its citizens and buildings but crushed them utterly. Baine had watched both friend and foe perish from arcane magic attacks far too often to feel anything but fury at what he beheld. The people caught in the blast had been blown apart inside, as magic distorted and re-formed them down to the last drop of blood. The buildings, too, were remade from the inside. So great had the blast been that Baine knew that every creature, every blade of grass, every handful of soil was now rendered dead and worse than dead.

And the awful magic would linger. Baine did not deal with magic. He did not know how long the eerie violet glow that marked Garrosh's calculated brutality would pulsate around the city of the slain. But Theramore would not be livable for a long time.

Tears ran down his muzzle, and he made no effort to wipe them away. He stood surrounded by throngs of cheering Horde, but as he looked around, he saw, illuminated by the ghostly arcane glow, faces that wore his own expression of shock and revulsion. What had happened to the warchief who had once said, "Honor . . . no matter how dire the battle, never forsake it"? Who had hurled another orc, Overlord Krom'gar, off a cliff to die for dropping a bomb on innocents and leaving nothing but a crater? The similarity was eerie and struck Baine to the marrow. Garrosh had gone from decrying such murders to committing them.

"Victory!" shrieked Garrosh, standing atop the highest ridge of the small islands in the channel. He lifted Gorehowl, and the axe's sharp blade caught and flashed the purple light over the assembled Horde. "First, I gave you a glorious battle in which we claimed Northwatch Hold for our own. Then, I harnessed your patience, so that we could fight an even more honorable fight—against the finest soldiers and minds the Alliance had to offer. Each one of you is now a veteran of a battle against Jaina Proudmoore, against Rhonin, General Marcus Jonathan, and Shandris Feathermoon! And to secure our victory, I snatched from beneath the very noses of the greatest magic wielders in this *world* an arcane artifact so powerful it has destroyed an entire city!"

He pointed at Theramore, as if any of those standing there were not riveted by the evidence of mass destruction. "This is what we have wrought! *Behold the glory of the Horde!*"

Did none of them see? Baine couldn't understand it. So many, too many, seemed happy at beholding the dead city, crowded with corpses of people who had died in a horrible and painful fashion. They were happy at being tricked into a battle against Theramore when all along, Garrosh had had the means to win without sacrificing a single Horde life. Baine was not sure which act he despised more.

The cheers were deafening. Garrosh turned and caught Baine's gaze. He held it for a long time. Baine did not look away. Garrosh's lip curled in a sneer. He spat on the ground and stalked off. The swell of the cheers followed him.

Malkorok, however, lingered. And then he began to laugh. It started slow and soft, rising to a maniacal cackle. Baine's sensitive ears were awash in insane laughter, in cheers at suffering, and in the imagined sounds of a whole city crying out in torment before obliteration mercilessly descended.

Unable to bear it, unable to bear his own self-loathing at having been a reluctant and even ignorant part of it, Baine Bloodhoof, high chieftain of the tauren, covered his ears, turned his back, and sought what illusion of respite he could in the warm dampness of the swamp.

Morning was unkind to the ruins of Theramore.

Without the gentling of the darkness, the stark devastation was blatant. Smoke still curled upward from the mostly dead fires. The arcane anomalies that had provided a show of lights at night were revealed to be evidence of realities and dimensions ripped asunder. One could even glimpse other worlds. Hovering in the air were not only rocks and chunks of earth that had been torn free, but the debris of buildings and weapons. Bodies turned slowly in the air, like grotesque puppets floating in water. The crackling and thundering were ceaseless.

Gharga surveyed the city with a chest that swelled with pride for his part in the battle. Surely lok'tras were already being composed about the glorious fight. He had heard that there were some mutterings about Garrosh's choices—rumor had it that they were coming mainly from the tauren and the trolls—but by and large, Gharga was proud that his orcs seemed as delighted as he by the outcome of the battle.

He waited on the bridge as the emissary from Warchief Garrosh was rowed over to the *Blood and Thunder*. Gharga stood even taller with pride as he realized that it was no ordinary orc but one of Garrosh's own Kor'kron, who now stood in the small boat and quickly climbed up the rope ladder.

The Kor'kron saluted him. "Captain Gharga," she said, "I have two missives for you as day dawns on the ruins of Theramore." The orcs could not suppress smiles as they regarded each other. "One is a private message from Warchief Garrosh. The other contains your new instructions. You, Captain, have a pivotal role to play in the next stage of the Horde's conquest of Kalimdor."

His eyes flashed in pleasure, but otherwise Gharga gave no response other than a polite bow. "I live to serve the warchief and the Horde."

"So it seems, and such loyalty has not gone unnoticed. I am instructed to wait while you read your orders and return with your response."

Gharga nodded and unrolled the second scroll. His eyes flickered over the brief message, and he found he could no longer suppress his delight. Garrosh was no idle boaster. He had backed up his promise to destroy Theramore in a fashion so dramatic and so utter that he had stunned everyone, even his most loyal followers. The Horde navy that now floated in Theramore Harbor was to disperse and form a blockade at every point on the continent. There would not only be no aid sent to Theramore—there would be none sent to Lor'danel, or Feathermoon Stronghold, or Rut'theran Village, or Azuremyst Isle.

Gharga's first stop would be Feathermoon Stronghold. And from there, he was to send word via his swiftest messengers to Orgrimmar that the Horde had been victorious beyond imagining and that the city was to prepare for the greatest celebration it had ever seen upon Garrosh's return.

Rerolling the scroll, Gharga said with confidence, "Tell our warchief that his orders are understood and the fleet will sail within the hour to obey them. And that I feel certain that, when I deliver the news to Orgrimmar, he will be able to hear the cheering all the way from here."

The first thing Jaina noticed as consciousness returned was the pain, although she had no memory as to why she was hurting so terribly. Every drop of blood, every muscle and nerve and inch of skin, seemed to be coldly aflame. Her eyes still closed, she moaned slightly and shifted position, only to hiss as the pain trebled. Even breathing hurt, and her breath seemed oddly cold as it escaped her lips.

She opened her eyes, blinking, and sat up. She brushed sand from her face, enduring the agony with gritted teeth, and tried to remember. Something had happened . . . something terrible beyond words, and for a second, she was cognizant enough to realize that she didn't want to remember.

A sudden wind blew her hair in front of her face. Instinctively she lifted a hand to brush it back, and as she did so, she froze, staring at the lock held captive in her fingers.

Jaina's hair had always been fair. "The hue of sunshine," her father had said when she was a child.

Now it was the color of moonlight.

She stood upon the edge of recollection, suddenly,

desperately not wanting to know, and then toppled over that edge.

My home . . . my people . . .

Jaina unsteadily got to her feet, her body trembling violently. Those who had accompanied her were nowhere to be seen. She was alone . . . alone with what she now steeled herself to behold.

She turned around. The sky was torn apart. It was mid-morning, but Jaina saw stars through the rents. Arcane anomalies winked in and out of existence. The colors, looking to her tear-filled eyes like open wounds and ugly bruises, danced mockingly above the ruins of what had once been a proud city.

A shadow fell upon her. Dazed, sick, she could not tear her eyes from the horror and cared not at all for what might be landing beside her. A voice shattered her trance.

"Jaina?"

It was a weary voice that held pain and concern and warmth, and she heard his boots crunching in the sand as he ran up to her.

She turned toward Kalec. Through tears standing in her eyes, she saw him clasping a hand to his side, though there was no blood. He was pale and looked exhausted but still found the strength to hurry toward her, limping slightly. As he drew closer, she saw his reaction to her changed appearance.

He reached for her just as her legs gave way, catching her and cradling her as she collapsed. Of their own accord her hands sought him, clutching him tightly as she buried her face in the crook of his neck. He held her just as fiercely, one hand on the back of her head and his cheek resting on her now-white hair. For a long, wordless moment, they clung to each other, and Jaina received the silent comfort.

"Gone," she murmured, her voice raspy with pain and shock. "All gone. Everyone, everything—we fought so hard, so courageously, and we'd *won*, Kalec, we'd *won* . . ."

He held her even more tightly. He did not attempt to soothe her with words. There were no words of comfort to offer, and she was glad he knew it.

"My kingdom—all the generals . . . Stoutblow, Tiras'alan, Aubrey, Rhonin, oh sweet Light, Rhonin. Why did he do it, Kalec? Why did he save *me*? I'm the one who was responsible for this!"

Now Kalec did speak, drawing back to gaze at her intently. "No," he said, his voice sharp with determination. "No, Jaina. This is not your fault. Don't you dare blame yourself. If it's anyone's fault, it's mine—my flight's, for allowing that cursed Focusing Iris to be stolen in the first place. That blast—you couldn't have fought it. No one could. The mana bomb was powered by the Focusing Iris. I was farther away than most, and the force of it hurled me clear out to sea. There was nothing you could have done—nothing anyone could have done."

One strong hand was wrapped around hers as they stood together. She clung to it as if it were a lifeline. And perhaps it was. Even so, she realized what she had to do.

"I have to go back," she said thickly. "Someone . . . might still be alive. I might be able to do something."

His blue eyes widened. "Jaina, no, please. It isn't safe."

"Safe?" The word exploded from her and she jerked in his arms, pulling back. "*Safe?* How can you talk to me of being safe, Kalec? That is—was—my kingdom. They were my people. I owe it to them to see if there is anything I can do!"

"Jaina," Kalec said, stepping toward her imploringly, "that place is reeking with arcane energy. You managed to escape, but the blast has already—"

"Yes," she snapped, the pain inside her heart far worse than the pain of her body. "What has it already done to me, Kalec?"

He hesitated, then spoke very calmly. "Your hair has been turned white. There is a single blond streak remaining. Your eyes are . . . glowing white as well."

Jaina stared at him, sickened. If the blast had done so much that was already so obvious, what else might it have done to her that *couldn't* be seen? Her hand went to her heart for a moment, pressing hard, as if she could somehow push the ravaging ache away.

Kalec continued. "I know you want to do something, to take some kind of action. But there are other things we can do. There's no one left there, Jaina. All you'll be doing is risking further harm to yourself. We can go back later, together, when it's safer, and—"

"There's no *we*, Kalec," she said bitterly. The hurt that appeared on his beautiful face only made her heart ache more, but she welcomed the pain now. It was suffering, and only her own suffering could ease the agony of the fact that she alone, of all the souls who had been in Theramore to help her, had survived. It felt good, cleansing, in a hard and brutal way. "There's only me, and my decisions, and my responsibility for those corpses back there. I'm going to see if there is anything at all I can do, any single life I might be able to save. And I'm going to do it alone. As I've always done. Don't follow me."

Swiftly she cast a teleportation spell. She heard him crying her name and refused to shed the tears.

They hurt her more when she kept them inside.

• • •

Jaina had thought she was prepared for what she would see. She had been wrong. Nothing could prepare a sane mind for what the mana bomb had done to Theramore.

The first thing she noticed was the tower—or rather, where it had once been. Gone was the beautiful white stone building that had housed her extensive library and her cozy parlor. In its place was a smoking crater, horrifically reminiscent of the one that yet lingered in Hillsbrad Foothills. Except that gash in the earth had been made by a city departing for war, while this one had been made by Rhonin's desperate attempt to avert disaster, an attempt that had been bought with his life.

She was surrounded by death, engulfed by it, overwhelmed by it. Death was in the line of listing buildings, not a single one of them intact. Death was in the feel of the earth beneath her feet, in the cacophonous and erratic sky above her. And most of all, death was in the bodies that lay where they had fallen.

Healers sprawled, the injured still in their arms. Riders and horses remained units in death, as in life. Soldiers had fallen with their weapons still sheathed, so sudden and inevitable had been the attack. The air crackled and sizzled and hummed around her, making her white hair float as Jaina, moving like a somnambulist, stepped carefully around the ruination of her life.

Jaina observed with a strange detachment the odd things that the mana bomb had strewn about. Over here was a hairbrush; over there, a severed hand. Near the edge of the crater fluttered leaves from a book. Automatically she reached to pick them up. One of them had been altered at so fundamental a level by the bomb that it crumbled to pieces as she touched it. By the armory, a soldier lay in a puddle of red blood . . . three paces away, another soldier floated at Jaina's eye level, globules of frozen purple liquid drifting upward from a rent in his armor.

Her foot stepped on something soft and she jumped back quickly, peering down. It was a rat, its body glowing violet. A piece of perfectly normal cheese was still gripped in its mouth. Kalec's warning that no one could have survived the blast echoed in her mind. Not even the rats, it would seem . . .

She shook her head. No. No, *someone* must have survived this . . . It couldn't possibly have killed everyone, everything. She moved with grim determination, sorting through rubble where she could, pausing to listen, hoping to hear a voice crying for help over the buzzing and crackling of a broken sky. She found Pained, who had fallen over the body of an orc she had clearly slain. Jaina knelt beside the warrior, brushing the long dark blue hair back, and then gasped as the strands shattered like spun glass. Pained had died with her sword in her hand, the familiar grim expression on her face. She had died as she had lived, defending Jaina and Theramore.

The hurt, numbed by horror, moved again like the awakening of a limb gone to sleep. Jaina forced it down and kept moving. Here were dear Aubrey, and Marcus Jonathan, Tiras'alan, and the two dwarves. On the top of one of the broken roofs was sprawled the body of Lieutenant Aden, his shining armor turned purple-black from the blast.

Suddenly Jaina's mind was clear, and rational, and her own.

You should stop. Kalec was right. Get out, Jaina. You've seen enough to know no one survived. Get out now, before you see too much.

But she couldn't. She had found Pained. She needed to find the others. Tervosh, who had been her friend for so long—where was he? And the guard Byron, and Allen Bright the priest, and Janene, the innkeeper who had insisted on staying—where were they? Where was—

The shape looked like a child at first, which was what drew Jaina's eye. The children had all been evacuated safely. Who—

And then she knew.

Jaina stood, barely breathing, wanting to look away but unable to. Slowly, jerkily, her feet moved, almost of their own accord, taking her to the body.

Kinndy lay facedown in a still puddle of her own blood. The crimson stain had tainted her pink hair, matting it, and Jaina realized she wanted to plop Kinndy into a hot bath and help her scrub herself clean, get her a fresh new robe—

She fell to her knees and placed a hand on the girl's shoulder, to turn her over. Kinndy's body crumbled into shining violet dust.

Jaina screamed.

She screamed in utter horror, frantically gathering up the crystalline powder that was all that remained of a smart, lively young woman. She screamed in loss, in grief, in guilt, and then most of all, in rage.

Rage at the Horde. Rage at Garrosh Hellscream, rage at those who followed him. Rage at Baine Bloodhoof, who had warned her but had nonetheless permitted this to happen. Had perhaps *known* this was going to happen. Her screaming turned to racking, hoarse sobs that ripped her throat. She kept lifting handfuls of the purple sand, trying to hold on to Kinndy, her sobbing increasing as the dust persisted in trickling through her fingers.

This wasn't *war*. This wasn't even *murder*. This was obliteration, done at a comfortable distance. Killing in the most brutal and cowardly fashion Jaina could conceive of.

Something glinted, like a sort of signal, on the dead earth. She stared at it for a moment, then slowly, unsteadily got to her feet. Staggering like a drunk, she made her way toward the strange gleam.

The shard of silvery glass was no larger than her palm. She picked it up. In her shocked state, Jaina didn't realize at once what she was looking at, and then pain stabbed her afresh. So many memories—Anduin's lively face as he chatted with her. Varian's scarred visage. Kalec standing out of sight in the corner when she used this mirror. Rhonin—

She caught movement out of the corner of her eye and whirled to look, hoping against all rationality that maybe someone had survived.

They were large, and covered in armor, and green. There were at least twenty-five, perhaps more than thirty of them, all orcs, and they were busily poking around the debris. One of them dropped something in a pouch, spoke to the others, and harsh orcish laughter punctuated the ceaseless ripping and popping sounds.

Jaina clenched her fists, including the one that clutched the shard of broken glass. She was only vaguely aware of the pain as the sliver sliced open fingers and palm.

It took a minute, but one of them noticed her standing in the midst of the devastation. He pulled back thick green lips from yellowed tusks in a grin and nudged one of his comrades. The biggest one in the best armor—clearly the leader of the little scouting party the coward Garrosh had no doubt sent to make sure everyone was quite dead—grunted, then said something in thickly accented Common.

"Little lady, don't know how you survive. But we correct mistake."

They all drew their weapons—axes, broadswords, knives that glinted dully with the slick of poison on their blades. Jaina felt her own lips stretch in a rictus of a grin. They looked at her more closely, at first clearly puzzled by her unexpected reaction, and then their leader began to laugh. "We get to kill Jaina Proudmoore!" he said.

"Bring her head back to Warchief Garrosh!" added another orc.

Garrosh.

Jaina didn't even deign to reply. She tossed away the mirror shard and simply lifted her hands. A wave of arcane energy, augmented by the lingering effects of the mana bomb, struck them all. They stumbled back, shaking and weakened. One of those clutching a dagger dropped the blade from nervous fingers and struggled to maintain her balance. Stronger orcs shook it off and again brandished weapons, hastening to close the distance.

A smirk curved across Jaina's face. The orcs froze, literally, in their tracks, their lower legs encased in ice. Jaina's fingers danced in the air, weaving a spell, calling fire out of nothing and hurling an enormous whirling ball of crackling flame right in their midst. Weakened from the blast of arcane energy, six of them succumbed at once, screaming in torment as they were burned alive. Ten more were severely scorched and spasmed in agony. They too would be dead shortly. The spell wore off, and the remaining orcs, somewhat more cautiously this time, continued to approach.

A cone of frigid air encircled them. They now moved as if through mud, and Jaina picked four more of them off with fireballs. They fell instantly. Another arcane blast, which felt almost effortless to Jaina, slew more.

Ten were left. Six of them were struggling; four were largely uninjured. Again fire sprang from her fingers, and all ten of them fell to the ground. She sent out another blast of arcane energy.

When she finally lowered her hands, sweat plastering strands of white hair to her face, they were all still. All save one. His chest heaved with ragged breaths, and he twitched and shuddered.

Jaina bent and picked up the mirror shard. She didn't look at it. Slowly, stiffly, a cold pleasure growing in her, she stepped over and on the bodies until she reached the lone survivor.

He was coughing, red-black blood streaming from his tusked mouth. Most of his body was covered in burns, the plate mail melted to his skin. It had to be terribly painful, Jaina mused.

Good.

She leaned over the orc, bringing her face close enough to his that she could smell his fetid breath as he gasped for air. He looked up at her, tiny eyes wide with fear. Fear of Jaina Proudmoore, the friend to orcs, the diplomat.

"Your people are despicable cowards," she hissed. "You are nothing more than rabid dogs, and you should be put down. You spit on mercy? Then you will have none. You want carnage? Garrosh will get more blood than ever he bargained for."

Then, with a savage cry, she brought the shard of mirror down into the small space between the orc's gorget and his shoulder armor. Blood spurted up, covering her hand, splashing her face.

The dying orc tried to roll away, but she held his head between her hands, forcing him to look at her as life ebbed with each heartbeat. When he at last was still, she rose. She left the shard of glass from the broken mirror embedded in the orc's throat.

Jaina continued her grim perusal of what the Horde had left of Theramore. The cold rage inside her burned stronger with everything she beheld. The dock was completely gone. Oddly, she felt better here, looking at the wreckage, than she did near the crater where—

She blinked. Not wanting to, but feeling compelled, she turned and walked back to where her tower had stood. She felt the tingling that was the hallmark of arcane energy growing stronger. The whole city was bathed in its residue, but she realized she was approaching the source of the disaster. Her heart rate sped up and she quickened her pace. She closed her eyes, then opened them. She did not want to look into the crater, but she knew she had to.

It was so simple and so lovely—a plain, glowing purple orb that pulsated with arcane energy. It looked delicate, but it had survived a blast that had reduced a city to ashes without so much as a scratch on its surface.

Kalecgos had not exaggerated the power of the item— or, she thought with a stab of fresh grief, the violence it could wreak in the wrong hands. She could feel the energy almost washing over her physically from the artifact's proximity. Her hair stood on end, and she felt her eyes strain for a moment, then adjust, and knew that they were glowing even brighter now. Purposefully she began to climb down into the crater. Rhonin's remains were nowhere to be seen. It appeared that he had succeeded in drawing the bomb directly to him. All that remained of Rhonin were two children, a grieving widow—if Vereesa had been far enough away to have survived the blast—and his memory. Jaina tasted bitterness in her mouth at the thought. He had died trying to save her. She would not let his death be in vain.

She reached the bottom. The Focusing Iris was at least twice her size and certainly heavy. She could teleport it with her and hide it for now, but the most pressing thing was how to conceal it from Kalecgos. The solution struck her almost at once. Kalec had come to know her well, had grown to care for her. Jaina bent down and placed her hand on the artifact, feeling a gentle thrum of energy. Coldly, calculatedly, she proceeded to ward it with her deepest sense of self, holding in her mind her greatest strengths and weaknesses. When he sought to find the Focusing Iris, he would sense only her. She would use Kalec's feelings for her to trick him. As the sole remaining survivor and ruler of Theramore, Jaina Proudmoore claimed the Focusing Iris for her own.

The Horde wanted war. They had gone to grotesque lengths to crush their enemy.

If war was what they wished, Jaina would give it to them.

With pleasure.

20

It was, finally, beginning to work.

There were still tremors from the wounded earth and sharp, angry lightning. The wind still wept and the oceans roared about the shaman as they stood, day after day, offering of themselves to heal the very soul of Azeroth. But there was progress.

Sometimes, the ocean seemed to becalm itself for a few moments. The rain would stop for longer and longer stretches, showing glimpses of blue sky. The earthquakes once ceased for three whole days.

The members of the Earthen Ring—Nobundo, Rehgar, Muln Earthfury, and others—took each little sign to heart. Just as with healing an injured body, it would take time to heal Azeroth. But the elements would, eventually, recover—as long as the care was maintained throughout the lengthy and grueling process.

Thrall stood strongly and securely on the shivering earth, at once rooting himself and drawing its pain from it. He envisioned his spirit, his union with the great Spirit of Life, soaring boldly upward to touch the very sky. He drew spray-damp air into his lungs, purifying it and breathing it out cleansed. It was hard work, demanding work, and, thus far, ceaseless work. But it was the most profoundly rewarding and, yes, joyous thing he had ever done in his life.

Calmed now, like a frightened child gradually drifting to sleep, the earth's trembling subsided. The winds, angrier, died down more sullenly. But the rain ceased. The shaman opened their eyes, returning to the simple physical reality, and exchanged weary smiles. It was time to rest.

Aggra's strong brown hand curled around Thrall's, and she looked at him with approval and admiration. "My Go'el has become a rock instead of a whirlwind," she said. "Since your return, we have made great strides."

He squeezed her hand. "If I am a rock, then you are the sturdy soil it rests upon, my heart."

"I am your mate, and you are mine," she replied. "We will be, like the elements, what each other needs when times are trying. Stone, wind, water—or fire." She winked. It had been Aggra who had pushed him toward his destiny when he had been ill at ease with the other shaman. There had been nothing of subtlety about her. Thrall had been angry at the time but had grown to see her wisdom. Since his return, they had been inseparable—working together as if in a dance, delighting in each other's company when at rest. He thought again of his words to Jaina and sent a silent prayer to whoever might be listening that she be blessed as he had been.

Thrall's good mood faded when they returned to camp and saw a young orc dressed in light leather armor, waiting at attention. The dust and mud on his clothing proclaimed him a messenger, and the grim look on his face spoke eloquently of the nature of the news he bore.

He saluted smartly. "Go'el," he said, bowing low, "I bring news from Orgrimmar. And . . . from elsewhere."

Coldness seized Thrall's heart. What had Garrosh done? Others, too, were approaching, looking mildly interested at the stranger in their midst. Thrall debated reading the news privately but decided against it. News was news for them all, for he was no longer warchief of the Horde.

He waited until the rest of the Ring had arrived, then motioned for them to come forward. The unfortunate young orc shifted his weight, clearly expecting the request that Thrall gave him. "Read your missive to everyone, my young friend," Thrall said quietly.

The messenger took a steadying breath. "'It is with a heavy heart that I inform you of nothing short of disaster to any thought of peace in this troubled continent—indeed, perhaps in the entirety of Azeroth. Garrosh gathered the Horde armies and marched on Northwatch Hold, razing it utterly. He then waited several days, allowing the Alliance to build up its defenses at Theramore. Against our navy and army, Theramore brought in the 7th Legion's fleet and several well-known military advisors, among them Marcus Jonathan, Shandris Feathermoon, Vereesa Windrunner, and Admiral Aubrey. The Horde fought bravely but was defeated—seemingly.

"'Go'el, Garrosh utilized enslaved molten giants to gain his victory in the Razing of Northwatch Hold. And to destroy Theramore, he—'"

The courier paused as a series of gasps rippled through the crowd. Former Horde and Alliance members were both gathered here, their loyalties placed aside in the face of the greater need, but still precious. And as shaman, to hear of the enslavement of elementals—and such elementals!—to wage war was horrifying. The words "destroy Theramore" hung in the air.

"Continue," Thrall said grimly.

"'To destroy Theramore, he stole an artifact from the blue dragons and used it to power the most potent mana bomb ever created. Theramore has fallen utterly, in an arcane ruin, and our scouts say that no one inside the city walls survived.'"

No one survived. Jaina, his friend, the constant voice of peace, was gone. Thrall found he had difficulty breathing, and Aggra squeezed his hand. He tightened his own grip until he knew it was painful; still Aggra held on, loving and supporting him, knowing more than most the stabbing pain that was in his heart.

Quiet sobbing could be heard as one of the draenei turned to her troll friend for comfort. The troll embraced the draenei gently but looked furious. Everyone was stunned, even those Thrall knew to be opposed to peace. Such wanton slaughter held no honor for the Horde. And such recklessness would have a dear price to pay.

Unbelievably, there was yet more to hear. Unable to speak just yet, Thrall motioned for the courier to continue.

The young orc's own voice was heavy with sorrow as he spoke. "'Our navy has dispersed, to form a ring around Kalimdor and blockade the Alliance. There will be no aid coming to Feathermoon Stronghold, or Teldrassil, or elsewhere, nor will any significant number of their inhabitants escape. Garrosh has openly boasted of conquering the entire continent and either driving out or *wiping* out all traces of the Alliance. The only light I can offer, my friend, is that not all the members of the Horde throng about Garrosh delightedly. Some of us see the dangerous path he is treading and fear that the Horde itself will suffer for it. With apprehension for my people, I remain your friend, Eitrigg.'"

Thrall nodded his comprehension of the dire words, but his mind was on other words, spoken not so long ago by a woman now dead.

Nothing is free, Go'el. Your knowledge and skills were bought at a cost . . . Garrosh is stirring up trouble between the Alliance and the Horde—trouble that didn't exist until he started it . . . You can control the winds as a shaman. But the winds of war are blowing, and if we do not stop Garrosh now, many innocents will pay the price for our hesitation.

And many had. For a long moment, Thrall simply stood, lost in painful, soul-searching thought while the rest of the Ring spoke their concerns. Had she been right? Could this have been avoided if he had let others do the working here?

There was a time when that question would have haunted him for days. Now he examined it, as the rational mind must, and dismissed it. Jaina had always maintained that it was as foolish to downplay one's abilities as it was to exaggerate them. Thrall had held the space of Earth for the four Aspects during the battle against Deathwing. He was most certainly not solely responsible for the healing that had taken place here, but he knew he had been able to significantly contribute.

To, quite literally, change the world by healing it.

He was as disturbed by the use of molten giants as the other shaman and as grieved as any by the honorless attack upon Theramore, the use of stolen magic to enact mass murder from a distance. But he knew that he could not—in fact, none of them could—leave now.

Nobundo was saying that very thing as Thrall's heavy

heart turned to the conversation. "We are seeing progress. We cannot stop now—none of us."

"What might he do next?" asked Rehgar. "To enslave molten giants for his own selfish purposes threatens to undo all that we have worked toward!"

"We united with the Cenarion Circle and the Aspects to heal Nordrassil," Muln Earthfury said. "This union was unprecedented and accomplished all we had hoped. With Nordrassil whole again, the world has a chance of healing. If Garrosh will do this, what might he do to our World Tree?"

Thrall looked over at his friends. Their faces reflected his own indecision. Nobundo and Muln exchanged glances, and then Nobundo approached.

"I am angered and saddened by this news," he said. "Not just word of the abuse of the elementals, but all of this. It is true that the earth may rise up in anger at being so mistreated, and even Nordrassil is at risk. But if we halt our work here now, in an effort to rebuke Garrosh—and I am not sure how such efforts would be received—we risk undoing what good we have managed to achieve. Go'el— the Horde was once yours. You chose to place Garrosh in charge of it. And all of us know of your friendship with the peace-seeking lady Jaina Proudmoore. If you feel the need to depart, no one here will question you. I would say the same to anyone else. We are here because we choose to be—because we are called. If you no longer hear that call, you may walk away with our blessings."

Thrall closed his eyes for a long moment. He was grieving, shocked, furious. He wanted nothing more than to don armor, pick up the Doomhammer, and march on Orgrimmar. To punish Grom Hellscream's son for all the foolish, arrogant, devastating things he had done.

Garrosh was his mistake, his responsibility, and no one else's. Thrall had tried to instill orcish pride in Garrosh, but instead of taking the best of his father's lessons, the young Hellscream had taken the worst of them.

But he could not go, could not satisfy his pain. Not yet. Even if Jaina Proudmoore's ghost were to show up and cry for vengeance right this moment, he would have to tell her no.

He lifted sad blue eyes to Nobundo and said, "I grieve. I am angry. But I am still called to be here. Nothing is greater than this duty, right now."

No one spoke, not even Aggra. They all knew what the admission had cost him. Rehgar reached out and clapped Thrall on the shoulder.

"We won't let anyone, Horde or Alliance, who fell in this ill-conceived abomination die in vain. Let us honor them by what we do here. Let's get back to work."

Jaina teleported into Stormwind's Valley of Heroes, directly beneath the statue of General Turalyon. General Jonathan used to patrol here, but there was no mounted soldier waiting to greet newcomers to the city or attend the king at a moment's notice. Jaina looked up at the scaffolding that supported several towers still under repair from Deathwing's attack.

She had hidden the Focusing Iris safely, close enough so that Kalecgos would continue to blur the artifact and her together, but other than that, she had not bothered to do much to "prepare" for her meeting with Varian. Her face and robes were dirty, her body lacerated by small cuts and discolored by bruises. She did not care. This was no formal dinner, no celebratory gathering, no occasion for baths and cosmetics or even clean clothes as far as she was concerned. Jaina had come for a more somber and colder reason than that. Her only concession to her appearance was to wear a dark cape with the hood pulled down to hide her newly white hair with the single remaining golden streak.

Stormwind, it seemed, had already gotten the dreadful tidings of Theramore's fate. The city was bustling at all hours, but now there was a precision and a grimness to it. Soldiers patrolled the streets, no longer nodding and greeting citizens casually but striding with purpose, their eyes scanning the rushing crowds. The bright banners of gold and blue had been taken down, replaced by simple, plain black ones of mourning.

Jaina pulled her cloak about her more tightly and set out for the keep. "Halt!" The voice was sharp, commanding. Jaina whirled, instinctively lifting her hands to cast a spell, but stopped herself. It was no Horde member assaulting her; it was one of Stormwind's guards. He had drawn his sword and regarded her, frowning. The frown turned into shock as the guard's eyes met hers.

Jaina forced a smile. "Your devotion to duty is to be commended, sir," she said. "I am Lady Jaina Proudmoore, come to have an audience with your king." She moved the hood back slightly, enough so that her features could be distinguished. Jaina did not recall meeting this man personally before, but it was likely she had encountered him during her many formal visits. If not, she was a familiar enough figure that he would recognize her.

It took a moment, but then he sheathed his sword and bowed. "My apologies, Lady Jaina. We were told there were no survivors save those on the outskirts of the city. Thank the Light you are alive."

It has nothing to do with the Light, thought Jaina. *It has everything to do with Rhonin's sacrifice.* She still did not know why Rhonin had chosen to die while ensuring that she survived. He was a husband and father of twins, the leader of the Kirin Tor. He had more to live for than she did. Jaina should have died with her city, the city she had been too trusting to truly protect.

Nonetheless, the words were meant kindly. "Thank you," she said.

The guard continued. "We are preparing for war, as you see. Everyone—we were all stunned to hear—"

Jaina couldn't bear any more and lifted a hand. "Thank you for your concern," she said. "Varian is expecting me." He wasn't. He thought her dead, lost with Kinndy and Pained and Tervosh and— "I know the way."

"I am certain you do, Lady. If you have need of anything, anything at all, any of the Stormwind guards would be honored to assist."

He saluted again and resumed his patrol. Jaina continued on to the keep. Here, too, the banners of the Alliance had been replaced with black ones, hanging on the front of Stormwind Keep behind the huge statue of King Varian Wrynn. Jaina had seen it before, and gave it and the fountain upon which it stood little heed. Quick footfalls carried her up the steps to the main entrance of the keep, where she announced herself and was told that Varian would, of course, see her shortly.

While she waited, Jaina had another visit she needed to pay. She slipped off through a side door and into the Royal Gallery.

It, and the art it housed, had suffered from the attack of the great black dragon. Some of the statues had been shattered, and several works of art shaken from the walls.

Anything damaged beyond repair had been removed, but other paintings, carvings, and sculptures remained here, awaiting attention.

Jaina stood still, as if she, too, were carved of stone. So painful were the emotions racing through her that she wished she was. Then her knees buckled and she found herself sprawled before a huge statue. It depicted a proud man, with long hair flowing beneath a sweeping hat. His mustache was neatly trimmed, and his carved gaze was fastened on something in the distance. One hand, now missing two stone fingers, was on the hilt of his sword. The other grasped his belt. A crack ran through the statue, starting at the booted right foot and zigzagging upward to end in the center of his chest. Jaina reached out with a trembling hand and touched the stone boot.

"Was it only five years ago that I chose my path?" she whispered. "I chose to ally with strangers, with the enemy, with orcs, instead of you, Papa. Instead of my own blood. I called you intolerant. Said that peace was the way. You said you would always hate them, that you would never stop fighting them. And I told you they were people. They deserved a chance. And now you are dead. My city is dead."

Tears slipped down her face. In a detached part of her brain, she observed that they were light purple and glowing—liquid arcane energy. As they splashed onto the stone base upon which the statue stood, the tears evaporated in violet mist.

"Papa . . . forgive me. Forgive me for letting the Horde grow so strong. Forgive me for giving them the chance to slaughter so many of our people." She lifted her eyes up again, seeing the implacable statue through a haze of purple-white. "You were right, Papa. *You were right!* I should have listened! Now, now that it's too late, I see that. It took . . . this . . . for me to understand."

She dragged a sleeve across her streaming eyes. "But it's not too late for me to avenge you. To avenge K-Kinndy, and Pained, and Tervosh, and Rhonin, Aubrey, and all the generals—to avenge everyone who fell last night in Theramore. They'll pay. The Horde will pay. I'll destroy Garrosh; you'll see. With my own hands, if I can. I'll destroy him, and every one of those cursed green-skinned butchers. I promise you, Papa. I won't betray you again. I won't let them kill any more of our people, *ever*. I promise, I *promise* . . ."

Jaina had taken a few moments to compose herself before returning to await her summons. That newfound composure was shattered when, after being announced and ushered into Varian's private chambers, she was greeted not by the tall, dark-haired former gladiator but by a slender, towheaded boy.

"Aunt Jaina!" said Anduin, relief on his face as he hurried toward her. "You're alive!"

He hugged her tightly. Jaina was stiff in the embrace. He sensed it at once and pulled back. His eyes went wide as he fully took in her arcane-altered appearance.

"What are you doing here?" she asked, more sharply than she had intended.

"I was worried about you," he said. "When word reached us about what happened in Theramore . . . I wanted to be here. I knew that if you had survived, you'd come to Stormwind."

She stared at him, mute. What could she possibly say? How could she speak to this child, who was so naive, about the true horror of what she had witnessed? He was so innocent, so ignorant of the real nature of their enemy. *As naive and ignorant as I was, once . . .*

"Jaina! Thank the Light!" She turned, relieved, to address the warrior king who strode into the room. Varian had long nursed a personal hatred of the orcs. Anduin was too young to understand, but he would, one day. Varian, she knew, would understand now—now, when it counted the most.

He was dressed informally and looked exhausted and harried, but there was relief and pleasure on his face. It too turned to surprise at her appearance.

Irritated, Jaina snapped, "The only reason I survived was because Archmage Rhonin pushed me through a portal to safety. I was affected at least somewhat by the blast."

Varian raised an eyebrow at the bluntness of her statement, but he nodded, accepting the explanation and not dwelling on it. "You'll be glad to know you weren't the only survivor," he said. "Vereesa Windrunner and Shandris Feathermoon and their scouting parties are also alive. They were far enough away from the center of the blast. They've returned to their respective homes and are talking to their people about war."

Jaina didn't want to think about the widowed Vereesa and her two fatherless children. "I am glad to hear that," she said, "all of it. Oh, Varian, I owe you an apology. You've been right all along. I kept telling you that we could somehow reach the Horde, find some way to peace. But we can't. This proves that we can't, and you knew it even when I was too blinded by hope to see it. We need to retaliate against the Horde. Now. They'll all go back to Orgrimmar. Garrosh won't be able to resist a celebration of his brave victory over the Alliance."

Anduin flinched slightly at the bitterness in her voice. She pressed on, the words rushing out of her. "The streets will run with ale, and the whole army will be assembled. There will be no better time to strike."

Varian tried to speak. "Jaina—"

She barreled on, starting to pace and gesturing with her hands. "We'll get the kaldorei to send their ships along with ours. We'll take them completely by surprise. We'll kill the orcs and raze their city. Make sure that they don't ever recover from this blow. We'll—"

"Jaina." Varian's deep voice was level as he caught hold of her wrists and gently halted her nearly frantic pacing. "I need you to be calm right now."

She turned her face up to his, questioning. How could he speak of calmness?

"I'm sure you don't know this, but the Horde has built up a very effective blockade around the entire continent. The kaldorei couldn't come help us even if they wanted to. I'm not saying we don't strike back. We will. But we've got to do so intelligently. Have a strategy. Figure out first how to break the blockade and then regain Northwatch."

"Don't you know what they did to it?" Jaina snapped.

"I know," Varian said, "but it's still a strategic foothold that we've got to get back before we can make a move. We've got to rebuild the fleet. We lost a lot of good people at Theramore; it's going to take time to call back others from their posts to fill their positions. We need to do this right, or we're just throwing more lives away."

Jaina was shaking her head. "No. We've got no time for that."

"We don't have time to *not* do it," Varian said. He kept his voice measured and calm. For some reason, it irritated Jaina. "We're looking at war that could stretch out over two continents. Maybe even into Northrend. If I am to enter into a world war, where there are no boundaries, I'm going to do so wisely. If we rush in now, we do the Horde's work for them."

Jaina looked over at Anduin. He stood silently, his face pale and his blue eyes sad. He made no effort to interrupt his father and his friend in their discussion about a world-wide war. She returned her attention to Varian.

"I have something that can help," she said. "A very great weapon has come into my keeping. It will destroy Orgrimmar just as surely as the Horde destroyed Theramore. But we will need to act now, when the armies are foolishly gathered together in Orgrimmar. If we don't, the moment will be lost!"

Her voice rose on the last word, and she realized she'd clenched her fists. It would be more than just, to use the Focusing Iris on Garrosh and his beloved Orgrimmar. "We can wipe out every one of those green-skinned sons of—"

"Jaina!" The word was a pained, sharp exclamation from Anduin. Surprised, Jaina fell silent.

"What happened in Theramore was more than a tragedy," Varian said, turning Jaina gently to regard him. "It was an irreparable loss, and a vile and cowardly act. But we mustn't compound the loss by losing more Alliance soldiers needlessly."

"There could even be some in the Horde who disagree with what happened," Anduin said. "The tauren, for instance. And even most orcs prize honor."

Jaina shook her head. "No. Not anymore. It's too late for that, Anduin. Far too late. There's no going back from what they've done. You didn't see what—" Her voice caught and she struggled to speak for a moment. "We must retaliate. And we can't wait. Who knows what atrocity Garrosh and the Horde will perpetrate if we do? We can't have another Theramore, Varian! Don't you see?"

"We will fight them, don't worry—but we'll do so on our terms."

She jerked free from his hands on her arms and stepped back. "I don't know what's happened to you, Varian Wrynn, but you've turned into a coward. And you, Anduin, I am sorry for my part in keeping you a gullible child. There's no hope for peace; there's no time for strategy. I have their ruination in my grasp. You're a fool for not seizing the chance!"

They spoke her name at once, father and son, so different but so oddly similar in how they stepped forward imploringly.

She turned her back on both of them.

21

It was with a wounded body and a heavy heart that Kalecgos returned to Northrend and the Nexus. He had, despite Jaina's words, followed her. Partially because he feared for her safety and her state of mind, and also because he sensed that the Focusing Iris was still in Theramore. It took him time—he had to fly, bearing not-insignificant injuries from the battle, and she had teleported.

He had beheld the huge crater and what the mana bomb had left of Theramore. It was sickeningly little. But the Focusing Iris was nowhere to be found. Someone had to have found it. He suspected Garrosh; the lives of a few loyal subjects of the Horde were nothing compared to the power of the Focusing Iris. Of course he would send a party to retrieve it.

Thus he had left Kalimdor, flying bleakly and laboriously northward with nothing to show for his efforts on the blues' behalf other than a dead city that was mute testimony to his failure. He had, unexpectedly but certainly, fallen in love. Now she, too, had been broken because of what he had done—or failed to do. Part of him simply wanted to head in a random direction and just keep going.

But Kalecgos could not do that. The blue dragons had put their faith in him. He had to tell them what had transpired and determine what course they wished him to take now.

Kirygosa met him as he approached from the south. She darted around him for a moment, showing her pleasure at his return, then settled in to fly beside him the rest of the way to the Nexus.

"You are wounded," she said worriedly. Many scales had been ripped from Kalecgos's azure form, and the skin beneath bore ugly bruises. He could fly still but ached with every wing beat.

"It is a little hurt," he said.

"It is not," she replied. "What has happened? We sensed something terrible . . . and you do not have the Focusing Iris."

"It is a story I wish to have to tell but once," he said, his voice revealing the deep pain of his heart. "Will you gather the flight, dearest Kiry?"

For answer, she dipped beneath him, nuzzling his head with her own, then flew off to obey. They awaited him, and he saw with renewed bleakness that their numbers had dwindled even further since his departure. He was pleased to see that Narygos, Teralygos, Banagos, and Alagosa had remained.

He landed among them, retaining his dragon form, and looked about. "I have returned, but the news I bear is grim." They stood quietly as he spoke, telling them of the cooperation he'd had from Rhonin and the Kirin Tor, from Jaina. Of his difficulty in pinning down the location of the Focusing Iris. And finally, keeping his voice emotionless because he could not bear to feel it all again, of the Horde using their artifact against the Alliance with so devastating an effect.

They listened in silence. No one asked questions. No one interrupted. He had expected anger, but instead they seemed to grow more melancholy than furious at the thought that their magic, their Focusing Iris, had been used to wreak such malicious destruction. It was as if something had broken inside each of them. Kalec understood that. It was a reflection of his own torment.

No one spoke for a long time. Then Teralygos lifted his head and regarded Kalecgos sadly. "We have failed," he said. "Our charge has ever been to ensure that magic was used wisely. To manage it. And look how badly we have executed that duty."

"The failure is mine, Teralygos," Kalec said. "I was the Aspect. I could sense the Focusing Iris, but I failed to locate it in time."

"It was stolen from all of us, not only you, Kalecgos. We all must shoulder the responsibility for this abhorrent event."

"I am your leader, as long as you will have me," Kalec said, though the words were like ash in his mouth as he spoke them. "I will do all that is in my power to recover it." *Even though it has gone missing—again. If only I had been able to destroy it when the sky galleon still bore it!*

"You are as lost as you were before this started," said Alagosa. There was only sorrow in her voice, not censure, but even so, the words stung. She was right.

"It was in Theramore," Kalec said. "It was not destroyed in the attack. Someone has spirited it away again, and I am certain that it is the Horde."

"I am not. I believe that it is in the possession of Jaina Proudmoore. You said she reached Theramore before you, and by the time you arrived, the Focusing Iris was gone."

It was not what was said that surprised Kalec so much

as who had said it. The accusation, spoken in gentle tones but no less stunning for that, came from Kirygosa. She had lingered in the back, listening quietly, but now she moved forward.

"Jaina helped me to find it," Kalec retorted defensively. "She knew even before the—even before, what kind of havoc it could wreak. Why would she willingly take it without telling me?"

"Perhaps because she doesn't trust you to keep it safe," said Kiry. Again, there was no attack in her voice or mien, but Kalec still felt wounded. "Or perhaps because she plans to use it against the Horde."

"Jaina would never—"

"You do not know what she would and would not do," said Kirygosa. "She is human, Kalec, and you are not. Her kingdom has been removed from the map as surely as if it had been blotted out with ink. She is a powerful mage, and the Focusing Iris—the very instrument of death to her people—was within her grasp. We need to consider this a possibility and prepare for it. If she has it, we must find out—and take it back. Whatever the cost. It is our artifact, and much of that blood is on our heads. We must not allow it to be used so again."

Her logic was unassailable. Kalec recalled how furious and grief-stricken Jaina had been when she teleported away from him. Too, she had been visibly affected by the arcane magic from the blast. It had whitened her hair, caused her eyes to glow; if it had done this to her body, what might it have done to her mind?

"I will find the Focusing Iris," he said heavily. "Whoever has it—Garrosh or Jaina."

Kiry hesitated now, glancing at Teralygos. "Perhaps it would be best if a party joined you in your search."

Kalec bit back an angry retort. Kiry had ever been a good friend; she was his sister of the spirit, although they were not clutch mates. She did not cast aspersions on Jaina to hurt him; she did so because she was worried. Worried that he might be too affected by his feelings for Jaina Proudmoore to complete his duty to his flight, and knowing him well enough to understand that if Kiry was right, Kalec would never forgive himself if something went wrong.

"I thank you for your concern," he said, "and I know you have only the good of our people in mind when you speak so. Please believe that I do as well. I can—I must—handle this on my own."

He waited. If there was too much of a protest, he would acquiesce to what the rest of the flight wished. He certainly had not done a faultless job by himself thus far.

Fortunately, most of the blues did not share Kiry's opinion. Kalec suspected that it was because they discounted Jaina, a single human, as a true threat. It was because Kiry recognized Jaina's abilities as being exceptionally strong that the dragoness did not follow suit.

"Then it is settled," Kalec said. "I will not fail you again."

He spoke the words with conviction, hoping beyond hope that he was right. This wounded world could not bear it if he wasn't.

Not so long ago, the former warchief of the Horde had held a celebration to welcome home the veterans who had fought against Arthas and in the Nexus War in Northrend. Garrosh well remembered the glorious parade to Orgrimmar—he himself had suggested it. It was at this celebration that Thrall had honored him, given him his father's weapon, which now rested securely against Garrosh's broad back.

Garrosh was proud of how he had fought in those wars. But he was even prouder of what he had done at Northwatch Hold and Theramore. In Northrend, at least part of the victory had been owed to the Alliance. The thought filled his mouth with ashy loathing. Now things were as they should be. Now the battle was against the Alliance. It was a war Thrall had had the power to start, but he had been too cowed by the fair-haired female mage. Instead, Thrall had fought for "peace," whatever that could possibly be between the orcs and their former oppressors. Garrosh was determined to be to the Alliance what Grommash Hellscream had been to the demons. As the father had overthrown obedience and enslavement to fel creatures by slaying Mannoroth, so the son would overthrow the subtler chains of "peace" with the Alliance. He was sure that even stubborn Baine and Vol'jin would come around eventually, and a true peace—on the Horde's terms, bought with blood and enforced with the same—would occur.

And so, he had given instructions that this celebration, this victor's triumphal march to the capital of the Horde, would put Thrall's to shame. Nor would the march and a single feast be all. No, Garrosh had ordered six days' worth of festivities. Raptor fights in the arena! Sparring battles, with heavy purses to the greatest warriors of the Horde! Feast after feast, set to the accompaniment of lok'tras and lok'vadnods, while the streets would flow with good orcish grog.

At one point, as Garrosh and his retinue headed toward the gates of Orgrimmar, he saw with satisfaction that the throngs of cheering Horde members would not part for him. They chanted his name until it rose like thunder, and Garrosh gave Malkorok a delighted look as he drank it in.

"*Garrosh! Garrosh! Garrosh! Garrosh!*"

"They love you too much to let you through, my warchief!" said Malkorok, shouting to be heard over the noise. "Tell them of your victory! They wish to hear it from your lips!"

Garrosh looked again at the crowd and cried, "Do you wish to hear my vision?"

He had thought it impossible, but the crowd roared even louder. Garrosh's grin widened and he waved them to silence.

"My people! You are blessed among orcs to live in a time of history. A time when I, Garrosh Hellscream, am poised to claim Kalimdor for the Horde. The human contagion that had taken foul root in Theramore has been cleansed by the essence of arcane magic. They are no more! Jaina Proudmoore will no longer emasculate us as a people with her soft-mouthed words of peace. They fell on deaf ears, and now she and her kingdom are but dust. But that is not enough. The night elves are next. For so long they have denied us the basic needs of life. We will deprive them of their lives, of their cities, and send what few we spare to become refugees of the Eastern Kingdoms. I, Garrosh, will humble them and reduce them to begging for mere morsels of food and a place to sleep, while the Horde avails itself of their riches. Their cities are cut off from aid by stout Horde battleships, and when we are ready to invade, they will fall before us like wheat before the scythe!"

More cheering, more laughter and clapping. And

another chant arose, spontaneous but inspired by his words:

"Death to the Alliance! Death to the Alliance! Death to the Alliance!"

Baine sat in the corner of the dank, dark inn at Razor Hill. What light came in through the door did nothing to illuminate the place, indeed only showed thick clusters of dancing dust motes. The beer was poor and the food worse. A few miles due north, he could have been enjoying a feast the likes of which he had never tasted. He was more than content here.

Garrosh had forbidden the army to disperse. All Horde fighters had to stay in Durotar, but the warchief had not commanded Baine to attend the feasts in Orgrimmar. The "oversight" was an insult, and Baine was intelligent enough to know it. He also knew he was thankful for it. He feared that if he were forced to spend another moment listening to cheers for Garrosh—cheers for placing the Horde needlessly in harm's way, cheers for mass murder enacted in the most cowardly of fashions—he would be unable to stop himself from challenging the green-skinned fool. And if he did, no matter who walked away from the fight, the Horde itself would be the loser.

He was not to be alone in his dark brooding. As he nursed the poor beer, he watched the doorway. More tauren came in, nodded to Baine, and took their seats. After a time, he saw Vol'jin. The troll did not sit with him, but their eyes met. Then, to his surprise, he saw the bright gold-and-red garb of sin'dorei . . . and the tattered clothing of Forsaken. His heart lifted. Others saw what he saw, felt what he felt. Perhaps there might be a way to halt

Garrosh's madness after all. Before the Horde ended up
having to pay the price.

The salt-tinged sea air was filled with sound. It had not
ceased since it began two days ago, when word of Theramore's fall had reached Varian, and would not cease until the task was complete. It was the sound of feverish
activity—boards being cut to size, nails being pounded,
engines being tinkered with. The barks of dwarves and
the cheerful voices of gnomes punctuated the noises of
industry.

Not a citizen of Stormwind complained of the noise,
for it meant hope. It was the sound of the Alliance refus-
ing to be broken by a single deadly but cowardly act.

Broll Bearmantle, Varian, and Anduin stood together,
gazing out at the harbor. The day had only just dawned,
and the sails being carefully raised on one of the great
new vessels were tinged with the pinkness of a sun peek-
ing over the horizon.

"I don't think I've ever seen quite so many workers all
in one place—not even in Ironforge," said Anduin. Per his
own request, Anduin was to remain in Stormwind until
the fleet had sailed, at which time he would return to his
studies with the draenei. Varian smiled down at his son,
glad that the youth had chosen to remain. The encounter
with Jaina had startled and upset both of them. Anduin
in particular reeled with the shock of seeing peace-loving
"Aunt Jaina" so full of hatred. They had talked long into
the evening, the man who had once identified with Jaina's new attitude and the boy who quailed from it, talked
about what grief and loss could do to someone, talked
about what war and violence, as well, could do.

Anduin had lifted sad but determined eyes to his father. "I know this is a horrible thing," he said. "And . . . I realize we have to attack the Horde. They've shown us what they are willing to do, and we must prevent them from harming more innocent people. But I don't want to be like Jaina. Not about this. We can protect our people—but we don't have to do it with hate in our hearts."

Varian's own heart had swelled with pride. He had not expected such acceptance, reluctant though it was, from Anduin. He was honestly surprised that he himself hadn't shared Jaina's feelings, and realized how far he had come from the man he had once been. There was a time when he had been filled with anger and rage, when parts of himself had been at war. He had been two beings, literally, and the rejoining physically was only a portion of the battle. He'd been taught to integrate those parts in his very soul, through the blessing of the wolf Ancient, Goldrinn. Truly, he had made great progress.

He might even be as wise as his son one day.

Broll had departed Teldrassil through magical means, an option not available to most of his people. The report of the blockade had been sobering but not unexpected.

"It is good, to see this construction," the druid said as the three stood together. "Do not think that you will sail alone, Varian. While we have many ships trapped by the Horde's blockade, there are many more elsewhere. Malfurion and Tyrande are more than willing to help you as best they can. You may look to see a few dozen of our graceful ships alongside yours in the not-too-distant future."

Anduin turned to regard the druid, craning his neck to look up at this friend of his father's. Anduin knew that Broll, too, had had to face loss and rage and hatred. Varian thought it must hearten the prince to see two former gladiators standing and discussing what had to be done with regret rather than glee. Light, it heartened *him*.

"You will not try to fight your way out of the blockade?" asked Anduin.

"No. Our energies are best put toward teamwork right now. What lives we must sacrifice need to count, Anduin. We have a better chance of winning when we focus together."

Anduin's golden head turned again to the ships in the harbor. "Why did the Horde do this? They didn't know we had relocated the civilians. They just . . ." His voice trailed off. Varian laid a gentle hand on his son's shoulder.

"The easy answer is that the Horde are monsters. What they did was monstrous, certainly. And I have a few choice words about Garrosh and his Kor'kron that I will not utter in front of young ears." Anduin gave him the ghost of a grin. Growing sober again, Varian continued. "I don't know why, Son. I wish I could tell you why people do such horrible things. The fact that I am certain many who are not Alliance are quietly muttering about Garrosh doesn't sway my hand."

"But . . . we won't fight like Garrosh did?"

"No," Varian said. "We won't."

"But if he is willing to do things we're not . . . won't that mean he will win?"

"Not while I have breath in my body," said Broll.

"Nor I," said Varian. "The world has become . . . unhinged. I saw violence and blood and madness in the pit. I did not expect to ever see anything like what Jaina was forced to witness."

"Do . . . do you think she will recover? From the hurt to her soul that seeing that gave her?"

"I hope so," was all Varian could say. "I hope so."

22

The Violet Citadel was somber and still as Jaina slowly walked up the stone steps from the entrance hall. Pain wrapped this place. Once, Dalaran had felt light to her. The designs and structures certainly were graceful, but more than that, it was a place where magic was integral. Now it felt . . . heavy in a way it never had before. Jaina, bearing her own burdens, sensed it, feeling kin to those who had lost so much.

Several extremely powerful magi, including the leader of the Kirin Tor. And one traitor, who was at least partially responsible for those bitter losses. No wonder the very air felt thick and sad.

"Lady Proudmoore," said a voice brittle with pain. Jaina turned, and she felt a stab of sympathy.

Vereesa Windrunner stood alone in the huge entrance chamber. She wore clean plate armor in shades of silver and blue, and any wounds she had endured in battle were either healed or healing. All but one, which Jaina felt would never fully heal.

The widow of Rhonin looked impassive, as if she were little more than an animated statue, except her blue eyes blazed with fury. Jaina wondered if that fury was directed at the Horde for murdering her husband, or at Jaina, or even herself, for surviving.

"Ranger-General Vereesa," Jaina said. "I . . . find I have no words."

Vereesa shook her head. "There *are* no words," she said flatly. "Only action. I have been waiting for you, since I heard you yet lived, for I knew you would come. And I come to you to implore that you will help me in obtaining that action. You survived; my beloved did not. You, I, and a handful of night elven Sentinels are the only ones who can give voice to the slaughter at Theramore. You have obviously come to speak to the Kirin Tor. May I ask what you intend to say to them?"

Jaina knew that Vereesa was leader of the Silver Covenant, a presence the high elf herself had formed as a precaution against possible treachery from the Sunreavers, blood elves who had been granted permission to join the Kirin Tor. As such, Vereesa was vocal and outspoken— but had no formal voice in the Kirin Tor. Neither did Jaina, officially, but as the sole living mage to report about the disaster—and as the one whom Rhonin had chosen to portal to safety even as he called the mana bomb down upon himself—she knew she would be given an audience. Now that Rhonin was gone, Jaina found herself remembering a particular conversation. How he had told her that many of the Kirin Tor wished she had not chosen the path she did, how they wanted her to be one of their number.

Jaina might not have been a member of the Kirin Tor. But she was certainly going to speak to them.

Vereesa was still looking at her, her face an implacable mask that doubtless concealed a maelstrom of anguish and rage. Suddenly moved, Jaina strode to the other woman and blurted out, "Rhonin cared about two things when he died. He wanted to make sure you would survive—and he made the effort to get me to safety. He bought both our lives with his own."

". . . What?"

"The bomb landed where it did because Rhonin called it to him. Rhonin used his magic to redirect it to the tower, which was heavily warded and magically protected, so the blast would cause as little damage as possible."

The façade was starting to crack. Vereesa lifted a trembling hand to her lips, listening.

"He—he told me that I needed to survive. That I was the future of the Kirin Tor, and if I didn't go through the portal he was struggling to keep open, we would both die—and his efforts would be for nothing. I refused to leave and—he pushed me through. Vereesa—I don't understand why he chose me. Theramore was my city; I should have died for it. But *he* was the one who died. And I will not forget that, not as long as I draw breath, and I will do all that I can to be worthy of his sacrifice. I was *there*, Vereesa. I know what they did. And I will urge the council to make sure the Horde is never, *ever*, in so powerful a position again. That no one else has to suffer as we have."

Vereesa's lips curved into a trembling smile, and the next thing the mage knew, the two women were hugging each other tightly, and Jaina felt warm tears against her neck.

For the second time in more than a week, Jaina stood in the Chamber of the Air. It looked the same, if something that constantly changed could be called "the same." The simple gray stone beneath her feet was the same, and the display of shifting sky from night to day, from storm to stars, was familiar. Yet everything was different. Jaina was no longer dazzled by the glorious vista, nor by the honor of being permitted to speak to the Council of Six. Five, now. She was unmoved as she looked about at the faces of the remaining members of the council.

Standing next to them, but not officially part of them, was the stone-faced Vereesa. Jaina was glad she had been permitted to attend. Surely she had earned the right by losing the one she loved best in this world.

"Sad is the occasion that welcomes Lady Jaina Proudmoore a second time to these chambers, but glad are we to see you survived." It was Khadgar who spoke, and this time he seemed to truly be the age his appearance proclaimed him as. His voice was weary; he leaned heavily on a staff; and even his formerly dancing eyes looked old. His companions, too, appeared strained. Modera had dark circles beneath her eyes. Disciplined Karlain was clearly having difficulty restraining his anger and pain. Aethas, the leader of the Sunreavers, who had recommended Thalen Songweaver, still wore his helmet, so Jaina could not see his face. But his body language was agitated.

"Thank you for seeing me," Jaina said. "Forgive me if I dispense with formalities. I came here not so long ago, asking for the Kirin Tor's help to defend Theramore. You granted it, and for that I am grateful. For the death of Archmage Rhonin, I grieve with you. He died a true hero. I am alive because of him. I am humbled by that gesture, and I vow to honor it as best I can. I will not mince words. I am here to ask you to join with the Alliance in attacking the Horde. The armies gather in Orgrimmar, to feast and drink and celebrate a massacre. If we strike now, we will destroy them so that they are unable to perpetrate such evil again."

"Dalaran is neutral," said Modera. "We went to Theramore only to protect and advise."

"And if you had done more than that, Theramore might be of note to mapmakers of the future," Jaina retorted. "Rhonin gave his life to stop the mana bomb as best he could. If there had been more—if the full force of the Kirin Tor had been brought to bear—he might still be alive!"

"I am . . . revolted by Garrosh's actions," said Aethas. "And I take responsibility for the harm done by one of my own Sunreavers. But attacking Orgrimmar is not the answer."

"You Sunreavers cannot be trusted," growled Vereesa. She looked imploringly at the other members of the council. "Why is he even still here? They are traitors, all of them! I warned you not to let them join the Kirin Tor!"

"There have been human traitors, and high elf, and gnome, and orc," said Aethas calmly. "I will do what I can to atone for the treachery of Songweaver. The irony that I sent him as a gesture of goodwill does not escape me. But we must not abandon our stance of neutrality for vengeance!"

Others were nodding. Khadgar looked thoughtful, as if he were turning things over in his mind. Jaina could not believe their reactions, their hesitation.

"What will it take for you to realize that the Horde will eventually turn on you? They do not understand 'neutral,' just as they do not understand 'diplomacy' or 'decency.' They will flow over Kalimdor, then turn on the Eastern Kingdoms, then come here. Your refusal to stop them will mean that one day soon, Horde will be swarming over Dalaran itself! Please, strike while we still can! We have uprooted the city once—let us do so now. Take it to Orgrimmar. Attack from above while they lie in a drunken stupor, dreaming of conquest! You've lost Rhonin and an entire city. Will you act when Teldrassil falls? When they are burning a World Tree?"

"Lady Jaina," said Modera, "you have been through the unspeakable. You have beheld horrors and watched a friend die while he saved you. There is no one here who approves of the actions of the Horde. But . . . we must meet, to decide what next to do. We will summon you when we have reached a decision."

Jaina bit her tongue against a flood of retorts and nodded. They would do the right thing. They *had* to.

Jaina found both Windle and Jaxi Sparkshine in a corner at the inn called A Hero's Welcome. The normally lively and bright tavern was quiet and solemn; there was little "welcoming" about it. Jaina hesitated in the doorway, wondering if she should intrude upon their grief. Wondering if she could bear the torment she knew she would see in their eyes. They had entrusted Kinndy to her, and she had failed them. There hadn't even been enough of the girl left to bury.

She closed her eyes against the sting of tears and turned to leave. As she did so, she heard a voice calling, "Lady Proudmoore?"

She flinched, then turned around. Both gnomes had slipped from their table and were walking over to her. How old they looked now, Jaina thought. Kinndy had come to them later in life, a little "miracle," they called her. Jaina's words floated back to her: *I give you my word, I will keep her as safe as I possibly can.*

She had planned to be eloquent, to praise Kinndy as

the girl deserved. To give her bereaved family comfort, to let them know that Kinndy had fought well and bravely, that she had been a light to everyone who knew her. That she died defending others.

What burst from Jaina's lips was, "I'm sorry. I'm so, so sorry." And for several long moments, it was the Sparkshines who gave Jaina Proudmoore comfort. They sat back down at the table, talking of Kinndy, wanting to be farther along in the healing process than any of them were.

"I've asked the Kirin Tor for help," Jaina said, her feelings too raw to continue speaking of her apprentice. "I'm hoping they will join the Alliance and attack Orgrimmar. To stop anyone else from—from ending up like Kinndy."

Windle glanced away for a moment, and Jaina realized he was listening to the chimes sounding the hour. Before she could apologize for keeping them so long, the gnome mage had slipped off his chair. "It's nine o'clock."

"Oh, yes," Jaina said, remembering. "You light all the streetlights in Dalaran. I should let you be about it."

The little mage swallowed hard, and his bright eyes grew even brighter with tears. "Come with me on my rounds," he said. "I've gotten . . . special permission. Only for a time, but . . . it helps."

Jaxi shooed them both along with a faint glimmer of her old self. "I've gone with him before," she said. "I think it's right you should go."

Jaina was utterly confused but still so racked with guilt and pain that she was more than ready to do whatever the Sparkshines asked of her. So she followed Windle out, keeping her steps slow and short so she didn't outpace him.

He shuffled outside and stood beneath one of the lamps,

then drew out a small wand with an almost childish-looking star on the end. Then, with more grace than she expected, he pointed the wand at the lamp.

A spark flew from the tip, dancing around like a firefly. It did not light the streetlamp immediately. Instead, the glowing magical flame began to draw lines in the space above the lamp. Jaina's eyes widened, then filled with tears.

The golden light was tracing the shape of a laughing gnome girl with pigtails. When the sketch was done, it came to life for a moment, small hands covering a giggling mouth, and Jaina could have sworn she heard Kinndy's voice. She glanced down with blurred vision at Windle and saw that the gnome, too, wept, though his eyes crinkled in a loving smile. Then the golden lines broke apart and re-formed into a larger ball of light, darting under the shade of the lamp. This lamp lit, Windle turned and trudged toward the next. Jaina stayed where she was, watching once more as Windle Sparkshine paid tribute to his murdered daughter, letting her "live" for a little while each night. No doubt when the tragedy had faded in others' eyes, Windle would be asked to light the lamps in the usual fashion. But for now, everyone in Dalaran had a chance to see Kinndy as Jaina and her parents had—bright and sparkling, her face alight with laughter.

The summons to return to the Chamber of the Air was not too long in coming. For the third time, Jaina stood in the center of the strange but beautiful room, regarding the council with enforced calmness.

"Lady Jaina Proudmoore," Khadgar said, "before I tell

you our verdict, know this: We utterly condemn the attack on Theramore with all our hearts, down to a member. It was cowardly and despicable. The Horde will learn of our displeasure and be cautioned against the usage of such wanton destruction. But this is a troubled time indeed. Especially for those of us who wield and would regulate and manage magic. A short time ago, we chose to offer our expertise and wisdom. We even agreed to help defend Theramore. Because of that decision, we were betrayed by one of our own and lost several fine magi, including our leader, Archmage Rhonin. Magic is in a dire state in this world now, Lady. No one is sure who's supposed to be doing what. The blues no longer have an Aspect; they have lost a precious artifact that has been used for destruction; and we don't even have a leader to guide us or take responsibility."

Jaina felt a cold sensation in the pit of her stomach and fought to keep her hands from clenching. She knew what they were about to say.

"We can't take care of Azeroth if we are in disarray ourselves," Khadgar said. "We've got to reform, examine just what exactly went wrong. We can't give what we don't have, Lady. And what we don't have is any real sense of what needs to happen next. You've come to ask us to throw the full force of our magi behind the Alliance. You've asked us to transport Dalaran to Orgrimmar and rain destruction down upon an entire city. We can't do that, Jaina. We simply can't. We've only just figured out we're grown-up enough to deal with having Horde representatives among us, Sunreavers, and now you want us to destroy Orgrimmar? The world would erupt in civil war, and our part in it would ensure this very city, which has endured so much, would also be divided. And even if we weren't, even if Dalaran and the Kirin Tor were in a state where we could handle this, there are merchants and craftsmen and innkeepers and travelers who never marched on Theramore. For pity's sake, there's an orphanage in Orgrimmar, my lady! We can't—we won't—obliterate innocents."

Jaina had to take a moment to make her voice steady enough to speak. "The orphans there will grow up to become Horde," she said. "They are being taught to hate us, to plot against us. There are no innocents in that Light-forsaken city, Khadgar. There are no innocents anywhere. Not anymore."

Before Khadgar could speak, she had conjured the portal. The last thing she saw before she stepped through was his young-old eyes filled with sorrow.

Jaina did not go far. Her destination was the main library. She had been here before, long ago, when she had lived and studied in Dalaran. As she crossed the threshold in the company of one of the Kirin Tor librarians, she felt the very air of the place brush against her body, then subside. In years past, she had cast a recognition spell in order to enter safely; the library wards still remembered her.

The librarian respected her request to be alone to peruse the books. He, as Khadgar had, looked at her with sad, sympathetic eyes. She did not want his sympathy, but she was willing to use it for her own purposes. Her request for solitude in this vast storehouse of books and scrolls had nothing to do with her alleged desire for quiet and reflection.

Once the sound of his footfalls had died away and she was certain she would not be disturbed, Jaina turned her attention to the books. It was a daunting task, to be certain. The room was enormous and filled with shelf after shelf that towered high into the air. Jaina knew from experience there was no real order here; chaos and illogical filing methods would help to confound more mundane thieves yet be no hindrance to magic.

She flicked her right hand. A small radiance appeared at the tips of the fingers, and she pressed the glowing digits to her temples for a moment. Then she extended her hand. The faint light-purple radiance left her fingers, like a tiny tendril of fog, and rose to the topmost shelf. While Jaina examined copies of books and read the labels of scroll cases with more ordinary senses, the arcane mist was seeking something else.

Time passed. Jaina found many tomes that, in the past, she could have happily curled up with for days. Now they held no interest for her. She was single-minded and pure of purpose. Title by title she read and discarded. This was Dalaran. It had to be here.

There came a sudden flash in the corner of her eye and she turned, smiling. The little arcane mist had accomplished its task. It had found something on a shelf that contained some of the library's rarest tomes, the most dangerous, the ones that were carefully locked with magical seals. Even the ones that weren't visible.

Jaina quickly scanned the titles. *Dreaming with Dragons: The True History of the Aspects of Azeroth. Death, Undeath, and In Between. What the Titans Knew.*

The Sixth Element: Additional Methods of Arcane Augmentation and Manipulation.

Gently, she placed her hand on the spine of the book. It felt as if she were touching a living thing. It almost . . . quivered beneath her questing fingers. She pulled it out, and immediately it began to glow violet as the protective wards hummed. Jaina gasped and nearly dropped the book as an image formed, made of purple smoke.

Archmage Antonidas's visage peered at her, stern and cautionary. "This is not for idle hands, nor prying eyes," the familiar, loved voice said. "Information must not be lost. But it must not be used unwisely. Stay your hand, friend, or proceed—if you know the way."

Jaina bit her lip as Antonidas's visage faded. Each mage who consigned a book to the great library put his or her own warding seal on it. That meant that Antonidas had discovered this book, probably before Jaina was even born, and placed it on this shelf. Judging by the dust, it had not been disturbed since. Was it a sign of some sort? That she was meant to find this?

The book continued to glow. She did not know the proper words to open it easily and so had to resort to a less pleasant method. She could force the seals to break, but she would have to act swiftly to avoid setting off magical alarms. Jaina sank into one of the comfortable chairs and placed the book on her lap. She took a deep, steadying breath and cleared her mind. Gazing at her right hand, she murmured an incantation of shattering. Her hand suddenly glowed bright purple.

Now she lifted her left hand and concentrated. The hand began to fade before her eyes, visible only because it was limned with pale violet light.

This could work, but only if she was very fast. She took another steadying breath, then placed her right hand down on the book.

Shatter.

The violet glow emanating from her hand danced and crackled over the book like lightning. She could feel it breaking the magical seal Antonidas had placed on the book, feel it . . . *hurt* as it was unwillingly forced open. She stared, not daring to blink. The very instant that the violet lightning started to subside, she slammed her left hand over the tome.

Silence.

A field flared to bright white life, encircling the book, silencing the magical cry it emitted. Slowly, the glow on both hands faded, and her left one gradually became visible.

She'd done it.

Quickly and carefully, mindful of the book's age, Jaina began to leaf through it. There were all kinds of illustrations of magical items. Jaina didn't recognize most of them. It seemed that many things had been lost to time and—

There it was. The Focusing Iris. She began to read, skimming over the compelling but now unnecessary details as to how the blue dragons had created it and the various things it had been used for. She didn't care what it had done. She knew firsthand what it had done. She wanted to know what could be done with it now.

. . . amplification. Any and all arcane commands will be augmented by proper directional usage of the object. In keeping with this author's theory that the arcane is an element unto itself, he humbly offers the fact that there is at least one documented occasion wherein the Focusing Iris was utilized to enslave, direct, and control various elemental beings.

Jaina felt almost giddy. She rose and looked around, making certain she was still alone in the vast chamber. Then, carefully, she wrapped the book in her cloak and moved swiftly out the door and down the steps. She had one more visit left to make in this city before she departed on what was looking to be a solitary venture of revenge.

23

I t had been Jaina herself who had designed the statue.
She had covered the costs and selected the artist. Now
Antonidas supervised the city he had given his life to
protect. The image of her friend had a spell cast upon it so
that it hovered about six feet off the grass. Below it was a
plaque:

ARCHMAGE ANTONIDAS, GRAND MAGUS OF THE KIRIN TOR
THE GREAT CITY OF DALARAN STANDS ONCE AGAIN—
A TESTAMENT TO THE TENACITY AND WILL OF ITS
GREATEST SON. YOUR SACRIFICES WILL NOT HAVE
BEEN IN VAIN, DEAREST FRIEND.
WITH LOVE AND HONOR, JAINA PROUDMOORE

Jaina now stood on the soft green grass and looked up
at her friend. The sculptor had been talented, able to capture Antonidas's combination of sternness and kindness.
In one hand ceaselessly turned a small orb, sparkling with
magic. In the other, Antonidas bore his greatstaff, Archus.

Jaina still kept the book hidden in her cloak, lest some
sharp eye spy it. She placed a hand on it as it lay, solid and
reassuring, wrapped in the fabric.

The memories flowed easily and, for the most part, painlessly here, in the shadow of her mentor's statue. This man had seen so much promise in her and had taught her with cheer, enthusiasm, and pride. She remembered long conversations with him about esoteric matters and the finer points of magic, such as the positioning of one's fingers and the angle of one's body. At that time, both she and he had been certain that in Dalaran she would progress far, even rise high in the Kirin Tor. And the beautiful city would be her home.

The soft smile that had touched her lips faded. So much—too much—had happened. She clung to the hope that somehow her mentor had reached past the grasp of death to guide her to the book that would tell her precisely how to use the Focusing Iris. She hoped he would bless her endeavor. Surely he would, if he had seen what she had seen.

A gentle touch on her shoulder caused her to start and almost drop the cloak-wrapped book. She caught it at the last second and turned.

"I'm sorry, I didn't mean to startle you," Kalecgos said.

Paranoia gripped her. "How did you know I was here?" she asked, trying to keep her tone light and casual.

"I returned to the Nexus, after we . . . after you left. I sensed your arrival here in Dalaran from there." His blue eyes were unhappy. "I think I can guess why you've come."

She looked away. "I came to ask for help from the Kirin Tor. Help to fight the Horde after what they did to Theramore. They refused me."

He hesitated, then said quietly, "Jaina . . . I went to Theramore too. If the bomb fell on the city, and we know it did, then the Focusing Iris should have been there as well. It was gone."

"I'm willing to bet the Horde sent someone to retrieve it," Jaina said. "I fought several of them."

"That's likely," he said in agreement.

"Can you still sense it?" she asked.

"No. But I would definitely know if it had been destroyed. So that means that once again, it appears that a powerful mage is hiding it from me—and doing an even better job this time. And as we have so tragically seen, if it still exists, it can be used to do great harm in this world."

So . . . her shielding spell had worked. "Then you'd better be about finding it." She disliked lying to him, but she knew he wouldn't understand. Or . . . would he? If he had been to Theramore . . . seen what she had seen . . . maybe he shared her feelings.

"Kalec—the Kirin Tor won't help me. You once said you would fight for me—for the lady of Theramore. Theramore's gone. But I'm still here." Impulsively she reached out and grasped his hand. He held hers tightly. "Help me. Please. We have to destroy the Horde. They won't stop with just this, and you know it."

She could see the struggle in his soul reflected on his face and understood how deeply he truly cared for her. As, she was coming to realize, she cared for him. But this was no time for the gentle sweetness of courtship, of romance. There was no room for love when the Horde still existed, was able to do such hideous things. She needed every weapon she could find, and regardless of her own desires, Jaina knew she had to make her heart turn to steel.

"I can't do that, Jaina," he said, and his voice was raw with pain. "This implacable . . . well, hatred—it's not you. The Jaina I knew still sought peace. Still tried to understand, even as she prepared to defend her people. I can't believe you truly want to perpetuate the same horror on them as they did to Theramore. No sane mind, no good heart, should ever wish that on anyone."

"So, you think I've gone insane?" she said lightly but angrily. She drew her hand back.

"No," he said, "but you are too close to the situation to judge your next course of action wisely. I think you would be acting out of pain, out of anger. No one blames you for feeling that way. But you mustn't act when you are in this irrational state of mind! I know you, and I believe you'd come to regret it."

She narrowed her eyes and stepped back. "I know you care for me, and you mean what you say in the kindest way possible. But you're wrong. This *is* me. This is who the Horde *made* me when they dropped that cursed bomb on my city. You don't want to help me? You don't hear the voices that cry out for justice? Fine. Don't help me. But whatever you do, do *not* get in my way."

He bowed low as she turned and strode off, clutching the book—the book that Antonidas had warded, the book that would help her let the dead rest in peace, the book that would give her the power to make the Horde taste what it had done—to her heart.

The inn at Razor Hill was raking in the revenue, and the innkeeper, Grosk, didn't mind at all. Razor Hill had always been a rough-and-tumble town, populated as it usually was with soldiers and transients who never stayed long. With so many coming in for meals and grog at all hours while the celebrating continued in Orgrimmar, Grosk thought—as he made his usual halfhearted effort to "clean" the glasses—that it was about time he got some of the spillover from the capital city. If some of the talk wasn't all praise and approval, well, so what? There had been grumbling about Thrall, too. People loved to complain. Discontent, about the warchief, the weather, the wars, the other races of the Horde, the Alliance, one's mate—it was good for business. There was a reason visiting a bar was called "drowning one's sorrows."

So with his grungy little inn filled to capacity with all the races of the Horde, Grosk was feeling very good indeed about life.

Until the Kor'kron walked in.

They filled the door, making the dark building even darker as their mammoth forms blocked out the light. Frandis Farley, having a poor excuse for a drink with Kelantir Bloodblade, turned at the sight.

"Trouble," Kelantir whispered.

"Not necessarily," Frandis replied in an equally soft voice. Before his companion realized what he was about to do, the undead was waving and calling cheerfully, "Friend Malkorok! Are you slumming? The contents of a chamber pot are probably better than the swill this rascal Grosk serves, but it's cheap and I hear it does the job. Come, let us buy you a round."

The Kor'kron looked to their leader, who nodded. "Grosk," Malkorok rumbled, "drinks all around." He clapped Frandis on the back so hard the Forsaken nearly fell forward on the table. "I might expect to find tauren or Forsaken here." He sneered as Grosk busied himself plopping down dirty glasses and a large jug of grog. "But I must say, you look sorely out of place."

"Not at all," said Kelantir, narrowing her eyes. "I have been in worse places than this."

"Perhaps, perhaps," Malkorok said. "But why are you not in Orgrimmar?"

"Iron allergy," Kelantir said. For an instant, Malkorok stared at her; then he threw his head back in a guttural laugh.

"It does seem that you and several others prefer more rustic environments," he said. "Where is that young bull Baine, and his toady, Vol'jin? I had hoped to speak to them."

"I have not seen them in a while," said Kelantir, putting her boots up on the table. "I do not much involve myself with the tauren."

"Really?" Malkorok looked puzzled. "Yet we have witnesses that put both you and Frandis right in this very inn just last night, in close conversation with both the tauren and the troll, among others. They reported that you were saying things like, 'Garrosh is a fool, and Thrall should return and kick him all the way to the Undercity, and it was cowardly to use the mana bomb on Theramore.'"

"And the elements," put in another of the Kor'kron conversationally as he reached for the jug of grog and refilled his cup.

"Yes, the elements—something about how it was too bad Cairne hadn't killed him when he had the chance, because Thrall would never utilize the elements in such a cruel and insulting fashion."

The blood elf and the Forsaken were silent now. Malkorok pressed on. "But, if you say you haven't seen Baine or Vol'jin recently, then I suppose those witnesses must be mistaken."

"Clearly," said Frandis. "You need better informants."

"We must," Malkorok said in agreement, "for it's obvious to me that neither of you would ever say such things against Garrosh and his leadership."

"I'm glad you understand that," said Frandis. "Thanks for the drinks. Can I buy the next round?"

"No, we had best be on our way. See if we can find Vol'jin and Baine, since, unfortunately for us, they are not here." Malkorok rose and nodded. "Enjoy your drinks."

The two watched them go. When the Kor'kron had departed, Kelantir closed her eyes and exhaled.

"That was far too close for comfort."

"Indeed," said Frandis. "For half a moment, I expected to be arrested, if not outright attacked."

The blood elf turned to signal for more drinks, then frowned. "That is odd," she said. "Grosk is gone."

"What? With such a crowded inn? He should be hiring more help, not skipping out with several thirsty customers waiting on him."

Their eyes met. No word was spoken between them, but as one, they rose and charged for the door.

They almost made it until a frost grenade locked them into position. Three frag grenades finished the job, and Razor Hill Inn exploded.

King Varian Wrynn and Prince Anduin stood in a large, open chamber in Stormwind Keep known as the map room, due to the enormous raised map that occupied most of the space. Two braziers burned, warming the stone chamber. Weapons of war lined the walls, everything from blunderbusses to swords to even three cannons. There were areas piled high with books about military strategy, but for now, Varian and the others gathered here had their attention on the map.

Assembled were representatives of all the Alliance races. Emissary Taluun represented the draenei. Broll spoke for the night elves, and King Genn Greymane for the worgen of Gilneas. Present as well were the gnomes' high tinker, Gelbin Mekkatorque, and three dwarves, one from each of the dwarven clans: jovial Thargas Anvilmar of the Bronzebeards, the dour Dark Iron dwarf Drukan, and cheerful Kurdran Wildhammer. Differences seemed to be put aside for the moment—even Drukan was willing to speak with courtesy and listened with interest.

The blockade concerned them all, including those who hailed from the Eastern Kingdoms. No one could afford to turn a blind eye to the potential conquest of an entire continent.

Varian stood as if lost in thought. Broll cleared his throat. Varian looked up and gestured to indicate that Broll should speak, then seemed to return to his own musing.

"I will speak for my people and, I am certain, all those Alliance who suffer from this action of the Horde," said Broll. "And while it may seem self-centered to recommend that Darkshore be the first site to be liberated, I have an offer as well as a request. We have several vessels and the elves to crew them standing ready to assist as soon as we are given the chance. Despite the hardship wrought by the Cataclysm, it is still a major hub. We have shipping lanes that connect us with Rut'theran Village and Feathermoon Stronghold. Once we free up Darkshore, we will have an advantage."

"Our spies report that the Horde seems to think we'd choose Feathermoon Stronghold," said Greymane. He grinned a little. "I'm continuing to let them think that. Did you know that the Grimtotem of Feralas are planning an attack on the Horde? Taking advantage of their distraction? How terrible for the Horde!"

Chuckles went around the room. Still Varian frowned slightly as he looked at the map.

"They think Shandris Feathermoon dead, as far as we can tell," Broll said. "They see the conquest of Feathermoon Stronghold to be more than a military victory—they see it, even more so, as a symbolic one. They will be in for a surprise when they find her at the head of her troops."

The mood sobered at once. Of all the brilliant warriors and tacticians sent to aid Theramore, only Shandris and Vereesa remained. So many had been lost. For all the passion in the room to strike back and halt the Horde's advance, there was still much grief.

"Has . . . has anyone . . . been to Theramore?" Gelbin asked quietly.

There was an awkward silence. "Lady Jaina," Anduin said.

"Yes indeed," said Gelbin, "and what a blessing that she still survives. Speaking of Lady Jaina, I assume there's a sound reason she's not here with us, strategizing today?"

"Lady Jaina is pursuing her own methods," Varian said, finally joining in the conversation. All eyes turned to him. "She is . . . too impatient to work with us. And I cannot pass judgment. What she deals with—even I cannot truly know how she feels, although I have known similar pain."

"What happened at Theramore must never be allowed to happen again," said Taluun. "Not by any being. All sane people must deplore such acts and forswear them utterly, or else risk destroying the very things that make us able to touch the Light."

There were murmurs of agreement. Varian looked at Anduin and nodded, almost imperceptibly. The boy's blue eyes had gone sad when talk of Jaina had come up, but now they crinkled slightly at the edges with a wan smile.

"I agree," Varian said. "But Lady Jaina may be right about one thing. I've spent a lot of time thinking about this, and . . . I believe we should not attempt to break the blockade. Not yet."

A chorus of surprised voices filled the room, protesting, some courteously, some angrily. Varian lifted his hands. "Hear me out," he said, raising his voice slightly to be heard above the din but not quite shouting. The others fell silent, looking unhappy.

He continued. "Wisdom would dictate that we do as Broll and Genn suggested: misdirect the Horde to think we are attacking the blockade at Feathermoon Stronghold, and then target Darkshore. Break the blockade, liberate the trapped elven fleet, then go on from there with more ships and soldiers."

"Wisdom would," said Drukan in agreement, disgruntled.

"I think instead we let 'slip' our plan to attack Darkshore, not Feathermoon Stronghold. It'll be all the more readily believed since we've already put out a false trail. Garrosh will order the bulk of his navy there. We, meanwhile, sail directly toward Orgrimmar. Attack Garrosh in his own capital. I have spies as well, Genn, and they tell me that not all are happy with Hellscream as their leader. It is . . . hard for me to believe, but there are some Horde who are as appalled at what happened in Theramore as we are. We take Garrosh and occupy the city. Chaos will erupt, and with any luck, the discontented among the Horde will see this as their moment to rise up. If not, then we still have disarray and hold their capital city."

"Our people suffer, Varian," said Broll quietly.

Varian softened. "I know, my friend," he said. "But this is a chance to cut the head off the beast. Regardless, the

Horde ships will leave Darkshore and come to the aid of Orgrimmar."

"It sounds like madness," said Genn, growling a little and looking at Varian with narrowed eyes. "But the audacity and unexpectedness of it—it just might work."

"It will save time as well," said Taluun. "It is faster to reach Orgrimmar than Darkshore."

Varian looked around. A few still seemed unhappy, but no one was protesting anymore. He hoped that he was right. If Garrosh found out what was being planned, or if for some other reason this attack failed, then he would lose nearly the whole of the Alliance fleet. All that would be left would be the elven ships still trapped in Darkshore and elsewhere.

But he couldn't shake the sense of rightness he had about it. And that was what made a king—the willingness to make decisions and bear the responsibility for either success or failure.

The ships in the harbor were finally ready. More had come to join them, exquisite elven and draenei vessels that had fortunately been traveling elsewhere when the blockade had been enacted, no less formidable for their grace and beauty than the more practical human-, dwarf-, and gnome-crafted ships. The cluster of proud vessels filled the harbor to overflowing and seemed to reach all the way to the horizon.

The docks were thronged with citizens. Most of them were from Stormwind itself, but many others had traveled to participate in this historic occasion. It was a sea of living beings next to the sea itself, Varian thought, and wondered how many of those gathered to see their loved ones off would have the joy of welcoming them home safely.

The weather could not have cooperated more fully. It was a bright day with blue skies and sufficient wind to harness but not enough to make the sea rough. A band played cheerful, inspirational martial music, and traditional anthems of each country and race to remind everyone that they belonged.

For all the air of celebration, as he scanned the faces in the crowd, Varian saw that there were somber expressions, even tears. This was war, not a mere skirmish with the soldiers back for supper. He had planned for it as best he could and was going himself to lead the troops, although his nobles had tried to convince him to remain. He could not send men and women off to face death without standing shoulder to shoulder with them. And when he walked out to the third tier of the harbor, beneath the great statue of the lion of Stormwind, the gathered populace cheered. For they knew he was one of them.

He lifted his arms as he marched out, with Broll, Greymane, Mekkatorque, Taluun, and the three Ironforge dwarves accompanying him. Banners of all colors were waved. Varian lowered his arms, calling for silence.

"Citizens of the Alliance," he said, his voice carrying to the eager listeners, "only a handful of days ago, the Horde perpetrated an act of villainy so calculated, so heinous, that it could only be answered by a call to war. And you have answered. You stand before me, ready to fight and die if need be, in order to preserve what is decent and good in this world. It is the Horde who started this war, not we . . . but by the Light, we will finish it!"

The crowd roared. Tears glinted on faces, but those faces were smiling.

"The attack on Theramore cannot even properly be described. There are opponents, and there are enemies; there are civilized beings, and there are monsters. There was a time when I made no such distinction. But being able to now makes our path even clearer and more righteous. By choosing to detonate a mana bomb over a populous city—an abominable act of utter cowardice—Garrosh Hellscream has clearly demonstrated what he is. And as he and those who follow him have chosen to be monsters, we will treat them thus."

He continued. "We will never retaliate in kind. For we choose differently. But we will fight. We will stop them so they cannot continue their methodical conquest. We will embody all the Alliance stands for, and we will do so united. I stand here not alone today, but with King Genn Greymane. His people have turned a curse into a gift. The worgen will battle with greater hearts than you have ever seen—proving that they, unlike our foes, are not monsters. Without the aid of our dwarven and gnomish brothers and sisters, these glorious vessels could never have been built in time to save the rest of Kalimdor from falling to the Horde. The kaldorei, long our allies and to whose aid we go, already have many ships waiting to join us as they fight to free themselves. And the draenei, who have been as sure a compass of righteousness as any that could be imagined since their arrival in our world, stand here ready to spill their blood for others."

He stepped back and spread his hands, indicating that the crowd should show its appreciation. His own could not have been more sincere. Never had Varian been more appreciative of both true friends and level heads. For long,

long minutes, there was no sound but the cheering of grateful people.

Varian resumed his position. "As is common knowledge, I will be with our brave marines as we depart today. I leave behind one who is worthy to lead you, if need be. One who has already led before."

Varian nodded. Anduin, who had been standing off to the side behind one of the massive cannons until he was called, stepped forward. The prince was dressed in the blue and yellow colors of the Alliance, a simple silver circlet atop his golden head, and was flanked by two draenei paladins resplendent in their glowing armor. And although he was much smaller than they, he was the one all eyes focused on. He was greeted by cheers and applause, and blushed a little; he was not used to public appearances. He lifted his arms, encouraging the crowd to quiet, and began to speak.

"I fear I will never be one to send off men and women into battle with joy," he said. "Even though there could scarcely be a more just reason for doing so. The Horde has acted against us in a manner too terrible to ignore. All who believe in justice and decency must take a stand against the horrors of Theramore." Varian, listening intently, recalled how the aftermath had been described, how it had turned Jaina from a rational, compassionate woman into someone who wanted—nay, hungered for—violence and revenge.

"If we do not act *now*—if these brave soldiers and sailors of the Alliance do not set forth *now*—then we condone what was done. We encourage, even invite, more violence, more slaughter of the innocent. Garrosh Hellscream has said bluntly that he wishes to drive out the Alliance from the entire continent of Kalimdor. We cannot meekly accept this. There comes a time when even the kindest heart must say, 'No, enough.' And that time has come."

He lifted his hands and closed his eyes. "And to prove the rightness of what we do, the purity of the purpose for which this fleet now sets sail . . . I call upon the blessed Light to touch all who would sacrifice to protect the innocent."

A soft light began to glow around his raised hands. It moved to envelop his body and then rose to hover above the crowd, showering down upon those who were prepared to fight and those who loved them.

"I pray that you fight with courage, and decency, and honor! I pray that your weapons be guided by the justness of what you do. I urge you to remember, as you go into the heat of battle, to refuse to allow hate entrance into your heart. Keep it a sanctuary, a temple to the memory of those so tragically slain. Remember at each moment you are fighting for justice, not genocide. Victory, not vengeance. And I know, I know with all my being, that if you go into battle with these things so firmly in your heart that no anger, no pain, can shake them, we will triumph. Blessings on you, soldiers of the Alliance!"

Varian felt the Light brush him almost like a physical thing. It seemed to caress him, to enter his heart, as Anduin had said. He felt calmer, stronger, more peaceful.

He watched his boy speak with the pure passion of his soul, watched how swiftly and sweetly the Light came to bless him. Saw how the people loved him.

Oh, my son, you are already the best of all of us. What a king you will make.

A horn sounded. It was time to embark. Everywhere were families making their farewells—older couples with grown children, fresh-faced youths saying good-bye to sweethearts. Then the milling throngs moved slowly toward the vessels. Handkerchiefs waved; kisses were blown.

Varian waited and smiled a little as Anduin, flanked by his two paladin friends, moved toward the flagship.

"You spoke well, Son," Varian said.

"I'm glad you think so," Anduin replied. "I spoke only what was in my heart."

Varian placed a hand on the youth's shoulder. "What was in your heart was perfect. I was and am very proud of you, Anduin."

An impish grin lit up the prince's face. "You don't think I'm a mewling pacifist anymore?"

"Ah, that's not fair," Varian said. "And no, I don't. I'm glad you realized the necessity of what we have to do."

Anduin sobered. "I do," he said. "I wish it were otherwise, but it's not possible. I'm—I'm just glad you're not like Jaina is. I've prayed for her, too."

Of course he had. "Anduin—this war we both think we have to fight—you know I might not come back."

He nodded. "I know, Father."

"And if I don't—you are more than ready to take my place. I know you'll rule well and justly. Stormwind could not be in better hands."

Anduin's eyes grew shiny. "Father—I—thank you. I would do my very best to be a good king. But . . . I'd just as soon not be for a very long time."

"Me too," said Varian. He pulled the boy into a tight, awkward embrace, pressed his forehead down to Anduin's, then turned and lightly ran down to the ships. He merged with the flood of sailors and headed to the flagship.

And to war.

24

Kalec flew with a heavy heart. He was terribly afraid that Kirygosa had been right about Jaina. Dragons did not have the ability to read minds, but Jaina's attitude when the Focusing Iris came under discussion was more than suspicious. He was almost certain now that she had absconded with the artifact herself and was intending to use it on her enemies as they had used it upon her. Reinforcing this unhappy conclusion was the fact that the Focusing Iris was once again hidden, even more expertly than it had been before. It was a bitter thought. He wanted to believe that the change he saw in this woman for whom he cared so deeply was due to the effect of the arcane energy of the bomb. But even if that was partially true, Kalec knew it could not explain everything.

So it was that he was returning, to the Nexus, to speak with his flight. And . . . he realized he wanted to go home.

He noticed as he approached that no one was wheeling protectively about the Nexus, as dragons had done from time immemorial. The sight saddened him further. He decided not to land immediately, but instead to speak with one who might have either balm for his soul or difficult words he would need to hear.

He found Kirygosa at her "pondering place," where he had been speaking with her when the news of the theft had first reached them. She did not seem surprised as she saw him approach. As before, she had opted for her human form, leaning against the shining tree, not feeling the cold even though she wore a light, sleeveless blue dress.

He landed on the hovering platform, transforming into his own bipedal form, and took the hand she extended to him as he sat beside her.

They didn't speak for a long time. Finally Kalec said, "I saw no one patrolling."

Kirygosa nodded. "Most of them are gone now," she said. "Each day, someone decides that his or her home is no longer here."

Kalec closed his eyes in pain. "I feel like I've failed, Kiry," he said softly. "Failed at everything. Failed as a leader, failed to recover the Focusing Iris, failed Jaina . . . failed to even realize how badly wounded she was by what happened at Theramore."

Her blue eyes held no hint of pleasure as she looked at him. "She has it, then?"

"I do not know. I can't really sense it anymore, not distinctly. But . . . I think she might."

She knew what the words cost him and squeezed his hand. "For what it is worth, I do not think you were wrong to have loved her. Or to love her still. Your heart is great, but it must also be wise."

"You know," he said, attempting to interject levity, "there are those who have said that you and I would be a good match. Prevent me from going after the wrong sorts of females."

Kiry did laugh at that, resting her head on his shoulder. "I do not deny that you will make a fine mate for someone one day, Kalecgos, but it is not me."

"And there goes my last hope of being a normal dragon."

"I am glad every day that you are not," she said, and his heart felt full with the affection in her eyes. He did love her—but not as a mate. He sighed, and the melancholy resettled upon him. "Oh, Kiry, I have lost my way. I don't know what to do."

"I think you know exactly what to do, and you know your path," she said. "You stand at a crossroads, my dear friend. As do we all. Either the blues need you to lead them well and wisely . . . or they need to be free to find their own paths, be the leaders of their own lives. Do we truly have a purpose higher than our duties to ourselves? Perhaps the younger races, too, have the right to be the leaders of their own lives. Make their own choices . . . and live with the consequences."

As Garrosh did, Kalec thought. *As Jaina is preparing to do.*

"Changes," he murmured, recalling what he had once said to Jaina. *There is a rhythm, a cycle to such things. Nothing stays the same, Jaina. Not even dragons, so long-lived and supposedly so wise.*

Supposedly.

"Where will you go?" he asked quietly, in those four words telling Kirygosa of his choice.

"I have not explored the world as you have," she said. "I am told there are oceans that are warm, not filled with ice. Breezes that are sweetly scented, not brisk and chill. I think I should like to see those places. Find a different pondering place."

There was no more need for words. She rose, as if she

had been waiting only to hear him release her. He too got to his feet, and they embraced tightly.

"Farewell for now, dear Kalec," she said. "If you ever have need of me, search for me in tropical climes."

"And if you have need of me, go to the most unlikely place you can think of for a dragon to be. I'm sure I'll be there."

His chest ached as he watched her change, catch the wind beneath her wings, and soar upward, wheeling for a moment in farewell and then heading south.

A half an hour later, Kalecgos stood alone at the top of the Nexus. His old adversary-turned-friend Teralygos had been the last one to leave. He headed northeast; unlike Kirygosa, the still peace of the cold lands, the traditional home of the blues, was what the elderly dragon craved.

None of the other dragons had been surprised at his decision; none of them seemed to blame him. Change. It had come, and all the struggling and resistance in the world, all the protesting, all the wishing for things to be the way they used to be—it was all futile. Change would come. What would it do to him, the sole citizen of a now-empty kingdom? Where did his path lie?

All things change, Jaina, whether from the inside out or the outside in. Sometimes with only a single shift in a variable, he had once said to the woman he fell in love with.

And . . . we are magic, too, she had replied.

"Yes," he murmured. "We are."

And he knew what he had to do.

Jaina had done what she could to disguise herself and had traveled by the usual methods to Ratchet rather than simply teleporting. Once there, she bought a gryphon from a traveler who seemed down on his luck and flew south. She fully realized that she was flying over the path the Horde had taken to march on Northwatch, and she let that bitter knowledge fuel her anger.

When the ruins of Northwatch Hold, now occupied by the Horde, came into view, she had to choke back a lump in her throat. The sight of the red-and-black banners of the Horde soldiers left behind to guard while the rest of the ships formed the blockade turned the pain cold.

She brought the gryphon to the earth and dismounted, taking care to hold the small pouch she always carried close to her. She then gave the gryphon a smart smack on his leonine rump. He flapped upward in irritation, and Jaina nodded. He would soon find his way back to Ratchet and a new rider, who would be very pleased at having him. Jaina had no further need of the beast. She turned to the east and murmured a teleportation spell. A few seconds later, Jaina arrived on Fray Island.

"Eh there, missy," said a rough voice. The human addressing her had cutoff breeches, an open shirt, and a cutlass. "Come to play with the pirates, have ye?"

She turned her glowing white eyes to him. "I've no time for this," she said. Almost absently, she directed a fireball at the thug. He screamed as his whole body caught fire, stumbled a few feet, and then fell, writhing.

Jaina was unmoved by the sight, turning her attention to the fellow's comrades as they rushed up, shouting angrily. They were not Horde—not all of them—but they were cutthroats and murderers and deserved no one to mourn them. Ruthlessly Jaina marched through the encampment, blasting her would-be killers with fire, ice, and arcane energy. She slew humans and trolls, dwarves and an ogre, who looked ridiculous with a tiny hat perched on his bald pate.

She scoured the buildings clean, so that she would have no distractions. Jaina turned toward the north. Her hand slipped down into the pouch and held the Focusing Iris—perfectly miniaturized, thanks to information gleaned from perusal of the tome she had stolen from the Dalaran library—and began to make her plans.

The Earthen Ring was exhausted. The elements seemed angrier today than usual, and while no one spoke the words aloud, Thrall was certain that he was not the only one to wonder if their efforts were starting to have less effect.

It did not make any sense. Progress had been very slow, it was true, but it had been measurable and consistent. The weary shaman retreated back to their encampment, in need of food and rest. Muln Earthfury, as the former leader of the Earthen Ring, seemed to be the most affected.

Aggra watched the tauren, frowning a little. "The silence troubles me," she said. "We all think the same thing, but no one speaks it. Come, let us talk to Muln."

Thrall smiled and shook his head. "We think along the same lines, my heart, but always you press for action first."

She shrugged. "Growing up in Nagrand will teach you to act quickly when you see trouble," she said, squeezing his hand as they walked.

Muln looked over at the two orcs and sighed. "I already know what you are going to say," he said. "And I do not know the answer as to why we seem to be backsliding. The elements are so distressed, and have been for so long, it is hard to hear them clearly anymore."

Thrall said, "Perhaps we should—"

Pain shot through him and he fell to his knees, clutching his skull.

Aggra dropped beside him, hands on his shoulders. "Go'el, what is it?" she cried.

His lips moved, but nothing came out. Aggra's face faded away. Thrall saw nothing for a moment, and then suddenly, he saw too much.

Water, blue-green and cold and angry, crashed over him. He choked, gasped, struggled to breathe. It lifted him up and then thrust him under, tossed and turned him. It was a great wave, and yet—Thrall saw here and there small, furious eyes, the shape of an arm, a head, the glitter of a manacle. This was more than a simple ocean wave—Thrall was at the mercy of enslaved elementals.

He was not alone. There were dozens, hundreds, of orcs caught up in the wave as well, all struggling to survive. Debris, too, was a danger in addition to the water itself. A hand made of seawater pushed Thrall downward, and he saw below him—

The roofs of Orgrimmar! How was that possible? But he could see the gate, the debris of the iron scaffolding that he had heard Garrosh had erected.

Help us, voices whispered.

Thrall couldn't breathe. He felt water filling his lungs.

Help us. This is not what we wish to do!

He felt the watery hand holding him down tremble, as if it was struggling itself against something, and then release. Thrall shot to the surface, coughing and gasping in clean air.

Stop this. Or else your people will die while we slay them and grieve, and we will live forever in servitude.

Thrall gathered his wits and, still coughing, asked, "Where?"

No words filled his mind, but there was an image: a chunk of land off the coast of the Northern Barrens. It was a long way from Orgrimmar, but what did the point of origin matter to the ocean, which touched all shorelines?

"Go'el," said the beloved voice, calling him back to the present. "Go'el!"

The horrifying image of drowned corpses and a ruined city faded. Thrall blinked, feeling a surge of relief at seeing Aggra's face instead of the vision—for such it had to be. She smiled and stroked his cheek.

"What did you see, my friend?" asked Muln. Others had gathered around now. Thrall struggled to rise, but Muln pushed him down. "Rest and speak—then rise and eat."

Thrall nodded. "You are right, of course, Muln," he said. "The elements granted me a vision. This may explain why they have grown so suddenly distressed." Quickly, succinctly, but leaving out no important detail, Thrall recounted what he had seen.

"Do you know the island?" asked Nobundo.

"I do," he said. "It is Fray Island, located due south of Durotar."

The shaman exchanged glances. "If the elements cry out so poignantly for aid, we must answer," said Muln.

But Nobundo shook his head. "No," he said. "If they wished aid from us all, we would all have had the vision. They know we cannot leave here. But . . . they did call for help."

Thrall nodded slowly. Aggra looked pained but resigned. "They spoke to me," he said. "And me alone. So it is I who must answer their cry and stop this slaughter of my people. Aggra, beloved, you know I would have you with me, but . . ."

She smiled around her tusks. "The task is yours, Go'el," she said, "and I will strike anyone who dares say in my presence you are not up to it."

He smiled wanly. "Up to it" indeed. Up to freeing hundreds of enslaved water elementals so that they did not eradicate an entire city? He hoped so. The elements were wise; he would trust them. Thrall got to his feet, embraced his mate, then headed to his small tent to pack what little he would need for the journey.

Vol'jin had had enough.

When word of the "accident" at Razor Hill Inn had reached him, he had seen it as a sign. He would risk no more "accidents" to his people. Long had he liked and trusted Thrall, and when that orc had urged him to stay with the Horde, he had agreed. Caution also had seemed to dictate such a choice, despite the insult Garrosh had offered him by forcing his people to live in the slums. Now the trolls were on the Echo Isles, and so too close for comfort.

But perhaps it was time for a withdrawal. Or at least time to plan for one. Garrosh and the "loyal" Horde—the ones who drank in taverns in Orgrimmar as opposed to Razor Hill—were still in the throes of self-congratulation for their despicable actions. The Kor'kron, or at least that filth Malkorok, had made it very clear that they were so convinced of ultimate victory that they were willing to eliminate those Horde members who dared speak against Garrosh in private and, presumably, public.

Under Thrall, the Horde had been good to the trolls.

But now—Vol'jin had lost many fine soldiers in the last two battles. And this was how he was repaid? No. Time to go home, at least for now, since home was so close; time to sink deep into meditation and see what the loa had to say. He recalled his words to Garrosh from some time ago, that the orc would spend his reign glancing over his shoulder—and that in his last moments, the warchief would know exactly who had killed him.

It seemed that the decision was the right one. Even before he reached the Echo Isles, he was met by a canoe. The shaman in the stern had his arms raised, and the water directly beneath the boat was moving faster than it should have; he was using the elements to bear him to his leader as swiftly as possible.

Vol'jin didn't even wait until the other boat pulled alongside him. Asking the loa to help him make his voice carry, he cried, "What is it, mon? What be wrong?"

The shaman answered, his voice borne to Vol'jin's long ears on the anxious wind, "Alliance! Dey comin'! A whole lot of dem!"

Garrosh roared in anger and threw his mug across the table. "Alliance? Here? Our intelligence said they were gathering at Darkshore!"

The hapless troll whose job had been to inform the warchief flinched slightly, although the mug had not been hurled in his direction. "I doan know about dat, Wahchief, but dey sure be closin' in on Bladefist Bay. Dere be dozens of ships. Whatchu wan' us to do?"

Garrosh recovered from his outburst almost immediately. "Tell Baine to send druids to every port that we are blockading. Our fleet needs to redirect immediately. And

Northwatch—order them here, every last ship! Now!"

And then, to the confusion of the troll messenger, a crafty smile crossed Garrosh's face. "And all the magi . . . bring them to me. The plan I have can work as well in Bladefist Bay as in Darkshore."

Varian stood on the deck of the *Lion of the Waves* as they approached Kalimdor. The draenei shaman had been doing a stellar job of imploring the wind and the waves for aid, and the fleet had crossed the ocean in record time with fair winds and calm seas. They were now but a few miles off the coast of Bladefist Bay. Varian was the leader of the Alliance forces but not the captain of the *Lion of the Waves*, and took care to let Telda Stonefist do her job. Indeed, it was an easy task—Telda knew what she was doing, and for all her small stature, every sailor jumped when she barked an order.

Now as Varian strode to stand beside her, the spray from the wind dampening both their hair, she handed him a spyglass. "There's yer first glimpse o' th' bay," she said.

Varian placed the instrument to his right eye. There was only one ship at the dock, though he knew the path through to Orgrimmar would be hard-fought. "Looks as if the single ship in the harbor is of goblin construction."

"Which means that one good shot should blow th' whole thing sky-high." Telda grinned.

Varian felt a tingle of unease. It was a remnant of Lo'Gosh, a heightening of all the senses, including those that went beyond the usual five. He turned to face into the briskly blowing wind, sniffing, and lifted the spyglass again to his eye. Only sea and sky, different shades of blue.

Slowly, he turned in every direction. Blue sea, blue sky . . .

Something that was not blue, a small speck on the horizon.

"There," Varian cried, pointing to the south. "Ships!"

Somehow, Garrosh had anticipated him.

"All hands, battle stations!" shouted Telda in a voice that seemed far too loud to have issued from such a short frame. Everyone jumped into action. Swiftly the well-trained marines leaped to the cannons. Magi climbed the rigging, the better to aim the devastating fireballs that wreaked such havoc on wooden sailing vessels. And the shaman rushed to the sides of the ship, more than any others putting themselves in harm's way, to urge the elements to assist them by showing they were willing to risk themselves as well.

The horns were sounded, and one by one, the ships that had been sailing due east swung about, ready to face the threat from the south. Varian scrambled up the rigging himself, holding on with one hand while bringing the spyglass to his eye.

There were several ships sailing steadily toward them, but the Horde was wildly outmatched. Varian nodded. He didn't know how Garrosh had expected them—perhaps a deep-sea fishing vessel had spotted the armada and hastened back to sound the alarm—but it didn't matter now. All that mattered was that the Horde had indeed focused on the blockade, and it was throwing all it had at the Alliance. Which was not much.

"Jaina," he murmured, quickly lowering himself to the deck, "you were right about one thing at least. Perhaps we can end this here and now."

At first, there was almost a giddy atmosphere. It was clear that the Horde had fallen for the disinformation spread by the Alliance spies and that its navy was busily engaged in guarding shores that would not come under attack. The few ships from Northwatch Hold were little more than practice targets. Bladefist Bay, still and quiet and nearly bored, now erupted into an ocean battlefield.

Heedless of his own safety, Varian climbed the rigging again and peered over the ocean. He could see a mere three or four ships, struggling in his direction as fast as they could. Their sails, too, billowed with wind; the Horde had had shaman far longer than the Alliance had and no doubt was demanding all they could give.

"Hard about port!" Telda shouted. Varian tightened his grip on the wet ropes as the ship swung hard to the left, turning to face the threat from the south. For a moment, he almost—almost—felt sorry for the crews in the ships the Alliance was about to blow out of the water.

"Fire!"

The *Lion of the Waves* was rattled by the sound of all its cannons exploding, disgorging their contents upon the enemy. Some cannonballs splashed harmlessly into the water, but most struck their target—the lead ship—dead on. Cheers went up as the side of the Horde vessel was nearly completely caved in.

And then the wood began mending itself. It would seem that in addition to experienced shaman, the crew of this ship also had skillful druids. Varian swore, climbed down swiftly, and dropped the rest of the way.

"Warlocks, at the ready!" he shouted. It was always uneasy when those who worked with demons were pressed into service for the good of the Alliance, but they had certain spells—and certain creatures in thrall—whose efficacy was undeniable. They hurried to the sides, their black and purple and other dark-hued robes flowing about them, and summoned their minions. As one, they lifted their arms and began to chant their ugly-sounding spells.

Fire rained down, steady and pervasive, on the already damaged ship. Small, cackling demons known as imps were sent to dance upon the enemy vessel, throwing fire hither and thither. The fact that they seemed to enjoy the destruction they wrought was an added bonus.

"Magi!" cried Varian, his eyes fastened on the Horde ship. Enormous fireballs joined the steady, deadly rain of flame. The cannons roared again, and the enemy vessel could take no more. It cracked in two, and Varian saw with satisfaction many Horde soldiers leaping frantically into the waters of the bay. Still more were going down with the ship.

The *Lion of the Waves,* victorious, swung slowly around. The shaman redirected the wind, and the ship bore down on its next target. "One doon; three tae go!" crowed Telda. "Come on, lads an' lassies! We'll be supping in Orgrimmar by sunset!"

And that was when a gray cloak fell over the ship.

Varian swore. This was shamanic doing. But already the warlocks were reacting, sending their glowing green orbs beyond the reach of the conjured fog and reporting back. One of them, a human woman seemingly too young for the shining white hair that draped over her shoulders, called to Varian, "Majesty—they're doing something in the ocean. It's churning fiercely. I can't quite make out what's going on."

More cannon fire, but this time, Varian didn't know which ships were doing the firing and which were being fired upon. And then there came a dreadful cracking sound—not the sound of ships buckling under cannon fire, but something new and horrible that was out there but unseen. And suddenly Varian understood that even though the Horde was vastly outnumbered, its forces were much more dangerous than he had anticipated.

25

It took time—more time than Jaina wanted to spend. But she needed to be thorough. Antonidas had taught her that. If you rushed through the studying of spells or their execution, you risked results where nothing happened—at best—or at worst, disaster. "It's every bit as dangerous as going into battle with a type of weapon you've never handled before," he had said, cautioning her.

So she sat on one of the small hills on Fray Island and reread everything the stolen tome could tell her about the Focusing Iris. She thought about what Kalec had shown her of magic, how it was logical and precise, and about what the book claimed, that arcane energy was so similar to an element it might as well be one, for all magical intents and purposes. As she read, Jaina would absently reach out to stroke the surface of the Focusing Iris, cool even in the hot sun.

She had already performed some experiments with the item, and successfully; its new, smaller size was testament to that. She restored it to its proper size and began other tests. She slept little and ate only conjured food. After two days of reining in her impatience, heartened by her success here, Jaina finally felt she was ready. She watched with narrowed eyes as the Horde sent most of its vessels from Northwatch Hold. Jaina expected they were going to Orgrimmar. The thought gave her pleasure.

Yes, go home, she thought.

She turned to face the ocean. The salty breeze stirred her white hair. Jaina centered herself, placing her hands on the Focusing Iris. If she understood correctly how the thing worked, it was a conduit—and, in the right hands, a magnifier—of arcane energy. She felt it tingling coldly. Then suddenly, a slender crack ran along its surface. And like an eye, it started to open.

Jaina gasped but did not break contact. As long as she was directing the flow of magic, it would obey her. There was a searing flash, and a beam of light shot outward from the Focusing Iris to the ocean.

With one hand on the Iris still, Jaina lifted the other and made the familiar motions of a certain spell.

Before, this spell had created a single elemental. Now, so quickly, there were ten. Ten shimmering, imprisoned water elementals standing on the surface of the sea, their eyes glinting, what served for their arms encased in manacles.

Jaina laughed. Then she made more. And more still, until there was scarcely any unenchanted water to be seen. Ordinarily such work would be beyond her, and if it were not, she would be quivering with exhaustion by this point. Instead, she felt as strong as when she had begun. The Focusing Iris did all the work for her. No wonder the Horde had coveted it, and no wonder Kalec had been so worried when it had been stolen.

For a brief moment, Jaina's concentration was elsewhere. The image of the blue dragon, beautiful to her in both his forms, appeared in her mind. She recalled his kindness, his laughter, how her heart had skipped a beat when he kissed her hand.

But it was only a moment. Grimly Jaina brought her attention back to the water elementals. There was no place for laughter and kindness in her world now. Not while a single orc yet breathed.

With little more than a thought and a twitch of her fingers, she re-formed those few elementals that had begun to lose cohesion due to her inattention. *Now to begin the binding.*

She had no spell for such a thing. To the best of her knowledge, it did not exist. But the Focusing Iris appeared not to be limited by such trivialities. Jaina concentrated hard on her intention, weaving her fingers in ways that came naturally to her.

And the Focusing Iris—and the elementals—obeyed.

They began to fuse together, thousands of them, not quite losing their shapes, but adapting to become part of a single, greater form. Jaina smiled. Her heart racing as she beheld her success, she wove them together even more. What had once been thousands of individual elementals, dancing on the top of the ocean, was now a single wave.

A tidal wave.

Higher it grew, and broader. Moving her hand in an upward gesture, Jaina caused the wave to rise. In the vast wall of water, she could still see individual eyes and enchanted manacles on watery arms. But they would not separate. Not while she bid them to stay together.

She took her time. It was no small distance from here to the tidal wave's ultimate destination. Jaina would need many elementals and would have to keep masterful control if she was to be successful. Finally, she was almost ready. A few more to gather up, another ten, perhaps twenty feet higher—

"Jaina!" said a voice, deep and rich and laced both with joy and pain.

The wave faltered as Jaina turned, keeping one hand still firmly on the Focusing Iris.

"Thrall!" Jaina shouted back. She deliberately did not use his "true name." "What are you doing here?"

The pleasure on his face faded. "I am so glad you live, my old friend. But I was called here . . . to stop you."

Old friend, he called her. That was what they were, wasn't it? Friends who had worked side by side, to stop wars, to save lives, both Horde and Alliance.

But they could be friends no longer.

The Doomhammer remained strapped across his back as he strode toward her, his arms outstretched imploringly. "I had a vision—of a tsunami unleashed on Orgrimmar. A tsunami that had its origins here. And so I came, as the elements begged me to, to stop this from occurring. In all my dreams and fears, I never thought to find you alive—and behind this horrible disaster about to happen. Please, Jaina—release them. Let them go."

"I can't," she said, and her voice cracked. "I have to do this, Thrall."

"I have heard about what happened to Theramore," Thrall said, still slowly approaching her. "I grieve with you at so many deaths in so brutal a fashion. But doing to Orgrimmar what the Horde did to Theramore—it won't bring anyone back, Jaina. All it will do is take more innocent lives."

"*You* grieve?" she snarled. "Theramore's destruction I lay firmly at your feet, Thrall! You left Garrosh in charge of the Horde! I begged you to come back, to remove him from power. I knew he would do something terrible one day, and he has. Garrosh may have done this—but I blame you for giving him the power to do it!"

Thrall stopped dead in his tracks, shocked by her words.

"Then—blame me, Jaina. Ancestors know, I blame myself. But do not seek to buy vengeance for the fallen of Theramore by killing my people!"

"*People?*" Jaina echoed. "I can't even call them that anymore. They're not *people*. They're *monsters*. And so are you! My father was right—it took an entire city of people slaughtered before I could see it. I was blind to what the orcs were, because of you. You tricked me into believing that there could be peace, that the orcs weren't bloodthirsty animals. But you lied. This is war, Thrall, and war *hurts*. War is ugly. But you started it! Your Horde obliterated Theramore and is now blockading the Alliance cities in Kalimdor. Whole populations are being held hostage, are being attacked. Well, as we stand here, Varian is leading the fight to break that blockade. And when I've completed my task, I'll help him. And then we'll see who holds whom hostage! But first—I destroy the city named for Orgrim Doomhammer, in the land named for your father!"

"Jaina! No, please, don't!"

With a smirk and a simple flick of her wrist, Jaina released the tidal wave.

A terrible sound, the cry of hundreds of enslaved elementals, shattered the air as the wave surged north.

"No!" cried Thrall. He shot out his arms desperately, pleading silently, *Spirit of air, hold them still! Do not let them be used to slay so many innocents.*

He reached in his pouch and touched the small carvings that represented the elements. Their essences manifested in glowing, pulsing images of these figurines. Such a totem appeared at his feet as air came willingly to his call, and the wind that suddenly sprang up wrapped itself around the writhing wave, attempting to restrain the tsunami.

Jaina growled and gestured. The elementals wailed in agony as they were forced to fight against the binding of the wind. Thrall grunted and found himself trembling with the strain. Jaina was a powerful mage, but she shouldn't have been strong enough to stand against him—especially not when it was the will of the elements themselves to resist her. Thrall had never seen the Focusing Iris, but he knew what it looked like. It had directed powerful surge needles that pulled arcane magic from Azeroth's ley lines to the Nexus; it had given life to a five-headed chromatic dragon. Now it was under the direction of a master mage.

Thrall sickly realized he had gotten things backward. The wonder lay not in the fact that Jaina was stronger than he was now. The wonder lay in the fact that he was able to resist her at all.

"Jaina," he said, the words coming out through teeth clenched with his body's strain, "your pain is justified. What was done was an atrocity. But the life breath of children should not be demanded for what Garrosh did!"

Her white head with the single gold lock turned to him. Her eerie eyes stared at him coldly. She splayed her fingers and shoved her hand forward. Thrall flew backward, slammed hard by something lavender-white and glowing. His world went gray for a second and he landed on his back on the sand, gasping for breath. His whole body shuddered, but he forced himself to rise and direct his energy toward holding back the tidal wave.

The attack had not been intended to loosen his hold over the elements. The attack had been meant to kill. Thrall could not bring himself to do that, not yet, not to Jaina, who had once been and might yet be a cherished friend. And thus he was handicapped in a way she was not.

Thrall asked the spirit of air for aid again. A gust of wind, raging at near-hurricane levels, blasted Jaina so fiercely that the mage stumbled backward, toppling to the sand. Her hand was torn from the Focusing Iris, and the whirling air snatched the words of command from her mouth.

Thrall used the precious seconds to direct his full attention to the towering wall of water. *Spirits of water, struggle against this spell that enslaves you. Take my strength; use it to—*

He heard and felt the heat behind him. Lamenting the need, he redirected his imploring from the spirits of water to a spirit of fire. Thrall whirled, his hands up to do what he could to protect himself from the massive fireball hurtling toward him. The spirit of fire was angry and tortured, and for a moment Thrall feared it would not hear him in time. Defensively he threw up three orbs of water that circled swiftly around him and granted him energy. Thrall could not help but close his eyes as he braced for the searing heat and pain. At the last second, the huge swirling ball seemed to fracture, flames going off in all directions. Only a very few struck the shaman, but those singed his robes and flesh painfully.

"I won't let you stop me!" Jaina shouted. She was on her hands and knees, crawling toward the Focusing Iris.

Before Thrall could react and disperse the groaning, straining elementals that composed the tidal wave, the mage slammed one hand down on the artifact, strengthening her spell. With the other, she twisted her fingers commandingly. Thrall was stunned as the two remaining globes of water were yanked from their protective orbit around him. They grew larger, magical bonds appearing on suddenly sprouted "arms," and then went to join their kindred—serving Jaina now. He realized that the artifact not only gave her own spells more power—it gave her power over his as well.

"Do you see, Thrall? Do you understand what you're up against?"

"I see, Jaina!" Thrall shouted back. He reinforced his totems and focused on keeping the tidal wave from being released. If only his words could reach her . . . "I see that you are broken and grieving. Don't let what Garrosh did to Theramore claim you as a victim too. I can help you!"

"Help me? Maybe you are helping Garrosh! How do I know that you aren't working with him? Maybe this has been your plan all along!"

So shocked was Thrall by the accusation that his spell faltered. The enormous tower of churning water elementals surged forward several yards. Thrall barely regained control of it by devoting his whole will to the task.

A huge pillar of fire suddenly appeared, whirling furiously and churning up sand as it bore down on Thrall. This he knew he could not dissipate, and nearly all his energy was being spent in holding back the crashing wave.

The wave—

Spirits of water, let me walk upon you, and embrace me!

He turned and raced from the sand onto the surface of the water, running as swiftly as if upon dry land. The orc headed straight for the huge, towering wave, thinking to use Jaina's own spells against her as she had used his against him. Just as he approached the quivering wall of water, he asked the element to hold him. He dropped like a stone into the ocean, and above his head, Jaina's pillar of fire crashed into her own tidal wave.

The fire was quenched at once and the wave severely weakened. Thrall dove deep, away from the churning chaos on the surface, and swam strongly back toward the shore. As he emerged from the sea, he saw Jaina frantically trying to repair the wave, creating more elementals and forcing them to merge.

Asking for the favor of the Spirit of Life, Thrall summoned two spectral beings—spirit wolves, transparent and misty, but every bit as dangerous as the more corporeal kind. He had created such manifestations before, but now, with the willing aid of the Spirit of Life, the wolves were even stronger. With howls that shivered along the air, the ghostly creatures sprang for Jaina, diverting her attention from her grim task.

"You just delay the inevitable," Jaina spat. She gestured, and suddenly lavender-white arcane energy exploded around her. With howls of pain, the spirit wolves returned to the plane from which Thrall had called them. "You can't beat me. Not while I have the Focusing Iris. It—" Her anger abruptly turned to pain. "You can't understand. You didn't see it. You don't know what it did—to Theramore, to me . . ."

Her torment was harder for Thrall to witness than her rage. She was an open wound, and she wanted to hurt those who had hurt her. More than that, she wanted to hurt everyone who had ever given her hope. Deep sympathy filled him but did not shake his resolve for an instant.

"You are right," he said, causing her to look at him with a surprised expression. "I wasn't there. But I can see what it has done to you. What Garrosh did to you. Fight Garrosh. I will not stop you. But do not make innocents—children, Jaina!—pay his blood price! You won't just kill them; you will kill the future!"

"There's no future for those who died in agony at Theramore," Jaina shot back. "Why should the orcs have one when they don't? When Kinndy doesn't, or Tervosh, or all those good and decent people?" Then, almost to herself, she said, "Why should anyone have a future?"

And the wave broke free.

Thrall arched his back and flung his hands up in the air. His muscles screamed and his lungs labored for breath as he poured all his strength into holding back the tide.

It halted in mid-surge, quivering against the strain as Thrall himself did. Air and water were in a conflict neither element truly wished as the tidal wave shivered. Thrall had no thought, no word, no gesture to spare for his own protection. He could feel the water struggling to break loose, feel the air fighting to hold it in place.

And he was entirely at the mercy of a woman who stood a few yards away—one he had once called "friend" but who now was striving to be death incarnate.

"Release the wind, Thrall!" Jaina shouted. One hand still on the Focusing Iris, she drew back the other. Arcane energy whirled about her, tossing her robes and white hair. "Or I will kill you where you stand, and you will still fail!"

"Do so!" gasped Thrall. "Slay me! Turn your back on everything that once gave you integrity and compassion! For I will not permit this wave to crash upon Orgrimmar as long as there is breath in my body!"

For an instant, it seemed to him that Jaina wavered in her determination. Then her face hardened.

"So be it," she murmured, and gathered the energy in her hand.

A shadow fell over both of them, and before either realized what had happened, a huge reptilian form dropped down on the sand. He interposed his massive blue shape between the orc and the human and cried out, "Jaina! *Don't!*"

Thrall could not believe it. Kalecgos—here! How had he found them? At once he answered his own question. The blue dragon had been searching for the Focusing Iris. The quest had come to an end—Kalecgos had found both it and its brutal mistress. Thrall now had an ally—and the orc continued to funnel all his energy into holding back the seething, straining tidal wave.

Jaina stumbled as Kalecgos landed in front of her. "Move aside, Kalec," she snarled, trying to recover. "This is not your fight!"

He changed into his half-elven form, still interposing himself between her and Thrall. "But it is, you see," he said. "The Focusing Iris is not yours. It belongs to the blue dragonflight. It was stolen, and something cowardly and horrifying was done with it. I cannot, I will not, let that happen again."

"It's not cowardly!" Jaina cried. "It's justice! You went back to Theramore, Kalec. You saw what was left. You didn't know them as I did, but Pained and Tervosh and K-Kinndy—they were your friends too! There was nothing left of her but sand, Kalec. *Sand!*"

Her voice broke on the word. He made no move to

fight her, even though she still stood in an attack pose. Even though she still had her hand on the Focusing Iris.

"I too have lost those I love," he said. "I understand at least a glimmering of your pain." Kalec took a step toward her, stretching out a hand imploringly.

"Stop! Don't you move!" Again arcane energy crackled about her. "You don't know *anything* about what I feel!"

"Are you so very sure?" Kalec had halted but not retreated. "Tell me if this sounds familiar. The initial incomprehension. The guilt, and the second-guessing, and the numbness, because you can't take it in all at once. You can only take it in a little bit at a time, like opening a dark lantern just a crack. The strange shock every single time as you realize, again and again and *again*, you will never see that beloved person anymore. And then the anger. The outrage. The desire to hurt the thing that hurt you. To kill the thing that killed them. But you know what, Jaina? *It doesn't work that way!* If you drown Orgrimmar, Kinndy still won't be waiting for you in Theramore. Tervosh won't be out tending his herb garden. Pained won't be sharpening her sword and glowering happily. None of them will come back."

Jaina's heart contracted in anguish. But she could not listen, because everything he said rang so sickly true. She could not agree, because then she would have to let go of the rage.

"They will have company," she spat.

"Then you had best plan to join them," Kalec said, continuing implacably, "because you wouldn't be able to live with yourself if you did this. Because, Jaina—all those things I described, I felt. I felt so deeply, so intensely, that I did not understand how my heart could bear to continue to beat. I know what it feels like. And . . . I also know that you can heal. It comes slowly, and in stages, but *you can heal*. Unless you've done something to yourself so that you'll never recover. And believe me—if you loose this wave upon Orgrimmar, you will be as dead as the ones you claim to mourn."

"I *do* mourn them!" Jaina shrieked. "I do! I can hardly *breathe*, Kalec. I can't sleep. I just see their faces, just as I remember them, and then their *bodies*. The Horde must pay!"

"But not by your hand, Jaina, and not this way." The voice came not from Kalecgos but from Thrall. Jaina turned stormy eyes upon him. "There is justice, and there is vengeance. You must see the difference between the two, or else you betray those who loved you."

"Garrosh—"

"Garrosh is a thief and a coward and a butcher," Thrall said calmly. "And you are doing precisely what he did— right down to using the same artifact that obliterated Theramore. Is that what you wish? Truly? To be remembered as that even by your own people?"

Jaina staggered back as if struck. No, he was an orc; he was just like the rest of them; her father had been right. Thrall was trying to confuse her. She shook her head wildly.

"I am doing what I know to be right!" she shouted.

"As did Arthas, when he slaughtered everyone in Stratholme," Kalec said. Jaina stared, appalled and disbelieving. He continued as if he hadn't noticed. "And he at least didn't act with hate in his heart toward those he killed. Is this what your legacy is to be, Jaina Proudmoore? To be another Garrosh, another Arthas?"

Jaina's legs buckled and she dropped to the sand, still keeping her hand on the Focusing Iris. Her mind was reeling, thick with fog and anguish.

Arthas—

I can't watch you do this.

She had said that to him, after begging him to change his mind. Had ridden off with Uther, weeping at what Arthas had become. Slowly, as if her head weighed a thousand pounds, she turned to look at her hand on the Focusing Iris. So simple a thing, to have so much power and to have caused so much pain. She thought of its energy being used to animate a five-headed monstrosity, Chromatus. To funnel all arcane energy to the Nexus. To fuel a mana bomb that incinerated innocent young girls.

To wipe out Orgrimmar—

She thought of Arthas mocking Antonidas before Archimonde destroyed Dalaran. And the face of her old mentor, crafted of purple smoke: *"This is not for idle hands, nor prying eyes. Information must not be lost. But it must not be used unwisely. Stay your hand, friend, or proceed—if you know the way."*

She had wanted justification so badly that she had seen his appearance as an invitation—even though she had been forced to break the magical seal. But it hadn't been.

Proceed—if you know the way.

But she hadn't known the way. She had been lost, blundering blindly. If anything, his brief appearance had been a warning, not a nod of approval. In her heart, Jaina knew what Antonidas's reaction would be to what she was about to do. And the knowing was like a knife.

The hand on the Focusing Iris clenched into a fist.

Jaina slowly got to her feet and lifted her tear-stained face first toward Kalec, then toward Thrall.

"For what he has done, Garrosh can be nothing but my enemy—and the Horde as well, as long as he is their warchief. I have hundreds of elementals enslaved to me. And I will *use* them."

Both Thrall and Kalec tensed.

Jaina swallowed hard, and the words crawled past the lump in her throat. "I will use them to aid the Alliance. To protect my people. I will not obliterate an entire city, for I am not Garrosh. I will not slaughter unarmed civilians, for I am not Arthas. I am my own master."

With those words, the tidal wave fractured. It was no longer a towering wall of water but hundreds of individual water elementals. They bobbed on the waves, awaiting Jaina's command.

"You have a right to wage war upon the Horde, Jaina," Thrall said. "But the blood on your hands will now be those of warriors, not children. In time, your heart will be glad of this choice."

"You do not know my heart anymore, Thrall," she said. "I am no butcher—but I will no longer call for peace at any cost. The Horde you do not lead is dangerous and must be challenged at every turn—and defeated. Then, perhaps, there can be peace. But not before."

Despite what she had said about her heart, she felt it ache at the sorrowful expression on his face. The lives lost at Theramore and Northwatch Hold were not the only casualties. This friendship of so many years, so cherished and championed by both of them, was another. It would be a long, long time—if ever—before she could call Thrall "friend" again. And she knew he knew it.

"The coming war will shake this world as the Cataclysm did, but in a different way," Thrall said. "And I have pledged to heal the world. I return now to the Maelstrom. Lady Jaina, I would we had parted another way."

"So do I," Jaina said, and meant it. "But that wish changes nothing."

Thrall bowed deeply. He transformed into a ghost wolf;

shaman as mystic creature departed, the ocean as solid as ground for him. She and Kalecgos watched him leave in silence. Finally, Jaina turned to the blue dragon.

"And what will you do, Kalecgos of the blue dragon-flight?" she asked quietly.

"I will bear Lady Jaina wherever she wishes to go," he replied.

"I will find where the Alliance fleet is engaged in battle," she said. "But first . . . I . . . I wish to see Orgrimmar."

26

Garrosh had ridden as fast as his dire wolf would carry him to Bladefist Bay as soon as he understood all the troll had told him. The ships had not yet arrived, so he commandeered the goblin vessel that seemed permanently moored there, to the surprise and pleasure of the small green captain. The craft chugged out to rendezvous with the other vessels approaching from Northwatch, with Garrosh, Malkorok, and many others on board.

It did not go unnoticed, but fortunately the Alliance was not yet within range. "Faster!" demanded Garrosh, but there were no shaman aboard to make the oceans obey. Garrosh itched to pull alongside one of the vessels, leap onto the deck, and start slaughtering Alliance, but he could not. Not yet. He roared with frustration as the Alliance quickly and brutally dispatched the first brave Horde ship. He watched it go down, blasted in twain and licked by fire, and let his anger fuel him.

Garrosh had been taken by surprise by the news but had recovered quickly. The Horde fleet might have been scattered over Kalimdor, but its secret weapon could be employed anywhere. Despite being so greatly outnumbered, he knew that vengeance would shortly be his.

As the goblin ship chugged valiantly toward the Alliance fleet, Garrosh laughed as several of the Alliance craft were suddenly swathed in fog. "Let them fear what is out there," he told Malkorok. "Let them feel the terror of not knowing what we do—until they behold our true power."

"Would that I could engage Varian myself, on his own vessel," growled Malkorok. "He would not taste a swift death, nor an honorable one."

"He deserves only to outlive the rest of those who accompany him, and watch them despair and die," Garrosh said in agreement. Some of the Alliance ships had managed to evade the fog or else had been out of range. They were bearing down hard now on the three remaining Horde vessels, but as the goblin craft finally pulled alongside the *Bonecracker* and Garrosh and the others leaped easily to the other ship's deck, the warchief was calm, even anticipatory.

"Summon them," was all he said to the captain. The troll took up the cry, and soon the call of "Summon them! Summon them!" was passed from ship to ship. The battle continued on and the air grew thick with smoke from cannon fire. On nearly every deck, Horde fighters were bleeding or dead, impaled by cruel splinters of wood the size of a human's forearm. Healers rushed about, tending to those they could while trying to avoid being casualties themselves.

The ocean's surface, already surging fiercely with the violation of cannonballs, shamanic enforcement, and the flotsam and jetsam of the battle, began to churn in earnest. White froth boiled, and then something exploded up from the depths.

The crew of the unfortunate Alliance ship only had time to gape in horror as the creature struck. Huge tentacles whipped about the mighty vessel, closing around it in a parody of a loving embrace. The kraken—for such it was—began to tighten the coils, squeezing, and the ship splintered. Garrosh threw back his head and laughed.

Other monsters arose from the cold heart of the ocean, angry and hostile at their enslavement but unable to vent their rage upon their masters. They turned their fury instead upon the Alliance ships, snaking out tentacles to seize and shake and sometimes fling the pieces they had made. Alliance soldiers of all races tumbled, screaming, off their broken ships and into the churning waters, where the kraken devoured them.

"Come, Malkorok!" cried Garrosh. "Let us take a few Alliance lives for our own. The kraken are powerful tools, but I do not wish all my foes to simply become food for the fish!"

"I am with you as ever, my warchief," Malkorok said. Up ahead there was one Alliance ship that had, thus far, evaded the grasp of the kraken. It had pulled about and, instead of firing its starboard cannons at the remaining Horde ships, was turning its full attention to blasting one of the kraken.

"Captain, take us there!" he cried. "I have a thirst for Alliance blood!"

Only too grateful to oblige, and with an uneasy glance at the blue-black, shiny, half-submerged *things* churning in the water, the captain pulled along the port side of the Alliance ship the *Lion of the Waves*. The crew cried a warning, but most of the attention was focused on the starboard side. With a grace belying their great size and muscular weight, the two orcs leaped the short distance between the vessels, and the fight began in earnest.

Malkorok was swinging as he sprang onto the *Lion*'s deck. A draenei priest, engrossed in healing the ship's crewmen, was cut down without even realizing the threat. Gorehowl sang its eerie song of slaughter, announcing Garrosh's presence and chopping off the furry head of a worgen. Sensing something behind him, the orc whirled, swinging, and Gorehowl collided with the oversized axe of a looming demon. The felguard's hideous gray face split in a yellow-toothed grin.

Garrosh laughed. "My father slew a demon far greater than you." He sneered.

The felguard laughed in return, a dark, sinister sound. "Enjoy it while you can," he rumbled.

Axe clashed with axe. The felguard was massive and powerful, but Garrosh was fueled by familial pride. He thought of his father fighting Mannoroth, one of the most powerful pit lords that had ever lived, and the tusks he wore in memoriam on his own brown shoulders. The felguard's laugh halted abruptly and he began to frown as Gorehowl struck home on his gray torso. Another strike, then another, and the felguard toppled in chunks to the deck.

"Warchief!" shouted Malkorok. His blades dripped scarlet, and there were no fewer than four bodies at his feet. "Behind you!"

He barely turned swiftly enough to get Gorehowl up between him and the large, black-haired, nearly impossibly fast human who came at him, wielding a massive sword—Shalamayne. Varian uttered a loud, furious howl, more suited to the ghost wolf for which he had been named than a human. Garrosh grunted as the unique blade bit his arm and drew blood. He parried in time to halt the blow from cutting deeper, and shoved hard. Varian staggered back, but Shalamayne descended again.

"The ancestors bless us indeed!" shouted Garrosh. "I knew you would die today, but I did not hope to have the luck to be the one to slay you!"

"I am surprised you have the guts to take me on," Varian snarled. "You've grown cowardly since we last met. First magnataur, then elementals, then kraken to do your dirty work. Did you run and hide when you dropped the mana bomb? I'm sure you were a safe distance away!"

Gorehowl sang again, sweeping low in a blow designed to cut off Varian's legs. The human jumped and whirled in midair, only to have Gorehowl nearly slice off his head as Garrosh followed through with the axe's movement.

"*You* are slower than you were the last time we met," sneered Garrosh. "You are growing older, Varian. Perhaps you should let that sniveling son of yours be king. I will march on Stormwind when the kraken have reduced your mighty ships to kindling. I will take your precious boy, slap him in chains, and parade him through Orgrimmar!"

He had thought to so anger the king of Stormwind that the human would explode in fury, fighting wildly instead of well. To his astonishment, Varian merely grinned, dodging the swing of the axe, measuring his next step. "Anduin might surprise you," he said. "Even lovers of peace despise cowards."

Garrosh suddenly grew tired of the taunting. "Thrice before have we fought," Garrosh snarled, "and it is three times too many. This time, you die—and so does all that you love." Garrosh charged, swinging Gorehowl, and Varian danced away. Garrosh followed, all finesse and strategy gone. The world had narrowed to this one man and his impending death. As the two closed in tight, their faces mere inches from each other, they were abruptly hurled into the air.

Garrosh flailed, holding on to Gorehowl by sheer will. He landed hard on the deck and then was suddenly sliding down it. He heard a massive cracking sound and then was falling toward the blue surface of the ocean. His armor was no friend now, and he sank like a stone as bits and pieces of the *Lion of the Waves* threatened to pin him to the ocean's floor.

Stubbornly, Garrosh refused to surrender to what seemed to be certain death. Still clutching his father's weapon, he used the sinking wreckage to his advantage, climbing up piece by piece as each one drifted. His lungs burned but he continued on, his face up toward the light until at last he burst through the surface and gasped sweet air, coughing violently.

Hands reached down and pulled him up, guiding him toward a rope ladder that had been tossed over the side of one of the ships—he knew not which—and, still holding Gorehowl, hauled himself up until he stumbled onto the deck.

"Warchief!" It was Malkorok, who had also survived. The two clasped each other's arms.

"V-Varian," gasped Garrosh. "What of him?"

"I know not," Malkorok said. "But look!"

Still coughing up seawater, Garrosh turned to gaze where Malkorok was pointing, and pride swelled inside him.

Everywhere he looked, Alliance ships were broken, burning, or desperately engaged in attacking the kraken. The water was littered with the debris of dozens of vessels. Garrosh threw back his head, roaring his victory.

"Behold the might of the Horde!" he cried. "Four ships against dozens! And it is we who triumph! For the Horde! *For the Horde!*"

Kalecgos held Jaina gently in his right forepaw, while she cradled the Focusing Iris next to her body. They headed north. Jaina was unsure why she wished so fiercely to see the Horde capital, but Kalec clearly trusted her change of heart and did not speak a word of objection. Did she want to reassure herself that there were indeed still innocents there and her choice was the right one? Did she wish to see if she could somehow spy Garrosh and blast him to pieces? She was uncertain.

Below them, following obediently and keeping pace with the swift flight of the dragon, were the bound water elementals. She could summon and dismiss them as she wished; Kalec had not asked for the Focusing Iris back, either. Jaina was more grateful for his unspoken, and apparently unshakable, trust in her than he could ever know.

Up they went, past the Echo Isles and the aptly named Scuttle Coast, where Jaina summoned a few angry, out-of-control elementals to join with their kin. The wreckage, though old, saddened and angered her, and she wished she knew where Varian had chosen to direct the Alliance attack.

As they approached Bladefist Bay, Jaina gasped, her eyes wide with shock and horror. The fleet—she had thought it would be attacking Feathermoon Stronghold or Darkshore, but it was here. Here . . . and under attack.

I would have destroyed the fleet, she thought. *If I had sent the tidal wave . . . I would have destroyed both Orgrimmar and the whole Alliance fleet . . .*

Nausea swept over her, and gratitude to both Thrall and Kalecgos. But now was not the time to feel faint and weak. She had to act. For the fleet was not under attack from mere Horde warships—Garrosh, it would seem, had summoned kraken to dispatch the fleet for him. As he had done with the molten giants in Northwatch Hold and the mana bomb in Theramore, he was acting in a cowardly and dominating fashion—wrenching the natural world or magic artifacts to obey him.

"Fly closer!" she called to Kalecgos. Kalec folded his wings and dove, opening them just in time and almost anointing them with seawater as he skimmed swiftly over the waves. Jaina held the Focusing Iris close with one arm and, murmuring the incantation, moved the fingers of her free hand.

Varian shoved the soaking mass of wet hair back out of eyes that stung from seawater. He clung to the wreckage of a ship—which one, he didn't even know—and tried to assess the situation.

So many ships had gone down, victims of the angry embrace of the kraken. He had watched, helpless, as sailors made it to the surface and struck out for shore or ship, only to have a gleaming, slimy tentacle reach out and pull them down into the creature's hungry maw.

He had no idea what had happened to Telda, or the white-haired warlock, or indeed any of the brave crew of the *Lion of the Waves*. Bitterly he amended that. It wasn't entirely true. He knew, had seen impotently, that some of them had met their violent ends. He could only hope that Garrosh and that hulking Blackrock orc were keeping those good people company in the bellies of some kraken.

A few ships were still intact and firing upon the sea beasts. But Light, there were so many of the cursed things, and each one wreaked such horror. Screams and the sounds of cracking timber filled the air. He recognized panic and despair trying to overcome him, and ruthlessly pushed the useless feelings back. They would not serve him now; even anger would not serve him now. He leaped to another remnant of a ship, his eyes now fastened on one of the few surviving vessels. He would be an easy target for a misplaced cannonball from one of his own ships, and only a morsel for a kraken. But he was one man and did not attract the notice of the great monsters, and by sheer will he made his way close enough to the ship called the *Ocean's Lady*. Cupping his hands around his mouth, he called out.

A worgen racing about on the deck heard him, sharp ears swiveling. He loped over to the side of the ship and leaned over, waving one of his powerful lupine arms. "Majesty! We'll send someone to—"

"Retreat! Now!" Varian shouted. If they stayed and fought the kraken, all that would remain of the once-mighty Alliance fleet would be a list of names and grieving families. "Those are my orders! Retreat, every last one of you!"

"We can send out a—"

"No! I'll make it to shore, as will the rest of us," Varian cried. "Take the ships and get to safety while you can!"

The worgen looked stricken and flattened his ears unhappily, but nodded. A few moments later, the *Ocean's Lady* began to turn slowly to port—heading east, back home to Stormwind.

But the kraken would not let them. As Varian watched, unable to stop it, the kraken followed the fleeing ships. The Horde victory would be complete after all.

Varian arched his back and let out a primal howl of fury and grief. This could not—should not—be happening! There had only been four ships! And yet Garrosh had won again.

Varian would not, as he had reassured the worgen, go quietly ashore, to live to fight another day. He would have done so if the fleet had survived. But now—now there was nothing left. No hope. Only a glorious death, achieved while taking as many of the enemy with him as possible. The kraken would not feast solely on Alliance flesh.

He still had Shalamayne, and now he drew it, clutching it tightly. He looked around, searching for any Horde fighter who, like Varian, had found reprieve in a piece of a broken ship. There—there, a sodden tauren was clinging to a curved chunk of wood that looked like part of a hull. He was attempting to clamber up atop it but failing. Snarling, Varian sprang, catlike, landing squarely on the floating debris, and brought his blade down. Blood spurted up, pattering him and adding a copper tang to the salty taste that was in his mouth.

One.

The king of Stormwind searched for another target. At that moment, a shadow fell over him. He looked up and saw the silhouette of—

A dragon?

The water around him surged upward, taking on form and shape. It bobbed up and down on the waves, a blue-green being with a small head, baleful eyes, and two manacled arms. A water elemental—no, no, hundreds of them, all suddenly dancing atop the surface of the ocean.

They flung themselves on the kraken attacking the

Alliance fleet. One of the monsters had surfaced so that its huge flat eyes were visible, and it let out a horrific, eerie wail as it was set upon by dozens of determined elementals. Varian suddenly leaped clear as a frantic tentacle slammed down on the water with an ear-splitting crack. Realizing he was safer in the ocean than on its surface, Varian filled his lungs and dove.

It was an astounding spectacle. The gargantuan kraken flailed with their massive tentacles while the smaller elementals swarmed around them. Incongruously pretty ribbons of dark red began to tinge the water as the elementals literally ripped the kraken apart. Varian swam away from the wreckage, into more open water. Another kraken struggled for its life, its sluggish brain no doubt more surprised than fearful that anything would dare to attack it. Still another floated on the surface, two of its limbs bobbing near it.

Varian's lungs burned and he struck upward, swimming strongly. As he broke the surface and gulped in air, he was suddenly seized and borne aloft. He started to struggle, but a familiar voice called out to him.

"Varian!"

Of course—the water elementals . . . He turned in the grip of the blue dragon to see her clasped in the leviathan's other forepaw. Her white hair was whipped about by the wind, and her eyes still had the strange arcane glow. But there was something about her—a sorrow, a resignation on her face, and yet a sort of peace that had not been there previously.

She pointed down, and he shook his head at the spectacle. There was not a single Horde ship, although he could now see that plenty of warriors were gathered on the shore, thinking to take the battle there if any stragglers survived. The kraken—fully eight of them—were no longer a threat. Their massive corpses bobbed on the waves, glistening in the sunlight. Varian felt a stab of loss as he saw how many ships the grotesque creatures had destroyed, but many yet remained.

Still obedient to Jaina's will, the water elementals, tiny from this vantage point, awaited their new commands.

"You attacked the kraken," Varian said. "Not Orgrimmar."

"No," Jaina said. "Not Orgrimmar."

He smiled faintly. "You saved the fleet, Jaina. Thank you. And now, if this good dragon will set me down on one of my ships—on to Northwatch!"

27

T he remains of the Alliance fleet sailed into the waters of the Merchant Coast unhindered. It seemed that Garrosh had indeed been taken completely unawares by the attack on Bladefist Bay, and the four ships that had attacked the fleet had been summoned from their no doubt relaxed postings at Northwatch. Without the kraken at its command, the Horde was no match for the Alliance fleet, damaged as it had been.

Still, that did not mean that the Horde would give up without a fight. There had been time to get word to those who manned Northwatch, and Varian's ships were greeted by the thundering of cannons and catapulted boulders.

"Return fire!" ordered Varian. Obediently the volley of cannonballs from the shore was met by those from the Alliance ships.

Overhead, Varian could see Kalecgos approaching. The dragon dove, and Varian saw Jaina perched atop the broad blue back. Kalecgos opened his massive jaws and breathed blue mist, and suddenly the volley of cannon fire ceased.

The catapults and ballistae continued to press their

attack. Varian rushed to the side of the ship, peering through his spyglass. He smiled. Garrosh had been arrogant. He had left only a very few to guard this key site, so confident had he been that his blockade of port cities in Kalimdor would break the Alliance.

He blinked as he saw several Horde soldiers clamber into small boats and push out to sea. For a moment, Varian thought they were trying to flee—then he realized they were heading straight for the nearest ship.

"By the Light," he muttered, "they mean to come aboard!"

It was suicide. He could not help but admire their courage, as troll and orc and tauren waved their weapons and shouted their defiance in the guttural Orcish tongue. Their bows and spells were not entirely ineffective, either—Varian saw several Alliance sailors topple to the deck with arrows in their throats, and others who were incinerated on the spot. The sails of the ship caught fire from a bolt that had killed one of the night elf sailors. Again the great shadow of the dragon fell as cold breath put out the flames.

And then, with no warning, dozens of water elementals formed at once. They rushed the small boats, easily overturning them, their manacled arms seizing the enemy and gleefully hauling the struggling Horde members down to a watery death. Other elementals swarmed ashore, targeting the attackers. There were cries of alarm and Varian saw a few orcs and trolls flee. But most of them stood their ground, snarling defiance and fighting to the last as arrows, cannon fire, and spells did their work.

There was silence for a long moment; then cheers went up from the Alliance vessels. Varian grinned, letting them enjoy this second victory, then shouted, "Ashore! The standard of the Alliance will fly once more over North-watch Hold!"

Boats were lowered, filled with happy crewmen and -women. Varian frowned to himself, then looked up. Kalec was hovering overhead. Varian waved his arms broadly, then pointed to the shore. The dragon's head dipped in acknowledgment. Varian hastened to one of the boats, to the honor and surprise of the crew.

By the time Varian reached the shore, lithely leaping out of the boat, Kalecgos had landed and transformed into his bipedal form. Jaina stood beside him. Varian strode up to both of them and offered his hand to each in turn.

"Twice today, the two of you have helped save the Alliance," he said. "We have regained a lost foothold in Kalimdor."

"I am glad to have been of help," Jaina said simply. "What now?"

"Something Garrosh will know to expect," Varian said, giving her a wicked grin. Jaina looked confused. "I've made no secret that I intend to bring the fleet to the various blockades. After the trouncing they've just received, and the loss of Northwatch, Garrosh is going to pull in tight. Which means we'll get our ports back without further loss of Alliance life." He sobered. "We took a beating ourselves," he said. "Those kraken would have wiped out the fleet if you hadn't arrived in time. And with Theramore, Northwatch, and the fleet destroyed . . ." He shook his head. "I don't want to think what would have happened to the Alliance."

Now Jaina looked uncomfortable. "About some of the things I said to you and Anduin—" she said, but Varian held up a hand.

"I am," he said wryly, "perhaps the absolute last person

to stand in judgment of behavior stemming from anger or a desire for revenge. And Anduin has been praying for you. I will be glad to tell him his prayers have been answered."

"Thank you," Jaina said sincerely.

"And you? What is next for you?" Varian inquired. He looked at both of them, and Kalec turned to Jaina.

"Theramore," she said quietly.

Varian nodded. "When we're done cleaning up here, I'll send a ship to Theramore. To . . . take care of things."

Jaina simply nodded. "I would be grateful. They deserve no less." She looked up at Kalecgos. "Let's go."

Garrosh saw the Alliance standard snapping in the breeze over Northwatch even as he pushed his laboring wolf to get there in time. Furious, he yanked his wolf to a halt, threw back his head, and screamed his fury. Wisely, Malkorok, Baine, and Vol'jin did not attempt to calm him down.

"How could this *happen*?" demanded Garrosh, his small golden-brown eyes staring at each of them. "We had every advantage! I destroyed Theramore to break their spirits. I trapped their people in blockades. I sent molten giants and even monsters of the deep after them, and still this happens!"

One of Baine's Longwalkers approached at a swift lope, then slowed, clearly loath to be the proverbial bearer of bad tidings. Baine nodded that he should proceed. The wary tauren knelt in front of—but not too close to—Garrosh.

"Warchief, I bring news from Northwatch," the Longwalker said.

"I can see the news from Northwatch," Garrosh snapped, pointing at the blue-and-white standard in the distance.

The tauren continued. "There is further news, over-heard by sharp ears." Garrosh made a visible effort to calm himself and waved for the messenger to proceed. "Varian intends for the fleet to sail to break the blockade. There are still ample ships remaining for the Alliance to be a threat to our captured ports. Sources reporting in seem to confirm this intention."

Garrosh leaped from his dire wolf, which actually darted back a step, ears flat. He reached for the Long-walker, grabbing him by the arm. "What sources?" he demanded.

"Garrosh," said Baine, his voice heavy with warning, "release my Longwalker. He will better be able to speak if he does not fear being attacked for bringing the truth."

The look that Garrosh shot Baine could have pierced armor, but the warchief saw the sense in this. He let go of the Longwalker's arm. "What sources?" he repeated.

"Druids have flown from Bladefist Bay, reporting that the Alliance fleet is heading out to break the blockade."

For a moment, Baine almost felt sorry for Garrosh. The orc's fury turned to visible pain and he sagged, as if all the life and passion had suddenly been bled out of him. At last, he said to Malkorok, "Order a full retreat. In our state, we cannot risk a battle on multiple fronts."

Malkorok's face was carefully blank as he replied, "As my warchief commands." He kicked his dire wolf and hurried off to speak with several other Kor'kron, who glanced back over their shoulders as Malkorok delivered the news.

"My thanks for your message," Baine told the Longwalker. "Go and eat, and have your wounds tended to." The other tauren bowed and gratefully left to obey. Baine turned to Garrosh. "I commend you, Warchief."

Garrosh looked at him askance. "Why?"

"For recognizing the folly of this path. This war was ill advised, and I am pleased that you have turned from—"

"I have not 'turned from' anything, tauren, and you tread on dangerous ground," Garrosh said warningly. "For someone with such large ears, you still manage to misunderstand what you hear. I do not intend to *end* this war. I intend to *escalate* it. This retreat is a regrouping, a reassessment of strategy—not a surrender to the 'power' of the Alliance!"

Baine attempted to hide his dismay. Beside him, Vol'jin did the same.

"We need to do more," Garrosh said, turning away from Baine and pacing as he spoke, clenching and unclenching his hands. Malkorok finished his conversation and returned to stand at attention while Garrosh continued. "*More* ships. *More* weapons. *More* elementals and beasts and demons obeying our commands. More soldiers need to be conscripted. Male, female, child—they can all contribute to the glory of the Horde."

His spirits were obviously lifting now, and his eyes were distant, focusing on the future and not the present with its stark message of ruination and disaster. "I thought too small—that was the problem. This is no longer about taking over Kalimdor. It is about crushing the Alliance utterly! Wiping their filth off the face of Azeroth! Burning Stormwind to the ground, and Wrynn with it! A war not for control of a single continent, but for conquest of this very world. We can do this; we are the Horde! But victory will be ours only if our plans are sound, our wills focused, our hearts strong and true!"

"Garrosh Hellscream," said Baine calmly, "I ride now for Mulgore with my braves. There are far fewer of them than when I rode out to answer the call of the warchief of the Horde. My loyalty to the Horde is deep, and you cannot gainsay me on that. But know this: I fight for the true Horde, not one that utilizes methods both unnecessary and shameful. There must *never* be another Theramore—not if you wish the aid of Baine Bloodhoof!"

Garrosh stared at Baine with narrowed eyes and a slight smirk that Baine could not interpret. "Duly noted," he said.

As he gathered up the reins of his kodo, Baine glanced at Vol'jin. The troll looked at him sadly and gave a nearly imperceptible shake of his head. Baine nodded slightly. He understood Vol'jin's reasoning. It was the same as Baine's own—Vol'jin needed to protect his people from the wrath of an offended Garrosh.

A world war.

As Baine headed west, toward home and the serenity of the rolling plains of his beloved Mulgore, he could not decide if Garrosh was mad with power . . . or simply mad.

How long had it been, Jaina wondered, since her own personal cataclysm? She had lost count of the days, but surely they had not been many; a fortnight would be too long. Only a fortnight, less, since she had been fretting about Thrall's disinterest in deposing Garrosh, the restlessness in her spirit. Since she had eaten delicious pastries with Kinndy, and her biggest worry had been the thought of her apprentice smudging books with frosting.

Like a sword, she had been tempered, ruthlessly and

efficiently—plunged into the coldness of hatred and revenge from the fire of anguish and back again, reshaped, remade, reforged. But now, like steel, she would withstand much. She would not break or shatter, not from grief or pain or rage. Not anymore.

She arrived in Theramore not by teleporting, and not alone, but on the broad back of a great blue dragon. Kalec landed outside the city limits, on the beach where once they had walked and talked, hand in hand. He crouched low to enable her to slip more easily to the earth.

Shifting into his half-elven shape, he stepped beside her. "Jaina," he said, "it's not too late to change your mind."

She shook her head. "No. I'm all right, Kalec. I just . . . need to see. With my own eyes—clearer now."

They were indeed clearer, both literally and figuratively. The arcane energy that had so poisoned her had faded. Her hair was still white with a single gold streak; that damage would not ever be undone. But the strange white glow was gone from her eyes. The arcane residue, too, had dissipated from Theramore. It was safe—physically, at least—for Jaina to return to the blasted city.

They walked up the slight hill to the path. There were no bodies here; there had been time before the bomb had fallen to gather Wymor and the others who had so gallantly defended the city by the sea, if not yet to bury them. The Horde, too, it seemed, had come for its dead. Though the glowing arcane energy had faded, the skies were still rent. Here and there, twisting ribbons of magic, glimpses into other worlds, could be seen, even in daylight. Jaina stared first at the wounded sky, then at the open gate, swallowing hard.

A warm hand slipped into hers. Kalec's grasp was

tentative; he would pull back if she wished him to. But she didn't. They walked, slowly, into the city of the dead.

Having seen the destruction once before, Jaina was at least somewhat prepared for the sight. Though familiar, it remained horrifically tragic, and her heart was ripped in twain again and again as she beheld the fallen. The buildings still listed, deformed or broken by the arcane. But at least the earth was starting to heal; she no longer felt the wrongness pressing up against the soles of her feet.

She shivered as a cold wind brushed past her. Curiously, she turned to Kalec, who had created it; then she understood and felt a rush of sorrowful gratitude. Both the coldness and the vigor of the wind kept the stench of so many corpses from becoming overwhelming.

"They c-can't just lie here," Jaina said, aware that her voice shook.

"They won't," Kalec said, reassuring her swiftly. "Now that it is safe, we can give them a proper farewell." He didn't say "burial." Not all the fallen had bodies left to bury. Those who had been peculiarly levitated had succumbed to gravity and now lay, more naturally, on the earth.

The items she had noticed on her first visit, which had been scattered with strange abandon, had mostly been scavenged. She felt a rush of anger but quickly damped it. The Horde had been defeated for now. Garrosh had been dealt a devastating and shameful blow. She wasn't here to rage and hate. She was here to observe and mourn.

Her foot slipped, twisting slightly as she stepped on something partially buried. The sunlight glinted on a silver, metallic shape. Jaina bent to work the weapon free from the earth, and as she did so, astonishment and something akin to awe filled her. She lifted it up, and the dirt simply fell away from the beautiful, ancient weapon, as if nothing so base could sully it. It looked as new as the day it had been forged. She held it reverently, but it did not glow at her touch, as it had done for first a human prince and then a tauren chieftain.

"Fearbreaker," she murmured, shaking her head in wonder. "I can't believe it."

"It is lovely," Kalec said as he regarded the mace. "It looks to be of dwarven make, if I am not mistaken."

"You aren't," Jaina replied. "Magni Bronzebeard gave it to Anduin, and he in turn gave it to—to Baine Bloodhoof."

Kalec raised a blue eyebrow. "How that came about is a story I should like to hear one day."

"One day," Jaina said in agreement, but did not add, *But not today.* "How odd that I should come across this now."

"Not odd at all," said Kalec. "It is clearly a magical weapon. It wanted you to find it."

"So that I could return it to Anduin," she said, and felt sad at how events had played out. Such hope the three of them had had, once. Hope that had been dashed to pieces, like a ship against rocks in a storm, by Garrosh Hellscream and the stark horror of the mana bomb. "It will give me an excuse to speak to him. To—apologize. I was very harsh, the last time we spoke. I regret that. I regret . . . much." She fastened the beautiful mace securely to her belt and nodded to Kalec that she was ready to continue.

They walked on, hand in hand, silent and respectful, and then Jaina's heart was wrenched yet again. Here was Pained's body, where Jaina had found it before. And Aubrey, and Marcus . . .

"Their bodies," she said. "They look . . ."

"Unchanged," Kalec said. "The arcane energy has faded from them." He said no more; he didn't have to. Jaina realized that if she were to gently stroke Pained's dark blue hair, it would not shatter like spun glass. Not this time.

A sudden grief seized her. "Oh, Kalec . . . If I hadn't touched Kinndy . . ."

"We will gather what remains of her, Jaina, gently and with love," Kalec said, forestalling her self-recrimination. "From what I hear, her parents have already found a sweeter way to honor her memory."

Jaina shattered. A sharp sound of grief, of helplessness, broke from her, and before she realized it Kalecgos had gathered her in his arms. They closed about her, warm and strong, and she pressed her cheek against his chest and sobbed. He rocked her, soothingly, as one might a child, and as her grief went from agonized sobs to subdued weeping, she realized she could hear two things: Kalec's heart beating steadily against her ear, and his voice, soft and low . . . singing.

Jaina couldn't understand the language, but she didn't have to. Sweet and sad, it was an elegy of some sort—a song to mourn the fallen, a song that had likely existed since before Kalecgos was born, perhaps before the Aspects had even been created. For as certain as there was always a new day dawning, that new day would eventually die in the west. Nothing was older than death . . . save life.

Kalec's voice was as beautiful as the rest of him, and the song wound its way into her soul, quieting it. She felt his lips press against her white hair. The kiss was loving yet gentle, a gesture of comfort that asked for nothing in return. Even so, and even in this tragic place, Jaina felt her heart stir. After what had seemed like an eternity—when it had lain, hard and cold, a sullen diamond in her chest—it was awakening. Now, like a seed in springtime, it was struggling toward light and warmth through the ice of winter.

Held safely and sweetly, Jaina thought of the last conversation she and Thrall had had as friends.

Did you . . . need healing? Jaina had asked.

We all do, whether we see it or not, Thrall had replied. *We bear the wounds of simply living in this life even if we never have a physical scar. A mate who can see one for who one is, truly and completely—ah, that is a gift, Jaina Proudmoore . . . Whatever journey you are on, whatever your path may lead to—I, at least, have found it to be sweeter by far with a life companion at my side.*

Kalec had helped her to heal, from more than just the wounds of simply living this life. He had seen her at her best and at her worst, had enabled her to find her true self when she was lost in a maze of anguish and fury. Would he become her life companion, as Aggra had become Thrall's? There was no way to know for certain. One thing Jaina knew now: nothing was for certain. The winds of change would blow as they willed.

But for now, she was content. She drew back and looked up at him. He gazed down at her, one hand brushing back the single lock of golden hair that yet remained.

"Rhonin," Jaina said.

He nodded. As they drew apart, Jaina felt cold as air moved between them, but Kalec's hand in hers was warm. They walked, slowly, reverently, toward the crater. Jaina winced as she recalled the archmage's last moments—his shoving her through the portal, the tower tumbling, the purple ash that the wind had doubtless swiftly snatched away to blow to the four corners of Azeroth.

"It was not in vain," Kalec said, reminding Jaina. "Had the bomb not been at least somewhat offset by the magic of the tower, the effect would have been much worse."

"He wanted to save Vereesa," Jaina said. "He wanted her to live . . . he wanted his children to have their mother, even if they couldn't have their . . ." She couldn't speak the rest of the words for a moment, then said, "He came . . . because I asked him to." She turned to face Kalecgos. "I was struggling so very hard just a short time ago. I felt so out of place, trying to push for peace when no one else seemed to care about it."

"Do *you* still care?" Kalec asked.

She thought about it for a moment, tilting her head to the side, her brow furrowing. "It isn't that I no longer care. I do. I'm not what I was—I don't burn for vengeance anymore. But . . . neither am I the woman who longed so much for harmony between the Horde and the Alliance. There . . . can't *be* harmony, Kalec. Not while Garrosh leads the Horde, not after what he has done. I don't believe peace is the answer anymore. Which means . . . I don't know where I belong."

He quirked an eyebrow. "I think you might, actually."

Jaina gave him a quizzical look and then realized that he was right.

She wanted to go home. Home to a place that had once been a nourishing sanctuary, one she had left reluctantly to follow her destiny. Jaina recalled what Kalec had said, about there being a rhythm and a pattern to things. Perhaps she had come full circle.

"Dalaran," she said. "The Kirin Tor. I did train very diligently, once upon a time. It feels right for me to be there now, in a way it never has before." She looked again at the rubble. "Rhonin thought so. He made sure I survived. He told me that he thought I was the future of the Kirin Tor. I should at least give them the chance to politely tell me to go away."

"You have become extremely powerful in your own right without them," Kalec said. "I think they would be lucky to have you—and I believe they would consider themselves so as well. Rhonin could not have been alone in his sentiments."

"And you, Kalec?" She braced herself for his announcement that he would leave her, return to the Nexus. He was, after all, the leader of the blue dragonflight. There was no place there for a member of the younger races.

"I think . . . if you have no objection . . . that I would like to accompany you to Dalaran." She couldn't hide her pleasure, and he smiled to see it, his eyes warm with affection. "I take it you don't?"

"No, I . . . I would like that very much. But what about the blues?"

His smile faded. "The flight has dispersed," he said. "We are all individuals now. I feel that we have a great debt to pay the Kirin Tor, for all that our poor stewardship has done to the world. I'd like to be the one to at least start repaying that debt." He gave her a lopsided grin. "They already permitted one dragon membership in their ranks, even though many didn't know exactly who Krasus was. Do you think I stand a chance?" he asked. Then he added, his voice unsure, "With them and . . . with you?"

Change, Jaina thought. *It brings pain; it brings joy; and it is completely inescapable. We are, all of us, our own phoenixes, if we choose to be. Out of the ashes, we can be reborn.*

She stepped forward and lifted her face for answer. With a gentleness that did not surprise her, and an intensity that did, Kalecgos of the blue dragonflight cupped her cheeks in his warm hands, searched her eyes, then leaned forward and kissed Lady Jaina Proudmoore . . . mage.

EPILOGUE

When Jaina and Kalecgos arrived in Dalaran and requested an audience with the council, she fully expected to be turned away or given a date in the future. Instead, the mage who greeted them assured Jaina and Kalec that the council would see them. At once. A very few moments later, Jaina and Kalec found themselves in the ever-changing, beautiful Chamber of the Air. Kalec could not help but glance around, marveling at the sights.

"The council welcomes Kalecgos of the blue dragonflight and Lady Jaina Proudmoore," said Khadgar, his voice aged and yet strong. "The world has wagged on since we last saw you here, Lady. Why do you and your friend come to see us this day?"

"For many reasons," Jaina said. "First . . . I owe you all an apology. This does not belong to me." She held out the tome that had enabled her to make use of the Focusing Iris. "I took it without—" She shook her head. "No. I won't mince words. I stole it, and I forced open the seal in order to utilize a dreadful weapon against my enemy."

"You did not use the weapon, though, did you?" asked Khadgar. "For unless my news sources have become uncharacteristically derelict in their duties, Orgrimmar still stands—with a shamed Garrosh Hellscream sulking in Grommash Hold."

"I did not use it against Orgrimmar, that much is true," Jaina said. "I was brought to my senses by Kalecgos and by Thrall. But I did use it to defend the Alliance fleet. I now return the book to you, and I have returned the Focusing Iris to Kalecgos."

"And I," said Kalec, unexpectedly, "would like to donate the Focusing Iris to the Kirin Tor."

A murmur went around the room. Even Jaina was startled. "Kalec—that has ever been the treasure of the blue dragonflight."

"Which is scattered now," Kalec said, "and no one is left to protect this treasure. We failed to keep it safe, to my shame, and I do not deem myself a fit guardian. Please— will you take it? I know there are many valuable artifacts in Dalaran. I can think of no safer place for it."

Modera stepped forward and accepted both the stolen book and the Focusing Iris, bowing slightly to Kalecgos. "Your concern is for the safety of others before your own ego, Kalecgos. This is duly noted."

Karlain drew himself up to his full height and regarded Jaina with folded arms. "Lady Jaina Proudmoore," he said, "you did not come here to simply return a book."

"No," she said. "I am . . . I humbly request permission to become a novice member of the Kirin Tor."

The council had to have been surprised, after she had stayed away for so many years, but it did not appear so. Khadgar gestured, and the other four approached him. They spoke in soft whispers. Jaina turned away politely, to give them as much privacy as possible. Kalec reached for her hand.

"I'd tell you not to worry, but that wouldn't do much good," he said.

She smiled a little, then said, "I'm . . . not sure what I'll do with myself if they refuse me. Even though I stopped short of destroying Orgrimmar——and I am glad that I did——I still believe Garrosh needs to be removed as warchief. That's not exactly neutral."

"You are skilled and intelligent and great of heart, Jaina," Kalec said gently. "There will always be a place for such as you."

"Lady Proudmoore?"

The voice belonged to Khadgar, and Jaina turned, her heart racing. "We must deny your request to be a novice member of our august body."

Jaina felt a sharp stab of disappointment, keener than even she had expected. "I understand," she said quietly. "My actions cannot be excused."

Khadgar went on. "They can, however, be atoned for. And you can't very well be a *novice* member of the Kirin Tor if you are its leader, now, can you?"

"What?" The word burst from her in a startled yelp more suited to the girl she had once been than the woman she now was. "But I've——I've not even . . ." Words failed her, and she stared at him, mute.

"Rhonin sacrificed his life to save you, Lady Jaina. He told you that you were the future of the Kirin Tor."

She nodded. "Which made no sense to me. I haven't even been a member."

"It made no sense to us either, when he kept pressing the point," said Modera. "But Vereesa found a box in his desk that contained several scrolls of prophecy given to him by none other than Korialstrasz himself."

Jaina and Kalec looked at each other. "And . . . I was mentioned in one of them?"

"Not by name," said Khadgar. He withdrew a scroll from his pocket and handed it to Jaina. "Read it aloud, please."

Jaina took the scroll with hands that trembled and read in an unsteady voice:

> After the red comes the silver,
> She who was golden and bright;
> The Proud Lady humbled and bitter,
> Shall now turn her thoughts to the fight.
>
> Sapphire to diamond she gleams now,
> The Kirin Tor leader who comes,
> "Queen" of a kingdom now fallen,
> Marching to war's martial drums.
>
> Be ye warned—the tides of war
> At last shall break upon the shore.

It fit. After Rhonin came Lady Jaina Proudmoore, whose gold hair had turned silver, and whose sapphire eyes had, for a time, gleamed white like a diamond. She had indeed been humbled and bitter, and still, in her own way, had a martial stance. She looked up at Khadgar, stunned.

"But—to choose me just based on this—"

"Not just on this. You have always been strong, my lady. In your power, and in your character," said Aethas Sunreaver unexpectedly. "Even when tested and tried. And when you faced both an unimaginable horror and an inconceivable temptation—and were perhaps yourself tainted by the effects of the mana bomb—you still chose a path that was fair and just, rather than vengeful and dark. It is, you must admit, unlikely that anything else will ever tempt you so again. And I do not think there stands among us anyone who, were he or she in your place, could have done better. Indeed . . . we might not have done even half so well."

"You misunderstand," she said. "I needed help to not become . . . something terrible. I could not have done it without Kalecgos."

"Well then," said Khadgar, turning to the blue dragon, "we'd best make sure he stays close to your side. You have already shown us your mind with regard to the Focusing Iris and the care you believe we would take of it. Would you like to become a member of the Kirin Tor yourself, Kalecgos? It sounds as if Archmage Proudmoore could benefit from your presence. Provided, of course, she accepts our offer."

And just that quickly, the Kirin Tor had a second dragon among its membership, and a still-reeling Jaina Proudmoore as its leader.

As soon as the investiture had been completed, the new archmage and leader of the Kirin Tor had returned to Theramore. Varian had been true to his word, sending a ship from Northwatch to respectfully gather the fallen bodies and even the purple sand. Outside the city limits there was now a mass grave, shocking and solemn in its size. It had been difficult for Jaina, but not as hard as she had feared; she had said her farewells earlier, standing with Kalecgos.

Now she presided over another ceremony she wished

with all her heart did not have to occur. It was a lovely sunset in Dalaran, the sky full of color yet transitioning to darkness, a poignant echo to the sorrowful nature of the ritual.

Today, they were saying farewell to Rhonin.

His children were there, one on each side of their mother, identical twin boys with their father's flame-red hair and their mother's eyes and slender build. Jaina had learned that they recently celebrated their birthday. She was glad that at least Rhonin had lived long enough to share that with them. Giramar, the elder by a few moments, seemed a bit more stoic than his brother, Galadin, whose lower lip quivered, though both pairs of half-elven eyes glittered with unshed tears. While both wore ornate robes for such a formal occasion, they did not match; Giramar's robe was indigo with silver trim, while Galadin had chosen dark green and gold.

Their mother wore not her familiar armor but a gown. Some were surprised to see that the garb was not black, nor even very conservative. Vereesa Windrunner was a proud and beautiful woman, and her marriage to the hot-tempered but good-natured archmage had been full of passion and devotion. It was his vibrant life she now chose to celebrate, not the ending of it, and so she was clad in a flowing red dress more appropriate to a ballroom than a funeral. Her eyes were dry; Vereesa had already done her mourning. Jaina's heart both ached for her and swelled with admiration. Rhonin's sons, though lacking a father, had a mother who would raise them well.

So many had gathered at the Violet Citadel. Jaina suspected that nearly every member of the Kirin Tor who could be present had come. And why should they not? Rhonin deserved it.

"Not all that long ago," Jaina said, "the Kirin Tor took

a bold step in selecting Rhonin to be its leader. He was unorthodox and outspoken—impetuous and stubborn. He had a tremendous sense of humor and great love of friends and family." She smiled a little at the twins, who sniffled slightly but who both shakily returned the gesture. Addressing the other members of the Council of Six, she said, "He took Dalaran in a new direction and led the Kirin Tor through a war with the very Aspect who had been chosen to guide and monitor magic. He died as he had lived—protecting and helping others."

Her own voice threatened to give out and she paused, collecting herself. "As his final act, he forced me through a portal—saving my life, even as he sacrificed his. He believed that I would be the future of the Kirin Tor. And because you agreed with him, here I stand. I can only succeed him; I can never replace him."

She looked out over the sea of purple robes, her heart hurting a little more as she saw the Sparkshines. "The winds of change blow fiercely; Azeroth is on the brink of war. The Kirin Tor can be the calm eye of the hurricane, if we choose to be. We can speak reason, when the rest of the world is going mad. We can remember that we have skills and knowledge, but so do others. I have at last come home, to Dalaran, though my path here has been a strange and winding one. Long have I been away, and I am glad to come back, bringing all I have learned, through love and through pain. And while I deeply regret some of my recent behavior, I do not regret who I have become because of it. I will lead you as best I may. It is time to bring the floating city down to the earth. I will do so with guidance, because I will ask your advice. I will do so with honor, because I will hold myself to the standard set by Rhonin. I will do these things—but I will continue to believe, as I know many here do, that this world cannot be safe with Garrosh Hellscream as the leader of the Horde. And how all these duties and beliefs will reconcile, I know not. But I have faith that they will." She thought of the prophecy and smiled a little. "Someone very wise seemed to think they would."

She lifted her arms to the sky. "There were not even ashes to scatter, my friend. But your spirit lives on. In the heart of your courageous wife, in the eyes of your beautiful sons, and in the wisdom of the Kirin Tor."

Jaina began to move her fingers in a weaving motion. Beside her, the other members of the Council of Six and Kalecgos did likewise, as did all the magi assembled. Jaina thought of a conversation she had had with Kalec, so long ago it seemed now, and again smiled slightly as a small, pale lavender ball of arcane energy formed in her hand.

"There is a rhythm, a cycle. There is—a pattern." She drew her fingers through the globe of arcane magic. It fragmented and re-formed, a whirl of signs and symbols and numbers. "All things change, whether from the inside out or the outside in. That is what magic is. And we are magic too."

She lifted her palm and sent the small orb floating upward. It was joined by dozens of its fellows, and then hundreds, as even those denizens of Dalaran who were unable to find space at the ceremony were still able to join in this gesture of farewell. The lights continued to rise, like fireflies of lavender magic against the deepening twilight, and despite everything—despite the tragedy of Theramore and the disaster she had almost been responsible for, despite the sorrow of losing Rhonin—Jaina felt her own heart lift with them.

All things change, she thought. *I, Thrall, Garrosh, Varian . . . Azeroth.*

A warm hand clasped hers, and she smiled up at Kalecgos. She was more than ready for the changes that awaited her.

Tink. Tink. Tink. Hisssssss . . .

A dwarf stood naked to the waist, firelight glinting off his sweaty torso, as he worked at the Great Forge of Ironforge. The forge had always burned, but it had seldom been utilized as it was now. There was no daytime or nighttime underground, and there was no cessation of the work to be done. War was in the wind, and the Alliance had to be prepared. The dwarf set aside the completed weapon, then placed his hands on his lower back as he stretched, wincing as he heard things pop and creak. He reached for a waterskin, wiped his red beard, and continued.

In Stormwind, they were building new ships. With each one, the designers refined the task of construction more and more, turning out crafts faster and faster. And Light knew they would be needed. While Garrosh had blinked, he could not be counted on to do so a second time. The Horde fleet was still intact, although it had retreated; the Alliance could not say the same thing. Varian stood near the harbor for a long moment, watching the activity, then returned to the keep.

He had a war to plan.

Garrosh paced in Grommash Hold. The orders were already being posted:

ATTENTION ALL ABLE-BODIED MEMBERS OF
THE HORDE! WARCHIEF GARROSH HELLSCREAM HAS
ISSUED A CALL TO ARMS FOR ALL CITIZENS!
MALE AND FEMALE ADULTS! YOU WILL
TRAIN TO FIGHT THE ALLIANCE IN A WAR
IN WHICH WE SHALL BE TRIUMPHANT!
CHILDREN AND OTHERS WHO CANNOT BEAR
ARMS—YOU WILL ASSIST IN CRAFTING WEAPONS
AND TENDING TO THE NEEDS OF THE WARRIORS!
ANYONE FOUND SHIRKING HIS OR HER DUTY WILL
BE ARRESTED FOR TREASON BY THE KOR'KRON.
NO EXCEPTIONS.
FOR THE HORDE!

The activity that had been afoot in Orgrimmar over the last several months had increased a thousandfold. Fires burned at all hours of the day and night, and the Kor'kron were rounding up conscripts.

Garrosh Hellscream stood alone in Grommash Hold. He stared down at a map of the Eastern Kingdoms spread on one of the tables, illuminated by the gleam of candlelight. He played idly with a dagger, thumbing its tip. His eyes flickered over the letters:

STORMWIND

Then he lifted the blade high over his head and brought it down nearly to the hilt in the middle of the *M*.

"I will watch your city burn around you, Varian Wrynn," he muttered. He grinned around his tusks. "After all . . . there can only be one victor in this war."

ACKNOWLEDGMENTS

Special thanks must go to Ed Schlesinger, James Waugh, Micky Neilson, and Russell Brower for their patience and support during a very difficult time. Thanks, guys.

Thanks must also go to the Puckett family—Rob, Bev, Chris, and Ryan. All authors should have such a place to go for a writing retreat.

NOTES

The story you've just read is based in part on characters, situations, and locations from Blizzard Entertainment's computer game *World of Warcraft*, an online role-playing experience set in the award-winning Warcraft universe. In *World of Warcraft*, players create their own heroes and explore, adventure in, and quest across a vast world shared with thousands of other players. This rich and expansive game also allows them to interact with and fight against (or alongside) many of the powerful and intriguing characters featured in this novel. Since launching in November 2004, *World of Warcraft* has become the world's most popular subscription-based massively multiplayer online role-playing game. The latest expansion takes players on a thrilling and never-before-seen corner of Azeroth: the mysterious continent of Pandaria. More information about *Mists of Pandaria* and previous expansions can be found on www.WorldofWarcraft.com.

FURTHER READING

If you'd like to read more about the characters, situations, and settings featured in this novel, the sources listed below offer additional information on the story of Azeroth.

- Lady Jaina Proudmoore's long struggle to broker peace between the Alliance and the Horde is depicted in the monthly *World of Warcraft* comic book by Walter and Louise Simonson, Ludo Lullabi, Jon Buran, Mike Bowden, Sandra Hope, and Tony Washington, as well as in *World of Warcraft: Cycle of Hatred* by Keith R. A. DeCandido and *World of Warcraft: The Shattering: Prelude to Cataclysm* by Christie Golden. Other details of Jaina's life are offered in *Warcraft: Legends*, volume 5, "Nightmares," by Richard A. Knaak and Rob Ten Pas, and *World of Warcraft: Arthas: Rise of the Lich King* by Christie Golden.

- Kalecgos's heroics, including his time as Aspect of the blue dragonflight, are chronicled in *World of Warcraft: Night of the Dragon* by Richard A. Knaak;

World of Warcraft: Thrall: Twilight of the Aspects by Christie Golden; *The Sunwell Trilogy* and *World of Warcraft: Shadow Wing*, volume 2, "Nexus Point," by Richard A. Knaak and Jae-Hwan Kim; and the short story "Charge of the Aspects" by Matt Burns (on www.WorldofWarcraft.com).

- Further insight into Warchief Garrosh Hellscream and his previous exploits can be found in issues 15–20 of the monthly *World of Warcraft* comic book by Walter and Louise Simonson, Jon Buran, Mike Bowden, Phil Moy, Walden Wong, and Pop Mhan; *World of Warcraft: The Shattering* by Christie Golden; *World of Warcraft: Beyond the Dark Portal* by Aaron Rosenberg and Christie Golden; *World of Warcraft: Wolfheart* by Richard A. Knaak; and the short stories "Heart of War" by Sarah Pine, "As Our Fathers Before Us" by Steven Nix, and "Edge of Night" by Dave Kosak (on www.WorldofWarcraft.com).

- More details about High Chieftain Baine Bloodhoof and his tense relationship with Garrosh Hellscream are revealed in *World of Warcraft: The Shattering* by Christie Golden, *World of Warcraft: Stormrage* by Richard A. Knaak, and the short story "As Our Fathers Before Us" by Steven Nix (on www.WorldofWarcraft.com).

- Before Vol'jin and his Darkspear trolls joined the Horde, they inhabited a small island chain between Kalimdor and the Eastern Kingdoms.

A glimpse into this period of Vol'jin's life can be found in the short story "The Judgment" by Brian Kindregan (on www.WorldofWarcraft.com).

- The infamous Banshee Queen, Sylvanas Windrunner, is featured in *Warcraft: The Sunwell Trilogy*, volume 3, "Ghostlands," by Richard A. Knaak and Jae-Hwan Kim; *World of Warcraft: Stormrage* by Richard A. Knaak; *World of Warcraft: Arthas* by Christie Golden; and the short stories "In the Shadow of the Sun" by Sarah Pine and "Edge of Night" by Dave Kosak (on www.WorldofWarcraft.com).

- Tales of Regent Lord Lor'themar Theron, the stoic ruler of the blood elves, can be found in *Warcraft: The Sunwell Trilogy*, volume 3, "Ghostlands," by Richard A. Knaak and Jae-Hwan Kim, and in the short story "In the Shadow of the Sun" by Sarah Pine (on www.WorldofWarcraft.com).

- A window into the devious mind of Trade Prince Jastor Gallywix, leader of the Bilgewater Cartel goblins, can be found in the short story "Trade Secrets of a Trade Prince" by Gavin Jurgens-Fyhrie (on www.WorldofWarcraft.com).

- Rhonin's earlier adventures are detailed in *Warcraft: Day of the Dragon*, *World of Warcraft: Night of the Dragon*, and the *War of the Ancients Trilogy* by Richard A. Knaak. His heroics as head of the Kirin Tor magi are also depicted in *World of Warcraft: Mage* by Richard A. Knaak and Ryo Kawakami.

- Varian Wrynn's path to become king was long and arduous. His early years are presented in *World of Warcraft: Arthas* by Christie Golden, *World of Warcraft: Tides of Darkness* by Aaron Rosenberg, and *World of Warcraft: Beyond the Dark Portal* by Aaron Rosenberg and Christie Golden. Varian's more recent exploits can be found in the monthly *World of Warcraft* comic book by Walter and Louise Simonson, Ludo Lullabi, Jon Buran, Mike Bowden, Sandra Hope, and Tony Washington; *World of Warcraft: The Shattering* by Christie Golden; *World of Warcraft: Stormrage* and *World of Warcraft: Wolfheart* by Richard A. Knaak; and the short story "Blood of Our Fathers" by E. Daniel Arey (on www.WorldofWarcraft.com).

- Thrall's exciting background—described in *Warcraft: Lord of the Clans* by Christie Golden—has allowed him to form strong bonds with heroes such as Jaina Proudmoore. You can learn more about Thrall and Jaina's friendship in *World of Warcraft: The Shattering* by Christie Golden, *World of Warcraft: Cycle of Hatred* by Keith R. A. DeCandido, and issues 15–20 of the monthly *World of Warcraft* comic book by Walter and Louise Simonson, Jon Buran, Mike Bowden, Phil Moy, Walden Wong, and Pop Mhan. His recent efforts to protect Azeroth during the Cataclysm and its aftermath are detailed in *World of Warcraft: Thrall* by Christie Golden and the short story "Charge of the Aspects" by Matt Burns (on www.WorldofWarcraft.com).

- In *World of Warcraft: The Shattering* by Christie Golden, Prince Anduin Wrynn turns to Jaina Proudmoore for advice on how to heal the rift between him and his father, Varian. More details about the prince are offered in *World of Warcraft: Wolfheart* by Richard A. Knaak; the monthly *World of Warcraft* comic book by Walter and Louise Simonson, Ludo Lullabi, Jon Buran, Mike Bowden, Sandra Hope, and Tony Washington; and the short stories "Blood of Our Fathers" by E. Daniel Arey and "Prophet's Lesson" by Marc Hutcheson (on www.WorldofWarcraft.com).

THE BATTLE RAGES ON

Tides of War marks the beginning of a dark era in Azeroth's history. Worldwide conflict between the Horde and the Alliance threatens to destroy what little stability remains. Having just recovered from the Cataclysm, does either faction possess the strength and resolve to survive more turmoil? The answer may be on Pandaria, a mysterious island shrouded in mist for thousands of years . . . until now.

In *World of Warcraft*'s fourth expansion, *Mists of Pandaria*, you can be one of the first Horde or Alliance heroes to forge into the heart of this exotic region, gathering new allies and battling ferocious enemies. You can also play as a noble pandaren (*WoW*'s latest playable race) and join the Horde or the Alliance, depending on which faction aligns more with your ideals. Regardless of the side you choose, your adventures will have impact on Azeroth's destiny. Ancient evils are on the rise across the enchanted isle of Pandaria, threatening to engulf the world in darkness unless *you* stop them.

To discover the ever-expanding realm that has entertained millions around the globe, go to www.WorldofWarcraft.com and download the free trial version. Live the story.